OTHERKIN'S HUNGER

Book 1 of the
Reclaimed Legacy Chronicles

Morgan Emerson Fox

RAINDROP BOOKS

Otherkin's Hunger - Book 1 of the Reclaimed Legacy Chronicles

Copyright © 2024 by Morgan Emerson Fox

All rights reserved.

ISBN-13: 978-1917185806

Raindrop Books LLC
8401 Maryland Drive, STE S
Richmond, VA 23294

This novel is a work of fiction. The events depicted in this
novel are not based on any real people or events. The names,
characters, places, and incidents are either the product of the
author's imagination or are used fictitiously. Any resemblance
to actual persons, living or dead, businesses, companies,
events, or locales is entirely coincidental.

The author has used real places in this novel, but any events
that take place in these places are fictional. The author has not
attempted to portray these places accurately, and any
resemblance to actual events that have taken place in these
places is purely coincidental.

The characters in this novel are completely fictional. They are
not based on any real people, and any resemblance to actual
persons, living or dead, is purely coincidental.

The author has created these characters and their stories for
entertainment purposes only. The author does not endorse or
condone the actions of any of the characters in this novel.

Otherkin.[1] /'əTHər͵kin/

n., sing. or pl. A person who holds the belief that they are not entirely (or not at all) human. Usually a spiritual belief pertaining to one's soul and the reincarnation thereof, but may also be a belief that one's genetics are descended from, for example, the Irish fae. The word Otherkin was coined to describe people who felt a connection to mythological humanoids such as elves and faeries, but has expanded in recent years to include dragons, gryphons/griffins and other supposedly mythical beasts as well as animals, angelic/demonic beings (<u>angelkin</u>/<u>demonkin</u>) and in some cases extraterrestrials.

adj. Of or relating to Otherkin.

<hr>

[1] Spiritedust. (2004, May 15). Otherkin. Urban Dictionary.
https://www.urbandictionary.com/define.php?term=otherkin

This book is dedicated to the ones we've lost to the inexorable march of time and age, whose memories linger like the faintest whispers of dawn. It is also dedicated to the families we were born into and the ones we choose, bound not by blood but by the depths of our hearts and the strength of our spirits. Here's to the friends who stand by us, embrace our quirks, champion our dreams, and hold us close in times of need.

This is a tribute to tolerance and acceptance, to the beauty of being true to who we are and the potential of who we can become. In a world riddled with division and hatred, this narrative stands as a beacon of hope, urging us to look beyond our differences and find unity in our shared humanity.

To our beta readers, editors, and every hand and voice that has touched this manuscript, your insights and dedication have sculpted this story into something far greater than it could have been alone. Your contributions are the undercurrents that give this tale life, depth, and resonance.

But most of all, to you, our readers and fans, to whom these pages belong as much as they do to us. Your enthusiasm, support, and love for this world and its characters fuel our passion and drive us to explore new horizons. We hope you find within these words the same joy, escape, and reflection we have found in creating them.

Thank you for joining us on this journey. May it inspire you, as it has inspired us, to reject division, embrace love, and always seek the light, even in the darkest times.

Prolog

As HE SAT, Grandmaster Eamon Vale glanced at the calendar that sat unobtrusively on his desk: the Ides of March. The date was not lost on him—a day of great historical import that resonated with the Sodality, long before it even took on that moniker. Julius Caesar had once been a rising star, with his expanding influence threatening to tip the balance of power in ways unfavorable to the clandestine organization that would one day evolve into the Sodality of the Thorns. On this very day, centuries ago, Caesar met his end in an orchestrated series of betrayals, his power abruptly cut, thereby tipping the scales back to the advantage they held so dear...

Though the event had evolved into legend, the Sodality's private archives told a more nuanced tale. Letters, some written in coded language, along with fragmented documents, pointed to the hidden hands that had guided the knives from the shadows on that fateful day. It was a potent reminder that sometimes the boldest moves were made in the dark, away from the glaring light of public scrutiny.

For Eamon, the date was a subtle affirmation of his life's work, a quiet nod to the powers he wielded from the obscurity of his chamber. On this Ides of March, he could not help but feel a particular resonance with the events that transpired on that distant day as he prepared to navigate a chessboard of intrigue. There was a symmetry to it, an elegant harmony that appealed to the grandmaster's sensibilities.

Leaning back, absorbing the weight of history, Eamon allowed himself a faint but unmistakable smile. Sometimes, the universe has a way of aligning events into a pattern so intricate and captivating that even he, who had seen much in his extended life, could only marvel at the spectacle. Today, on this auspicious day, Eamon Vale felt entirely in his element.

Before delving into the intricate machinations of global and otherworldly affairs that filled his days, Eamon allowed himself a moment to reflect on his rise to power within the Sodality of Thorns. His predecessor had met an untimely demise that was gruesome and was orchestrated down to the finest detail by Eamon himself. There was a certain poetic justice in it; his predecessor had thought of himself as untouchable, secure in his grip on the Sodality's many tendrils of influence. But in the shadowy world they operated in, even a flicker of hubris could be fatal.

The following power vacuum could have easily led to chaos and fractured the Sodality's influence as it had before. Rival factions had eyed the vacancy with rapacious gluttony, but Eamon was always one step ahead. His purge of potential contenders had been equally brutal and necessary, conducted with a precision that left no room for reprisal. It served as a purging fire that forged the Sodality into a fearsome weapon, honed to eliminate all supernatural threats by any means. Its origin, conceived in ancient Sumerian times, was rooted in controlling mystical arts only accessible to the elite.

No living human knew Eamon's secret—that he was more than human. Much more!

Centuries had passed since he became the grandmaster, and not a single individual had risen that could challenge his mastery over the Sodality. He had ushered the organization through multiple eras, assuming new names and faces, always adapting and staying ahead of the countless threats that sought to undo the order he had imposed. The satisfaction it brought to him was immense, but even he had to admit that a sense of ennui occasionally would settle over him like a shroud.

Now that his control was complete and all otherworldly powers virtually eliminated, he often found himself yearning for a new diversion, an intricate challenge to elevate the stakes and set his wits ablaze once again. Sometimes, the diversion was in flesh or blood.

Other times, it was provoking wars or genocides to help purge or purify the human race.

Recently, a new problem had caught his attention. Lucian David Miller, the prodigious founder of Coruscant Technologies, Inc. Reports indicated the young entrepreneur was on the cusp of unlocking genetic enigmas that could disrupt the control Eamon had so painstakingly maintained. Lucian was probing into territories Eamon had actively suppressed. Lucian's biotech empire was poised to potentially unlock legacies that were best left…buried.

The name Lucian Miller sparkled like a gem in a mound of ordinary stones. The young CEO, it seemed, had a knack for delving into dangerous knowledge. In doing so, Lucian had unwittingly painted a target on his own back, making him an object of acute interest for the grandmaster.

The corners of Eamon's lips lifted ever so slightly. This could very well be his new diversion, a wild card that promised to make the game not just interesting but exhilarating. Eamon's keen eyes flickered back to the other intelligence briefings that had accumulated on his desk. Each one seemed like a trivial concern compared to the dossier on Lucian Miller. Was it possible that Lucian was unaware of the Pandora's box he was trying to crack open, or did he suspect— arrogance and greed driving him? In either case, it could not stand.

Lucian's escalating curiosity, ambition, and wealth signaled a turning point. The grandmaster couldn't deny a certain admiration for the young man's audacity. But he was playing a dangerous game— one that involved not just the boardrooms of corporate skyscrapers but the shadowy corridors of supernatural realms, whether he knew it or not. If Lucian continued on his current trajectory, he would become an unacceptable threat. And threats, Eamon knew from centuries of existence, had to be neutralized. It would be best to eliminate it now before it could grow even more dire.

Eamon closed the Lucian dossier and turned his attention to the world map displayed on a massive touchscreen on the wall, showing current points of interest and the web of influence between them. Lucian Miller had entered his calculus now—a variable that could alter the equation entirely. Eamon leaned back in his chair. Patience had always been his strongest ally; it had to be, when one had lived as long as he had.

Though he was thousands of miles away from the hustle and bustle of New York City, technology and sorcery kept him well-connected. His fingers danced over the slick surface of his encrypted tablet, multitasking between apps designed for maximum security.

A second screen displayed a real-time feed from his operations around the globe. His attention, however, was focused on New York City, particularly on Richard Kael, one of his regional controllers stationed conveniently close to Lucian Miller's corporate headquarters.

The corner of his lips twitched upward as he composed a coded message for Richard. "Initiate a new operation: Icarus. Gather comprehensive intelligence on Lucian Miller, CEO of Coruscant Technologies, Inc. Identify vulnerabilities and prepare for action." Richard's task was unambiguous—prepare a blueprint for Lucian's downfall.

Recalling their single meeting, where oaths were sworn and loyalties sealed, both mundanely and mystically, Eamon was confident in Richard's capabilities and loyalty. The controller was bound to him not just by the oaths he swore but by ties wrought through ancient rites, weaving the oaths with dire consequences.

He pressed send, automatically encoding and encrypting the message, watching as it traveled the digital aether to reach Richard in New York. Eamon then returned his gaze to the display mounted on the wall. Digital threads connected points of interest, assets, and ongoing operations—each node integral to his global web of influence.

Lucian Miller had become another point on this complex network, unaware of how entangled he was about to become. And while Richard would deploy traditional methods of intelligence gathering, Eamon had a plethora of otherworldly options at his disposal. Those resources were rarely used now; modern techniques were nearly as effective but carried far fewer risks.

The board was set, and Lucian Miller had just become an unwitting player. He had yet to realize how tightly these strings could constrict.

But he would. Oh, he most certainly would. With that thought, Eamon's lips curved slightly upward, a ghost of a smile touching the corners.

Part One

One

Mrs. Thompson glanced at the antique clock.

"Five minutes to closing, Anja. I trust you will follow the proper procedures for finishing up?"

"Of course, Mrs. Thompson," Anja replied.

The library had closed to the general public earlier, and only pre-approved researchers were allowed to remain inside. Anja almost always had the closing duties, and the last of the researchers had already departed.

"Do not procrastinate or allow yourself to be sidetracked. I shall not tolerate any aimless meandering throughout the premises," Mrs. Thompson admonished, punctuating her words with a disapproving arch of her finger.

"I promise I'll head straight home after locking up," Anja said, her words a comforting half-truth. She planned on going straight home, of course, just not immediately. In her mind, she mused, *As if curiosity were a crime.*

Mrs. Thompson studied Anja briefly before adding, "The archive rooms remain strictly off-limits."

"Of course," Anja replied innocently.

"See that you remember that, dear. The priceless knowledge in our care here is not for trifling amusements," Mrs. Thompson said as she donned her coat and gathered her belongings. "Have a good evening then. Lock the front gate securely behind you when you leave."

"Yes, ma'am," Anja said. "Goodnight, Mrs. Thompson."

But as soon as the librarian departed, a subtle smile crept across her face. Rules had never really constrained her thirst for knowledge. Her real research was about to begin. Tonight, curiosity compelled her to linger.

The amber glow of the library lamps cast flickering shadows on the polished wood panels as Anja made her final rounds through the shelves and display cases. Her footsteps echoed softly on the floors, blending with the imagined whispers of turning pages from the ancient tomes surrounding her.

As the chimes marking the closing hour filled the halls, Anja finished her last checks around the library. Her eyes lifted to the third-floor balcony as she returned to the central hall. Up there, among polished oak shelves, she knew the Blackwell Heights Repository's volumes waited—gifts from an esoteric library long since shuttered.

As Anja made her way toward one of the staircases, her gaze was drawn upward to the magnificent, frescoed ceilings. The intricate designs, emulating the artistry of long-forgotten masters, depicted scenes that seemed to whisper the secrets of history, philosophy, and the mysteries of the universe. The colors, though faded over time, still held an ethereal vibrance.

The main hall of the library seemed a cathedral of knowledge, and its multi-tiered shelves were the sanctuaries. On each of the three levels, rows upon rows of dark, polished oak shelves held the tomes that spoke of the world's collective wisdom. Every shelf was a world of its own, laden with ancient texts and rare historical documents, each carefully bound and patiently waiting for the inquiring mind to unlock their secrets.

Anja felt enveloped by the library's walls, as if they held her close, whispering secrets only she could hear. For her, the silence wasn't empty; it thrummed with a life of its own, as though echoes of past scholars still lingered in the air. The scent of old books, the subtle creaks of the balcony floors, and even the soft rustle of turning pages seemed like dialogues with kindred spirits from bygone eras. This wasn't just a building with books; it was her sanctuary, her escape from the mundane. With each book she opened, she felt as if she were unlocking a new world, and every page she turned took her one step further into the labyrinth of the past.

That night, as she climbed a brass spiral staircase toward the upper levels, a sense of eager respect washed over her. The view from the balcony impressed her, filled as it was with rows of ancient books and striking architecture. She knew the library was a place where she could both lose herself and find something more.

Tracing her fingers along the closed cases, intricate designs of brass grillwork adorned the special glass that safeguarded the books. Through the transparent barrier, she moved her gaze past aged almanacs, collections of folklore, and rare astrological charts. Disregarding well-known sagas and records of the past, her thoughts briefly flitted to more provocative narratives waiting for her at home. However, she zeroed in on a more enigmatic volume instead.

Near the last of the shelves, Anja noticed a text bound in time-worn leather with strange glyphs on its spine that she had not examined yet. It hinted at ancient mystic symbols and their occult meanings. She carefully opened the case and took out the heavy tome, bringing it downstairs to a secluded nook by a mullioned window, settling into a worn velvet sofa.

As she thumbed through the vellum pages, her thoughts drifted to moon phases and planetary transits. She then noticed a scrawled sigil in the margin. The title beneath—penned in a spidery script—was hard to decipher, but it led her to another: the Ashton Grimoire. Its name stirred something within her. Consulting the library catalog, she discovered, to her delight, that it was housed right here in the library.

Satisfied but ever curious, Anja closed the tome with a reverential touch. She reached for her notebook, its pages filled with meticulous entries written in elegant strokes. Today's discoveries would occupy a special place in her ongoing compendium of knowledge. She penned her thoughts concisely, noting key symbols and references for future exploration.

Once her fountain pen stopped dancing across the paper, Anja let out a soft breath. A sense of accomplishment and an insatiable appetite for more swirled within her. Closing her notebook, she rose from the velvet sofa, cradling the ancient tome carefully in her arms, and made her way back up the staircase.

Upon reaching the enclosed glass case, she returned the book to its designated space with the respect it deserved, aligning it perfectly with the other mystical tomes. The diamond patterns of brass grillwork seemed to shimmer momentarily as if acknowledging the return of its valued resident.

Locking the case, Anja took a final sweeping look at the rows of oak shelves that surrounded her. Her subtle smile returned; the library was a vault of endless possibilities where every book was a door, and she held the keys.

After returning to the main level and preparing to secure the library for the night, she paused momentarily by the security panel, and her eyes flickered with a different sort of illumination. The night's research couldn't quite be deemed complete—not yet. With a quick glance at her wristwatch, she calculated the minutes she could afford to spend on what she considered a rather clandestine pursuit.

She bypassed the panel, opting not to activate the security system just yet. Making her way to a less frequented corner of the library, she arrived at a door unassuming in appearance but weighty with implication. It was the entrance to the restricted archive in the basement. Few were aware of its existence, and fewer still had access. Anja had the keys, both literal and metaphorical, to this hidden alcove.

Inserting the key into the lock, she felt the tumbler turn smoothly, as if beckoning her into the room beyond. As the door swung open, the air grew noticeably cooler, redolent with the scent of aged parchment and bound leather.

Descending the narrow staircase that delved into the lower reaches of the library, she couldn't help but feel the pull of something greater —unseen but palpable. The ambient temperature dropped with each step, but it was a cold that invigorated rather than chilled her senses.

Her eyes adjusted to the soft light emitting from the strategically placed, low-wattage bulbs. It offered just enough illumination to navigate the labyrinthine arrangement of shelves, cabinets, and trunks that filled the subterranean chamber. This archive was a repository of esoterica so potent, so dangerously insightful, they were kept separate, even from the likes of Blackwell Heights' impressive collection.

The Ashton Grimoire sat ensconced behind bars of wrought iron and silver. Access to the grimoire was secured by an ornate gate of interlaced iron bars and bright silver filigree. She traced her fingers over the cold metal, examining the intricate craftsmanship. A heavy padlock engraved with mystic symbols held the bars firmly in place.

Examining the lock, she noticed markings denoting lunar phases and astrological signs corresponding to metal elements. A puzzle: it seemed the padlock would open only when certain celestial conditions aligned. "Well, someone seems to have had a sense of humor," she chuckled, thinking of the crotchety curator for this collection.

Recalling the moon phases and planetary transits from the text where she had found the sigil, she felt certain she knew the correct lunar and planetary alignments. She carefully aligned the symbolic dials on the padlock to the proper configuration.

Holding her breath, she pulled on the lock. The padlock clicked, and the latch released with a resounding clank that shattered the silence. Removing the lock from the hasp and hooking it over a bar, she looked at the gate. With a gentle push, the gate swung slowly inward with a groan. The way was now clear, and she reverently retrieved the ancient Ashton Grimoire from its sanctuary, eager to unveil its secrets. She donned a pair of cotton gloves from her pocket and reached forward.

Her hand trembled slightly as she withdrew the ancient text, its leather cover etched with arcane symbols long forbidden. She reverently set the book down on a nearby table and opened its creaking binding. The cryptic script flowed across the tattered pages in spidery scribbles and curious diagrams. Her light cast a small pool of illumination, faintly revealing the secrets held within. She took a deep breath and traced a finger down the ancient incantations, sounding out the harsh syllables under her breath.

Turning a page, she froze. An elaborate circular seal marked the vellum, seeming to writhe in the light unsteady in her hand. The occult symbols hypnotized her. Her eyelids grew heavy as she gazed at the otherworldly design. She thought she heard whispers emanating from its depths, murmuring an incomprehensible tongue. None of the languages she had studied seemed to fit.

"Odd," she thought, shaking her head sharply to break the trance. This grimoire was potent—she could feel the energy radiating from it. It was almost as if her thoughts were rearranging. She knew from her previous research that ritual, intense study, or training could rewire a brain somehow. There were plenty of research papers on that topic.

What long-hidden secrets might it reveal to one brave enough to delve deeper? A dark hunger shifted inside her. She knew that getting caught here could jeopardize Mrs. Thompson's trust. She pushed down that hunger even though the danger was starting to excite her, but now was not the time. She also needed more information to start deciphering the obviously hidden meanings. There would be time enough to return later.

She carefully placed the tome back in its place and closed the gate. Glancing around, she realized she had never actually been in this corner before. Latching the lock back in place with a loud clack and setting the dials back to how she found them, she looked around one last time to make sure everything was as she found it.

Quickly ascending, making her way into the main gallery, she paused and looked around. Especially late at night, the sight of the library and museum pieces struck her with awe. She never got tired of that sight.

The old clock chimed midnight as she gathered her belongings into her messenger bag to leave. She had lingered longer than intended over the Ashton Grimoire, losing track of time. Moving through the shadowy rooms, she made sure all windows were tightly fastened and the exhibit lights were switched off. At the front entrance, she methodically set the alarm by entering the security code into the keypad. The system beeped reassuringly to the instructions.

Turning off the last desk lamp, she opened the ornate door to step out into the night air. She secured it behind her, hearing it clink into place and lock. The sound echoed with a note of finality down the empty street.

She glanced back at the imposing edifice of the library one last time, with the Ashton Grimoire still lingering in her thoughts. But she had done as instructed, ensuring the repository of precious knowledge was fully locked up and protected until the morning. Mrs. Thompson would remain oblivious to her extra research. Pulling her coat tighter against the chill, she set off towards home, the streetlights casting long shadows.

The piercing shriek of her alarm jolted Anja awake. Catching her breath, she tried to shake the unsettling images from her dreams. The strange symbols from the grimoire had haunted her slumber, swirling through ominous landscapes. She wondered what it all meant.

Dragging herself out of bed, Anja brewed a strong cup of tea. As the kettle hissed and rumbled, her thoughts returned to the arcane seals that had now become an obsession. What secrets lay buried behind their occult ciphers?

While sipping her tea, she considered the many rare books and artifacts that filled the dusty shelves of Raymond's shop. Perhaps he had some forgotten tomes that might provide clues to the grimoire's origins. It was worth a visit.

Reinvigorated by this spark of hope, Anja busied herself getting ready for the day. She chose her clothing carefully—a flowing peasant skirt, a white lace blouse, and pendant earrings made from antique keys. Standing before the mirror, she began to brush her long hair, which cascaded down to the middle of her back. Although naturally dirty blond, she had dyed it a deep shade of burgundy that complemented her green eyes, making them even more striking. As she looked at her reflection, the deep hue of her hair seemed to capture the essence of who she felt she was.

Satisfied with how her hair framed her face, she spritzed herself with her favorite perfume. The soothing notes of jasmine and sandalwood filled the air, lending her an extra layer of confidence.

With a final swipe of red lipstick, she felt ready for the day. Donning her boots and grabbing her worn leather messenger bag, Anja set off for Archambault Antiquities.

Securing the lock on her apartment door, Anja slipped the key into her worn leather messenger bag that rested on her shoulder. A glance at her watch told her it was fifteen minutes shy of ten—just about the time Raymond should be unlocking the doors to his antique shop.

Stepping down the weathered stone staircase, Anja drew in a breath of crisp morning air. With skies unblemished and birds offering melodic greetings, the spring day beckoned her. Opting to cover the ten blocks to Archambault Antiquities on foot, she welcomed the opportunity for a quiet walk to collect her thoughts.

Anja's knee-high boots carried her briskly along the sidewalk, winding her way through the Brooklyn streets. The neighborhood was just beginning to stir—people moving their cars, shops raising metal gates. She offered friendly nods to familiar faces.

As she drew closer to the antique shop, Anja felt a flutter of anticipation. Ahead, the vibrant green sign reading "Archambault Antiquities" came into view. She peered through the window at the treasure trove of books and antiques as she passed before arriving at the intricately carved wooden door. Just in time for opening!

Taking a breath, Anja turned the tarnished handle and stepped inside; the shop's bell softly announced her arrival. Dust particles danced in the rays of morning light streaming through the windowed façade. It was time to continue the hunt.

The familiar aroma of aged paper greeted Anja as she stepped inside. At the back of the shop, Raymond glanced up from an open crate and gave a friendly wave.

"Morning, Anja! You're just in time; I've got some new sixteenth-century books fresh in from an estate sale," he said, beckoning her over.

Anja nodded in appreciation as she approached, although her mind was clearly elsewhere. "Raymond, I have to tell you what I discovered last night in the archives at the Morgan." She went on to describe uncovering the Ashton Grimoire, hidden away behind its sealed gates.

As Anja spoke, Raymond's face took on a grave cast. "Among those who traffic in occult artifacts, that grimoire has a dark reputation," he remarked, his voice dropping to a hushed tone. "Word has it Ashton ventured into perilous rites—sorceries that should remain untouched. Meddling with such energies never comes without a price."

"But what happened to him exactly? The history is so vague."

Raymond lowered his voice even more, almost a whisper, "Rumor has it Ashton's experiments went too far; the depths of magic he explored led to a terrible end. His mangled body was found in his study."

Anja was intrigued and pressed on, "And others have died mysteriously after encountering his grimoire?"

Raymond nodded grimly, "Over the centuries, yes. Accidents, suicides, madness—it leaves a trail of death. I'd wager good money there are those who sought to keep it hidden."

Anja processed this with frustration. "Please, Raymond, there must be something more about the grimoire that can help me unravel its secrets."

Raymond paused, then replied, "I have an old diary here, recovered by one of Ashton's fellow scholars and eventually sold to a dealer like me. It may provide insight, but, Anja, be wary of tugging at unknown threads."

He placed a hand gently on her shoulder. "I know that look in your eyes, my love. But take care in tampering with forces you do not fully understand. The pursuit of hidden knowledge has often come at a grave price."

Anja pondered his words but felt undeterred. "I know there are risks, but the secrets locked within those pages...they're unlike anything I've seen. Please, Raymond, if you know of anything that could help decipher it..."

Anja felt Raymond's gaze linger on her before he finally spoke. "Very well, but promise you'll be cautious." He vanished into the maze of bookshelves and reappeared holding a weathered text, which looked like an old diary. "Maybe this will offer you some clues."

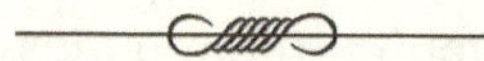

Touching the diary, Anja was filled with conflicting emotions. Fear, yes, palpable and cold, but it was mixed with something that burned hot within her chest. A strange excitement also tingled at the edges of her awareness, something that she couldn't quite place. She tried to suppress it firmly as she talked with Raymond, but it lingered, adding an edge now.

Clearing her throat, Anja looked back up at Raymond. "Wait. Did you say you thought there were those trying to keep it hidden?"

Raymond nodded gravely. "There are rumors about those determined to suppress anything occult. Silencing those who delve too deep into magical arts and other phenomena beyond this world. Witch hunts, staking vampires, hunting werewolves, and the like. Just look at the Inquisition or other religious institutions."

He lowered his voice further. "Maybe they just use other names now. If there were an organization behind it all, they would operate in secret. I would find it difficult to believe that they were all part of one entity. These are just rumors and whispers, mind you. But still..."

The notion that there might be an organization bent on suppressing occult knowledge was both intriguing and terrifying. Just the thought of it sent a creeping feeling up Anja's spine, but she maintained a calm demeanor, her mind sharp and analytical.

She turned the diary over in her hands. "Then I must unravel the grimoire's secrets carefully," she declared, meeting Raymond's eyes squarely. "Dark secrets have hounded me my whole life; it's time I stopped hiding from them."

Raymond looked at her, his eyes filled with concern yet softened by empathy. "I understand, my love. The path of light can be a lonely one, especially when the darkness beckons. You walk between both worlds." He gently squeezed her shoulder reassuringly. "Speak of this to no one else. Whether such a thing exists or not, it's wise to take no chances. Guard what you discover and hold those secrets close."

Anja gingerly nestled the diary into her leather messenger bag. As she tucked it next to her notebook, the worn leather binding gave a faint rustle, like whispers from the past. After securing the brass clasp with a satisfying click, she slung the bag's long strap over her shoulder, feeling its reassuring weight. Then, with a determined stride, she headed out of Raymond's shop, stepping onto the bustling Brooklyn sidewalks.

The subway station was only a few blocks away. Anja wove through the crowds jostling along the busy streets. Descending the concrete steps underground, she swiped her MetroCard and passed through the turnstile to board the uptown train.

Finding a seat as the car clattered forward, Anja contemplated the diary nestled in her bag. What revelations about the grimoire's origins might be contained within its aged pages?

Emerging from the subway near the Morgan Library, Anja decided to stop at her favorite sidewalk café to refuel. The rich aroma of coffee enveloped her as she sat down with a rich chocolate almond croissant and a latte. Opening her bag, Anja carefully lifted out the diary.

The sounds of the city faded away the moment she turned the pages. Anja's focus narrowed to the slanted handwriting as she slowly deciphered the text. References to Ashton's studies of ancient runes and celestial sigils fascinated her. She periodically stared off into the distance, absorbed in piecing together clues.

The clink of dishes and hiss of the espresso machine briefly drew Anja's attention back to the present. But soon, the cryptic diary again consumed her thoughts as she sought its hidden knowledge.

Skimming through the diary, she noticed a shift in Ashton's writings near the end. His usual script became hurried, even frantic in places. He wrote of shadows following him, of seeing strange figures on the edge of his vision.

She continued reading and found that Ashton claimed to hear whispers in the night, voices uttering foreboding warnings. He believed he was stalked by a sinister entity intent on stealing his life's work—the encoded grimoire. She came across multiple references to a secretive cabal known as the 'Empty Hand,' though who or what they were remained unclear. Maybe 'Empty Hand' was another group he was consulting for knowledge. Either way, Anja realized she needed more information.

Anja felt uneasy reading Ashton's growing paranoia in those final entries. He wrote of other prominent occultists who had vanished or died abruptly under mysterious circumstances. Ashton was certain some faceless group was targeting him for delving too far into occult secrets. In an agitated scrawl, he vowed to use every tool of talismanic magic at his disposal to ward off those who hunted him. But the measures apparently proved futile, as his writings ended abruptly.

Anja lowered the diary, with her mind spinning with these dark revelations. She gazed across the bustling street, wondering if danger and deception lurked behind its vanilla appearance. What menacing forces had cut short Ashton's obsession? Was it supernatural forces or beings that had killed him, or was it some cult or organization trying to suppress his knowledge? The potential danger sent a charge through her. She had been frustrated by her sedate life of late and hungered for something more.

Glancing at her phone, Anja tucked the diary back into her bag and hurriedly gathered her things. It was a quarter till noon—time for her shift at the Morgan Library. She briskly walked the few blocks, and the stone edifice of the library soon loomed into view down the tree-lined street, its ornate façade casting shadows that danced with the sun.

Inside, the rich smell of leather, parchment, and old wood greeted Anja as she briskly crossed the cool marble floors, the echoes of her footsteps blending with distant whispers of scholarly conversation. At the front desk, Mrs. Thompson was sorting through paperwork. She glanced up at Anja over her spectacles.

"There you are, right on time. We've got a full slate of researchers scheduled today, so I'll need you to retrieve some archived periodicals from the annex once you've put your things away," she said, her voice infused with a hint of urgency.

"Of course, I'll take care of it," Anja replied, making her way to the staff lounge filled with the faint aroma of coffee. She stowed her messenger bag securely in her locker and straightened her library name tag, the glint of its metal catching the light.

Anja moved through the grand rooms, her footsteps softened by the rich carpeting, preparing for the steady stream of patrons. She smiled politely at scholars already settled in the reading rooms, immersed in their work beneath the soft glow of antique lamps. Despite the looming questions raised by Ashton's diary, she focused on her tasks at hand. There would be time enough after closing to further her covert research.

The hours passed swiftly as Anja assisted patrons, re-shelved books, and handled various administrative tasks. She enjoyed being immersed in the tranquil scholarly atmosphere, her mind at peace. Before long, it was a quarter till six—time for her dinner break.

Making her way to the central court, Anja admired the café's elegant mix of marble, glass, and greenery, evoking a European alfresco style. Elegant chandeliers cast a warm glow, creating a serene oasis within the busy library. She ordered roasted salmon with vegetables and a glass of Pinot Grigio, the flavors dancing on her palate. The discount and tab for employees made dining here a welcome and convenient perk, a tasteful end to a day filled with the ever-present allure of hidden knowledge.

Settling at a small table amidst the quiet clink of flatware and a gentle murmur of conversations, Anja finally allowed her mind to wander back to the diary in her locker. What knowledge had cost Ashton his life?

As she ate, the delicate flavors of her meal were muted by her thoughts. Anja contemplated her next move. If she could just decipher a few more symbols from the grimoire, it might shed light on the cryptic references in Ashton's diary. The coinciding details hinted at some larger significance, like distant stars forming an unknown constellation.

Glancing at her phone, Anja realized her break was nearly over. She would review her notes about the diary after closing. If she could break the right sequence, its secrets might begin to unravel. The answers seemed so close now, almost tangible, like a fragrance she couldn't quite place. She just needed a way to reach through the veil of the past and grasp them.

As Anja finished her last few bites, lost in thought and the soft clatter of a bustling café, she noticed a lanky teenage boy approaching her table. Dressed in a hoodie and jeans, he had an anxious air about him, his eyes darting as though expecting to find answers in the room's corners.

"Excuse me, you're one of the research librarians, right? Could you help me find information on something called Otherkin?" he asked.

Anja paused, the unfamiliar term stirring her interest. "I'm not sure I've come across that before. Why don't you explain it to me?"

The boy shuffled, looking down, a blush coloring his cheeks. "Well, I think it's sort of like…people who believe they're…not fully human. That their soul or spirit comes from an animal or mythical creature… or something."

Anja's looked at him in interest. "Hmmm. I take it you feel an affinity with this Otherkin concept?"

Not meeting her eyes, he nodded. "I've always kinda felt out of place like I'm meant to be something more than just plain old kid. Do you think there could be books here that talk about it?"

"I don't think it would be in our traditional archives, but the internet, if you can believe anything you find there, may provide some information. The social sciences collection here may have something as well," Anja said, her voice soft and accepting. She smiled warmly, sensing the teen's isolation. "I'll be happy to help you search for information. Don't ever feel alone in who you are."

The boy smiled back gratefully before being called away by an older gentleman, likely his father, who waited patiently in the distance. Anja watched him go thoughtfully, her mind flickering back to her own adolescent existential crises. Her grandmother had helped her before she passed, but even before she died, she didn't get to visit her as often as she would have liked.

As the boy walked off, Anja called out, "Wait, I didn't get your name."

He glanced back, a shy smile playing on his lips. "Oh, it's Dillon."

She smiled warmly in return. "Nice to meet you, Dillon. I'm Anja, and I'm usually here around this time if you ever want to talk more. Or just ask for me at the research desk inside."

Dillon nodded gratefully before heading off to join the older man, his steps lighter. Anja watched him go, reflectively, a sense of kinship settling within her. She certainly understood feeling out of place, like her true self was something more, a hidden fire waiting to be discovered.

From a young age, Anja had sensed mystical undercurrents calling to her, dark impulses that both frightened and exhilarated her. She had never felt at home in the mundane everyday world and never quite fit in. Pursuing the arcane had become her purpose—her passion. That was what had driven her to her books and research. She had never quite considered things from that angle before—Otherkin. If he sought guidance in exploring his inner feelings, Anja hoped to provide support. Too often, those who walk between worlds must find their way alone. She wished Dillon a journey free of the torment and isolation she had known.

With a thoughtful smile, Anja headed back to the front desk, the boy's unease still lingering in her mind.

Two

Lucian sat at the head of the polished mahogany conference table as the board room filled with directors from selected Coruscant's corporate entities and headquarters' staff.

As the last of them sat, he leaned forward, resting his forearms on the desk in front of him; his fingers formed an intricate pattern as his thumbs and index fingers touched, creating a steeple. The rest of his fingers intertwined in a web of contemplation, his usual silent gesture of deep focus. It was an intimidating gesture.

His gaze methodically swept across the room, settling on each individual for just a moment before moving on. Clad in a finely tailored suit that highlighted his broad shoulders and lean frame, Lucian embodied a sense of authority that was nearly palpable. His dark eyes, keen and calculating, scanned the room. His dark hair, neatly styled, added a layer of sophistication. Finally, his gaze settled on the CFO, locking eyes as if zeroing in on a key piece of a complex puzzle.

The CFO started with an overview of earnings, projecting steady growth across Coruscant's public-facing subsidiaries, from VedaCorp's new generics to Panacea's clinics. Lucian smiled at her. "Wonderful, Victoria, thank you."

Revenue streams from these above-board enterprises weren't just ends in themselves; they were crucial stepping stones to something far greater, something rooted deep within his psyche. Lucian's ultimate ambition was audacious—enabling people to unlock the maximum potential of their DNA. This far-reaching vision, which always seemed to echo in the back of his mind, had been influenced by his eccentric uncle. He inspired Lucian on a course of relentless pursuit and extraordinary choices, each one a calculated risk to achieve a dream that transcended conventional understanding.

Lucian fixed his piercing gaze on the acting VedaCorp director further along the table during his presentation. "You seem to gloss over production delays in your Bengal facilities. Tell me, Robert, what's the real issue?"

Robert swallowed nervously. "Well, we've had some supply chain setbacks recently, but we're working diligently to resume full production..."

Lucian smiled coolly, resuming his steepled fingers, "Ah, quite the setback, isn't it? Please explain, Robert."

Sweating under Lucian's penetrating stare, Robert stumbled over his words. "There may have been a...an internal security breach. But my team is conducting a full review, implementing new protocols..."

Lucian slammed his palm on the table, startling Robert. "A breach? And I'm only learning of this now?" His dark eyes bored into him, and Robert withered further. Composing himself, he continued. "I expect a complete report, with full details and what you have uncovered to date, in my hands before I leave for New York tomorrow morning, as well as detailed daily reports until this 'setback' is fully rectified. Our own operations and our partners rely on smooth operations." He gritted his teeth. "Am I clear?"

"Of course, Mr. Miller," Robert replied nervously.

"Excellent. I know you won't disappoint me again, but you better get started immediately." Lucian flashed a disarming smile that didn't reach his eyes.

Robert hurried from the room as Lucian dismissed him with a wave of his hand. After he left, Lucian chuckled softly to himself in satisfaction, steepling his fingers once more.

HelixGenetics CEO Angela Chen summarized growth in customer sign-ups and sample intake. "I've identified several potential university partnerships that could expand our data access substantially…"

Lucian leaned forward. "Make those partnerships happen. Size matters, doesn't it, Angela? I want your team to maximize our reach with aggressive marketing pushes," Lucian instructed Angela. "Spare no expense. Do it."

Lucian smiled, satisfied. "Excellent work, Angela. Draft a proposal for new staff hiring and send it my way. Also, let me know if you need anything else."

Lucian sat back in his chair, contemplating the strategic implications of their next moves. Angela's marketing pushes weren't just about brand expansion; they served a larger, vital role in the grand scheme of his ambitions. By obtaining a more diverse range of DNA samples from different ethnic and geographical backgrounds, he would enhance the dataset to guide their genetic research. It wasn't merely a question of unlocking human potential—it was about understanding the very fabric of human variability. With this treasure trove of information, they could push the boundaries of what was scientifically possible.

"Yes, sir," Angela nodded seriously.

Next, the chief legal counsel summarized regulatory challenges facing certain subsidiaries. Lucian detected a sliver of defiance in the woman's eyes as she spoke. He made a mental note to keep an eye on her. Although not attracted to her, he thought it might be entertaining to force some of that defiance down.

"Thank you, Simone," Lucian turned toward the next down the line.

As each presenter finished, Lucian subtly probed them, taking their measure, pleased that he could read them so easily. That is why these face-to-face sessions were so critical.

Afterward, Lucian retreated to his private office for more confidential discussions. Everything was proceeding as expected, but he reminded himself that patience was still required. The future could not be rushed. Not yet!

Robert placed a thick report on Lucian's desk. Security and production issues in VedaCorp's Bengal facilities filled the pages. Lucian skimmed quickly, absorbing the essentials. He needed to monitor the situation closely.

"Remember—daily," he instructed Robert, catching the man's weary gaze.

A series of virtual meetings later, Lucian exchanged his suit jacket for a leather coat and dark sunglasses. His limousine awaited in the executive garage. The tinted windows secluded him from the world as the car headed for the private airstrip.

As the jet reached cruising altitude, Bella approached with a tray carrying a glass of his favorite old Irish whiskey. Two cubes of spring water shimmered in the glass, catching the cabin lights.

"Your drink, Mr. Miller," she said, placing it on the table beside his laptop. "Aged eighteen years, just how you like it."

Lucian looked up, meeting her eyes. "Ah, well, they say some things improve with age, don't they?"

Her lips twitched as if holding back a smile. "Indeed, they do," she replied, her voice laced with something that caught his interest.

Lucian took a sip of the whiskey, savoring its complexity. "Exceptional, as always, Bella. Your ability to know just what I need is unparalleled."

She offered what seemed like a practiced smile. "That's what I'm here for, Mr. Miller. To make your flight as pleasant as possible."

Watching her walking away, Lucian's lips eased into a satisfied smile. She had a way of making the long flights feel just a bit shorter.

Pulling his attention back to his laptop, the first report from Akar Labs in Iceland appeared on his screen. His biometric tracking project was progressing as planned.

The next Akar Labs update excited Lucian, which was about EpiCRISPR studies using his custom gene templates. Thanks to new supercomputing hardware, the team was advancing quickly and even showed promise in integrating quantum computing.

The last Akar report made him pause. It discussed weaponizing prion proteins against certain genetic traits. Lucian decided to secure that data, repurposing it for prevention or treatment instead. In the wrong hands—hands not his—the data could be catastrophic.

Rumors of Russian interest in similar research caught his attention. Given the situation in Russia and Ukraine, he considered recruiting more of their scientists. He'd already poached some virologists for Iceland, where vodka was just as good but the conditions far better.

Scrolling through the data from HelixGenetics, Lucian evaluated the algorithms. More genetic markers would soon be identified. Then, not just ordinary folks but even those with potential psychic or paranormal traits would be within the reach of his ever-expanding network.

He made a mental note: HelixGenetics should focus on populations with historical associations to the extraordinary. Every bit of anomalous data would be another step toward his objectives.

After reviewing the rest of the reports and being satisfied with the updates, Lucian closed his laptop and sat back, savoring the last sips of whiskey. His vision was steadily becoming a reality. At this point, it appeared as though nothing could stand in his way.

An hour later, the jet descended into Teterboro Airport, a convenient hub for wealthy travelers headed to Manhattan. It taxied to a private hanger away from prying eyes.

Stepping onto the tarmac, Lucian spotted his NYC chauffeur waiting beside his Rolls-Royce. "Good to have you back, Mr. Miller," the driver greeted him.

"Thank you, Thomas. Let's head directly to the penthouse," Lucian replied as the driver held the door for him.

The Rolls glided out of the airport, its dark windows obscuring Lucian from view. As they drove through crowded, early evening streets out of New Jersey and toward Lower Manhattan, he looked forward to returning to his luxurious apartment overlooking the city.

Arriving at the skyscraper, the Rolls-Royce pulled into the private garage. Thomas stepped out of the driver's seat and walked over to open the door for Lucian. "I'll take care of the car, Mr. Miller. Have a good evening."

"Thank you, Thomas," Lucian replied, exiting the vehicle and making his way to the private elevator.

As the elevator ascended, Lucian's anticipation built. The doors opened to the top floor. He stepped inside, pleased to be back in New York, the true heart of his growing empire.

Lucian sat at his large mahogany desk overlooking downtown Manhattan as he reviewed documents related to Coruscant Technologies, the new Delaware entity managing his US interests.

He often chose mahogany furnishings in appreciation of the wood's origins from his family's plantation holdings in the Solomon Islands, which he had visited during his childhood. He still remembered those excursions vividly.

A while later, still in the office reviewing market reports, his cellphone rang. Checking the caller ID, he saw it was his mother, Eliza, and answered, "Mother!"

"Lucian, darling! I wanted to invite you to the estate the last weekend in March," Eliza said in her breezy, entitled tone. "We're having a family celebration for my birthday."

Lucian suppressed a sigh. "Mother, that's less than two weeks away. My schedule is quite full with Coruscant business."

"Nonsense, I insist you come," Eliza pressed on. "Your brother and sister will be here. Your father is eager to speak with you as well."

The mention of his stern father, Bartholomew, made Lucian pause. Perhaps some advice on navigating the family company's European connections could prove useful, or perhaps more insight into the family businesses in general would be good.

"Very well, I'll make it work," Lucian conceded. "But I can only stay one night. I'll fly up next Friday. Could you have your driver pick me up from the field?"

"Absolutely! We'll see you soon, darling," Eliza said happily. Lucian just shook his head as he hung up. He supposed one wasted weekend might benefit him in the long run and it was her birthday after all.

After ending the call with his mother, Lucian buzzed his secretary, Ava, on the intercom. "Ava, could you please assist me with some personal business?"

"Of course, Mr. Miller," came the reply. Ava soon appeared in the office doorway, tablet in hand, ready to take notes.

Lucian explained, "I need to have a gift for my mother, Eliza, for her birthday next weekend. She has opulent taste—perhaps a piece of jewelry or something that projects status. Please identify a few options and send me your recommendations."

"Right away, sir, I'll reach out to some of the usual providers for options," Ava responded, making a note. "Any particular budget for this gift?"

Lucian waved his hand. "Cost isn't a concern; just find something that befits her level of affluence. I trust your taste."

Ava nodded. "Understood. I'll compile some choices that meet her sensibilities." She added, "Should I also arrange for a floral delivery the day you arrive?"

"Oh—Yes, an impressive arrangement—her favorite blooms are white roses and calla lilies," Lucian specified.

"Of course, I'll make sure they're delivered Friday morning ahead of your arrival that afternoon," Ava replied. "Please let me know if any other needs come up, and I'll be happy to make the arrangements."

"Also, inform the office staff that I'll be out those days. Tell them to hold any business matters for me unless it's an emergency."

Later in the afternoon, when he was reading some recent developments in epigenetics, Ava entered, holding her ever-present tablet. "Mr. Miller, I have some options for your mother's gift," she said.

"Very good, let's see what you've found," Lucian replied.

Lucian glanced over the options Ava had curated for his mother's gift. The sapphire cocktail ring caught his eye; its platinum setting showcased an opulent oval sapphire flanked by diamond baguettes. It felt most aligned with his mother's style.

"Arrange for the ring to be gift-wrapped and brought to me before Friday afternoon," he instructed.

"Excellent choice, sir. I will contact the jeweler right away and confirm the ring's delivery," Ava responded.

Lucian was satisfied. The gift was sure to please his mother. Satisfied, Lucian turned his attention back to the documents on his desk, glad that trivial personal matters were in competent hands.

After an exhausting day, Lucian was eager for his dinner date with Vanessa, the captivating woman he'd met at a charity gala last year. Vanessa had been a dazzling presence on the arm of an older socialite, but what truly captured Lucian's attention was her shared love for fine cuisine and stimulating conversation. Over time, she'd become intimately familiar with his preferences. As a high-class escort, she was very accommodating, and relationships requiring commitment had never quite suited him.

Upon arriving at Le Grand Étoile, he saw Vanessa already seated at their reserved table. She looked stunning, her black cocktail dress accentuated by the velvet choker he'd given her. "You look stunning tonight," he said, leaning down to offer her a light kiss.

Her eyes, a vivid shade of green, sparkled in the dim candlelight as she smiled. "You're too kind. How about we start with the Château Margaux?" She arched an eyebrow, posing a playful challenge.

Throughout the evening, the two enjoyed an array of exquisite dishes paired perfectly with wines. Their conversation flowed effortlessly, from travel to philosophy to art, reaffirming to Lucian that Vanessa's intellect was as enticing as her beauty. Time seemed to evaporate in her company.

Finally, as the evening progressed, Lucian looked at her and said, "I've immensely enjoyed our time. Shall we move on to the main course?"

Vanessa met his gaze, then looked down, a coy smile forming on her lips. He offered his arm, and they made their way to his waiting Rolls-Royce, where Thomas, his driver, held the door open for them.

Lucian felt the Rolls-Royce glide to a stop in front of his penthouse building. The door opened, and Thomas gave him a nod, silent but always professional. Lucian stepped out, then extended his hand to assist Vanessa from the car. She accepted, her fingers lightly touching his.

Inside the building, the elevator whisked them skyward, leaving the city's noise far below. As the doors opened to his penthouse, Lucian sensed Vanessa's subtle intake of breath at the sparkling view across the city.

Once inside, he offered to take her coat, which she graciously accepted. "Can I offer you a drink?" Lucian asked, his eyes meeting hers.

"Something light," Vanessa responded, her lips almost attempting to suppress a smile.

He moved to the bar, pouring champagne into two fluted glasses. With a casual stride, he returned and handed her a glass, their fingers brushed briefly. The unspoken electricity between them seemed to shimmer in the air.

Lucian guided her to the panoramic windows that offered an expansive view of the Manhattan skyline. The night had draped the city in its inky cloak, punctuated by the flickering lights of towering skyscrapers. He relished the view but found Vanessa's presence equally captivating.

Lucian felt a sensation he couldn't immediately identify, a sort of excitement mixed with a comforting familiarity. For a moment, he felt as if they were the only two people in a world of endless possibilities. Then, with a nearly imperceptible nod from both, Vanessa knelt in front of Lucian.

Their interludes were not frequent, but the times they spent together were always fulfilling in more than a monetary way. She truly enjoyed his company; with him, she could almost be herself. At times, she wished there could be more between them but harbored no illusions. Someday, someone would come along that would capture his heart and she would mourn her loss. She had other clients and savings enough to retire at any time, but this was her life and she honestly enjoyed it.

Vanessa looked up at the billionaire in front of her. The lights of the city reflected off his eyes, glittering like small sparks of desire. This was a scenario that had played out before and was known to both. He was the executive producer and she the innocent starlet trying to get a leading role. Simple enough, but she was in the mood for a bit more of the dominance he so naturally exuded. She wanted to feel all his passion to fill the place of the love he could not feel for her.

With her head already tilted back, she closed her eyes and shook her head. She put into her expression the sorrow she imagined from the loss when he moved on. "No. No role is worth this…"

Lucian looked down at her, appraising. "It's too late to back out now. You said you wanted this, so it's happening—one way or another."

Turning her head, she whispered, "No, I can't."

"Look at me!" He was obviously picking up on her cues and responding to her mood.

She heard a whisper of cloth and then felt his silk tie wrapped over her eyes to be roughly fastened behind her head, her hair feeling the bite of it. Hotness began to pool between her legs.

"If you don't want to look at me, then see nothing." The heat in his voice was what she wanted to hear. "Strip. I want to see what you have to offer."

Vanessa tried to feign timidity, forcing her hands to tremble as she slipped the straps off her shoulders.

Lucian, with his voice dropping lower and rougher, commanded her. "Faster. I want to see you naked." She could feel him grab her arm, pulling her to her feet.

She could imagine his dark eyes on her as she slipped off the dress. She quickly unhooked her black strapless bra and let it drop. She stepped out of her thong, dropping it as well before trying to cover herself and lowering her head to the side. She couldn't hide her arousal as her nipples tightened.

Grabbing the ends of his tie with a handful of hair tightly, he led her toward the side of the room. "Good, but it's much too late for modesty now."

Feeling the edge of a soft leather couch as he pushed her back onto it, letting his grip go, she sat back. Not being able to see amped up all her other senses. It was what she liked best about being blindfolded. They had a safe word, but she had never used it with Lucian.

"Now, while I get ready, I want to see more. Spread your legs and open yourself up to me." Lucian ordered.

The leather couch beneath her felt soft and inviting, and the scent of sex filled the air. She could hear the sound of a zipper being pulled down, followed by the rustling of clothing as Lucian prepared himself for her pleasure.

As she complied, tentatively at first, she could hear him moving and the rustling of clothing, a shoe being tossed to the side with a thump, then another. She leaned into the vulnerable feeling and started to move her fingers along her opening, and the slick wetness began to form. Moaning softly, her other hand moved up and cupped one breast.

"That's right, Vanessa, you can let that star in you shine," he said, close to her now.

She could feel the air move near her face and smelled his cologne, a scent she had come to know. Not knowing what he would do next was getting her wetter by the moment.

This. This is what I wanted, she thought, feeling a surge of desire and reached out to explore him with her fingertips. His skin was smooth and warm, and she could feel the heat emanating from his body as he stood over her.

"You are so beautiful," he said, his voice low and husky. Vanessa could feel the weight of his gaze on her, even though she couldn't see him. She shivered with anticipation as he began to touch her; his fingers traced a path across her skin.

Each touch aroused her more and more. His hands moved over her body, exploring every inch of her skin, while his lips and tongue did the same. Bites, pinches, and light scratches mixed with the soft touches at unexpected intervals were driving her arousal. She could feel him pushing her limits, taking her further into the headspace she wanted. And she loved it.

Faking her pleasure has never been a problem with Lucian. He has always been able to tell, reading her with uncanny ease. Pleasure for him always required a matching pleasure of her own.

Once she was writhing and moaning under his ministrations, she could feel him kneel on the couch next to her. With one hand, she reached out to grip his erection to guide it to her mouth, the other going to her slick folds. As he began to trust, she matched the movement with her own and continued to pleasure herself. She could feel her own climax nearing and felt his scrotum tight and tucked in close. Yes, he was near, too.

He ripped the tie off her face and she blinked up at his face as he drove into her mouth. His motions started to turn ragged as he stared down at her. She was near her peak already, and the sight of him was glorious.

Sensing the right moment, she pulled back. "Now, Lucian, please..." She opened her mouth, ready for it, wanting to feel the hot splashes of his pleasure.

He grabbed the back of her head and hair, holding her in place, and wrapped the other hand around himself, stroking himself slowly, drawing out his pleasure as he continued to look down at her.

Eyes locked together, he came; pulses of hot seed painted her face and tongue in cream-colored lines. The tangy taste of him pushed her over the edge as she rubbed her clit.

Lucian continued to stroke himself and looked down at Vanessa, watching her face as she tasted him. She moved closer and licked up along his shaft and to his fingers there, lapping up the few strands still clinging, her other hand still teasing out the last vestiges of her own climax.

Looking down, she saw the flush on her chest was mottled with some splashes, which she gathered on her fingers. Returning her gaze to Lucian's face, she could feel the heat of his gaze as she brought those fingers to her lips and licked them slowly, tasting herself along with thick and slippery traces of his essence. The scent was as tangy as the taste.

She could feel her body almost glowing with satisfaction as they came down from their high, knowing it had been a wonderful conclusion to their nights. Yes, this was the main course indeed, with a delightful desert.

Sunlight bathed the city in a radiant glow as the controller of the

Northeastern region of the US stepped into his secure office in a nondescript building somewhere in Manhattan. Yesterday, a message had pinged onto his encrypted network—a dossier on Lucian Miller. The man was not new to the Sodality's files, but the grandmaster's instructions were clear. Lucian's activities had suddenly escalated from a minor concern to a top-tier priority.

Further intel had trickled in from a mole within Lucian's organization. It outlined an upcoming trip Lucian was planning, a move that might provide the vulnerable moment needed to neutralize him effectively. Seating himself behind a desk cluttered with tech, the controller pondered his options.

Scrolling through a list of his field operatives, his eyes paused at a particular name: Smoke. A versatile agent, well-suited for complex assignments that required a knack for improvisation and capable of violence. Smoke was ideal for the task at hand.

With a few keyboard strokes, he drafted an encrypted notice of activation. Upon clicking 'Send,' he knew that across the city, in some nondescript location, Smoke would receive the message, decrypt it, and prepare to take action.

For the controller, it was one step closer to solving the issue of Lucian Miller, a problem that had evaded their grasp for far too long. But now, with the right operative activated and a potential chink in Lucian's armor, the board was set, and the pieces were moving.

Leaning back in his chair, Richard allowed himself the brief luxury of a satisfied smile. Even his lips seemed reluctant to betray his emotion, twitching ever so slightly as they formed the expression.

Three

As Anja returned to the front desk, her encounter with Dillon stirred memories of her grandmother, Madeline. When she was young, Madeline would share stories of their Scottish lineage, the McGregors with a mystical heritage, tales passed down from her grandmother, Elspeth, Anja's great-great-grandmother.

Madeline possessed a touch of 'second sight,' able to sense things beyond this world and in the flow of life. Anja recalled long talks with Madeline as a teen, confiding her feelings of being different.

"You have the gift as well, Anja," Madeline told her, her voice tinged with a gravity that made Anja listen intently. "Our family descends from ancient bloodlines. The magical arts could flow strongly through you. Trust your feelings." Madeline didn't just stop at revealing their lineage; she also taught Anja about old rituals designed to focus her thoughts and energies. According to her, Anja was on the cusp of a great destiny, one that could only be fully realized if she embraced herself and accepted what lived within her.

After Madeline's death, Anja felt lost. Her parents' divorce added to her upheaval, but she was committed to upholding her grandmother's legacy. Although she struggled with her magical abilities, she felt a subtle connection growing. Her work with the grimoire hinted at greater power if she could just unlock it. A bittersweet smile crossed her lips when she thought of Madeline. She wished her grandmother could see her now; she would be proud of her granddaughter. Anja had become a keeper of ancient wisdom in a world that seemed to have forgotten its value.

Anja thought about her late grandfather, Patrick Kinzey, whom she had never met. He was a successful real estate developer from a line of Scottish immigrants. Despite his busy career, Patrick had always prioritized his love for Madeline. To show his devotion, he bought a countryside estate where they planned to retire together in peaceful surroundings.

On her twenty-first birthday, Anja received a sealed envelope from the family lawyer. Opening it, she found not just a deed to the grand manor and its gardens but also a heartfelt letter from her late grandmother. A wave of awe and gratitude washed over her. The letter detailed an inheritance that went beyond property; a trust fund, the product of her grandfather's savvy investments, would offer her financial freedom.

Even more touching were provisions for Anna and Carl, the manor's loyal caretakers. They'd get to keep their cottage and continue their roles with a separate trust fund set up for them. The knowledge weighed on Anja, filling her with a sense of purpose and responsibility. This inheritance allowed her to leave her father's apartment, providing her the autonomy to delve deeper into her arcane studies.

The estate beckoned in her thoughts, a place where she felt her grandmother's comforting aura. Madeline's legacy offered her more than material wealth; it provided a sanctuary.

Anja wondered briefly if the library's Mrs. Thompson could be related to her maternal grandparents, the Thompsons, whom she'd never met. The thought faded quickly; maybe it was better not to know. Family relationships had always been complicated for her.

Her father, Geoffrey Kinzey, was a finance man, dismissive of his Scottish heritage and out of touch with Anja's peculiar interests. Her mother, Elizabeth, was a prim attorney who couldn't fathom Anja's nonconformist leanings. She often felt like an outsider at home, more so after her parents' acrimonious divorce.

Her older sister Amanda was another strain, always playing the obedient daughter and pointing fingers at Anja. With Amanda siding with their mother during the divorce, their already tenuous sibling relationship further deteriorated. Anja chose to live with her father, gaining some freedom due to his indifference. Amanda moved across the country for college and all but cut ties with her sister, something Anja didn't really mind.

Anja sometimes wondered if she would feel more connected to her family if not drawn so strongly to the arcane and mystical. But she could not pretend to be someone she was not. Their differences seemed irreconcilable. In some ways, she felt liberated by the distance from her relatives but would always miss her grandmother.

After finishing her studies at Columbia, Anja found a home in the academic world, particularly in medieval esoterica. Earning her MLS opened doors, leading her to a position at the library. It was an environment where her unique interests weren't just tolerated but celebrated. Here, among scholars who shared her fervor for uncovering lost wisdom, she felt seen. Her work allowed her to dig into ancient texts, offering her the freedom to explore her theories without ridicule. It was as if the library's walls provided a sanctuary for her unending quest for knowledge.

"Anja! Did you hear me?" Mrs. Thompson's sharp tone cut through Anja's ruminations, making her jump.

"Oh! I'm sorry, Mrs. Thompson. My mind was wandering," Anja replied apologetically.

The head librarian adjusted her spectacles and gave Anja a scrutinizing look. "Clearly. As I was saying, it's nearly closing time. The last researchers will be packing up shortly."

Anja glanced at the old clock, surprised to see it was already a quarter to nine. The day had flown by in a blur of tasks and contemplations.

"Of course, I'll start closing up as soon as the patrons clear out," she assured Mrs. Thompson, hoping her eagerness wasn't obvious.

Seemingly satisfied, Mrs. Thompson gathered her coat and

handbag. "Very well. Good night then," she said, making her way out.

Her lips allowed a brief smile as the librarian disappeared through the grand doors. Finally, the time had come. She hurried to retrieve her messenger bag and the diary from her locker.

Soon after ensuring all the researchers had left and the doors were locked, Anja made her way back to the locked archive room that housed the Ashton Grimoire. A rush of anticipation surged through her veins as she opened the iron gate and retrieved the ancient text once more. Settling at the table, she turned the brittle pages with care.

Some of the arcane seals and sigils called to her. Anja copied them into her notebook, meticulously tracing each line and curve. Replicating the occult symbols, she felt an odd energy tingle through her fingers, but their significance still eluded her.

Try as she might, Anja could not decode any new revelations in the grimoire that night. Her thoughts continued to swirl back to her conversation about the Otherkin. Closing the heavy tome, Anja decided to conclude her research for the evening. Perhaps fresh eyes in the morning would unveil new insights from her notes and the diary. Tonight, she would delve into learning more about otherkin instead.

After ensuring the library was securely locked and the alarms set, Anja headed home to her studio apartment. She brewed some tea and opened her laptop, drawn to explore this concept resonating with Dillon. If she could better grasp it, maybe she could help him and learn something about herself as well.

Anja scrolled through websites and forums, captivated by the diverse experiences and struggles self-proclaimed otherkin described. A wistful thought crossed her mind: if only she had access to such perspectives when she was younger. The phenomenon seemed both widespread and astonishingly varied.

In the past, she had dismissed forums such as these as nothing more than popular conspiracy theories—Q-Anon and its ilk were viewed as dangerous nonsense. A preference for published and printed work had always guided her; the internet, after all, teemed with charlatans and 'alternative' facts.

Sipping her tea, Anja delved into the various online forums and articles about Otherkin. She learned the word originated in the 1990s BBS elf fandoms but had expanded to encompass all who identified as part- or non-human.

Many participants described feeling a fundamental difference from humanity from a young age. Like herself, they grew up sensing they did not belong. The communities attempted to provide comfort and understanding among kindred spirits.

Some posts discussed the concept of body dysphoria—a disconnect between their physical and mental self-image, very much like gender dysphoria. Anja was familiar with the sense of not fully fitting into her own shell, but she was definitely feminine.

Others wrote of phantom limbs and sensations—feeling wings, tails, or other non-human appendages. Anja was fascinated but couldn't quite relate to that particular experience. She wondered if dreams counted. According to several posts they did count—so maybe she could relate after all.

The most prominent shared thread was a yearning for belonging and self-discovery. Finding similar people—their tribe. Anja understood that desire all too well. While she did not identify as otherkin herself, Anja felt great empathy for their journeys. She hoped to provide guidance to young Dillon as he navigated his path to self-acceptance. Maybe she should reassess her own feelings about the Otherkin.

Delving deeper, Anja came across subgroups like angelkin, demonkin, therians, and vampires. She found the demonkin communities most intriguing, given her own occult interests. Perhaps part of her fascination with the dark arts stemmed from an innate connection to infernal realms. Although skeptical, she could not outright dismiss the possibility of her soul, or part of it, originating beyond the human sphere.

The more Anja read of demonkin, the more she identified with their descriptions of shadowy impulses and sensing innate preternatural talents. If a person's spirit could align with angelic energies, why not infernal ones too?

She wondered if embracing this side of herself could unlock new cognitive doors and offer insights into deciphering old texts like the Ashton Grimoire. There was much overlap between her esoteric studies and the experiences described by otherkin of diverse kinds.

Anja stifled a yawn, her body's quiet protest against the late hour research. She decided to wrap up her digital exploration of Otherkin for the night. Shutting her laptop, she washed up and changed into a black satin chemise.

Climbing into her plush bed, Anja's thoughts continued to swirl with those of demonkin, therians, and the like. She identified more closely with them than she had expected. Reaching to turn off the bedside lamp, Anja wondered if she would dream herself in some non-human form tonight.

Resting her head on the pillow, she smiled softly in the darkness. Her talk with young Dillon had unlocked a new path of discovery. She looked forward to learning more, perhaps finding fresh means to access her own gifts.

Anja drifted off, surrounded by mystical texts and strange curios, opening her mind to whatever realms—demonic or otherwise—her spirit felt drawn to. If embracing her shadow self could illuminate her purpose, she would not shy away from the darkness. Its temptation had always beckoned her…just on the other side of sleep.

Anja was shelving books when her cell phone vibrated. She glanced at the caller ID—it was her old college friend and roommate, Zoe Ananda.

"Zoe! It's been too long," Anja answered warmly.

"Anja! I'm back in New York and ready to hit the town with my best bookworm friend," Zoe replied excitedly.

Anja smiled. "What brings you back to the city?"

"I just transferred here as an FBI special agent with the New York field office. So I'm officially a resident again!"

"That's amazing. Congratulations!" Anja said, aware that Zoe had long aspired to join the Bureau.

Zoe continued, "I officially start next week, but first, we are going out to celebrate properly! What does your Friday night look like?"

"Fridays are a late shift for me at the library, but I could sneak away and be ready by ten p.m.," Anja replied.

"Perfect! We'll party like it's still senior year. Get ready for a night on the town with your old gal-pal, Zoe!"

They made plans to meet up. Anja smiled as she hung up. Zoe's bubbly enthusiasm was infectious, as always. She looked forward to catching up with her vibrant friend and former roomie.

The rest of the week seemed to fly by in a blur of mundane library tasks for Anja. Her additional research into the Ashton Grimoire had stalled, adding to her frustration. Anja also had not seen Dillon back at the library yet.

By Friday afternoon, she felt restless, the tedium of work weighing on her. Anja found herself looking forward to her evening out with Zoe. It had been too long since she let loose and had some mindless fun. At precisely nine p.m., Anja grabbed her coat and messenger bag, waving to Mrs. Thompson.

"Heading out early for once?" Mrs. Thompson asked, surprised.

"Yes, I'm meeting an old friend tonight," Anja replied with an eager smile.

Mrs. Thompson raised an eyebrow. "Hmm, not going to get into any trouble, are you?"

"No, just drinks and catching up with a friend," Anja assured her. Seeing Mrs. Thompson's skepticism she added, "I'll be sure to be in on time tomorrow, not to worry."

Seemingly placated, Mrs. Thompson nodded. "Very well. Do enjoy yourself then—you could use an evening out with friends your age, I suppose."

Anja grinned. "I will, thank you! Good night!" She hurried out before Mrs. Thompson could say anything else.

Leaving the library, Anja rushed home to change. A spritz of perfume and a brush of her hair later, she donned her clubbing dress and boots. On her way to the subway, she found the cool night air invigorating, fueling her rebellious mood.

With her unique blend of Indian and American heritage, Zoe's features were striking—warm brown skin, dark almond eyes, and silky black hair flowing down to her shoulders. She had an aura of confidence and sensuality. Zoe wore dramatic winged eyeliner and red lipstick, along with golden hoop earrings that swung as she waved excitedly to Anja. Knee-high boots with stiletto heels completed her eye-catching ensemble.

Anja smiled, both amused and impressed by her friend's daring outfit as always. Though Anja had chosen a slinky black dress and boots for the night out, Zoe's revealing ensemble was far more bold and vivacious by comparison. While Anja tended to favor darker, understated styles, Zoe clearly relished showing off her colorful personality. Her red minidress with a metallic sheen, boasting some revealing cutouts and boots, showcased the perfect blend of her South Asian beauty and daring American attitude. Anja was thrilled to reunite for a carefree night of fun with her gorgeous, spirited friend.

Approaching Zoe outside the neon-lit club, Anja greeted her with a fierce hug, squealing with delight. As they laughed and made their way inside, Anja exhaled, letting the pulsing music wash away the stresses of the week.

Relieved to dance away her worries for a night, she surrendered to the beat. With shots flowing and Zoe's arm wrapped around her shoulder, Anja allowed herself to live in the moment. The answers she sought would come when they were ready... For now, she would savor this small freedom.

The dance floor was a mass of writhing bodies as the DJ spun intense House Techno beats. Strobing lights flashed wildly through plumes of artificial smoke, giving the packed club an otherworldly vibe. Anja and Zoe danced with abandon, swept up in the frenetic energy.

During a break, as they headed to the restroom, the pulsating music muted slightly. Anja asked Zoe, "Looking forward to your new assignment? What will you be doing now?"

Zoe waved her hand vaguely. "Oh, it's probably just going to be piles of paperwork. But I don't want to talk shop tonight—this is about cutting loose!" She twirled dramatically in her minidress.

Anja laughed. "You're right; work talk can wait. But we should catch up over lunch once you're settled."

Just then, the next song dropped, vibrating the walls. "For now, let's dance!" Zoe shouted, pulling Anja back towards the dance floor.

Anja and Zoe danced wildly as the night wore on, attracting attention from those around them. At one point, Zoe leaned in close to Anja's ear and shouted over the music, "Go ahead and give one of these guys your number! You need to get laid."

"What? Really, Zoe?" Anja gave her a friendly poke while Zoe just grinned.

Anja simply smiled and shook her head politely at the hopeful admirers hovering nearby. She appreciated her outgoing friend's encouragement, but casual hookups had never appealed to her, though she did feel a longing. Hot romance tales would have to do. Anja needed a deeper connection before opening up so intimately, and she had never found anyone who called to her that way. Ever since that time in high school when... No, she locked down those memories.

The pulsing beats and swirling lights carried the two through the early morning hours. Anja let the music's energy course through her, washing away her everyday restraints, if only for the night.

As she danced, Anja's thoughts drifted to arcane symbols from the Ashton Grimoire and secret watchers hunting. She imagined otherkin beings moving through the flickering lights, ancient chants echoing beneath the rhythmic bass.

Zoe's arm was draped around her shoulder, keeping Anja anchored in the moment. But the mystical thoughts still swirled through her mind, as persistent as always. For a few hours, she had escaped into youthful frivolity. But the shadows were waiting when she closed her eyes.

As closing time neared, Zoe gave Anja a tight hug. "One of my admirers is hosting an afterparty. Come with!"

Anja smiled but shook her head. "Not tonight. But we'll meet up soon!"

Zoe nodded, looking disappointed, before smiling and hugging her.

With a wink, she headed off into the night on the arm of a handsome stranger. Anja felt suddenly alone as she left the club's pulsing energy behind. The night air was still as if the city held its breath.

Walking to the subway, the hairs on Anja's neck prickled. She imagined unseen eyes tracking her every move. Hidden threats seemed to lurk in every shadow—but then again, it was midtown Manhattan in the middle of the night.

A cab pulled up, one among the many hunting for revelers heading home, and Anja quickly jumped in. As it carried her through the empty streets, she stared out the window into the darkness. What dangers awaited those who dared to seek forbidden answers? For now, her questions would remain unspoken.

The cab dropped her at her apartment entrance. Anja ascended the stairs, reassured only once behind her own locked door. Tonight had been a thrilling but brief escape. Tomorrow, it would be back to her world of secrets and rituals hidden in dusty pages.

As Smoke loaded his 9mm Glock and slipped the silencer into his go bag, the words from his controller played on a loop in his head: surveil, identify, eliminate. There was no room for error. The all-black SRK and other tools felt heavy, a weight that went beyond the physical.

He thought back to his initial days in the Sodality, how he'd committed to protecting humanity from the supernatural. The vow was not just a ritual; it was a personal pledge.

Double-checking his gear, his mind filled with the faces of past Sodality members whose courage fueled him now. For the greater good, he was willing to blur some lines. With his senses heightened, Smoke focused on the mission ahead. His training and commitment made him feel capable and ready to face the challenge.

Satisfied that he'd left no traces in his apartment, he closed the door behind him. This place had served its purpose. Now, he needed to disappear. He navigated the shadowed streets, looking for an older, nondescript car. Finding one, he hot-wired it with practiced ease and drove off. As dawn broke, Smoke felt a sense of resolve. Information on the estate's security measures fortified his confidence. He had a job to do, one that might go unheralded but would matter nonetheless.

It was time to get into position and wait. He'd rest and prepare, mindful of the gravity of his mission but not burdened by it. Tonight, he'd do what he had been trained for, safeguarding a world that would never know his name.

Four

Lucian's sleek jet touched down on the private airfield near his mother's estate. He patted the elegantly wrapped ring box in his pocket, anticipating how happy his mother would be receiving it. He saw the family's longtime driver beside the green Rolls-Royce Phantom. "Good to see you again, Mr. Miller. Let me take you to the manor."

During the drive, his eyes wandered over the sprawling lawns and gardens, each contour of greenery reminding him of the inheritance that awaited him. As they reached the grand entrance, Lucian spotted the stately butler. "Welcome home, sir. Your mother is in the sunroom with your father."

Lucian followed the butler, feeling the familiarity of the ornate halls around him. His mother's enthusiastic embrace greeted him as he entered the sunny glass-enclosed sitting room. "Lucian, darling!"

His father, appearing as solemn as Lucian had expected, stood and said, "Son, walk with me. We have business to discuss."

Nodding, Lucian turned to his mother. "First, happy early birthday." He handed her the wrapped ring box.

Her eyes widened, a response that Lucian had hoped for. "Oh, Lucian, you shouldn't have! May I open it now?"

"Absolutely," he replied.

As his mother unwrapped the gift and discovered the sapphire cocktail ring, Lucian felt a swell of pride at her reaction. "It's absolutely exquisite! You do have such taste. I can't wait to show it off tomorrow."

"Your brother and sister have arrived already, and Abigail has brought along her new boyfriend. I had to allow it, or she refused to come at all," she said, prompting Lucian to raise an eyebrow. This was news to him, but he simply nodded in acknowledgment. Looking at her husband, "Remember you two, supper will served in a little while; don't get too wrapped up in business!"

His father gestured toward the hallway, signaling it was time to go. Lucian felt the weight of expectation as he followed, knowing all too well that tardiness was not an option when Bartholomew Miller IV was concerned.

Soon, they were seated in the dark, wood-paneled study. His father fixed him with a firm stare, steepling his fingers. It was a gesture Lucian had learned from him, one that signaled serious discussion ahead. "Now then, about family business. Your brother concerns me. Winston lacks any sense of direction or work ethic. And his drinking has grown worse. And Abigail, well…"

Lucian nodded, choosing his words carefully as he met his father's penetrating gaze. "I assumed as much. He has made no effort to better himself or live up to our legacy."

His father harrumphed, words laced with disdain. "Indeed. A layabout parasite, undeserving of his privilege." Lucian felt a momentary pang at the harshness but couldn't disagree. "I updated the documents last month to clarify this so there would be no questions. Winston will retain his trust fund but be removed from any leadership role in the business, not that he has been much part of it anyway."

Lucian suppressed a smile. It was the kind of news he had expected but was relieved to hear. "I appreciate your faith in me, Father. I swear I will expand and empower the Miller name."

His father continued, "As I've stepped back lately, your Uncle Edward in London has taken over daily operations."

"I know. He's been doing an admirable job managing things," Lucian responded, nodding.

"Quite so. But Edward and I agree it's time for you to join the board and take a larger strategic role. I have heard many things about the successes you have had on your own and the influence you have had on our pharmaceuticals and biotech firms."

His father's words carried weight, and Lucian felt the swell of responsibility and potential. "I appreciate you entrusting me with this."

With a pat on Lucian's shoulder, his father seemed to confirm his approval. "Excellent. Ah, we'd best head back. Your mother will be cross if dinner is delayed!"

As they arrived back in the sunroom, the butler entered, "Pardon the interruption, but supper will be served in the dining room shortly."

"Wonderful!" Eliza exclaimed.

Sharing a knowing glance with his father, Lucian extended his arm to his mother. As he escorted her from the sunroom, his mind shifted gears, bracing himself for the intricate dance of family dynamics that awaited him.

Lucian, his mother holding his arm, and his father entered the grand dining hall. Across the table, Winston already had a drink halfway to empty, his gaze as unfocused as his life ambitions. Lucian couldn't help but think how the family's initial hopes had all but evaporated when it came to Winston.

After ensuring his mother was comfortably seated, Lucian took his place, setting his eyes on the seat opposite him where Abigail would soon sit.

Last to make their entrance were Abigail and a young man who, to Lucian's initial surprise, looked a bit like him. *Interesting.*

His mother announced, "Children, this is Abigail's new beau, Thomas. Make him feel welcome."

Lucian appraised Thomas with mild curiosity. Abigail had always been crafty when it came to relationships. This dinner was shaping up to be anything but dull.

The appetizer was one of Eliza's favorites: oysters on the half shell. As everyone tucked in, Eliza didn't waste time inquiring about Abigail's charity ventures. "You should throw a grander event this year, darling," she insisted, to which Abigail responded with a nod, barely hiding her annoyance.

By the time the second course arrived, the focus had shifted to Winston's latest indiscretions. Lucian's lips twitched at the corners as he listened to his father's stern reprimands, Winston drowning his humiliation in more wine.

Thomas attempted to impress the table with his social connections when the main course came around, but Lucian caught Abigail's discreet eye roll.

As the conversation shifted to the topic of family trusts, tempers flared. Winston slammed his fist on the table. "You can't just cut me off!"

"I've had enough of your reckless behavior. You haven't been interested in the business and can't seem to find any ambition. I haven't cut you out of your trust yet, but just might, if you can't get your act together! Maybe that will provide the drive you need," Bartholomew replied icily.

Eliza intervened, trying to diffuse the situation by turning the attention to the activities planned for tomorrow. However, Lucian couldn't help but feel amused by the spectacle. It was high drama, and for once, he wasn't at the center of it.

Lucian wrapped up the meal by sharing news of his latest business ventures, earning nods of approval from his mother. When coffee and petite fours were served, the tension had ebbed, but the emotional undercurrents in the room were palpable. Lucian stood up to leave the table satisfied, having navigated the family gauntlet without a scratch. But Abigail's hand shot out, gripping his arm.

"A word, dear brother?"

Abigail's smile never met her eyes as she escorted Lucian away from the dining hall and into a lavish sitting room. She closed the door and faced him, arms crossed.

"Alright, Lucian, I think it's time we have a chat, just the two of us."

Lucian raised an eyebrow. "Oh? And what did you wish to discuss, dear sister?"

Abigail fixed him with a piercing gaze. "Let's talk frankly, shall we? I know you've been whispering in Father's ear."

Ah, so this was about the inheritance machinations Lucian had set in motion. He met her stare coolly. "Dear sister, I'm sure I don't know what you mean."

Abigail laughed. "Please, I know you're planning something with Father. If you think I'll stand idly by, you're very mistaken." She began pacing, visibly fuming. "You won't sideline me in this family."

"Why wish for more when you're already excelling in your own sphere?" Lucian asked, his tone as smooth as silk.

Abigail's expression tightened. "I won't be cornered into being a mere socialite."

Lucian could almost see her internal struggle. "You have your trust fund and Mother's ear. What more do you want?"

The silence was answer enough. Lucian decided to press further. "Your current beau, Thomas, seems to lack a certain…ambition, wouldn't you say?"

Abigail looked like she might explode. "You dare question my choices?"

"Even you couldn't resist an eye roll when he was name-dropping. I can't be the only one who noticed."

Her face turned a shade redder, but Lucian wasn't finished. "He does bear a curious resemblance to me, don't you think? Aspirational, perhaps?"

"What are you implying? Just go," she spat out.

Lucian rose, feeling a sense of accomplishment. "I'll say goodnight to Mother."

As he left, he couldn't help but think he had hit a nerve, revealing a chink in Abigail's usually impenetrable armor. Lucian felt a smirk pull at his lips. The night had turned out to be quite enlightening after all.

After closing the door behind him, Lucian felt an urge to see his mother before retiring. He found Eliza in the sitting room. The laughter of Winston and Thomas echoed from the billiards room down the hall. Father had retired, leaving mother alone with her evening sherry.

She brightened as he entered. "Ah, Lucian, come sit."

He took a seat next to her. "You were quiet at dinner, Mother. Is everything alright?"

Eliza dismissed his concern with a wave. "Oh, family gatherings stir the pot, that's all. No need for me to add any more spice." She looked at him with a warmth only a mother could muster. "Your steadiness is a comfort, Lucian."

He patted her shoulder gently. "I'm always here for you, Mother."

"Such a good son," she replied, touching his knee.

Lucian's lips twitched in a half smile, but then he sobered. "It's late, Mother. You need your rest for tomorrow."

"Ah, yes, the ravages of time," Eliza sighed, standing with his help.

He kissed her cheek. "Sleep well. I'm off for a brief walk by the lake."

"Just don't be out too long. A storm is coming," she warned and headed upstairs.

Once alone, Lucian adjusted his jacket and made for the door. The lake had been his sanctuary since youth, and tonight, it called to him again. Unencumbered by his usual digital tethers—laptop and business phone back in Manhattan—only the night and the lake awaited. And should any emergency arise, Ava had his number. With that assurance, he stepped into the night.

Lucian made his way down the sloping lawn. A familiar path through the trees led him to the lake, the same path he'd trodden since boyhood whenever he yearned for peace and quiet. He settled atop a flat rock near the shore, his eyes drifting across the water, losing himself in thought.

In the distance, clouds were slowly rolling in, intermittently obscuring the luminous moon. Occasional droplets plinked the lake's surface, expanding in rippling rings—much like the reach of my empire, he mused.

Crickets and night birds filled the air with their nightly chorus. These moments of serenity were a rare gift, a brief respite from the ceaseless demands of his ambitions. The raindrops grew more persistent, confirming the approaching downpour. Lightning split the sky, and seconds later, thunder rolled. His mother had been right; it was time to head back. Yet he lingered, inhaling the scent of the impending rain, the trees shimmering as the moisture gathered on their leaves.

As fat drops began to fall in earnest, Lucian stood. He had better leave now, lest he'd be soaked. He cast one last look over the lake, now pockmarked by the quickening deluge, the rush of sound taking over the night air. Turning his collar up, he made his way back through the trees as the wind lashed the limbs and thunder echoed. Within the tumult, Lucian's mind was already calculating, planning again.

Lucian picked up his pace as the rain intensified, the trail now a muddy mess. Flashes of lightning periodically lit his path, and he marveled at how well he still knew the way, even in darkness. As he neared the tree line, ready to emerge onto the lawn, Lucian noticed odd lights flickering through the boughs. Drawing closer, he felt his pulse quicken. Multiple sets of lights, mostly blue but some red, were flashing in the night, diffused by the falling rain. Police cars?

Ducking behind a large maple, Lucian peered out cautiously. Two police cruisers were parked near the manor's side entrance, their lights still flashing. Dark figures moved furtively in the downpour, their flashlights sweeping. A cascade of thoughts flooded Lucian's mind: calculations, contingencies, and potential threats. Had his secret activities been discovered? He quickly dismissed the thought. The local county sheriff's cars wouldn't be the ones to come for him.

Remaining concealed by the shadows, Lucian edged around the lawn's perimeter. He needed more information before revealing himself. Pausing beneath a balcony, he noticed the lights were on in his father's upstairs room, shadows flitting across the curtains.

Making a decision, Lucian left his hiding spot and approached the side entrance just as another bolt of lightning lit up the sky. An officer raised a hand, halting him. "Stop right there, sir! This is a restricted area. State your name and business."

His confusion deepening despite the grim signs, Lucian replied, "I'm

Lucian Miller. This is my family's estate. What's happening?"

The officer scrutinized Lucian before speaking. "There's been a...an incident. We're securing the scene. Are you carrying any weapons?"

His stomach tightening, Lucian answered, "No, no weapons. An incident? Which of my family is hurt? I need to see them right away."

The officer rested a hand on his weapon. "The detectives will want to speak with you, and so will the sheriff. For now, you can wait inside."

Lucian nodded, feeling the chill and damp seep into his bones yet maintaining his composure. An officer from the hallway was called over to accompany him, guiding him to the sitting room to await further news.

Lucian paced the room, each step radiating his growing impatience and frustration. Heavy footsteps echoed in the hallway before Sheriff Bowman finally appeared, water dripping from his hat.

"Mr. Miller? I'm Sheriff Bowman. My apologies for the wait; I needed to assess the situation myself first."

Struggling to maintain an even tone, Lucian said, "Sheriff, what is going on? Has something happened to my family?"

The sheriff's eyes were unyielding. "An incident occurred tonight. Detectives are on their way."

"This is unacceptable. I want to see my parents, now!" Lucian's voice tightened with each word.

"Stay here, sir. You'll be questioned soon." The sheriff turned, ignoring Lucian's plea for more information as he retreated down the dark hallway.

Left alone, Lucian resumed his pacing. His family's standing should afford him more answers. For now, his thoughts spiraled, constructing multiple scenarios about tonight's events. He'd need to be calculated in his responses to the detectives.

Questioned? Thinking of the worst possibilities, Lucian understood the likely implications: suspicion would naturally fall on him, especially given his father's recent adjustments to his will and trust.

Deciding that complete cooperation was the wisest course for the moment, Lucian felt the immediate need for legal counsel. He glanced at his phone; it was two-twelve a.m. Corporate lawyers wouldn't suffice; this was a situation demanding specialized expertise. Within moments, Lucian was on the phone, dialing his lawyer's emergency line. The time for waiting was over; now was the moment for decisive action.

"Charles, this is Lucian. There's been an incident at my family's estate, some…altercation. The details are unclear, but it's serious enough that detectives are en route."

Charles replied with alarm, "My god, that sounds ominous. What can I do?"

Lucian responded calmly, "While I appreciate your capabilities, this matter requires specialized assistance. Please contact Horace Reed immediately. He has represented my family previously, and ask him to come here to Granite County. I need strong counsel present before speaking with the authorities."

Charles answered, "Of course, completely understandable. I'll call Reed right away and keep you informed. In the meantime, say nothing further until he arrives."

"Thank you, Charles. Please have him contact me when he's on his way." Lucian ended the call, hoping he had set in motion the first steps to limit his exposure.

For now, all he could do was impatiently prepare for the investigation process. The night's events would require adaptable strategy and discretion to navigate.

Lucian heard footsteps and muted voices approaching down the hall. He discerned the sheriff speaking with two newly arrived detectives.

"With this high profile, we'll need all hands on deck," the sheriff said. "I'm requesting the BCI's forensics team and additional personnel for assistance."

A female voice replied, "With respect, my partner and I have handled dozens of major cases."

"I know you're capable, Cruz, but this one requires extra care. I'm not sure you realize yet just how big this will be," the sheriff responded firmly. "You wanted to advance your career, right? This is the kind of case that makes reputations...for better or worse."

After a pause, Detective Cruz answered, "You're right, Sheriff. It's just..."

"Good. Keep me in the loop. This will take cooperation between agencies, but you'll lead the investigation," the sheriff affirmed. He then added, "I also need to give the state AG a heads-up on this. No pressure, though, Nina. Just take a good look at the scene, then have a chat with Mr. Miller. He's a big shot, too, so watch out."

"Sheriff," Detective Cruz replied. Their voices faded down the hall again.

Lucian took a deep breath, preparing himself mentally. He would need to be at the top of his game to navigate the scrutiny ahead. Adversity had yet to stop him; this would be no different.

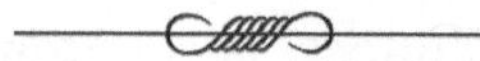

Leaving the room with Horace Reed, Lucian felt the weight of the situation press down on him. Determined to find answers, he knew he had to explore every angle and follow every lead. The truth was waiting to be uncovered, and Lucian was determined to bring justice to his family's name. He was angry, barely containing his rage.

He couldn't help but feel a sense of relief, though, knowing his cooperation had been beneficial. He could imagine the weight on their shoulders, trying to solve this case. He did not think they would succeed or were as motivated as he was now.

His lawyer gave him a reassuring pat on the back. "You handled that well, Lucian. We'll keep cooperating and do everything we can to clear your name."

He nodded, "Thank you, Horace. This is a nightmare, but I want to do whatever it takes to find the truth. No, I will do whatever it takes!"

Horace glanced around, then lowered his voice, "Given the high-profile nature of this case and the media attention, I suggest we consider hiring personal security for you."

Lucian nodded in agreement. "You're right. It's better to be safe. I'll need to arrange that. Also, Horace, can you arrange for a couple of private investigators to start some inquiries of our own?"

"Consider it done," Horace replied, making a note in his pad. "I'll get my best team on it right away."

As they walked through the busy police station, Lucian's mind was racing with everything he needed to handle. He had to arrange for the funeral for his family, a task that weighed heavily on his heart.

Once he returned to his family's estate, the reality of the loss hit him harder. He was not only dealing with grief he had not expected but also handling immense responsibilities that had unexpectedly fallen upon him. He knew the days to follow would be filled with countless arrangements, interviews, and constant media attention.

Alone in the hotel, the estate still closed off for the investigation, Lucian used his business phone sent with Horace by his secretary to call his Uncle Edward in England.

"Uncle, I'm afraid I have tragic news," Lucian began solemnly once Edward answered. He proceeded to explain what happened to Edward's brother Bartholomew and the rest of the family.

Edward was audibly shaken, asking probing questions Lucian did not have answers for yet. After offering his condolences, Lucian continued gently, "I know it is a heavy burden, but the family business needs you now more than ever. I'm still tied up with the investigation here."

"Of course," Edward replied, composing himself. "I will start making arrangements to have your father and the others brought back to the estate for burial. And releasing statements to the British press with dignity."

Lucian asked delicately, "Could you also handle telling the rest of the family? I'm just so overwhelmed right now."

"I'll do that," responding somberly.

"Thank you, Uncle. My team will assist you however needed. Call me anytime," Lucian said before hanging up.

Next, Lucian called Charles. "Charles, I wanted to thank you again for connecting me with Horace on such short notice," Lucian began. "He appears to be very capable and has handled matters here well."

"Of course, I'm glad I could help quickly, given the horrific circumstances," Charles replied solemnly.

Lucian continued, "I also need to get the estate and will matters handled smoothly. Can you recommend a probate specialist?"

"Genevieve Lee is the most seasoned estate attorney in town. I'll get a contract drafted right away," Charles assured him.

Lucian agreed. "Excellent. Please have her expedite transferring all applicable assets into my name. I want protections in place under the circumstances. Also, could you coordinate with public relations to have someone start on that aspect? Have them contact me to get my thoughts?"

"Right away, sir, you can count on me to facilitate everything," Charles said.

After ending the call, Lucian sat back, satisfied at having set that in motion.

Five

Anja hummed to herself as she prepared for her Sunday shift at the library. After grabbing a light jacket, she headed out to the breezy spring morning. She stopped by the corner newsstand to purchase a copy of the Sunday paper. Her neighborhood was just beginning to stir awake, with the sunlight coaxing residents outside.

Reaching the subway entrance, Anja descended into the muted underground. As expected, the station was less crowded than during the weekday rush. Finding a seat on the train, she settled in and retrieved the newspaper from her worn leather messenger bag. Unfolding the first section, Anja began perusing the headlines and latest news. She hoped for some interesting article to enliven the sleepy Sunday commute. Soon, she would be immersed in her work at the quiet library. But for now, Anja was content to catch up with goings-on in the world.

As Anja casually unfolded the paper, the chilling front-page headline grabbed her attention: 'Prominent Miller Family Found Slain Upstate.'

She inhaled sharply, goosebumps rising on her arms. This was far from the Sunday morning news she anticipated. The article provided scant initial details about the 'horrific incident' at the Miller family's upstate estate. It named the victims—Bartholomew Miller IV, his wife Eliza, and their adult children Winston and Abigail. One additional victim remains unnamed pending next of kin notification.

Police had provided no information about the causes of death or suspects. The local Granite County sheriff was quoted saying the Bureau of Criminal Investigation was assisting with what was now a high-profile homicide investigation.

Anja shuddered, reflecting on her father's stories about the powerful Miller family's business empire. For such elite socialites to meet a violent, inexplicable end sent shivers down her spine. With her trying to find out more about Ashton's horrific death and thoughts of secret societies running through her head, she couldn't help but wonder. Folding up the paper, Anja's mind spun with unanswered questions.

Anja resolved to stay vigilant for any developments relatable to her own arcane pursuits, unlikely as that seemed. For now, she tried focusing her uneasy thoughts back on the day's work ahead. She seemed unable to focus on that, though. The story just kept pulling her attention back to Ashton. In her mind, she reviewed what she had learned so far:

The Ashton Grimoire said to have been authored by Edward Ashton, a little-known English scholar and occultist in the late sixteenth century. He spent years traveling Europe and the Middle East, collecting esoteric knowledge before compiling it into the encrypted grimoire.

Ashton was said to belong to several secret societies and mystery schools throughout his travels, gaining access to rare magical texts and rituals. He became convinced that certain occult forces could transform humanity if properly harnessed.

The grimoire contains a mix of transmutation alchemy, astrological casting, summoning rites, and other arcane material Ashton synthesized from obscure sources now lost. He hoped it could unlock the potential of humanity.

However, Ashton grew increasingly paranoid near the end of his life. His diary indicates he felt targeted by unknown sinister forces wishing to suppress his grimoire's power.

His writings stopped abruptly in 1591. In the same year, historical records show Ashton met an unsolved, horrifying demise that halted his occult work permanently.

The nature of Ashton's final fate remains unclear.

Still unsettled by the news article, Anja retrieved her leather journal and fountain pen from her bag and began jotting down leads to follow and questions to answer:

March 26, 2023

- *Look into death records/texts regarding Ashton's demise in 1591 —likely in London. How did he die?*
- *Review Ashton's diary again for clues on his travels and occult studies. Make a list of any ancient texts he references or hints at.*
- *Maybe some references to other works/sources are encoded in the grimoire itself.*
- *Cross-reference those text names with the Morgan Library archives and other collections. Locate copies to study.*
- *Research groups/secret societies Ashton may have joined for esoteric knowledge during his journeys.*
- *Research groups/secret societies that may have been hunting/ trying to stop Ashton, as alluded to by Raymond (another visit??).*
- *Background and biography on the Miller family—maybe the paper would have more details. See what their writers would dig up.*
- *Explore connections between the Millers' deaths and Ashton's fate. Too similar to be a coincidence? Or just a feeling?*

Anja's pen moved across the page hurriedly. A grim but urgent sense of purpose drove her—more lives had been lost, and these were clues she could not ignore. Somehow, she felt certain they were connected. That feeling settled in.

There must be meaning in the intersecting lines between Ashton centuries ago and the Miller tragedy now. Anja had to uncover the truth before darker forces stymied her progress. She would begin her investigation in earnest once this Sunday shift was complete.

The train screeched to a halt at Anja's stop, jolting her from her racing thoughts. Hurriedly gathering her things, she ascended to the bustling city sidewalks above. Briskly walking the blocks to the library, Anja paid little mind to the people and noises around her. The morning's revelations still kept coming back to her.

Approaching the imposing edifice, Anja took a deep breath to clear her mind before stepping inside. She was greeted by the stern but familiar voice of Mrs. Thompson.

"There you are, Anja. We have a full slate today." She gestured to a cart of books awaiting shelving and boxes of new acquisitions.

"Of course, I'll get started right away," Anja replied, stowing her messenger bag and notebook in her locker. There would be time later to process all she had learned. For now, she shifted her attention to the tangible tasks before her, hoping work would distract her restless thoughts.

The morning passed swiftly as Anja assisted patrons and processed new acquisitions. During an afternoon lull, she managed to devote some time to the newspapers. Skimming through, she pieced together more about the Miller family's prominence—their vast business empire, political clout, and ties to Britain's elite circles.

One article provided a timeline of events at the estate that night but no definitive details, mostly just the time the security monitoring company notified the sheriff's office due to some anomaly and when the first deputy arrived at the estate. Bartholomew, his wife Eliza, oldest son Winston, and daughter Abigail were named as victims.

Anja noted Lucian Miller, Bartholomew's younger son, was not mentioned among the deceased. She raised an eyebrow at this. As the sole surviving heir, suspicion would surely fall his way.

She learned the Bureau of Criminal Investigation was supplementing the local sheriff's department in the investigation. But no leads or suspects had been named yet. Anja leaned back, pondering the implications. If other forces were at play, there must be clues she could decipher. Why did she feel there was something there? She couldn't name it, but there was a strong feeling. She was sure it wasn't based on her recent obsession with Ashton, although that might be coloring her thoughts a bit. She just knew she had to find out what was going on.

For now, she had more questions than answers. But she felt the key to unraveling this mystery lay in the past—with Ashton's own tale centuries prior.

"Doing a little light reading on the job, I see?"

Anja looked up from the newspaper to see Dillon smiling down at her. She quickly closed the paper, not wanting to alarm the boy with the macabre story.

"Dillon, nice to see you again! How are you doing?" she asked warmly.

Dillon shuffled his feet a little. "Oh, alright, I guess. I actually have a question for you. Did you learn anything more about, you know, otherkin?"

Anja gestured for Dillon to take a seat nearby. "I have been reading up more. There seem to be a few common threads—feeling out of place, sensing something integral is missing from one's self. But experiences vary greatly."

Dillon nodded eagerly as Anja related what she had learned about the community's desire for belonging and the wide variety of types and experiences.

She continued, "But the most important thing is finding people who understand and support you. If I come across anything that seems useful, I'll be sure to pass it along."

Anja adopted a more serious tone. "Now, I want you to be careful in online groups. There are some who prey on those seeking belonging. If anything ever worries you or feels off, please come talk to me."

Dillon nodded. "I will, thanks."

Appraising, Anja asked carefully, "What type of 'kin' do you relate to, if you don't mind me asking?"

"I actually feel closest to…wolves. And the moon, like my energy is tied to its cycles. Is that strange?" he asked self-consciously.

"Not at all," Anja assured him. "Our spirits take many forms. Yours simply longs for the wild forests under lunar light. There's beauty in that."

Dillon smiled, seeming to find solace in having someone understand his feelings. Anja hoped she could continue guiding him somehow, whatever shape his journey took.

"Thanks, Anja," Dillon smiled as he got up to leave, seeming relieved to find someone open to his identity that he could relate to in person.

Returning to her newspaper reading, a name caught Anja's eye—Howard Miller, a brother of the deceased Bartholomew IV. The article described Howard as an eccentric scholar ostracized by the prominent family for his occult obsessions and unconventional beliefs. Though born a Miller, he had lived in self-imposed exile from the dynasty that scorned him.

Anja leaned back thoughtfully. Here was a relative with esoteric pursuits not unlike her own. Perhaps he had insights into the influences that seemed to be swirling around the Miller tragedy. Maybe he even knew secrets about Ashton. She jotted Howard's name in her journal. Once she had gathered more background details on Ashton's demise, reaching out to Howard could provide an inside perspective from someone tied to, yet separated from, the influential family.

Anja tapped her pen absently. Each thread she pulled seemed to unravel new connections between past and present. The path ahead was coming into focus, albeit dimly. Glancing at the clock, Anja realized her break was nearly over. She quickly folded up the newspapers and returned to the front desk.

In between assisting patrons, she managed to begin some preliminary online searches on sixteenth-century English death records that could contain clues about Ashton's death. When free, Anja also delved into the Morgan Library's catalog of digitized medieval manuscripts and rare Renaissance texts. If any accounts of Ashton's death existed, they would likely be found in these archives.

As closing time neared, Anja felt she had reached the limits of what this initial dig could uncover. Perhaps reaching out to Howard Miller could provide additional clues.

Richard scrutinized the encrypted report from Smoke, detailing the unexpected, ongoing investigation at the estate. It appeared that their target had somehow escaped the ensuing chaos, mistaken for an unforeseen visitor.

This was troubling news. A high-profile inquiry of this nature risked exposing the Sodality. Thankfully, Smoke had adhered to protocol, disappearing into hiding as per long-established contingency plans. But this left the organization momentarily understaffed should urgent needs arise.

He decided to fast-track the activation of a new operative, Raven— someone who had been vetted and trained for years, awaiting her opportunity to serve. Her unique skills could fill the gap efficiently if swift, discreet action was required.

Just as he was finalizing plans, an alert came through from London. Their digital monitors had detected queries about Edward Ashton in the archives. The name of the long-dead occultist had not surfaced for centuries until the recent incident. Someone seemed to be picking up Ashton's trail, seeking details about his final days. That someone was traced to be Anja Kinzey in his region. This could simply be academic curiosity. However, given Ashton's ties to certain perilous rituals and texts, any revived interest warranted scrutiny.

He added this development to Raven's briefing. Her priority would be to cautiously track any leads on who was investigating Ashton's past. Until they had more information, standard procedures for deterring and redirecting such research could be implemented through back channels. Ashton's legacy would remain shrouded in history's fog.

Composing an encrypted message to activate Raven, he hoped this complication would resolve swiftly. Patience and care were paramount.

Miller, however, could still pose a serious threat, and his newfound wariness would significantly complicate matters. If he were to join forces with Kinzey, as unlikely as it seemed, it could prove disastrous. A final solution might become necessary, which would only be more challenging now. With a curse, he turned his attention to other matters.

Since the library was closed on Mondays, Anja lingered over the morning paper and tea when her phone rang. She smiled when she saw it was Zoe calling.

"Anja! How's my favorite bookworm?" Zoe's bubbly voice came through the speaker. "Listen, I have to head out of the city later today for a work thing. But I was hoping we could do a quick lunch to catch up?"

"I'd love that," Anja replied warmly. "Did you have a place in mind?"

"Oooh, how about that bistro place we used to go to near campus? Around noon?" Zoe suggested.

Anja agreed readily. She hadn't seen her vivacious friend since the night at the club. "Sounds perfect. I can't wait to hear all about your new job."

"It's been…interesting, that's for sure. Save me a seat on the patio —I've got so much to tell you!" Zoe said.

After finalizing their plans and saying goodbye, Anja leaned back contentedly. She was looking forward to their lunch—Zoe's bold spirit never failed to invigorate her. And Anja could use a dose of that carefree warmth before plunging back into the obsessive darkness of her research.

Around noon, Anja made her way to the cozy French bistro that was a favorite campus haunt. The ivy-covered brick façade looked unchanged from their university days. Stepping inside, Anja inhaled the aroma of fresh bread and aromatic coffee. She asked for a table out on the sunny patio, taking a seat where she could watch for Zoe's arrival.

The patio was dotted with round metal tables shaded by striped umbrellas. Planter boxes overflowing with colorful flowers lined the edges. Couples and students chatted leisurely over wines and baguettes around her. It felt nostalgic being back at their old haunt. She hoped Zoe's high spirits would counteract her own increasingly gloomy disposition.

Soon enough, Anja spotted Zoe sailing through the front door and out to the patio, dressed sharply as always. She waved enthusiastically when their eyes met, and Anja's mood instantly lifted.

"Anja!" Zoe called out brightly as she arrived at the table. They exchanged a quick hug before Zoe settled into her chair.

A waiter came by for their order—Zoe chose her usual chicken crepe and Anja went with a roasted vegetable galette, just like old times.

Once the waiter stepped away, Anja leaned in curiously. "So tell me, how's the new job going? Is it everything you hoped for?"

Zoe sighed, though still smiled. "Oh, you know, glamorous special agent work, long nights on stakeouts, high-speed car chases...," she said dramatically before laughing. "Honestly, it's been pretty dull so far, but...I have been assigned to a high-profile case upstate. Details are being kept very hush-hush, so I can't share anything. But let's just say I'm making up for lost time very quickly!"

"That sounds incredibly exciting!" Anja replied. She wondered if it might be related to the Miller murders but knew not to pry despite her desire to do just that. Still, something seemed to pull her.

Their food arrived shortly after. As they ate, the conversation flowed easily between the two, just like their college days. Anja treasured these uncomplicated moments with her spirited friend before returning to her increasingly ominous studies. Despite herself, Anja's curiosity got the better of her. "So...does this new case have anything to do with the Miller murders? It was big news, after all." Maybe it was her looking into Aston's death coloring her thoughts, but she couldn't help thinking there was more to it.

Zoe looked surprised, then quickly composed herself. "You know I can't confirm or deny that." She smiled slyly over her crepe.

Anja nodded. "Of course. But if you do find yourself up there, keep an eye out for any...strange...aspects. I have a feeling about this."

Zoe raised her eyebrow. "A feeling, huh? You always were uncannily intuitive. Is there anything else you want to tell me?"

Anja hesitated before responding vaguely, "Nothing concrete. Just what I've read in the papers so far. But I suspect there may be more going on beneath the surface. Darker forces, obscure history—things the usual authorities may overlook."

Zoe studied her friend closely. Over the years, she had learned to trust Anja's unexplained 'feelings' about phenomena beyond the norm. If Anja said this case had unseen elements, Zoe would stay alert.

"I'll keep that in mind," Zoe said. "Can't hurt to keep an open perspective." She smiled wryly. "I may have an odd update for you soon if those premonitions prove right!"

Assessing what she had observed of Anja in the years since they became friends, Zoe has always found her an intriguing mix of open and impossible to read. That had been what had first drawn her to Anja. It was refreshing to have a friend that she couldn't always predict. Her constant habit, she realized now, of profiling everyone around her tended to take the fun out of things, especially now.

Looking at her, Zoe could see that Anja was holding back. Something important. She decided to press just a bit, "So…, what are you not saying? Nothing concrete?"

"Umm, not yet. Wait, are you profiling me now? Again? I thought you had given up on that—well, for me, at least," Anja responded with an exaggerated pout, but her eyes crinkling.

Grinning, "Yeah, guilty as charged. Hazard of the job. I have never been able to turn it off."

Anja couldn't resist, "Always turned on, eh?" Waggling her eyebrows and grinning.

"Anja!" Zoe laughed, rolling her eyes, then added, "well, not always."

The rest of their lunch passed enjoyably over dessert and light chatter. When the check came, Zoe insisted on treating since she made the invite. As they strolled outside, Anja grasped her arm warmly. "Be safe out there. I know you can handle anything, but still…"

Zoe patted the holster hidden discreetly beneath her stylish blazer. "Don't you worry; I've got all the protection I need if things get hairy."

They exchanged one more quick hug before parting ways—Zoe off on her upstate assignment and Anja returning home to her occult texts and growing unease.

"Stay in touch!" Anja called after her. "Let me know what you find up there. And if you need any help figuring out the inexplicable, you know who to call!"

Zoe laughed, flashing a thumbs-up as she walked away. Anja smiled, cheered by her vibrant energy. But alone again, she took a deep breath to steel herself before heading out.

Anja returned to her apartment after her lunch with Zoe, the weight of her research and thoughts pressing on her. She was also concerned about Zoe but knew she could handle herself.

She knew that to delve deeper into the mysteries she was uncovering, she needed guidance. One name repeatedly emerged as an authority on the occult and esoteric knowledge—Professor Howard Miller of the London School of Mystical Arts and Esoteric Sciences.

Sitting down at her desk, she fired up her laptop and began searching for his contact information. Various papers and treatises by him had left an impression on her. She hoped he might be willing to offer insights into the enigmatic path she was treading. After a few minutes of searching, she finally found a contact number for Professor Miller.

She quickly stored the number in her phone, her excitement growing, anticipating the possibility of speaking with someone who shared her passion and might shed light on her discoveries. Taking a deep breath, she composed herself, ready to make the call.

As she stared at the digits on her phone screen, she couldn't help but feel a mix of nervousness and eagerness. With a determined deep breath, she pressed the call button and put the phone to her ear, the line ringing on the other end. The seconds felt like an eternity as she waited for someone to pick up.

Finally, a voice answered on the other end, "Hello?"

Anja's heart raced as she realized she was speaking to the legendary Professor Howard Miller. "Um, hello. Professor Miller, my name is Anja Kinzey. I'm a researcher in the field of esoteric studies, and I've come across your work and writings. I was wondering if I could possibly have a moment of your time to discuss some matters related to the occult?"

There was a brief pause on the other end; Anja held her breath. Then, to her relief, the professor responded, "Anja Kinzey, you say? Well, it's not every day that a young researcher reaches out with such enthusiasm. I must admit, I'm intrigued. Very well. Let's have a conversation."

Exhaling, Anja plunged into her inquiry. "I've been researching the life of Edward Ashton, a figure whose history intersects with the realm of the esoteric. I've come across some rather cryptic information about his death and its possible connection to something more… disturbing."

She could almost hear the professor's curiosity piquing on the other end. "Edward Ashton, you say? A name that holds significance in certain circles. What kind of information are you seeking, Anja?"

Anja's words came out in a rush as she explained, "I'm trying to uncover the circumstances of his death. Some accounts suggest it was not a mere accident. Rather, it was tied to something hidden, something beyond the ordinary. I was wondering if you have any insights, any knowledge, or perspectives on Edward Ashton and what might have led to his demise."

There was a moment of thoughtful silence before Professor Miller responded, his voice measured and thoughtful. "Edward Ashton's story is indeed one that has intrigued many seekers of the hidden. While I cannot claim to possess all the answers, I can share with you what has been passed down through generations of esoteric enthusiasts."

Anja sat up straighter as she listened intently, her pen poised to capture every word.

"Edward Ashton was a man of exceptional intellect and deep curiosity. His research led him into realms that most would deem fanciful or even dangerous. He believed in the existence of ancient forces and arcane knowledge that could reshape the very fabric of reality. It is said that he stumbled upon writings and artifacts that hinted at secrets that could lead men to madness or enlightenment."

Anja's mind whirred with the weight of the information. "And his death?" she pressed.

Professor Miller's voice grew somber. "Edward Ashton's end remains shrouded in ambiguity. Some say he was pursuing a truth that some wished to remain hidden. Others claim he delved too deeply into matters best left alone. Whether his demise was a sinister conspiracy or a tragic consequence of his own pursuits, one thing is clear—his legacy and the questions he posed endure."

Anja felt uneasy at the professor's words. "Is there any documentation, any specific texts or sources that might shed more light on his findings or his end?"

The professor's reply was careful. "Anja, I do possess certain texts and accounts that delve into the enigmatic world that Edward Ashton inhabited. However, I must caution you—this is a path fraught with danger. The truths you seek are not for the faint-hearted."

Anja's resolve remained unshaken. "I understand, Professor. I'm prepared to face whatever lies ahead. If there's any information you can share, no matter how cryptic, it could be crucial to understanding the larger picture."

There was a brief pause before Professor Miller spoke again, his voice carrying a hint of respect for her determination. "Very well, Anja. I'll gather what I can and send it to you. But remember, the path you're on may lead to revelations that will challenge your very understanding of the world. Please proceed cautiously."

"Thank you, Professor Miller. Your guidance means a lot to me," Anja replied sincerely. "Professor. I'm also curious about your relationship with Lucian David Miller, the CEO of Coruscant Technologies. I've heard he is your nephew." Anja inquired, her mind racing with possibilities.

"Yes, you are correct. Lucian is my nephew," Professor Miller confirmed. "We weren't very close when he was growing up, but I did share stories of the supernatural with him when he was young. He always had a curious mind."

Anja absorbed the information. "Thank you for sharing that with me. I heard about your brother Bartholomew, Lucian's father. I'm so sorry for your loss. It must be an incredibly difficult time for you."

"Thank you, Anja. Your kind words mean a lot to me," Professor Miller replied, his voice tinged with sadness. "It's been a trying time, but we are managing as best we can. I will be attending the family funeral soon. Dark times indeed."

"I can only imagine how hard it must be. Please know that if there's anything I can do to help, even in a small way, I'm here for you," Anja offered sincerely.

"Thank you. Your support is much appreciated," Professor Miller said gratefully.

As the call ended after exchanging email addresses, Anja couldn't help but feel a renewed sense of purpose.

Raven stood outside the Morgan Library, calmly observing the building from a distance. Anja Lee Kinzey, the research librarian, had caught the organization's attention with her recent inquiries into the long-dead occultist Edward Ashton. As the evening sun cast long shadows across the street, Raven knew it was time to pay Anja a visit. She approached the library's entrance and presented herself as a curious visitor. Inside, the hushed atmosphere of the historic building enveloped her as she discreetly made her way to the information desk where Anja was currently stationed.

As Raven approached, she noted Anja's eyes lift from her work to meet her own. Although the librarian maintained a composed exterior, Raven sensed a subtle shift in her posture, as if her arrival had set some internal alarm bell ringing. Anja's smile seemed almost too professional as if she were making an effort to conceal something.

"Good evening, ma'am," Raven said politely, "I'm new to the city and heard this library was a treasure trove of information. Mind if I ask you a few questions?"

Anja glanced around, making sure no one else was within earshot before replying, "Of course, I'll do my best to assist you."

Raven carefully steered the conversation toward the topic of Edward Ashton, subtly probing for any additional information that Anja might not have shared. Anja, however, already wary, was not so easily taken in. She had frequently concealed her 'questionable' research from her parents and others she felt would not understand.

Though her mind was racing, she responded with practiced ease, "Oh, yes, Edward Ashton. Fascinating figure, but my research on him was merely a fleeting interest. I'm more focused on other subjects now."

Raven maintained a façade of interest in the casual conversation while making mental notes of Anja's guarded responses. She knew Anja was holding back, and the librarian's change of tone hinted that there was more to her questions than she was willing to reveal.

Raven knew the importance of maintaining her anonymity, even in seemingly harmless encounters. When Anja asked for her name, she responded with a well-practiced smile, "You can call me Emma."

The name was simple, unremarkable, and one she had used before in similar situations. It served its purpose of deflecting any suspicion while keeping her true identity hidden. To anyone else, she would appear to be just another friendly visitor touring the library.

After a few minutes, Raven artfully steered the conversation away from sensitive topics, discussing unrelated matters that seemed to put Anja at ease. As she prepared to leave, she felt her own words and actions had painted her as nothing more than a casual tourist, curious but largely indifferent to the occult or Edward Ashton.

As she gave Anja a departing smile and turned away, she picked up a subtle shift in the librarian's posture, a slight tension that hadn't been there before. Raven couldn't help but wonder if her alias 'Emma' had struck Anja as somewhat contrived. She tucked that observation away for later analysis; it could be relevant in understanding how alert Anja really was.

As Raven prepared to leave, she took a final, sweeping glance around the library, mentally mapping the faces of everyone present. Her eyes flickered toward Anja one last time, committing the librarian's face to memory.

Once outside, she immediately melted into the crowd, her posture relaxing only slightly. She was already thinking ahead, her mind whirring with plans and contingencies. Raven knew she had to adapt her strategy. Anja was proving to be more perceptive than she had initially estimated, which called for a change in approach. For now, the shadows were her sanctuary, and in them, she'd continue her watchful surveillance.

As Anja finished her shift at the Morgan Library, she caught Mrs. Thompson's scrutinizing gaze. "You seemed rather distracted this afternoon, Anja. And less than welcoming with our patrons."

"I apologize," Anja murmured, her thoughts already drifting to the door. Ever since her encounter with the woman who called herself Emma, her nerves had been stretched thin.

Mrs. Thompson's voice hardened. "I expect your full attention during work hours. No more daydreaming."

"Of course. It won't happen again," Anja assured her, grabbing her messenger bag and making a hasty exit.

The setting sun cast long shadows that seemed more ominous than before. Anja felt as if invisible eyes followed her. Quickening her pace, she headed home. Once inside her apartment, she bolted the door and sank into her thoughts. Emma's subtly pointed questions had left no doubt; her research had attracted attention. Attention from quarters best left undisturbed.

She paced her living room, unease spiraling into outright worry. How much did they know? Was her every move now under scrutiny?

Regret surged through her. She should've been more cautious with Professor Howard Miller. His emails had been like breadcrumbs leading deeper into a perilous forest. Raymond could help. Eccentric as he was, he'd always appreciated her unorthodox pursuits. He'd given her the diary and even hinted at the others.

The grim fate of Edward Ashton was a cautionary tale, but it only fanned her hunger for knowledge. Her attraction to the hidden power in Ashton's Grimoire was no longer a simple academic curiosity; it felt like a magnetic pull.

Frustration and a touch of anger brewed inside her, provoked by the realization that she was tantalizingly close, stymied only by petty gatekeepers clutching their secrets tightly. Her grandmother

Madeline's voice seemed to echo in her ears: "Embrace your true self, and you will achieve greatness." Years of muffling her natural inclinations and mystical urges felt like wearing a too-tight corset, restricting her every breath.

A steadfast resolve filled her, diluting any residual fear. She'd decode those ancient symbols, unleash forgotten magics, and snatch back the knowledge others jealously guarded. Let them dispatch their shadowy agents. She was ready to seize what she believed was her birthright. In that moment, Anja felt more alive than ever before.

Come morning, she would visit Raymond. Her information gathering would be relentless and uncompromising. A heady exhilaration washed over her. But she welcomed it, just as her grandmother had foretold.

Done with her introspection, Anja changed into a satin nightgown, bypassing her usual nighttime ritual of note-taking and reading. She needed to still her swirling thoughts.

Slipping under the covers, she reached for the lamp switch, plunging her room into inviting darkness. The distant noise of the city offered a quiet undertone. Eyes on the ceiling, her thoughts galvanized her, making her feel ready.

Sleep overtook her at last, but it was restless, filled with the fleeting visions of arcane symbols and rites long buried in the sands of time.

Six

ZOE ARRIVED AT the Miller estate early in the morning, accompanied by Detective Chad Owens from the Granite County sheriff's office and another BCI detective. The sun had barely risen, casting long shadows across the grand mansion, creating an eerie atmosphere that matched the gravity of the crime scene. Approaching the entrance, she met Detective Cruz, who she knew was heading the investigation.

"Morning, detective. FBI; I'm here to help," Zoe greeted, offering a handshake.

"Good morning, Ms. Ananda," Cruz replied, lips trying not to twitch up into a smile, grasping her hand. "Thanks for coming all the way from the city to help us with this one."

"I'm here to assist in any way I can," Zoe said. "Let's go see what we're dealing with."

Her eyes swept the interior as they navigated through the mansion. Every detail could be a clue, a piece to a complicated puzzle. Cruz briefed her on their findings so far, showing her crime scene photos as they went. Though the bodies had been removed, the haunting stains remained. She found the absence of the corpses a small mercy, given the unsettling atmosphere and lingering scent of blood and decay.

On the upper floor, they found signs of each victim in separate bedrooms. Thomas' room was empty, but his belongings were still there, suggesting he was supposed to be there instead of where he was found. In a chilling revelation, Zoe viewed photos of Thomas' body in Lucian's sister's room. She noticed that Thomas bore a strong resemblance to Lucian, an observation that begged further explanation.

The background information began to form a hazy picture in her mind. Thomas was an unexpected guest at the gathering. Lucian, the likely target, had various potential motives tied to him—his groundbreaking biotech research, his wealth, or even something related to Abigail. Added to that, Lucian's recent favor in his father's will made him look suspect. More information would be needed to untangle the complex web of possibilities.

Zoe studied the photos intently. Both victims were found naked, the scene far more gruesome than in his mother's, father's or brother's rooms. "An escalation," Cruz suggested, "probably indicating a personal vendetta."

She had to agree. Such brutality usually marked a crime of passion. Thomas' missing heart was especially jarring, a deeply personal and symbolic act that spoke of unfathomable rage. The removal of his genitals suggested an even more specific kind of fury. It was as if the killer had assumed Thomas was Lucian, the true object of this macabre message. It also suggested he knew the victims and their relationship. In this case, they may have been assumed to be brother and sister.

As she tried to make sense of the chilling tableau, Zoe pondered the murder weapon, a likely silenced 9mm, which hadn't been recovered. Also missing was a combat knife of some sort, as indicated by the preliminary autopsy findings. A professional killer, then? Yet, the emotional intensity of the crime scene seemed inconsistent with the cool detachment one would expect from a hired gun.

She also noted the missing ring—a sapphire and diamond piece from Lucian's mother. It was the only valuable gone, leading her to believe that theft wasn't the main objective. Instead, it might be a twisted trophy, adding yet another layer to the killer's profile.

Her thoughts circled back to Anja, who'd urged her to look out for the unusual. This case was quickly becoming a labyrinth of peculiarities and unsettling details. She made a mental note to consult with Anja later, valuing her friend's knack for understanding the inexplicable.

As hours stretched on, Zoe combed the mansion, their focus sharpened by the estate's eerie stillness. Then came the revelation about the disabled alarm system. The security company had attempted to contact the house via an integrated intercom and phone but had failed, ultimately alerting local authorities. This breach could have tipped off the intruder—no, the killer—that their time was running out. Perhaps "assassin" was the more fitting term, she thought.

Zoe adjusted her blazer, making sure her badge was visible as she stepped out of her car. Detective Cruz joined her, looking focused and determined. Today, they were to interview Lucian Miller again, the surviving member of the prominent Miller family, about the gruesome murders at the upstate estate.

The sheriff's building loomed ahead, and Zoe could feel the weight of the case on her shoulders. It was high-profile, sensitive, and shrouded in mystery. She knew they needed to tread carefully to get to the truth. As they entered the building, Sheriff Bowman greeted them with a nod.

"Cruz, Special Agent Ananda, thanks for coming in. This is a big one, so we want to make sure everything is done right."

"We're ready, sheriff," Cruz replied confidently.

Sheriff Bowman led them to an interview room where Lucian Miller sat, flanked by his lawyer, Horace Reed. He seemed composed, but his face betrayed a mix of grief and confusion. Zoe could understand how overwhelming this situation must be for him. She also studied his reactions and his appraisal of her. A slight half-Indian, half-American woman with warm brown skin, dark almond eyes, and silky black shoulder-length hair. She knew she was attractive; Lucian's gaze took that in but did not linger in any sexual way. Points to him, she thought.

"Mr. Miller, this is Detective Nina Cruz, whom you have met, and

Special Agent Ananda from the FBI. She is advising and is here to help add more insight from any potential national level interests," the sheriff introduced.

Lucian nodded politely. Zoe could see no indication of evasion in his reactions, more than would be expected in this situation. She had observed no reason to doubt his sincerity. Despite the high-profile nature of the case and the risks involved, he had willingly provided his cell phone for analysis to clear any suspicion against him. He had also volunteered information on the recent will changes. He was intelligent, PhD, successful, and extremely wealthy already. Was he playing the game this deeply? She didn't think so.

Horace Reed, the seasoned criminal defense attorney, sat next to Lucian, observing every detail of the proceedings with a keen eye.

"Mr. Miller, we understand this is a challenging time for you," Zoe began, maintaining eye contact. "We need to revisit the night of the tragedy for a more coherent picture of the events."

Taking a deep breath, Lucian nodded. "Of course, Agent Ananda. I want nothing more than to find who did this to my family." His words carried a tinge of fury, his expression hardening momentarily.

Zoe and Cruz systematically worked through the timeline of the night. They questioned Lucian about his activities, corroborating his statements with interviews from the house staff and driver, who had been oblivious to the horror unfolding within the mansion walls.

"I was at the lake," Lucian reiterated. "I find peace there, especially with the pressures of my businesses. But a storm came, so I had to return."

Cruz chimed in, "Officers noted you arrived back during the heavy rain. Is that correct?"

"Yes, that is correct," Lucian confirmed. "I had to navigate through the downpour and the lightning to get back."

Throughout, Zoe and Cruz diligently compared his answers with evidence and previous testimonies. Horace Reed was quick to jump in when necessary, carefully advising his client while also facilitating cooperation with the investigators.

By the end of the interview, Lucian's alibi seemed to hold water. His being at the lake, his return only after the incident, and his cooperative demeanor—all these factors worked in his favor.

"Thank you for your cooperation, Mr. Miller," Zoe concluded. "We'll reach out if we have any more questions."

Once the door closed behind Lucian and Reed, Cruz turned her gaze to Zoe. "What's your take?"

Zoe weighed the situation. "Lucian's alibi is mostly dependent on cell phone data, which does put him away from the scene. He also seems genuinely eager to help. I don't detect deception, but we can't ignore the possibility that he might have orchestrated this, knowing he'd have an alibi of sorts."

Cruz nodded, her lips pulling taut as she processed Zoe's analysis. "I'll have the tech team examine the cell phone data immediately. That should help clear up whether he was directly involved or not. But I agree; we need to keep an open mind."

Zoe felt the weight of unresolved questions tugging at her mind. She was missing something crucial—some piece of the puzzle was eluding her grasp. As they left the room, her gaze remained focused; her mind was a sieve, letting irrelevant details drain away while trapping the valuable nuggets of information.

"I need to review everything," Zoe said. "Can I use an empty space here to go over the case files and notes before I head back?"

Cruz gave her a supportive nod. "Of course. Take your time. I'll see what the tech team has found so far and join you afterward."

Seated alone in an empty room, Zoe spread the case files before her. She took her time, meticulously taking notes and revising timelines. The details could easily be overlooked, but not by her. Her mind whirred as she sifted through the evidence, and her notes began to paint a shadowy profile of the killer.

Cruz joined her, and the two women engaged in a brainstorming session. Cruz's keen eye for detail and knack for intuitive leaps dovetailed well with Zoe's methodical approach.

"Time for me to head back and start on that preliminary report," Zoe finally said, gathering her notes. "I'll also work on the suspect's profile."

Cruz straightened, her face a mask of resolve. "I'll continue on this end. I'll coordinate with the local forensics and see if we can identify any suspicious movements on surveillance cameras, either heading north or south."

Before departing, Zoe dialed her supervisor to summarize the developments in Lucian Miller's interview. She requested extra resources and support, keenly aware that unearthing the truth would demand collective expertise.

Once back in the city, Zoe hit the ground running. She initiated calls to a forensic psychologist and a cold case expert to tap into their specialized knowledge. She sifted through FBI archives for any cases bearing resemblances to the Miller estate murders, seeking elusive connections. Her research took her down various paths, including exploring the enigmatic occult angles that Anja had subtly alluded to. All the while, she communicated frequently with Cruz and the local team, mutually updating each other on emerging leads.

The more Zoe delved into the case, the more intricate it appeared— a kaleidoscope of secrets, complex family dynamics, and veiled agendas. They were inching closer to the truth, though gaps in the puzzle still yawned wide. Every new discovery fueled Zoe's tenacity. She knew the task was beyond her lone efforts. It would take her team, external experts, and investigative partners to sift through the maze of this complicated case. Despite the progress and collaboration, Zoe knew she was standing on precarious ground with insufficient concrete evidence. Feeling the encroaching frustration but unwilling to capitulate, she petitioned her superiors for permission to consult Anja, a civilian whose expertise lay in realms unconventional yet potentially revelatory.

Intrigued by Anja's early assertions that something far from ordinary was afoot, Zoe sensed her friend's unique insights might provide the much-needed breakthrough. With a green light from her supervisor, she readied herself to contact Anja, hoping to illuminate the shadowy contours that so far defied easy understanding.

Anja awoke the next morning feeling unrested. Her dreams were filled with unseen perils lurking in the darkness. Shaking off the haunting images, she rose to prepare for the day. Walking to Raymond's shop, she paid closer attention to her surroundings than usual. The city seemed cast in suspicion now. She scrutinized every passerby, watching for any sign of surveillance. But the neighborhood's morning rituals continued as always.

Arriving at the antique store, Anja hesitated before entering. She studied the shopfront, peering into the windows for anything amiss. Within, Raymond was going about his typical morning tasks. Taking a breath to toughen her nerves, Anja stepped inside to the cheerful ring of the bell.

"Anja, you're back. Did Ashton's diary provide any revelations?" Raymond asked, rising to greet her.

"It certainly shed light but also raised more questions," Anja replied, lowering her voice. "Ashton referenced a secret society stalking him—the 'Empty Hand.' I found mentions too of the 'Brothers of the Thorn'—connected?"

Raymond nodded grimly. "Ah yes, whispered legends tell of such a hidden order guarding dangerous knowledge throughout history."

Anja continued, "I also read about the Miller family's horrific incident upstate. I have a feeling somehow that this is not just a coincidence."

"You may be right…"

Raymond pondered her theory about the Miller incident and disappeared into the stacks, to return with a crackling bundle tied in twine. "These letters belonged to a former associate of Ashton's that I acquired at auction some time ago. They may provide clues about his dealings."

Handing them to Anja, he added, "But be very careful, my love. Tugging at these threads could unravel more than you anticipate."

Accepting the letters gratefully, Anja replied, "About that—my inquiries may have already garnered…unwanted attention. There could really be an organization trying to bury Ashton's secrets along with anything…or anyone…connected with the supernatural."

Raymond regarded her. "That is troubling. I've heard whispers of such a cabal but thought them conspiracy theories. If real, they are not to be trifled with."

He squeezed Anja's shoulder. "I know I can't dissuade your pursuit of truth. Just promise you will be vigilant. Some knowledge comes at too high a cost. Are you sure you want to pay that price, my love? Perhaps I can offer some other distractions. Let me show you a few books I think you may like…"

Anja nodded, feeling a sense of comfort as their ritual played out once more. Their friendship had grown over time, and this familiar routine helped ease her mind. She considered Raymond as he led her through the maze of bookshelves in his shop, her fondness and respect only growing.

The scent of aged leather and musty parchment filled the air, creating an ambiance of mystery and intrigue, grounding her with their familiar presence. She felt a release of tension she hadn't even realized was there, grounding her in the familiar presence of the books. As they reached a secluded corner, Raymond turned to Anja with a warm smile.

"I've been gathering some books that I thought might catch your interest," he said with his eyes twinkling with mischief. "I know you have a penchant for Gothic romance and the darker tales of old. I've set aside a few volumes for you."

She had eagerly followed him to the back room. The dimly lit space was stacked with dusty books, some with faded titles and ornate covers, reminiscent of a bygone era.

"These books are true gems, carefully preserved for those who appreciate the artistry of words from a different time," Raymond said, running his fingers gently over the spines. "Take your time, my dear, and borrow as many as you like. They might serve as a delightful distraction from your inquiries."

Anja's eyes widened as she scanned the titles. The selection ranged from classic Gothic novels to obscure works that hinted at the forbidden. She picked up one volume and read the title, *The Secret Garden of Pleasure and Pain*, and another, *Whispers of the Night: A Collection of Sinister Tales*.

"These are fascinating," Anja said with gratitude. "I truly appreciate your thoughtfulness, Raymond, but I think you are getting to know me too well."

Raymond chuckled softly. "It's my pleasure, my dear. Sometimes, diving into the realms of fiction can provide an escape from the weight of reality. And who knows, you might stumble upon hidden treasures within these pages," he added with a smile.

Anja nodded, feeling a sense of comfort in the old man's presence. Selecting a few books, she couldn't help but wonder if he knew more about the secrets she was chasing. Wisdom in his eyes hinted at a lifetime of knowledge, but Anja knew better than to pry into matters that might be better left undisturbed. Like what he knew about these books and… Nope, not going there!

With the borrowed books securely tucked into her now crowded messenger bag, she bid Raymond farewell, promising to return soon. Once she was back on the busy city streets, the oppressive weight of her investigation seemed momentarily lifted, even as her bag grew heavier with the newly acquired volumes. She knew she couldn't let these distractions keep her from the truth. Yet, for now, the allure of Gothic romance and dark fiction offered a welcome, albeit brief, respite from the lurking shadows that seemed to dog her. She walked briskly along her usual route through the bustling streets to the Morgan Library, still keeping a watchful eye out, the feeling of being watched diminished but not gone.

Inside the magnificent building, Anja was pleased to see Mrs. Thompson's desk vacant—the stern librarian must be away for the moment. Anja carefully stuffed her now bulging messenger bag safely in her staff locker and quietly went about her typical morning tasks of tidying shelves, logging new acquisitions, and preparing the reading rooms for patrons. Despite the normalcy of her routines, she felt a restless energy propelling her movements. The tantalizing clues from Ashton's past called to her from her locker, awaiting her. She hoped for a few undisturbed hours to unravel their secrets.

For now, Anja maintained her façade of professionalism, keeping her true preoccupations concealed. But her thoughts could not be tamed so easily. She knew how close the answers lurked—if only she could break the final seals guarding Ashton's ancient truth from her grasp.

As Anja closed up for the evening, she rushed to her locker, eagerly retrieving her leather messenger bag. At the front desk, she quickly wrote a note for Mrs. Thompson: "What a hectic day! I'm quite worn out, so heading home to rest this evening. See you tomorrow, Anja."

Satisfied, Anja hurried out before Mrs. Thompson could come up with any last-minute tasks. Now, there would be no distractions from diving headfirst into Ashton's mysterious correspondence. The secrets had waited centuries—she could wait no longer.

Clutching her messenger bag tightly, Anja descended the steps with resolute purpose. By necessity, she had played the part of dutiful librarian all day, but now, her new resolve drove her once more. She would not stop until the shadows relinquished their deadly truths. Yesterday, her journey had crossed the point of no return.

Back in her apartment, Anja carefully laid the contents of her bag on the kitchen table: her notebook, the bundle of Ashton's letters, the antique diary, and two other books loaned by Raymond. She was eager to delve in but was also drained from the hectic day. Deciding some relaxation would sharpen her focus, Anja drew a warm scented bath, lighting candles around the edges. She soaked pleasantly, feeling the day's tensions dissipate as soothing music played.

After drying off and changing into a loose, comfortable robe, Anja brewed some calming herbal tea. She took a deep breath, gazing at the promising pile of documents.

No more distractions. Glancing at the other two books...well, maybe... She needed to immerse herself in Ashton's world tonight, centuries past, but...relaxed and fresh from the bath, her skin still tingling from the bath salts and oils, her mind drifted to other needs and hungers too long suppressed.

In the soft glow of her bedside lamp, Anja placed the book, 'Forbidden Desires: A Collection of Sensual Secrets,' on her nightstand. The cover was adorned with intricate patterns and alluring symbols that seemed to beckon her into its pages. She took a deep breath, feeling a mixture of anticipation and nervousness, unsure of what lay ahead.

She paused and lit a few candles around the room, choosing from scents complimenting the fragrances from her bath. The candles' flickering flames danced on the walls, softened by her lamp's soothing light, casting mesmerizing shadows that seemed to echo the forbidden tales that awaited her. After laying back on her bed and retrieving the book, Anja carefully opened it, letting her eyes wander across the pages filled with tales of passion, longing, and exploration of desires that seemed to mirror those that had been hiding away in the depths of her heart.

As she began reading, the words on the pages painted vivid scenes of enchanted gardens where lovers met under the moonlight, their desires intertwining with the enchanting fragrance of forbidden blooms, the scent of her candles drawing her deeper into the tales. The stories whispered of tender caresses and the intoxicating thrill of surrendering to the allure of another's touch.

Her mind and body were transported to a realm of fantasy, where she could indulge in the eroticism of the tales without judgment or restraint. The words sparked a fire within her, awakening long-suppressed feelings and arousing a hunger she had ignored for too long. She thought back to her first explorations of her body in her youth, only fourteen, the first time she discovered the hidden delight within the folds of her body. Those early explorations were now colored by darker and more explicit readings and the years of practice since.

She had never been with a man, or woman, for that matter, but the longing had been growing sharper. She knew she was missing something but had never found that someone to give herself to. For now, she would lean into her fantasies. She knew, though, that her newfound determination to accept herself and let her wild side—her hunger—free would not be pushed back down easily. Yes, she would embrace her true self and set herself free.

With each turned page, Anja allowed herself to drift deeper into the world of 'Forbidden Desires.' The stories were a dance of intimacy and vulnerability intertwined with the torrid and explicit, urging her to embrace her desires and needs, to no longer suppress them for fear of judgment. Anja felt a fire igniting within her. She had always known that she was different, that her desires didn't fit neatly into society's box of normalcy. But now, as she devoured the words on the pages before her, she realized it was okay to be different—that her desires were valid.

As she finished the next tale, her heart pounding with arousal, she knew that she couldn't go back to living a half life, denying her true self. Instead, she made a promise to herself to fully embrace her sexuality, to explore all of the taboo fantasies that she had buried deep within herself.

Standing from her bed, she let her robe slip off her shoulders to pool on the floor, appraising her nakedness in the mirror on the wall. She ran her hands and fingers over her body, feeling every curve and contour and feeling the cascade of hair down her back. She knew that she was beautiful and deserved to be desired.

Turning down the duvet and pulling back the top sheet, she crawled slowly back onto her bed, lying down on the plush sheets and turning over onto her back. She spread her legs wide, revealing herself to the mirror, as shadows and light danced across her skin. Touching her skin, she thought back to the stories she had read. She remembered the intensity of the characters' emotions and the way they gave themselves entirely to each other. And as she closed her eyes, she knew that she, too, could experience that kind of passion. She could feel the heat building within her.

The flickering light from the candles enveloped her, reflecting the growing heat within her. She let her fingers trace the curves of the book, almost as if they were caressing a lover's skin. The softness of the sheets beneath her heightened her senses, as did the scent of the candles. The more she read, the more she submerged in the sea of sensations. Each word seemed to spark a reaction within her, and she felt herself falling deeper into her own mind. She could feel her heart pounding in her chest as she imagined herself in the scenarios described on the pages before her.

She could imagine herself being dominated by a powerful partner, submitting to their every desire, pain, and ecstasy mixing as one. Or, perhaps, watching as another woman sucked her lover's cock while she pleasured herself.

As she read, she felt her body responding to the images in her head. She grew wetter with each passing minute and could feel her clit tingling with anticipation. She ran her fingers over her lips, imagining sweet kisses. Circling her nipples with her nails, she felt them harden even more. Flicking them, then a sharp pinch, the sensations echoed down to her clit.

Tracing her fingers down her belly, Anja felt herself growing ever more excited. She could hardly contain the energy coursing through her veins. She reached down between her legs, touching herself directly for the first time since she started reading. She circled her clit with her index finger, feeling it harden and thrum against her touch. She added more pressure, rubbing across and around. The sensations built within her until she could hardly bear it anymore. Then, without warning, she reached her first climax of the night. She cried out in surprise, but the feeling was too sudden and intense to stop. She rode out the waves of pleasure, letting her orgasm consume her completely.

After finally regaining her ability to focus, her mind wandered to her own longings again, to the touch of another against her skin, to the taste of a forbidden kiss, to the ecstasy of surrendering to the passionate dance of intimacy.

As she lay there, Anja couldn't help but think about all the times she had hidden away her true desires. All of the time, she had denied herself the pleasure of exploring her own body and mind. It wasn't right, she realized, to deny herself the opportunity to experience love and intimacy as she had for many years. She wanted to find someone who could accept her for everything that she was. Someone who wouldn't judge her for her kinks or desires but instead celebrate them. Someone who would embrace her fully, both in body and soul.

The idea of such a person filled her with hope, and she resolved to keep searching. To put herself out there, to risk rejection, because the possibility of finding that genuine connection was worth it. She sensed that somewhere out there, there was someone who would appreciate her for exactly who she was.

Another narrative called to her: a story of a visitor in the night, slipping into the beds of men while they slept and sliding into their dreams to ride them to oblivion. A dark and beautiful demon of sex. A succubus. Drawing out strength and power from her nocturnal lovers to feed upon to sate her hunger. Insatiable, powerful, and irresistible —like the siren's call of this tale to her. A fleeting sense of destiny brushed across her skin, sending a new flush of heat to her core.

Again, she wound herself higher, continuing to pleasure herself. She felt like she was reaching new heights of ecstasy. With each stroke of her fingers, she felt herself getting closer and closer to the edge again. She inserted a finger into her vagina, feeling the warmth and moisture of her own juice. She slid her finger in and out, adding another finger soon after. Finding her G-spot and caressing, feeling the waves of pleasure crash over her again and again as she kneaded it, her thumb finding her clit again.

Anja's body felt alive with sensation as she continued to play with herself. She felt unstoppable, as if she had unlocked some deep reservoir of desire within herself, and it would never let her go.

She rubbed her clit furiously, feeling the heat building once again. She added a third finger to her vagina, stretching it wider and wider. She could feel herself getting closer and closer to another orgasm and reveled in the sensations.

Finally, as she hit her peak yet again, she arched her back and let out a cry of pleasure. She felt a surge of liquid flow from her, squirting across the bed. This time, she felt like she had truly broken free of all the restrictions and limitations that had held her back before. She felt like she was discovering new parts of her body, new sensations that she never knew existed. She felt like every part of her was alive and vibrating with electricity.

She squeezed her breasts, feeling the weight of them in her hands. She pinched her nipples, feeling the sharp sensations spread. And then, finally, she returned one hand down, fingers stroking her clit, rubbing it fiercely again until she reached another climax. This time, she felt like she was floating. Like she had transcended her physical form and became ethereal —something greater than herself. And in that moment, she knew that she would never look back. She was ready to embrace her desires—her darker desires seemed all the more alluring.

As the night wore on, Anja lost herself in the world of the book and the desires it awakened within her. Again and again, the outside world faded away, leaving her immersed in a realm of sensuality and pleasure. In her private sanctuary, she found release after release as she had never let herself before, allowing her body and soul to finally embrace the forbidden fantasies that had been waiting for this moment of liberation. She knew she was lost to it now...and found.

As the night went on, Anja felt like she was entering a different plane of existence. She was no longer simply a woman reading a book; she was a creature of pure sensation, existing only to experience pleasure in all its forms, much like that succubus.

As the sun began to rise, casting its warm light across her bedroom, Anja finally fell into a deep and dreamless sleep, exhausted and tender but deeply satisfied. She knew that she had undergone a transformation, after which nothing would ever be quite the same again.

Seven

Lucian received a call from Detective Nina Cruz, updating him on the investigation's progress.

"Mr. Miller, analysis of cell phone logs and tower pings supports your statements so far," Cruz stated matter-of-factly. "As such, we are authorizing your return to New York as per Mr. Reed's request."

Lucian adopted a grateful tone. "Thank you, detective. My legal counsel, Mr. Reed, impressed upon me the need to return for business matters. I appreciate your understanding."

"Of course," Cruz replied. "We'll expect continued availability for any further questions. And if you could have Mr. Reed coordinate with us on information releases moving forward."

"Absolutely, I aim to help however I can to find justice for my family," Lucian said sincerely.

After finalizing the arrangements and expressing her condolences, Detective Cruz ended the call. Next, Lucian called Jonas Richter, head of security operations for Coruscant Technologies.

"Jonas, I have an urgent request. Given recent events, I need discreet but robust personal security arranged," Lucian stated without preamble.

"Completely understandable, sir; we'll get your protection detail sorted immediately," Jonas replied efficiently.

Lucian continued, "Pull team members from our executive division.

I want seasoned professionals with military or law enforcement backgrounds. Ideally, ex-special forces."

"Of course. I'll personally vet and select four of our best to cover you twenty-four seven until the threat passes," Jonas assured confidently.

"It may be long term. Do it swiftly and keep arrangements need-to-know. Report only to me on this," Lucian ordered.

"Absolutely, sir. Consider it handled," Jonas said.

Satisfied the request would be enacted quickly, Lucian ended the call. He disliked relying on guards, but caution was prudent until the perpetrator was caught. And Coruscant's security teams were loyal only to him. With a brief nod, Lucian began to pack his belongings, both relieved to leave and burdened by the gnawing realization that this was far from over.

New York City's skyline stretched out before Lucian's office window, its shimmering lights contrasting with the darkened room. He sat behind his desk, floor plans of his penthouse, office space, and building with security details spread before him. The events at the family estate weighed heavily on his mind, and the need for security remained ever-present.

Knocking on the door, Jonas Richter entered first, followed by the four members of the security detail. Lucian stood to greet them, a sense of gratitude mingling with the gravity of the situation. Lucian referred to his notes provided earlier by Jonas and nodded to the group to start things off.

1.   Name: Captain Ian MacGregor
2.   Background: Former SAS operative

Captain MacGregor stepped forward, his demeanor poised. "Mr. Miller, it's an honor to serve as part of your security detail. I spent years with the SAS, handling covert operations and security details for high-profile individuals. My experience in assessing threats and devising tactical plans will ensure your safety. With your approval, I'll be leading your detail."

Lucian's took in his appearance and stance. The captain stood tall, a sculpted figure of discipline with well-defined muscles apparent even beneath his formal attire. His hazel eyes were intensely alert, observing every detail of the room as if constantly assessing threats. His dark brown hair, almost black, was of moderate length and neatly styled, with grey beginning to show at his temples. This lent him an air of experience and authority that only bolstered Lucian's initial impression. Lucian nodded and looked at the next in line.

3. Name: Former Special Agent Emma Turner

4. Background: Former undercover FBI agent

Special Agent Turner smiled, her keen eyes scanning the room with a hint of confidence. "Mr. Miller, my background is in undercover work for the FBI. I've successfully infiltrated criminal organizations and managed to gather crucial intelligence. I'll blend seamlessly into the background while keeping a watchful eye on any potential threats."

As Emma took her turn, Lucian assessed her with the same discerning gaze. She was of medium height, her body toned and athletic, a clear indication of her rigorous training and discipline. Her posture exuded self-assurance, as if in control of her surroundings. Her movements were always fluid and balanced, as though her body and mind operated in perfect synchrony.

Her dark black hair was pulled back in a style that was both practical and effortlessly elegant, a reflection of her professional and personal duality. But it was her eyes that commanded the most attention. They were piercing green, intense and laser-focused. They moved not nervously but observantly, always analyzing and calculating. Those eyes suggested she could dissect a complex situation or a risky environment in a mere heartbeat. Lucian took all this in, filing it away as he nodded in acknowledgment, turning his gaze to the next.

5. Name: Sergeant Carlos Ramirez

6. Background: Former Marine Recon

Lucian studied Carlos as he stepped forward. Square-jawed with a neatly trimmed beard, the man had an air of rugged masculinity that seemed both inviting and intimidating. Just a few inches shorter than

Ian, Carlos' dark, short hair and dark skin added another layer of seriousness to his appearance.

And then Carlos smiled. The warmth in that gesture was a surprising contrast to his otherwise stern demeanor, hinting at a depth of character that went beyond mere duty. He was dressed sharply in a well-tailored suit, something that didn't go unnoticed by Lucian. Clearly, the man could blend into any high-profile event without causing a stir, all the while fulfilling his role as a bodyguard to the fullest.

In that moment, Lucian felt a sense of assurance. Carlos' composure and the subtle details of his appearance spoke volumes about his dedication and experience. This was a man he could trust to do his job exceptionally well.

"Mr. Miller, I've served in Marine Recon, where adaptability and precision are essential. I have experience in handling a variety of security situations and am well-trained in close protection. Your safety will be my top priority."

Again nodding, he appraised the last.

   7. Name: Lieutenant Claire Anderson

   8. Background: Former elite member of the Royalty Protection Detail

As Claire took her turn stepping forward, Lucian's gaze shifted to her, assessing her features with precision. She stood just a tad taller than Emma, lending her a poised, almost regal, air. Her striking light amber eyes met his, revealing a presence and self-assuredness that he found intriguing. Her hair, a rich golden brown that appeared entirely natural, was pulled back into a neat ponytail, a practical choice that nonetheless showcased her elegant neckline.

Those eyes, though. They were something else—confident and calm, yet capable of being piercing if need be. Lucian felt like those eyes would miss nothing, and that reassured him. Claire appeared fully capable, her entire bearing reflecting a calm readiness he highly valued.

Claire met Lucian's eyes with a steady gaze, her demeanor exhibiting a mix of confidence and composure. "Mr. Miller, as a former member of the Royalty Protection Detail, I've provided security for high-ranking officials and dignitaries. My expertise lies in identifying and neutralizing potential threats. Rest assured, I'll do everything in my power to keep you safe."

As the introductions concluded, Lucian shook hands with each team member in turn, sensing a unique presence emanating from each one. Whether it was Ian's unwavering poise, Emma's keen eyes, Carlos' intense readiness, or Claire's quiet confidence, each individual held an element that transcended mere skill. It was as if some intangible quality, woven into the fabric of their beings, set them apart.

"Thank you all for joining me in this challenging time," he said, maintaining eye contact to emphasize his sincerity. "Based on Jonas' word, I trust your abilities." His gaze lingered a moment longer on each face as if trying to discern the source of that extraordinary air about them.

It wasn't just the sum of their impressive resumes; it was the sense of synergy he felt among them, a collective strength amplified by unique attributes. Lucian couldn't put his finger on it, but whatever it was, it fortified his confidence that he was in the safest hands possible. And in times like these, that unspoken assurance meant everything.

Jonas Richter chimed in, "Mr. Miller, I handpicked these individuals for their exceptional skills and proven track records. They will operate with utmost discretion while providing you with the highest level of security."

"Excellent," Lucian replied, taking a moment to gather his thoughts. "I feel more at ease already. Let's go over the details of the building and the security plan for any meetings and travel. Since any overseas travel will be by private jet, weapons should not be an issue. Ian, I'll leave the details to you. Look into the legalities of that.

"I trust that you all have passports and have no issues traveling. In the near term, I'll be attending my family's burials in England soon," he added gravely.

The four nodded.

"I am fortunate I'm not dead, too. I have a feeling this could be very dangerous...for all of us," Lucian added seriously. "There are rooms available here that you may all use while off duty or resting. And

Jonas, please make sure everyone has what they need: cards and access, contact information for coordination, communications gear, phones, anything... Remember that this is to remain low profile. Now, let's move to the conference room and get started."

They spent time going over details, but it was getting late and Lucian needed rest. Gathering his notes and papers, Ian, the leader of the security detail, briefed the rest of the team on their duty rotation. Afterward, Ian and Jonas departed to finish coordination and equipment arrangements. Carlos and Emma headed for their assigned rooms, leaving Claire to follow Lucian to his room for some much-needed rest.

As the morning sun cast a warm glow through the windows, Lucian sat behind his desk once again, reviewing some documents. Ian, his head of security, stood outside in the foyer near Ava's desk, keeping a watchful eye on the office entrance.

Just then, the intercom buzzed, and Ava announced that the investigator Lucian was expecting had arrived.

"Send him in and have Ian join us," he replied, pressing the button.

A man in his late thirties with a strong and composed demeanor entered, followed by a watchful Ian. He was neatly dressed in a dark suit, and his pale blue eyes conveyed a sense of determination. This was Mark Donovan, the investigator assigned to delve into the background of the Miller family and the incident at the estate.

"Mr. Miller, good morning," Mark greeted with a firm handshake. "I've compiled some initial findings based on your yesterday's directions, and I'm here to update you and discuss our next steps."

"Good morning, Mark," Lucian replied, gesturing for him to take a seat. "Please, tell me what you've discovered so far."

Mark sat down, placing a folder on the desk. "I've started digging into Thomas' background, as well as his immediate family. So far, no glaring issues or red flags have surfaced. They seemed to be well-regarded, with no known enemies or disputes. So far, your assessment of Thomas as a social climber wanting to ride your sister's status seems to be spot on."

Lucian nodded thoughtfully. "Keep digging. We need to be thorough. Find out how involved or how serious they were. Where was it going? Was that the reason my sister wanted to insert herself into the family business even though she had little interest or involvement in the past?"

Mark nodded, made a note, and then continued, "Regarding the incident at the estate, I've requested copies of all police reports and notes from the Granite County sheriff's office and the BCI. Mr. Reed was able to call in some favors and a nudge from the AG to break them loose. It might take some time, but I'm confident we'll get a comprehensive overview of the investigation."

"Good," Lucian responded. "I want a detailed analysis of everything they've gathered so far."

"Now, about the sheriff, Detective Cruz, and Zoe Ananda," Mark said, glancing at the notes he had prepared.

"Sheriff Bowman has been with the department for over two decades and has a clean record. No suspicions or controversies linked to him."

Lucian interjected, "Still, check if he has any personal connections or conflicts that could be relevant."

"Of course," Mark acknowledged. "As for Detective Cruz, she's been recognized for her work on previous cases. No indications of any wrongdoing or personal agendas so far."

Lucian leaned back in his chair, deep in thought. "Keep an eye out for any unusual patterns in her investigations."

"Understood," Mark replied. "And Zoe Ananda, the FBI Special Agent, has shown promise and has had very promising reviews and was chosen to receive additional training as a profiler. This is her first real assignment up from Quantico."

Lucian nodded thoughtfully. "So Zoe has training in criminal profiling?"

"That's correct," Mark confirmed. "It's a specialized skill set, and she must have shown promise during her training to be assigned to a field office."

Lucian leaned back in his chair, absorbing the information.

"Interesting. I want to know more about her background and how she ended up in the FBI…associations and any other details that might give us a better understanding of her."

"Of course," Mark replied. "I'll dig deeper and provide you with a comprehensive report on her background and career."

"Good," Lucian said, a sense of determination evident in his voice. "Keep me informed of any developments, no matter how small."

Mark stood up, folder in hand. "You can count on it, Mr. Miller."

As Mark left the office to begin his work, Ian approached Lucian. "If you need anything else, sir, don't hesitate to ask."

Lucian glanced at Ian and offered a small smile. "Thank you, Ian. Keep an eye on everything here for now. There may be other… services…that might be needed."

Ian nodded, looking at Lucian appraisingly. "Yes, sir." Lucian recognized that look. As Ian was stepping back out, he asked him to have Ava send Jonas up as soon as he was available.

A soft chime echoed through the room, signaling an incoming communication. Lucian tapped a button on his top-of-the-line computer system, and the NexGen Pharmaceuticals logo showed on the screen. In a moment, Dr. Isabelle Sinclair appeared.

"Good evening, Lucian—well, afternoon your time. I hope all is well on your end," Isabelle greeted.

"Good evening, Isabelle. Let's get straight to it. How is the progress on our mutual endeavor?" Lucian replied with his characteristic directness.

"We've made remarkable strides, thanks to the resources you've provided," Isabelle said confidently. "Your modified CRISPR technique, EpiPhase CRISPR, has shown promise in targeting animal-related genes in our test subjects. We've successfully activated a few dormant genes responsible for enhancing sensory perception and agility."

Fascinated, Lucian leaned forward, his eyes bright with interest. "Continue."

"The transformations are controllable, albeit temporarily," Isabelle continued. "We've managed to induce partial therianthropic shifts in some of our subjects, but without a clear understanding of the missing factors, the effects are inconsistent. Some subjects exhibit partial animal traits, but we are yet to achieve full therianthropy."

Lucian's interest increased further, but he remained cautious. "Incomplete, but promising. Tell me more."

"In our attempts to regulate the transformations, we've implanted Flux-Stabilizing Crystals, but they're behaving unpredictably," Isabelle explained. "Our researchers still haven't found the key quantum effects needed, and we're still exploring how to stabilize them further. It's some unknown magic we're missing."

"Magic?" Lucian's skepticism surfaced. "Stick to the scientific facts, Isabelle."

"Of course, that was just a figure of speech," Isabelle nodded, understanding his perspective. "Our lack of understanding in this area is a significant obstacle. We require more data to refine the process, but we've been met with several ethical challenges, considering the unpredictable nature of these transformations. Some…unfortunate outcomes."

Lucian's face darkened, recalling the concerns raised by his own doctoral advisor during his academic days at Oxford. Yet, his ambition pressed him forward. "I expect results, Isabelle, even if we must push the boundaries of ethics. Our wealth and influence can shield us from prying eyes."

Isabelle hesitated, torn between her scientific pursuit and ethical considerations. "I understand your drive, Lucian, but we must be cautious. We don't want our research to spiral out of control."

"Cautious, yes, but never hesitant," Lucian replied, his voice unwavering. "Forge ahead, Isabelle, and remember: the rewards for success will be boundless."

Isabelle nodded, her determination tinged with apprehension. "Understood, Lucian. We'll press on and keep you updated. But be prepared for anything; the secrets of therianthropy would lead us into uncharted territory."

As the video conference ended, leaving Lucian deep in thought—his ambition converging with his thirst for power—he found himself recalling tales from his uncle Howard in his youth. Howard's sincere belief in the supernatural was evident, even though he was shunned by the rest of the family. With a nostalgic smile, Lucian's mind wandered back to those cherished moments when he used to sit in Howard's study, captivated by the tales of magic and the supernatural. Howard's passionate storytelling had left an indelible mark on his younger self's imagination; his uncle's belief in the occult had been unwavering despite all the opposition.

As Lucian's thoughts drifted back to one particular tale, the legend of the "Celestial Nexus," he couldn't help but wonder if there was some truth to his uncle's stories. The idea of a hidden location where lay lines of magical energy intersected with the physical world, granting unimaginable powers to those who could harness it, now seemed somehow less far-fetched. Yet the scientist within him was torn. How could he reconcile his logical, evidence-based approach to research with the fantastical stories he had heard as a child? Could there be a connection between his biotechnological advancements and the elusive factors he sought?

Lucian knew that as the CEO of a biotech empire, his reputation and credibility were on the line. Venturing into uncharted territory, where science and magic merged, could be seen as reckless or unscientific—indeed lunacy. But the allure of the unknown, the desire to uncover secrets of life, beckoned him forward. He realized that true progress often required taking risks and challenging conventional boundaries.

With a newfound sense of determination, Lucian made a decision. He would continue his research, exploring the possibilities that transcended the confines of traditional science. The legacy of his eccentric uncle, Howard, would forever be intertwined with his own quest for knowledge, propelling him into unexplored realms of discovery. He wasn't comfortable consulting with Howard and really had no idea how to proceed along these other lines of inquiry. He did sense a path forward, but it seemed out of his reach, at least for now.

Still lost in thought, his intercom buzzed, and Ava announced a visitor—the lead investigator with an update.

Mark entered, followed by Claire, with a stack of files and documents, ready to provide Lucian with the latest findings. Lucian gestured for him to sit. As Mark laid out the files, he began sharing the latest developments.

"We've made some headway in our investigations," Mark began, his voice steady. "The police reports and notes from the Granite County sheriff's office and the BCI have shed some light on the incident at the estate."

Lucian leaned forward, his face serious. "What have you found so far?"

Mark flipped through the files, organizing his thoughts. "It appears the sheriff's office conducted a thorough investigation, but there were no immediate leads or suspects. They've ruled out any involvement from you, at least for now, as well as from the employees and household staff."

Lucian nodded, taking it in. "And what of Detective Cruz? Anything unusual in her work?"

"Nothing suspicious so far," Mark replied. "Detective Cruz seems to have conducted her duties professionally. Her focus has been on gathering evidence and interviews."

Lucian's brow furrowed. "Keep an eye on her. I want to cover all bases."

"Of course, sir," Mark said. "As for Zoe Ananda, she's a promising agent with a strong background in criminal profiling. She has submitted a draft profile; here's a copy for your review. Be aware it contains some graphic details." Mark reached over, passing Lucian the document.

Lucian took the file, nodding. "I'll go through it later. Keep digging into her past, her connections—anything that might offer a clearer picture."

Noticing a thoughtful expression cross Mark's face, Lucian asked, "Something on your mind?"

Mark hesitated briefly. "Actually, yes, Mr. Miller. It's about SSA Zoe

Ananda and her recent actions in the case."

Lucian's eyebrow lifted in interest. "Continue."

"It appears that SSA Ananda reached out to one Anja Kinzey, a librarian at the Morgan Library and Museum specializing in Medieval, ancient, and arcane history," Mark detailed.

Lucian's eyes narrowed. "That's an unusual direction for her investigation. Are there similar threads in other FBI cases, perhaps?"

"Exactly," Mark confirmed. "There's no mention in team discussions of why she'd consult someone in such a field. It raises questions. She seems to be profiling the killer as an agent or contract killer for an unknown, possibly powerful, organization with religious or occult overtones."

Lucian's brow furrowed further as he processed the information. "Any idea how Zoe and Anja are connected? Is it personal or professional?"

"We haven't found any direct ties between them so far," Mark replied. "However, they did attend the same college at the same time —Columbia. It's possible they know each other then or crossed paths in some other way, but without more details, the nature of their relationship remains unclear."

Lucian pondered this, weighing the implications. "Continue your search, Mark. I want to know how deep this connection goes and its relevance to the case."

"Absolutely," Mark assured him. "I'll delve into their backgrounds and inquire at the Morgan Library and Museum."

"Excellent," Lucian said. "And see if the museum has any insights on Anja's role in the investigation. She might have shared something."

"I'll get right on it," Mark confirmed, jotting down a note. "It's worth pursuing."

Lucian valued Mark's meticulousness. The intertwining of science, violence, and arcane history puzzled him, but he sensed that the answers might lie within these disparate elements.

"Understood," Mark said, logging Lucian's instructions. "Regarding connections between the Millers and other significant parties, we're compiling a list. Jonas and the security team are also gathering intel."

Lucian reclined in his chair, his mind a swirl of possibilities. "Report back if you find anything substantial."

"Will do," Mark said. "It's a complex tapestry we're trying to weave. It might take some time to see the whole picture."

Lucian exhaled, recognizing the long road ahead. "I get it. Just keep going."

As they delved deeper into the case, time slipped by. The sun sank, filling the room with dusky light. Lucian felt his exhaustion mounting; he'd need rest to be at the top of his game.

"Thank you, Mark," he said, his voice tinged with fatigue but also gratitude. "Your commitment is exemplary."

Mark nodded, eyes filled with resolve. "Thank you, sir. We'll get to the bottom of this."

As Mark exited, Lucian gazed out the window, his reflection mirroring his inner uncertainty. The case had grown increasingly intricate with SSA Zoe Ananda's involvement and her link to Anja Kinzey. The unknowns were many, but he sensed that these seemingly disconnected strands would eventually converge unexpectedly.

Could the answers be tucked away in some long-forgotten past? As more pieces fit together, Lucian hoped they'd unveil the obscured intent behind the calamities that had plagued his family.

Eight

Anja woke up feeling refreshed; her body and mind had rejuvenated after the intense release of tension the night before. The lingering scents of exotic oils and candles from her readings still filled the air. She fixed herself some tea, sat at her kitchen table where she had left the bundle of letters the night before, and laid them out carefully. They alluded to a wide array of topics, reflecting Edward Ashton's vast and enigmatic interests. Anja sorted them carefully, arranging the correspondence into distinct categories to make her review more manageable.

She first delved into the letters related to secret societies and occult groups Ashton had been a part of. His discussions on rituals, alchemy, and symbolism intrigued her. Anja could almost sense the weight of the secrets within those pages, as if the words themselves held a mystical aura. Next, she explored the letters from Ashton's known associates, like the Elizabethan scholar and astrologer John Dee. These exchanges offered glimpses into their metaphysical studies and provided insights into Ashton's intellectual circle.

Her curiosity only deepened as she discovered writings from unknown mystics and sages that Ashton had met on his travels through Europe and the Middle East. The letters that intrigued her the most were those written by Ashton himself. They revealed heated debates with fellow occultists and academics on topics ranging from magical arts to Hermeticism. Anja admired his passion for seeking knowledge and understanding the mystical forces that shaped the world. However, the tone of his later letters changed, reflecting his frustration after falling out of favor with the establishment. Anja sensed desperation in his words as he sought patronage to support his research.

The final set of letters held a chilling weight. Ashton's paranoia was evident in his desperate pleas to trusted confidants, warning them about threats to his life from unknown adversaries. These notes were a grim reminder of the dangers he faced in his pursuit of knowledge. Anja pondered the phrases used, such as "ceaseless pursuit," "safehouses across the foggy moors and misty fens," and "wretched hounds." Ashton's language painted a vivid picture of his predicament, with imagery that seemed straight out of a gothic novel.

The letter's tone shifted from fear to defiance as Ashton expressed his determination not to go quietly into oblivion. He spoke of "protective wards and spells," revealing his dedication to defending himself against the unknown forces wanting to eliminate him. The mention of a desperate ritual to "rend the veil" added an air of mystery and mysticism to the letter, leaving Anja with more questions than answers.

Ashton's plea for his friend to avenge him and preserve his legacy showcased the depth of his convictions and the righteousness he felt about his work. The use of "obloquy" to describe how he feared his name would be tarnished after his demise demonstrated his command of language and his desire for his accomplishments to be understood and appreciated by the world. The closing lines, "Perhaps in time, I shall return from beyond the veil…but for now, this is my farewell. Yours eternally, Edward Ashton," held a haunting finality. Anja couldn't help but feel a sense of sadness for the enigmatic occultist and a burning curiosity to uncover the truth behind his fate. Checking the date on the letters, she found they were written just before his demise.

With a deep breath, Anja set the first letter aside and picked up the second one that had caught her attention. It was more of a note, almost like Edward Ashton's private confession. In this letter, he delved into the depths of his writings and the measures he took to safeguard its secrets. The language used had a scholarly precision, reflecting Ashton's meticulous approach to his life's work.

The letter began with a sense of reluctance as Ashton acknowledged the pain of obscuring his life's endeavors and knowledge he had accumulated within the Grimoire's pages. He had intentionally used his personally devised languages and symbols, ensuring that the unveiled truths remained hidden from all but the most enlightened minds. He expressed doubt about the readiness of his era to comprehend the profound revelations he had discovered.

Despite his reservations, Ashton couldn't bear the thought of his labors being lost to time. In the Sigrum Animus chapter, he embedded subtle clues—references to ancient numeric systems, alignments, and lexicons—hoping they might guide a future seeker toward unlocking the Grimoire's secrets. The use of the word "seeds" hinted at the cryptic nature of these clues, small yet potent enough to inspire someone knowledgeable in ancient arts to undertake the arduous task of deciphering the text.

With the letters before her, Anja knew that she held a glimpse into the life and mind of a man who had delved into the realms of the unknown, leaving behind secrets waiting to be unraveled. Continuing her study of the letter, she felt a growing sense of responsibility to fulfill Ashton's wish—to be the one patient and wise enough to illuminate his true legacy and reveal the hidden light within the Grimoire. The path ahead was daunting, yet she felt an unyielding determination to unlock the ancient pages' secrets.

After reading through the bundle of letters, Anja's mind raced with questions and possibilities. Each piece of correspondence offered a unique piece of the puzzle, and she knew the answers were hidden within those pages and his diary. She was certain she could unlock the secrets of the Grimoire.

Unanswered questions lingered. *Was there a society targeting Ashton?* Howard Miller might have more insights. He had given her clues that helped her uncover details of Ashton's death and might know more about those Ashton had feared.

Anja took a deep breath and dialed the number she had saved

under "Professor Miller—LSMAES." After a few rings, a warm and familiar voice answered.

"Professor Miller speaking. How may I assist you?" he asked politely.

"Professor Miller, it's Anja Kinzey again. I hope I'm not interrupting anything important," Anja replied, trying to sound composed despite her swirl of emotions.

"Ah, Anja! It's always a pleasure to hear from you. Not interrupting at all. How may I be of service?" he responded warmly.

"Firstly, I want to thank you again for your previous help with my Edward Ashton research. Your insights were invaluable. Today, I have a few more questions, and it's about something much more delicate," Anja began, knowing she needed to be cautious with her words.

"Of course, my dear. You know you can always count on me for assistance. What is it you wish to know?" Professor Miller asked, his tone indicating genuine interest.

Anja took a moment to collect her thoughts before proceeding. "You see, Professor, I've come across some information that might indicate a connection between Edward Ashton and a secret society maybe known as the Hidden Hand or perhaps the Faceless Watchers. They seem to be somehow involved. I wanted to know if you have any knowledge about them or if they have any historical ties."

There was a brief pause before Professor Miller replied; his tone turned more serious. "Anja, if they truly exist, they are deeply secretive organizations, and it's true that they have dabbled in matters that some would consider dangerous or forbidden. However, their true intentions and motives have always been shrouded in mystery. There have been rumors that they were involved with actively suppressing anything supernatural—viciously. I must advise you to tread carefully, for delving too deep into their affairs could attract their unwanted and potentially very dangerous—even deadly—attention."

Anja nodded with a shiver, even though the professor couldn't see her. "I understand, Professor. I have the feeling they were involved with or orchestrated Ashton's death. That's why I'm being cautious. I believe there may be dangers involved, and I don't want to put myself or others at risk. Especially you."

"Thank you and very wise. It's essential to exercise caution when dealing with such matters. If you have any more questions or concerns, please let me know. In the meantime, I will start digging discreetly into this secret society to see what more I can find," Professor Miller assured her.

"Professor, please be careful."

As their conversation drew to a close, Anja felt thankful for Professor Miller's wisdom and guidance. She knew that navigating the dangers of this unknown group and the questions surrounding Edward Ashton's work would require all the help she could get. With determination in her heart, she hung up the phone.

Coming back to her table, Anja carefully packed the letters, notes, and documents, securing them in her messenger bag. As she gathered her belongings, excitement and trepidation churned within her. The puzzles she was unraveling were both fascinating and dangerous.

Dressed for work and with her bag in hand, Anja stepped out into the bustling city streets. The cool morning air invigorated her, and she felt a renewed determination to continue her pursuit of knowledge and truth. The path ahead was uncertain, but she was resolute.

As she reached the library, Anja's mind was already racing with thoughts about the day's research. She greeted her colleagues with a warm smile, disguising the excitement brewing within her. The library was her sanctuary, a place where she could lose herself in the world of books and forgotten lore.

Throughout the day, Anja diligently attended to her duties, all the while keeping her mind alert for any clues or connections that might shed light on "Hidden Hand" activities or Edward Ashton's seemingly impenetrable demise.

Later in the day, Anja noticed a woman she didn't recognize approaching her desk. She glanced around to make sure no one was eavesdropping before giving the visitor an acknowledging nod.

"Umm, Anja Kinzey, right?" the lady asked quietly, trying to be discreet. "My name is Emma Turner. My employer would like to meet with you in his office."

Anja's eyes widened slightly, and she let out an exasperated sigh.

"Really? Another Emma? Sure..., um, no, not interested, and I don't even care who your employer is," she responded, frustration and worry clouded her thoughts. She couldn't shake the feeling that these encounters were related.

Emma could sense Anja's apprehension, but she had been instructed to insist on the meeting. "I understand, but he's concerned about your well-being. It won't take long, and he just wants to talk."

Anja hesitated for a moment, considering the request. She didn't want to be rude, but she also didn't want to be pulled away into an unknown situation. "Look, I appreciate the concern, but I really need some time alone to focus on my work. Tell your employer I'm fine here at the library."

Emma nodded, knowing she had to respect Anja's wishes and that this approach had somehow gone off the rails. "Alright, I'll let him know. But if anything changes, if you need anything or feel unsafe, don't hesitate to reach out." She passed Anja a card with only a phone number on it.

"I will," Anja replied, still feeling a bit uneasy about the situation. She watched as Emma walked away, her mind filled with questions and suspicions about the encounters with these mysterious "Emmas."

After slipping the card into a pocket, Anja returned to her research, trying to shake off the distraction. She knew she had to stay focused and determined if she wanted to uncover the truth about Edward Ashton and the "Hidden Hand." However, the encounters with the two "Emmas" had left her on edge, and she couldn't shake the feeling that there was more to the story than she knew.

A little while later, Anja's phone buzzed, and she saw Zoe's name flashing on the screen. Relief and curiosity bubbled within her as she answered the call.

"Hey, Zoe! It's so good to hear from you," Anja greeted her.

"Anja, it's great to talk to you too," Zoe replied. "I just got back from upstate, and I couldn't wait to catch up with you. There were some strange details in that case, and I remember you mentioning you had a feeling about it before I left."

Anja felt goosebumps as she recalled her premonitions before Zoe's assignment. "Yeah, it was odd. I can't explain it, but I just had this feeling that your case had something to do with the Miller murders. And then, well…"

Zoe's voice turned serious. "It does, and it's been haunting me. Those were some of the most bizarre and disturbing crime scenes I've ever seen. Something is not adding up, and I can't shake the feeling that there's more to it than meets the eye."

"I feel the same way," Anja admitted. "There are so many unanswered questions."

"Exactly. I think we need to put our heads together and see if we can make sense of this. Can I come to see you at the library? We can go over everything in more detail," Zoe suggested.

"Oh, that sounds ominous. Aren't you not supposed to share details with us civilians? But, of course, I'd love that," Anja replied, relieved to have Zoe's expertise to help unravel the mysteries surrounding the Miller murders. "Why don't we meet at the café here at the library? We can grab some dinner and have a private spot to talk."

"Sounds perfect. See you there in an hour?" Zoe confirmed.

"Absolutely. I'll be waiting," Anja said with a smile, looking forward to having Zoe by her side to navigate the secrets complicating her life.

After ending the call, Anja couldn't help but feel grateful for her friend's support. Still, she couldn't shake off the unsettling encounters with the two "Emmas" earlier. There was something off about those situations, and she knew she needed to share her concerns with Zoe, too.

At six p.m., Anja made her way to the café in the central court. The library's atrium was an elegant space with natural light filtering through the glass ceiling, casting a warm glow over the diners below. Anja found a table in the back, tucked away in a cozy booth, providing a sense of privacy away from other patrons. A few minutes later, Zoe entered, and their eyes met in recognition. They exchanged smiles as Zoe joined Anja at the booth.

"Hey, it's good to see you," Anja greeted.

"You too," Zoe replied. "I'm glad you're here. I have some

interesting updates to share."

As they settled into their seats, Zoe explained, "I asked for and got permission to bring you in as an expert consultant on this case. With your knowledge of occult history and secret societies, I believe you could provide valuable insights."

Anja was somewhat taken aback by the offer but quickly realized that having Zoe's official support would also grant her access to resources she might not have otherwise. "Wow, I didn't expect that, but I'm honored, Zoe. If it helps us get to the bottom of this, then I'm in."

"Great," Zoe smiled. "Let's get started then. Here are some details from the scene that you might find interesting..."

As Zoe shared the details, Anja's mind began to race with possibilities. Her expertise in the occult and her premonitions might hold the key to unlocking the clues surrounding the Miller murders.

After discussing the scene, Zoe paused and looked at Anja. "Hey, I know this has been a lot to take in, and it's getting late. Are you still up for some food? I can't think on an empty stomach."

Anja chuckled softly, realizing she had forgotten about her appetite amid all the intense discussions. "You're right; I could use a bite. Let's order something."

As they ate, Anja sensed their investigation getting complicated. Yet, she felt a glimmer of hope, knowing that with Zoe's unwavering determination and her intuition, they might just uncover the truth that had eluded so many before them. She explained her findings about Ashton's murder and the eerie similarities to historical cases. Zoe listened attentively, her profiler's mind working overtime to connect the dots. The mention of a secret society known as the "Hidden Hand" aroused Zoe's interest, and she looked thoughtful.

"The Hidden Hand...I've also heard rumors of such an organization before," Zoe mused. "A powerful group with an unsettling agenda. Nazi related, I believe. It sounds like they see themselves as the protectors of humanity, but their methods sound extreme. Like some kind of supremacist organization."

Anja nodded in agreement. "Exactly. From what I've gathered, they seem to view anything hinting at the supernatural as a threat that must be eliminated, It's as if they believe they alone have the moral authority."

Anja leaned back in her seat, deep in thought. "You mentioned connections to Lucian and some kind of genetic or bio-enhancement research. That could be a possible motive. Perhaps the Hidden Hand sees such research as an affront to their beliefs and aims to put an end to it."

Zoe considered the possibility. "It does fit. If Lucian is involved in research that challenges their ideology, they might see him as a threat. I also can't shake the feeling that he might be the main target for another reason. Maybe he's stumbled upon something he shouldn't have, something that implicates this group in some way." Her eyes widened like she had found the missing link as she continued, "You think they might be after him for more than just his research?"

"It's a possibility," Anja replied. "I've heard whispers that their influence extends far beyond just suppressing knowledge. There are rumors of darker secrets, hidden agendas, and ruthless actions in their history."

Zoe leaned forward, donning a serious expression. "If that's the case, then Lucian might still be in grave danger. We need to find a way to stop this organization before they cause more harm."

Anja nodded. "Agreed. But we have to be careful. If they have been operating for centuries, they must have considerable resources and connections. We don't want to draw their attention to ourselves or make any rash moves."

Zoe sighed. "It's a delicate balance, but we'll figure it out. I trust your instincts, Anja. You've already proven your insights are invaluable. I will also have to limit what I put in reports. I'd likely be put in an asylum if I start talking supernatural or magic in the FBI."

Anja smiled appreciatively. "And I trust your investigative skills, Zoe. Together, we make a formidable team. Let's keep digging and see where it leads us."

They continued brainstorming ideas and theories. Anja sensed the weight of their shared responsibility, and the knowledge that Lucian's life hung in the balance only fueled their determination to uncover the truth.

"Speaking of Lucian...," Zoe said with a mischievous twinkle in her eyes, leaning in closer to Anja. "I have to admit, he is quite the catch if anyone dared. Those dreamy dark eyes and that charm—you've seen his pictures in the paper, but trust me, they don't do him justice—HOT!"

Anja couldn't help but chuckle at Zoe's playful tone. "Oh, come on now, Zoe. You're making him sound like a romance novel protagonist."

Zoe laughed, nodding in agreement. "Well, maybe he could be the protagonist of our own little romance novel. A forbidden love story with a secret society backdrop, perhaps? Oh...have you gotten laid recently?"

"Zoe!" Anja rolled her eyes playfully. "We have enough drama in real life without adding a romantic subplot. But I won't deny that Lucian might have a certain allure."

"Exactly!" Zoe exclaimed, playfully raising an eyebrow. "And if we were in a romance novel, I'd be the sassy sidekick."

Anja smirked, playing along. "Oh, no doubt about that. You'd keep the mood light and add a splash of humor to every perilous situation."

Zoe grinned. "And you'd be the brilliant and mysterious heroine with hidden powers and a heart of gold, unraveling ancient mysteries and outsmarting the bad guys, getting laid by the protagonist..."

Anja chuckled, shaking her head.

Zoe nodded. "We should write this novel someday. It could be a bestseller. But for now, let's focus on the real-life mystery we're dealing with this secret organization and its dangerous agenda. I think our adventure will have enough twists and turns to rival any romance novel."

Anja's smile softened as she looked at her friend. "You're right, Zoe. Our need to uncover the truth is far more important than any fictional romance. Sometimes, Zoe, you can go over the top on those splashes of humor, though."

With a sigh, Zoe conceded, "Yes, I know...the darker things get, the more the stress piles on. I try to compensate with the jokes. Like on a crime scene. You should hear what gets said..."

"Yes, and like for finals in college. I understand and don't worry. A little stress relief is needed," Anja admitted.

"Okay, now...," Zoe raised her glass in a playful toast. "...To the dynamic duo—solving mysteries and fighting the forces of evil! See? Stress relief!"

"To the dynamic duo!" Anja echoed, clinking her glass against Zoe's with a smile.

As they enjoyed their meal and the camaraderie that had grown between them, Anja was grateful to have Zoe in her life again for friendship and support. In the midst of danger and uncertainty, their playful banter and shared determination provided a sense of comfort and strength.

In a dimly lit, nondescript apartment, Raven sat at her computer, meticulously typing her report on Anja's recent activities. Her fingers moved swiftly and purposefully as she detailed Anja's interactions with Howard Miller and Zoe Ananda, noting how Anja had ventured into the dangerous territory of the Ashton case despite the discreet warning. Raven mentioned Anja's phone call to Howard Miller in London, a conversation she couldn't decipher due to its encrypted nature. She also noted an unexpected meeting between Anja and Emma, Lucian's bodyguard. Despite her best efforts, she was frustratingly unable to overhear their conversation. She also related her suspicions that all of these occurrences were related.

Emma, why did it have to be Emma? she thought wryly.

After completing her report, Raven encrypted the message and sent it through the secret communication channels to the controller, the hidden figure who oversaw their operations. The message would reach him, masked by layers of encryption and digital shadows.

In an undisclosed location where the controller resided, Richard received the encrypted report. He skimmed the words on the screen, absorbing the information with calculated precision. Frustration and concern clouded his expression as he contemplated the situation.

"Blowing up from multiple angles," he muttered to himself. "Complications we cannot afford."

He leaned back in his chair, weaving fingers together, contemplating the course of events. The prophecy he had once read in ancient texts came to mind, a foreboding warning of events set into motion long ago, destined to collide in the present.

"This was not how it was meant to unfold," he whispered to the shadows. "We were meant to safeguard humanity, not be entangled in such intricate webs of deceit and revelation."

His mind raced with the possibilities and potential consequences of the situation. Anja's curiosity and connections to the Ashton case were becoming increasingly problematic, and her meeting with Zoe added another layer of complexity.

"We need to maintain control," he mused, his voice low and commanding. "We cannot let her delve deeper into our secrets, nor can we allow her to unravel the truth behind the Sodality."

He composed a reply to Raven with instructions and promptly sent the encrypted message…

Nine

After the dinner with Zoe, Anja made her way back to the library proper, her mind still swirling with thoughts and speculations. Little did she know that another encounter awaited her amongst the aisles of ancient tomes and beautiful museum pieces.

Just as she reached a particularly secluded section, she heard footsteps approaching from behind. Turning around, she saw Lucian, flanked by a woman she did not recognize, and Emma 'number two,' walking toward her with a determined look in his eyes.

"Anja," he said curtly, "we need to talk. I don't appreciate being turned down like that."

Anja's heart quickened seeing him, feeling a mixture of attraction and apprehension. She took a step back, trying to regain her composure. "Mr. Miller, it's not a good time. I'm busy with work; I need to focus and don't need the distraction."

Lucian's expression clouded, and he took a step closer. "I don't believe you," he said, his voice tinged with frustration. "I need your help. What do you know about my family's past?"

Anja's eyes darted between Lucian and his two imposing bodyguards. She knew she had to be cautious with her words. "I don't know anything that would concern you, Mr. Miller. I'm just a librarian doing my job."

"Really?" Lucian scoffed. "Then why did you turn away Emma

when she tried to talk to you? And why did you meet with Agent Ananda? What are you doing with the investigation?"

"Keep your voice down! Library—remember?" Anja whispered harshly.

Anja felt a chill run down her spine as she realized Lucian had been keeping tabs on her. She decided to answer carefully, hoping not to reveal too much. "I have no idea what you're talking about. Emma approached me, and I had no idea who her 'employer' was, but I have no interest in whatever you and your family are involved in. I am sorry for the loss of your family. Perhaps that is what has you so wound up. As for Zoe, we're old college friends and we were just catching up. If you are so in need of help, then perhaps a bit of manners would do you well."

Lucian's eyes narrowed, and he took another step closer, invading her personal space, a quiet menace in his voice. "Don't play games with me, Anja. You're involved in some way. I need to find out why I was targeted…why my family was targeted. I won't stop."

Anja swallowed hard, trying to maintain her composure. "I assure you, Lucian, I'm not involved in anything. I'm just a researcher. I have no intention of causing any trouble for you or your family."

Lucian's lips were in a flat line. "Good," he said, his tone dripping with malice. "Because you wouldn't want to be on the wrong side of me."

Anja's heart pounded in her chest as she sensed the veiled threat in his words. She knew she had to be careful but couldn't back down. "I'll keep that in mind," she replied, trying to sound defiant despite her fear.

With one last look in his unreadable eyes, Lucian turned on his heel and walked away, followed by his two guards. Anja let out a shaky breath, feeling dismissed and uneasy. She couldn't deny the magnetic pull she felt, but she also couldn't ignore his arrogance and the danger he represented.

Danger to her self-control was a real possibility. As Zoe had said—he was HOT, and she was right that his photos did not even come close to doing him justice. Anja could feel his presence calling to something inside her. Something she had never felt before. But still—

the nerve.

She resumed her work in the library but couldn't shake the feeling of being watched. She couldn't help but wonder what secrets Lucian David Miller might be hiding. And she couldn't help but wonder what Lucian's touch would feel like.

As Anja gathered her things to leave for the evening, she was taken aback when Mrs. Thompson approached her with a stern and disapproving expression.

"Anja, we need to talk," Mrs. Thompson said, her voice firm. "I've been noticing a change in your behavior lately, and it's not acceptable. You've been acting darker and more assertive, and it's affecting your performance and attitude at the library."

Anja felt a mix of guilt and defensiveness, but she knew she had to remain composed. "I'm sorry if I've seemed different lately, Mrs. Thompson," she replied, trying to sound sincere. "It's just been a stressful time, and there have been some…intrusions in my life that I'm trying to deal with."

Mrs. Thompson crossed her arms, not entirely convinced. "Intrusions? What kind of intrusions?"

Anja hesitated, not wanting to reveal too much. "Just some people approaching me and asking questions about things I'm not comfortable discussing," she said vaguely.

"Well, whatever it is, it's not an excuse for letting your work suffer," Mrs. Thompson admonished. "You need to maintain a professional attitude and focus on your responsibilities here."

Anja nodded. "You're right, Mrs. Thompson. I apologize for any lapses in my performance. It won't happen again."

"It better not," Mrs. Thompson warned. "We value our staff here, but we also expect them to conduct themselves appropriately. I don't want any more issues, do you understand?"

Anja nodded again, this time with a more determined expression. "Yes, I understand, and I'll do better. I expect the intrusions will stop soon, and I'll be able to focus on my work without distractions."

Mrs. Thompson looked skeptical but seemed willing to give Anja a chance to prove herself. "Very well, but I'll be keeping an eye on you," she said sternly. "Don't disappoint me."

As Mrs. Thompson walked away, Anja let out a sigh of relief. She knew she had to be more careful and maintain a façade of normalcy at the library. She had wanted to stay late after closing to take a look at the Grimoire with the new revelations she had found in the package of letters and notes, but she also couldn't shake the feeling of being watched. Danger seemed to lurk around every corner and she wasn't bold or strong enough to risk it. Yet.

Leaving the library, she couldn't help but wonder how she had become entangled in this web of secrets. She knew she had to be cautious, but she also couldn't resist the pull of the Grimoire and the secrets it held. Anja vowed to be more discreet, but deep down, she knew her curiosity and determination would lead her further down dark paths.

As Anja sat in her reading chair back in her apartment, surrounded by the comforting presence of her beloved books, she tried to push away the thoughts of the day's events. She poured herself a glass of wine, hoping it would help ease her tense nerves. Just as she was starting to relax, her cell phone rang. Hesitatingly she answered the unknown number.

"Hello?" she said cautiously.

"Anja, it's Lucian," came the familiar voice on the other end of the line. "I wanted to apologize for my behavior in the library earlier."

Anja was taken aback by his call and felt a mix of surprise and curiosity. "Apologize? Well, that's unexpected," she replied, trying to keep her tone cool and unaffected.

Lucian chuckled lightly. "Yes, I admit I may have been a bit miffed by your refusal to meet me, but I claim extenuating circumstances. I hope I didn't come across as too…overbearing."

Anja couldn't help but feel a flutter of something in her stomach at the sound of his voice. "No, not at all, well, kinda," she said, trying to sound casual.

Oh, gah! That's how to sound cool, Anja. What's wrong with me?

"But just so you know, my number is unlisted, so I'm curious how you got it."

Lucian brushed past her comment. "I have my ways," he said, his voice tinged with amusement. "But that's not why I called. I wanted to make it up to you for my behavior. How about we meet tomorrow night for dinner?"

Anja considered for a moment before countering, "How about Monday night? I'm off work then and won't be so tired."

"Monday night it is then," Lucian agreed; she could almost hear the grin in his voice. "I'll have my driver pick you up at your address at eight."

Anja couldn't help but be affected by the unexpected turn of events. There was something about Lucian's voice that stirred things inside her, and she couldn't deny the intrigue and attraction she felt toward him. But she was also cautious, so sarcastically remarked, "You know where I live, too? Great, now I have another stalker…"

There was a momentary pause before Lucian responded, lowering his voice, "Another? Wait…never mind, we can discuss that later."

Anja was surprised by the almost possessive or maybe protective tone in his voice; she also couldn't help but be intrigued. "Jealousy doesn't suit you, Mr. Miller," she teased, trying to hide the effect his words had on her.

He chuckled softly. "Perhaps you'll see a different side of me Monday night," he said cryptically.

"We'll see…"

"Good night, Anja."

"Good night…"…*Lucian,* she added to herself.

Anja's life was becoming more and more entangled with Lucian's, and she couldn't help but look forward to it.

Anja stood naked before her closet, contemplating her options for the evening ahead. The dinner with Lucian at a fancy restaurant in Manhattan called for something elegant yet alluring. After a moment's consideration, she chose a knee-length, silky, deep emerald dress with a subtle V-neckline accentuating her collarbones and setting off her green eyes and burgundy hair. She chose a black lace thong and bra after discarding the thought of going without. He wasn't going to see them, she vowed…but, just in case.

The dress hugged her figure in all the right places, the fabric draping gracefully down to her knees. She slipped into a pair of black stiletto heels that added a touch of height and sophistication.

Then, she moved to the vanity to apply light makeup. Soft, smoky eyes accentuated her gaze, and a rosy hue adorned her lips. Leaving her hair down after a brush, Anja saw herself in the mirror and was pleased with the result. She wanted to look and feel confident, knowing that Lucian's dark eyes would surely be upon her.

Finishing her preparations, she dabbed her favorite perfume on her wrists and neck, savoring the delicate and alluring fragrance. Its jasmine and sandalwood notes made her feel sensual and empowered —a perfect choice for the evening's dinner.

Promptly at eight, the buzzer sounded, and Anja pushed the button by the door to acknowledge her readiness. She heard a man's voice on the intercom. "Miss Anja? I'm here to take you to Mr. Miller."

She replied, "Thank you. I'll be right down."

Exiting onto the street, Anja was greeted by an imposing figure, likely another bodyguard. He was tall for a Hispanic man, which seemed unusual. His dark hair was neatly trimmed, and his well-tailored suit emphasized his lean and athletic physique. He introduced himself as Carlos.

As they approached the sleek and elegant Rolls-Royce waiting by the curb, Anja couldn't help but admire its opulence. The black exterior gleamed under the city lights, and the iconic grille gave it an air of regal sophistication. The driver stood by the open rear door, impeccably dressed in a chauffeur's uniform, his demeanor exuding professionalism and courtesy.

Stepping into the car, Anja asked with a smile, "What's your name?" to the driver holding the door.

"Oh, sorry, Miss, it's Thomas."

As she settled into the plush interior, Thomas got in to drive, with Carlos getting in the front passenger seat after scanning the people and surroundings. *Shotgun,* Anja mused to herself.

Inside, she couldn't help but notice the attention to detail. The soft leather seats cradled her, and the refined wood finishes added a touch of warmth to the luxurious setting. The smell of leather was welcoming. The ambiance was nothing short of enchanting, making her feel like she was part of a romantic fairytale. *Okay, Zoe, you have your moments...* Anticipation tingled in Anja's veins as she considered the night ahead. She couldn't help but wonder what the evening held in store, feeling a mixture of nerves and excitement.

Soon, the Rolls-Royce glided to a halt in front of a stately building adorned with ornate golden lettering that read "Le Grand Étoile." The restaurant's elegant façade exuded sophistication and charm, drawing in discerning patrons seeking an exceptional dining experience. Carlos stepped out of the car before she did, his eyes sweeping the area. Anja couldn't help but note his vigilance, which made her feel both reassured and slightly unnerved.

Anja stepped out, feeling a touch of nervousness as she looked at the impressive entrance of the restaurant. Thomas, the courteous and composed driver, bid her a pleasant evening before driving away, leaving her in Carlos' capable hands.

With an air of quiet assurance, Carlos led Anja into the restaurant, past a well-dressed clientele enjoying cocktails and conversation in the elegant lounge area. They were met by a poised and attentive maître d', who offered a warm smile at the sight of Carlos. "Good evening, Mr. Ramirez," the maître d' greeted with a smile of recognition.

"Good evening. Mr. Miller's party," Carlos replied, and the maître d' nodded, guiding them through the restaurant with practiced grace. They passed by intimate candlelit tables adorned with fresh flowers, each setting contributing to the ambiance.

As they approached a private room tucked away from the main dining area, Anja noticed a figure sitting outside at a table with a steaming cup of coffee. It was Emma, Lucian's bodyguard. She smiled in greeting, and Anja nodded in acknowledgment as they passed by.

Carlos knocked lightly on the door to the private room before opening it for Anja. She stepped inside, and there he was—Lucian Miller. He was dressed impeccably in a well-tailored suit, his eyes turning to her as she entered.

The sight of Lucian elicited a response from the pit of her stomach, a subtle flutter that seemed to echo throughout her body as his dark eyes locked onto hers. For a moment, time seemed to stand still, the world outside their private room blurring into inconsequence. "Anja," Lucian said with an apparently genuine smile, rising from his seat to greet her. His voice had a captivating quality that stopped her breath for a moment. "I'm so glad you could join me."

Anja couldn't help but smile in response, the atmosphere of the private room creating an inviting setting. "Thank you for inviting me," she replied, taking in his presence.

She noted Carlos stepping back, his departure almost inconspicuous, before he left the room.

Lucian gestured to the chair opposite his. Anja settled into it gracefully as he scooted the chair forward for her. "Thank you," she murmured.

The private room offered a cozy and intimate space adorned with elegant décor and soft lighting. It was clear that every detail had been carefully considered to create an atmosphere of refined elegance.

Before returning to his seat, Lucian poured from a bottle on the table into crystal glasses for them, the wine's vibrant red hues capturing the light and reminiscent of her hair. As he handed a glass to Anja, he began, "This is Beaujolais Nouveau, a young and lively red wine. It's known for its fruity flavors and smooth character. I hope you'll enjoy it." The air was charged with anticipation, and Anja could feel the electricity between them, a subtle tension that seemed to thicken the atmosphere.

Lucian's eyes sparkled as he took in her appearance, "You look like a dream tonight, a level of beauty that would cause a riot in the library if you appeared there dressed as you are."

With a wry expression, "You caused a stir earlier there when you came to call." She added a smile to take the sting off just a bit.

"I would like to sincerely apologize again for my rudeness during that episode. I would genuinely like to forget that happened. Events have conspired to put me on edge, but I will promise to work on my manners for you from now on."

"Well, I think I may be able to forgive you if you can hold to that promise," she replied, her eyes now matching her smile.

As the conversation continued, Lucian's compliments flowed effortlessly, his words weaving a captivating web around Anja. She couldn't help but notice the genuine look in his eyes. The way he spoke about her beauty and intellect stirred something deep within her.

Anja tried to maintain a composed demeanor, reminding herself that this was not just an ordinary dinner but a chance to gather more information. Yet, despite her attempts to focus on that intent, she found her thoughts drifting.

Lucian's magnetic presence enveloped her, drawing her closer with an allure she couldn't quite put into words. There was undeniable chemistry between them, a connection that seemed to transcend the strict boundaries of logic. Anja found herself wondering if Lucian felt the same pull.

As Lucian continued, his gaze never leaving her, Anja felt a flush of heat spreading through her body. The room seemed to shrink, and the world outside faded away, leaving only the two of them in this private space.

He leaned in slightly, his voice becoming a soft whisper. "Anja, you're not just incredibly talented, but you have a unique appeal that has captured my attention," he confessed, his eyes locked onto hers.

Anja almost shivered, her breath catching in her throat. She was caught off guard by the intensity of his words, and a part of her wondered if this was all just a part of his charm, his ability to draw people in with his words. But there was something genuine in his gaze, something that spoke of a deeper connection, a shared understanding of the things that lay hidden inside her.

Before she could understand that feeling, Lucian shifted the conversation to more practical matters, broaching a potential project he had in mind. He mentioned specific historical and occult details he needed to unravel and how he believed her expertise would be invaluable in shedding light on the enigmatic past.

"I'm still not completely convinced that your meeting with Ms. Ananda...Zoe, was entirely personal and not related to the murder investigation?"

"Um, guilty, but you were coming on rather strong," she admitted since he seemed to have a line to inside knowledge.

He went on to confirm those feelings as he mentioned a call he had with his uncle Howard. "He was impressed with your knowledge but was also concerned for your safety concerning your inquiries." At her surprised look, he added, "He is family, after all, and he did confirm that I should ask you for your help."

As they delved into some surface details of the proposed project, Anja's professional instincts took over, and she listened intently to Lucian's requests. Her mind raced excitedly at the prospect of delving deeper into things she was already thoroughly immersed in.

But beneath the surface of their more professional discussion, the undercurrent of desire and attraction lingered, impossible to ignore.

She was torn between the temptation of the unknown, the thrill of stepping into uncharted territory with this powerful man and the rational voice inside her, warning of the potential dangers of getting too close. She had committed to putting herself out there to find someone she could let loose with, but was he the one? Was she willing to take a chance with him? She was sure she could resist him, but the question lingering in her mind was—did she even want to resist?

Anja took another sip of her wine, the subtle taste of strawberry on her tongue, a distraction from the whirlwind of emotions inside her. Lucian watched her, a hint of a smile playing on his lips as if he could read the thoughts racing through her mind.

The evening wore on, the intimate setting and the shared ideas creating a silent bond between them. Anja found herself opening up, sharing more than she had intended as if the weight of the Grimoire had spilled over into their conversation. She also shared her feeling of being watched and her uneasiness with another visitor. "I had another Emma visiting me before yours. I had a really bad feeling about her. She was the other stalker I mentioned on the phone."

Lucian grinned, then sobered. "Glad as I am that your stalker was not another man seeking your attention, I am very worried about your safety. I will have to look into that. I would bet that it's also connected to the murders."

"I got the same impression," Anja replied with the same sober expression.

Lucian leaned in closer. "I wouldn't want anything to happen to you unless it involves me."

Anja chuckled softly, her humor finding a way to lighten the weight of his last statement. "Well, you can rest assured that there's no queue of men seeking my attention. You're the only one stalking me at the moment," she teased, winking playfully.

Lucian raised an amused eyebrow, a glint of mischief in his eyes. "Oh, I'm not stalking you, Anja. I prefer to think of it as…persistent interest," he replied, his voice tinged with amusement.

Anja laughed, enjoying the playful banter. "Persistent interest, huh? Well, I'll keep that in mind when I spot you lurking in the shadows," she quipped, her tone light but with a hint of intrigue.

Their playful exchange was momentarily interrupted as they both remembered the gravity of the situation and the dangers that surrounded them. Lucian's expression grew serious, and Anja's smile faded.

"I don't mean to make light of it," Lucian said earnestly. "I genuinely worry about your safety, especially with that odd visit."

Anja appreciated his concern, the sincerity in his words evident. "Thank you."

Their conversation eventually turned back to the matter at hand, the potential collaboration on the research project. Lucian offered her to work directly for him, but Anja hesitated, explaining the conflict with the library's employment policy.

"I appreciate the offer," she said, meeting his gaze with sincerity. "But I can't give up my position at the library; it provides me with access to research materials and books that would otherwise be out of reach." Thinking of the Grimoire, "However, I am open to finding a way to collaborate on this. We could work together and share information and resources. I believe our combined expertise could be mutually beneficial."

Lucian nodded, understanding her position. "I'd be happy to explore that option," he said, a smile playing on his lips. "I have a feeling we make a…formidable pair, Anja."

She was resisting the pull Lucian seemed to exude and her desire to let him have his way with her right here. Her hand, under the table, trembled slightly.

Fuck me, she thought, wanting him to do just that. *What is getting into me? Err, rather, what I want in me. Sheesh…* She felt a flush of heat as her mind flashed to images from her recent date with the books from Raymond.

Forcing her mind back to the present, Anja felt a potent blend of desire and trepidation, knowing that her life had taken an unexpected turn and that she was stepping into a world of secrets and desires she hadn't seen coming.

Lucian thanked Anja for her time and expertise, and they bid each other farewell. Anja knew the meal they had shared was exquisite, yet the flavors and dishes blurred in her memory, overshadowed by the intensity of her emotions.

"Good night, Anja."

"Good night…, Lucian," she added, taking one last look into his eyes.

Carlos was waiting outside, his watchful gaze meeting Anja's as she stepped out of the private room.

By the time Anja and Carlos left the restaurant, Thomas was just opening the back door of the Rolls for her.

She entered her apartment with the scents of the evening's encounter still lingering on her skin. She couldn't shake the feeling that the path ahead would be painted with uncertainty and intrigue. And maybe more.

Ten

The morning sun cast a golden hue over the city as Lucian prepared to meet with Ian. Despite the beautiful day, his thoughts were consumed by Anja. She had bewitched him in a way no other woman had before. Her resistance to his charms both frustrated and fascinated him, adding a new layer to their interactions. He found himself drawn to her; her intelligence, wit, and the sibylline aura that surrounded her. Sitting in his office, he couldn't help but dwell on their dinner together. Anja's presence had captivated him, and he sensed a mutual attraction simmering beneath the surface. It was a tantalizing dance, yet she held herself back, only increasing his interest further.

Lucian's thoughts were momentarily interrupted as Ian entered the room.

After returning a nod, Lucian picked up the phone and called Mark. "Mark, it's Lucian. I need you to assign someone or a team to keep a close eye on Anja twenty-four seven. After my conversation with her last night, I'm concerned about her safety. I want to know everything about this other 'Emma' she mentioned approaching her in the library and anyone else who might be taking an interest in her. I don't want to take any chances."

Mark's efficient and focused tone came through the line, "Understood, Lucian. I'll make it a priority. We'll keep tabs on her starting as soon as I can brief them and get them started. We'll gather any information we can."

"Thank you, Mark. I appreciate your quick action," Lucian replied.

As he hung up, Ian made a teasing comment about stalkers, to which Lucian replied with a smirk, recalling Anja making a similar comment. "I prefer to think of it as persistent interest. She's an intriguing woman, and I want to make sure she's well-protected."

Ian chuckled, understanding Lucian's sentiment. "Well, whatever you call it, I'm sure she'll appreciate your concern. Just be careful, my friend."

Lucian nodded thoughtfully. But he couldn't deny the pull he felt towards her: intellectually, physically, and emotionally.

"I know, Ian. But sometimes, you just have to trust your gut," Lucian said resolutely.

Ian nodded in agreement but added with a grin, "Are you sure it's your gut? Or is it some other piece of your anatomy, just a little lower?"

Lucian rolled his eyes and tried to keep from grinning.

Richard read Raven's encrypted message carefully, his face betraying no emotion. He knew that Anja and Lucian's potential collaboration could indeed pose a significant threat to the Sodality's secrecy. Anja's knowledge and expertise, combined with Lucian's resources and influence, made them a formidable duo.

He weighed the risks carefully. Eliminating Anja now, with her heightened sense of caution and additional security measures seemingly provided by Lucian, would be difficult. Any attempt on her life might draw unwanted attention and expose the Sodality's existence.

But allowing Anja and Lucian to continue unchecked could be just as dangerous. Their cooperation could lead them closer to unraveling the secrets of the Sodality, something that must be avoided at all costs.

The controller's fingers danced across the keyboard as he composed his response to Raven's report.

Proceed with caution, he wrote. *"You are correct in your assessment of the situation. Anja and Lucian must be handled delicately. Eliminating them directly is risky. Instead, focus on subtle manipulation and misdirection. Plant seeds of doubt and discord between them. Use their emotions against them. If done skillfully, they may become adversarial, and that may prove to be an opportune time to strike, eliminating Anja.*

Attached are notes and photos that Smoke obtained prior to his missteps. The woman seen with Lucian is a high-priced escort that Lucian frequents and might provide some leverage. Her name is Vanessa Delacroix. In the attached files, find her address and phone number. You should be able to use this to your advantage. With your expertise, you should be able to generate some incriminating photos. Use your best judgment.

He paused for a moment, considering his next words carefully. *But be warned, Raven. I will not tolerate any mistakes like Smoke's. He will not be able to assist you with this. You must act with precision and discretion. Failure is not an option!*

With a final click of the send button, the message was encrypted and sent on its way to Raven. The controller knew that the delicate balance between protecting the Sodality's secrets and neutralizing potential threats had now shifted. It was a high-stakes game where every move could spell triumph or catastrophe.

As he sat back in his chair, Richard knew that the future held great uncertainty. But he was committed to maintaining control and safeguarding the Sodality's existence, even if it meant making difficult decisions and sacrifices along the way. The game was far from over, and he had every intention of winning.

Raven's eyes scanned the attached files, studying the notes and photos that Smoke had obtained before his mistakes had cost him dearly. She noted Vanessa Delacroix's name and description; she was a high-priced escort to whom Lucian had taken a liking. A cunning smile shaped her lips as she considered the possibilities that lay ahead.

Vanessa could be the key to unraveling Lucian's carefully crafted image. With generative AI at her disposal, Raven knew she could create a web of deception that would sow doubt and mistrust. The thought of manipulating them through Vanessa excited her, and she couldn't help but relish the task.

She, though, also knew to proceed carefully. Lucian was no fool, and he would not be easily swayed by just any fabricated evidence. Neither would Anja. Raven needed to ensure her plan was seamless and her manipulations undetectable.

Raven's mind flooded with ideas as she began to devise her strategy. She would start by gathering more information about Vanessa Delacroix, learning everything she could about her background, interests, and vulnerabilities. Looking over the photos that Smoke had provided—some nude shots of Vanessa, others of Lucian escorting her into a restaurant—Raven thought they could serve as a starting point. With more information, she could tailor her manipulations to strike at the heart of Lucian's weaknesses and Anja's vulnerabilities.

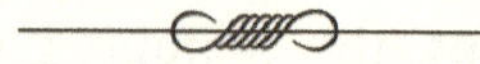

Lucian leaned back in his chair as Ian departed. Ava announced over the intercom, "Your uncle Edward is on the line."

"Thank you, Ava," he said, picking up the phone.

"Hello, Edward," he began the call.

The phone call between Lucian and Edward took on a somber tone as they discussed the arrangements for the family's remains. Edward began with the updates, "Lucian, with the assistance of Horace Reed and Ava, I've managed to secure the release of the family's remains from the coroner's office in Granite County. They will be transported to England for burial at the family estate there. We've also made arrangements to have the extended family attend, and press releases have been prepared to address the situation. The funeral has been scheduled for this Saturday morning."

Lucian sincerely thanked Edward for taking care of these sensitive matters. "Thank you. I'll arrive on Friday afternoon. I can't express how much I appreciate your help, Edward. It means a lot to me during this difficult time."

Edward's response was grudging, with a hint of disdain. "Well, it had to be done. And speaking of family, Howard insists on attending the funeral. I can't say I'm thrilled about it."

Lucian understood Edward's reservations but replied calmly. "Howard is still family, no matter how you may feel about him. Besides, I wanted to speak with him anyway. There are some matters I need to discuss with him."

Edward let out a sigh. "Very well. Just be careful, Lucian. You know how he can be."

Lucian acknowledged Edward's concern. "I'll handle it, Edward."

"Actually, Edward, I'll be bringing a special guest with me to the estate," Lucian said, surprising his uncle. "Her name is Anja Kinzey, and I believe her presence could prove quite beneficial. Please arrange for a room near mine for her."

Edward couldn't hide his curiosity. "Anja Kinzey, you say? What's her relation to us, and why would she attend the funeral?"

Lucian decided to gloss over the details for now. "Let's just say she may be able to assist in the investigation of this tragedy. I thought her insights might be valuable during our stay at the estate. And now that I think about it, I may be able to convince her friend, an investigator attached to the case, to observe. She will have no legal authority there, and I can ensure she will not cause issues."

Besides, he thought to himself, *I believe a conversation between Anja and Howard could be enlightening.*

Edward grunted but didn't press further. "Very well, I'll make the arrangements for rooms, though they may need to share one...Is there anything else you'll need?"

"Actually, yes, two to four rooms for my security detail, depending on the space available. They can also assist with security for the funeral and services. They are very capable. And one room for Ava, my secretary."

Edward responded, "I think I can handle at least two for security and one for Ava, but can't promise more yet. I'll see what I can do."

"Thank you, Edward. I'll see you at the estate," Lucian replied, keeping his thoughts to himself. In truth, he saw this as an opportunity to spend more time with Anja, to convince her of the importance of their shared research, and perhaps to explore the undeniable chemistry between them. Her companionship during this difficult time might bring a much-needed sense of comfort and understanding. Lucian was going to make the most of the situation and see where it might lead.

"Thank you again for taking care of everything. I'll see you soon."

The call ended with a sense of cautious optimism. Lucian knew that dealing with family drama would require patience and diplomacy.

As Lucian sat alone in his office, he called up the latest results from NexGen in Switzerland. Frustration gnawed at him as he reviewed the data once again. Despite their state-of-the-art technology and sophisticated analysis, the research seemed to have hit a dead end. The answers he sought remained elusive, buried beneath layers of genetic complexities.

Lucian sighed, reclining in his chair as memories of discussions with Isabelle from NexGen, his uncle, and Anja surfaced. The puzzle's pieces lay before him, challenging him to connect them. Between the murder reports, his talk with Anja, and the occult ties, everything seemed to converge toward something he couldn't overlook.

He recalled his uncle's stories, ones he would have once dismissed as fantastical or absurd. Howard had always been drawn to the unusual and paranormal, exploring ancient beliefs and forgotten practices. But now, faced with the current situation, Lucian couldn't help but wonder if there was more to his uncle's beliefs than he understood.

Could it be possible that ancient knowledge, passed down through generations, concealed some truth? He couldn't dismiss the possibility that there might be truths hidden within ancient tales and texts.

His mind drifted to Anja, with her vast knowledge of history and genuine passion for the supernatural. She could hold the key to unlocking those secrets, but he wondered if she held more significance than he had previously realized.

Lucian considered the implications of genetic markers and the potential for extraordinary capabilities encoded within their DNA. If there was some knowledge of ancient practices that could enhance human abilities, it might explain the supernatural elements in history and still be attainable or rather within reach again with his guidance.

He began to piece together a daring supposition—a theory that once seemed unthinkable but now felt compelling. What if the secrets to unlocking latent genetic potential, allowing individuals with the proper genetic legacy to possess extraordinary talents, intelligence, and insight, were actually linked to the supernatural?

In an era marked by technological marvels and scientific breakthroughs, the fusion of archaic knowledge with contemporary insights seemed plausible. Could Anja, with her research into medieval occult practices, fit the pieces together if they worked together?

Lucian knew that he couldn't allow his emotions to cloud his judgment. He needed to approach the situation with caution and scientific rigor. If there was any truth to his theory, it had to be tested and scrutinized. He resolved to pursue the truth. The path ahead might be filled with uncertainty and challenges, but he couldn't turn away from potential discoveries that lay just beyond his grasp.

As he closed the files on his computer, he was now, more than ever, determined to convince Anja to accompany him to the funeral and bring her friend Zoe along. He also planned to take her to Switzerland and pay a visit to NexGen in person.

He summoned Ava and Ian. "The funeral for my family will be this Saturday. Ava, I need you to coordinate travel arrangements from here to the family estate in Kent. I need you to attend as well if that's not a problem."

"I can do that," she replied.

Lucian added, "Ian and his team will be attending as well. Also, plan for Anja Kinzey and Zoe Ananda, the FBI profiler working on the case, to travel with us. After the funeral, I intend to take a trip to Switzerland personally to visit NexGen and further investigate the results they've obtained."

Ava nodded, her fingers already tapping away on her tablet. "Of course, Mr. Miller."

Lucian continued to lay out his plans and finished with, "I want to make sure everything is taken care of for a smooth trip."

"I'll take care of everything right away," Ava confirmed.

Lucian then turned his attention to Ian. "I need you to handle the security arrangements for the trip."

Ian nodded.

With the necessary arrangements set in motion, Lucian felt a sense of excitement. The trip to Switzerland would be a pivotal moment, and he could hardly wait to explore the possibilities that awaited them.

After receiving the assignment from Mark Donovan, Dan had been on the night shift vigilantly watching over Anja Kinzey for any lurking threats. The previous evening had passed uneventfully, and tonight appeared to be headed in the same direction.

From a discreet vantage point opposite the library, he observed as Anja secured the premises and embarked on her walk home. The vibrant pulse of the city's nightlife would easily cloak anyone aiming to blend in. Yet, thanks to his acute senses and refined skills, he wasn't easily deceived.

After examining the information Anja provided about Emma, Dan felt a jolt of anticipation when he noticed someone shadowing Anja. This could be the clue they needed to figure out the stranger's intent. Dan trailed the woman discreetly, his expertise enabling him to meld into the night. He observed her, gauging if she posed a threat or was just coincidentally walking the same route. Her consistent distance from Anja was suspicious. As they wove through the city, Dan kept a careful distance but ensured he could still see her. Years on the job had taught him to rely on his instincts.

She eventually veered into a dim alley. Dan chose to stay at the entrance, not wanting to corner her or lose her in the twisty streets.

While he waited, he called Ian to update him on the situation. Amidst the city's ambient sounds, Ian instructed him to continue tailing the mysterious woman.

Time passed, and Dan's eagerness mounted. The moment felt crucial, and just as he questioned if she had evaded him, he heard a subtle sound from the alley's depths. The woman soon appeared. Dan studied her and an ominous feeling engulfed him. Her approach was purposeful. She suddenly spun around, wielding a knife. His reflexes, sharpened by years of experience, propelled him into action. The blade nicked his arm, but he swiftly countered with a forceful punch to her face.

Even as he readied his firearm for defense, she had already bolted. Her speed was astonishing, and he realized chasing her down wouldn't be easy. Shooting her in the back was out of the question. Unfortunately.

Dan's pulse quickened after the unexpected altercation. Without delay, he updated Ian. "Ian, had a confrontation with our subject. She attacked me, but I'm okay. Lost her, though. She must've noticed I was on her tail."

Ian's response was swift and reassuring, "Hold your position, Dan. Reinforcements are on the way. Stay alert."

Dan took a defensive stance at the alley's entrance, anticipation and anxiety pulsing through him. He was about to call in again when a familiar figure approached: Emma, one of Lucian's bodyguards. She assessed the situation with a quick glance, her sharp eyes landing on the blood on his arm.

"Are you alright?" she inquired.

Dan's jaw tightened, and he nodded. "I'm fine. She cut me, but Anja's safety concerns me more. We need to figure out who this woman is and her motive."

Emma's gaze was firm. "We'll get to the bottom of this. First, let's collect any evidence. Once we've done that, we can update Ian and Lucian. Claire's already with Anja. She's upset after hearing about this."

As they began collecting samples, the encounter replayed in Dan's mind. This wasn't his first dangerous confrontation, but something about this woman deeply unsettled him. Her skill and intensity made him question her nature. She was well trained.

Later, back at the office, Emma cleaned Dan's wound with practiced care. "You were fortunate," she remarked, her voice carrying a weight of warning. "We have to be on guard. This isn't over."

Eleven

ANJA'S HEART RACED as she descended into the subway station. Her uneasiness lingered, but the source of her discomfort remained elusive. She had quickened her pace through nighttime Manhattan, trying to shake off the uneasy feeling gnawing at her. As the subway train arrived, Anja boarded with a sigh of relief. The enclosed space of the train felt safer, and she could feel the tension in her muscles beginning to ease slightly. Still, she remained on edge, her eyes darting around.

The ride was uneventful, and the feeling of being watched clung on. Anja knew Lucian had assigned his security detail to keep an eye on her, but the thought of being constantly monitored unnerved her. She tried to convince herself that it was for her safety. Nonetheless, the eerie feeling was unsettling.

As she approached her apartment building, Anja was startled to see Claire standing nearby.

"Anja, good evening," Claire greeted her with a nod. "I apologize if I startled you. Mr. Miller asked me to keep an eye on you."

Anja's tried to regain her composure. "Oh, it's fine," she replied, forcing a smile. "I appreciate the concern. I guess I'm just a bit on edge tonight."

Claire glanced around the area, searching for threats. She noticed Anja's nervousness and suggested, "Why don't we go inside?"

Anja hesitated for a moment, then nodded in agreement. "You're right. Thanks, Claire. Come on up."

They made their way to Anja's apartment, and as they entered, Anja felt she wasn't the only one uneasy. Claire's presence and heightened alertness only reinforced the sense that something significant was unfolding around her. Anja hoped that with Claire's watchful eyes, she could relax a bit now after a stressful trip home.

After settling into the apartment, Claire turned her attention to Anja. "I need to fill you in on something concerning. We believe the woman you encountered in the library, the one you had a feeling about, has been following you. She attempted to attack one of our agents, Dan, earlier tonight. He was injured, but he's okay. We lost her in the chase, but we're doing everything possible to track her down. Dan was trying to spot anyone interested in you. It appears he did."

"Oh, damn, I had a feeling something wasn't right! Is he going to be okay?" Anja asked.

Claire nodded reassuringly. "Yes, he'll be fine. He's tough. But we need to be extra cautious now. Ian just called with some updates and instructions. He wants us to bring you to the penthouse. A car will be here shortly to pick us up. Lucian will explain everything there."

Anja nodded, her emotions torn between anxiety and relief. "Alright, I'll get ready. Thank you, Claire."

Claire gave a small smile. "Sure. Just stay close, and we'll get you through this."

Waiting for the car, Anja couldn't help but wonder about the mysterious woman following her. Conflicting emotions of fear, curiosity, and a wave of dark anger engulfed her.

The city seemed to take on a more sinister mien as they headed to the penthouse. The empty streets, dark windows, and shadowy alleys hid unknowable threats. She focussed on the anger to keep her fear at bay.

When they arrived, Claire led Anja directly to Lucian's office, where he was waiting along with the rest of his security team. She couldn't help but be captivated by the luxury of Lucian's residence and the breathtaking views of Manhattan below. The city lights twinkled like stars, casting a warm glow over the vast skyline. The sight gave her a brief respite from the turmoil of the evening.

Anja was still on edge but couldn't deny feeling safe and comfortable being with Lucian. As he discussed the events of the evening and the attack on Dan, her emotions swung between fear and intrigue. She watched Dan, who was trying to make light of the situation despite the bandage on his arm and the sweatshirt he was wearing.

"Well, if I knew I was going to end up in a borrowed sweatshirt tonight, I would've at least brought my own," he quipped with a wry smile, sniffing at it.

She heard a few chuckles escape from some of the security team members. They seemed to appreciate Dan's dry humor even amid a tense situation. Lucian cracked a small smile as well.

"You wear it well, Dan," Claire said, playfully patting him on the back. "But let's hope you won't need more borrowed clothes anytime soon."

"Agreed," Dan replied, his tone still light but with a sense of determination. "Next time, I'll just wear my 'superhero' outfit. That should scare off any potential attackers, right?"

"True," Emma said. "But I don't think it would help you avoid being spotted. Again."

The team laughed. Despite the seriousness of the situation, Dan's humor seemed to help them relax and focus, much like Zoe would have done.

Lucian's worried expression didn't escape Anja's notice throughout the conversation. She appreciated his concern but also sensed that there was something he wasn't telling her. As the night wore on, exhaustion started to take its toll on Anja; she knew she needed rest to process everything that had happened.

When Lucian suggested she stay in a guest room at the penthouse, Anja hesitated. "I appreciate the offer, Lucian, and I understand it's probably the safest option right now, but I need to know more about what's happening. Who was that woman, and why was she following me? And what does all of this have to do with your family?"

Lucian sighed, his expression torn between wanting to protect Anja and the need to be honest with her. "I promise to answer all your questions in the morning, Anja. Right now, you need rest, and we all need to regroup. It's been a long night for all of us, and we'll need a clear mind to figure this out. Please, just trust me for tonight. You're safe here."

Anja looked into Lucian's eyes, searching for any hint of deception. Ultimately, she decided to trust him, at least for the night. "Alright, but you tell me everything first thing in the morning. Deal?"

Lucian smiled softly. "Deal. Now, let's get you settled in a guest room. Ava will take care of anything you need. And don't worry, we'll figure this out."

As Ava led her to a luxurious guest room, Anja's mind buzzed with questions and uncertainty. The comfort and safety of the penthouse did offer some relief, and she hoped that come morning, she would finally get some of the answers she needed. Settling into the bed, Anja pondered her life's unexpected turn and the potential revelations awaiting her in the morning. Her thoughts drifted to Lucian and his undeniable allure. His commanding presence and a hint of vulnerability she had glimpsed during their interactions fascinated her. Something about him captivated her, drawing her in like a moth to a flame.

She found herself indulging in fantasies about exploring a darker, more intimate side with him. Imagining herself in one of her dark romance fantasies, where passion and desire intertwined, she felt something deep inside her stir. In her imagination, Anja saw herself in his arms, their bodies entwined as they succumbed to the irresistible pull between them. The touch of his lips on her skin, the intensity of his gaze, and the thrill of surrendering to him aroused her immensely.

Yet, amid the seductive fantasy, a hint of caution remained. She knew that getting involved with Lucian would be dangerous in more ways than one. The mysteries surrounding him and the shadowy world they seemed to be entangled with were no mere fantasies, and the risks were real.

Even as she acknowledged the dangers, Anja couldn't deny the attraction she felt. It was as if she had stumbled upon a realm of darkness and secrets she had only explored through her readings. The lines between history, the supernatural, and reality seemed to blur.

With a sigh, she tried to push the enticing thoughts to the back of her mind. There were more pressing matters to attend to in the morning. She needed to uncover the truth about the elusive group known as the "Hidden Hand," decode the significance of the ancient grimoire, and understand her link to them. And how and why the hell was Lucian entangled with this?

As sleep finally began to claim her, she hoped the morning light would bring clarity and, perhaps, a glimpse of her new path. In the darkness of the night, her dreams continued to dance between the realms of passion and peril, leaving her heart and mind swirling in a lacework of desire and fascination.

As Anja woke up in the morning, she felt surprisingly refreshed despite the tumultuous events of the previous night—the sun's soft rays filtered through the curtains, casting a warm glow in the room. The sumptuous surroundings of the guest room reminded her that she was in Lucian's penthouse. Feeling the need to clear her head, she decided to take advantage of the shower attached to her room. The marble-clad bathroom was a sight to behold, adorned with lavish soaps and shampoo that exuded tantalizing fragrances. The fluffy white bath sheet enveloped her in a cocoon of softness as she stepped out of the shower, providing a small moment of indulgence amid uncertainty. She couldn't help but let out a playful giggle upon noticing a soft, fluffy white robe hanging on the back of the door. Imagining Lucian in such a robe made her smile, and she couldn't help but wonder how it would suit him. The image was both amusing and strangely appealing.

After dressing in fresh clothes she had packed, Anja noticed, with a pang of regret, that she had forgotten her perfume. It was a small oversight, but she had a particular attachment to that scent—it made her feel confident and composed. She sighed, realizing that in the rush of the previous night, she had left a piece of herself behind. Nonetheless, she pushed the thought aside, knowing that there were more pressing matters to address. Lucian had promised to answer her questions this morning, and she was eager to learn more about the world he belonged to and the secrets that had entangled her life with his.

Anja entered the living room feeling anxious and saw Lucian sitting in the corner nook with a laptop. The sight of Lucian's striking presence and the penthouse surroundings compelled her to take a deep breath. Lucian stood up and greeted her with a warm smile, gesturing to a seat for her.

"Good morning, Anja," he said, his voice inviting. "Please, have a seat. I hope you slept well."

Anja nodded, her mind still buzzing with questions but determined to take things slow. "As well as one can in such surroundings," she replied, her tone playful.

Lucian chuckled. "I'm glad to hear that."

As she settled into her seat, Lucian called Ava and requested a breakfast tray. It had a delicious spread of bacon, sausages, eggs, fruit, and other inviting treats. The enticing aroma of assorted breakfast items filled the air, and Anja's stomach growled in response.

"You really know how to make a girl feel special," Anja teased, casting a sidelong glance at Lucian.

He smirked, leaning in slightly, his eyes twinkling with mischief. "Only the best for my beautiful...guest," he replied with a hint of innuendo, playing along with her banter.

Anja's cheeks flushed slightly at his compliment. She couldn't deny the thrill of attraction coursing through her veins. She decided to push the envelope a bit further. "Oh, so now you're trying to charm your way into my heart with...breakfast?" she retorted, a playful glint in her eyes.

Lucian feigned innocence, his lips curling into a devilish grin. "Who said anything about hearts? I'm just hoping you'll be captivated by the...food...and maybe a bit more," he replied, his tone suggestive.

Anja laughed, enjoying the playful wordplay and the tension between them. "Well, I suppose I can't resist good...fruit," she quipped, reaching for a strawberry and taking a slow bite.

After they had finished their breakfast, Anja couldn't resist bringing up the topic again. With a playful glint, she said, "So, you promised to tell me all your secrets this morning."

Lucian leaned back in his chair, a mischievous smile dancing on his lips. "Ah, but some secrets are meant to be savored slowly," he replied. "Besides, I wouldn't want to overwhelm you with too much at once."

Anja laughed. "Fair enough," she said, playing along. "But I hope you'll be generous with your revelations when the time is right."

Lucian's gaze held hers, intensity in his eyes. "I promise you'll get all the answers you seek," he said.

Anja felt a rush of emotions looking at him, her mind buzzing with questions. She knew there was so much more to uncover about Lucian and the world he lived in, and she was determined to learn more. She savored the breakfast and the playful banter with the man, capturing her passions and mind. There would be time for more serious conversations shortly; for now, she was content to enjoy the moment.

After breakfast, Lucian led Anja from the nook to his office, where he settled into another soft leather chair mirroring the one she had occupied the night before. He took a deep breath, breaking the silence that had settled upon them. "Anja, I want you to know that I value your presence," he began, his voice steady and sincere. "You're not just someone caught up in the chaos of my world. There's something unique about you, a spark I've rarely encountered."

Anja felt her cheeks flush at his words. She realized that she tended to blush far too often in his presence.

"I believe there's a reason we've crossed paths," Lucian continued, his gaze unwavering.

Her mind wandered for a moment as she absorbed his comment, feeling a connection that transcended the bounds of their situation. Lucian's words touched a part of her that had been hidden away, an aspect of herself that craved adventure and discovery—even danger.

"And as we move ahead," Lucian said softly, "I promise to be honest with you, to share what I can."

Anja nodded, acknowledging that although she had stepped far from her ordinary life, something about Lucian made the risk seem worth taking.

"I want to trust you, Lucian," she replied, her voice steady.

"It all began with my fascination for biotechnology," Lucian explained. "I was driven to explore the possibilities of enhancing human capabilities, pushing the boundaries of what we believed was possible—through genetics. I delved into research that some might deem controversial, even bordering on the unethical."

As Lucian spoke, Anja listened attentively, her curiosity intensifying with each revelation. She leaned forward in her chair, absorbing every word as he painted a picture of his research and aspirations.

He paused for a moment as if contemplating how to continue. "You see, I've always believed that humans possess untapped potential, hidden capabilities that lie dormant within us. My goal was to unlock that potential and bring forth abilities beyond the ordinary."

Anja's mind raced with possibilities, envisioning the implications of such research. "And what did you uncover?" she asked.

"I made some significant breakthroughs," Lucian replied, pride evident in his expression. "I discovered ways to manipulate certain genetic markers and activate dormant abilities in human DNA."

He leaned back in his chair, a hint of sadness in his eyes. "The knowledge I had amassed seemed to have attracted the interest of a secretive and dangerous organization. I don't know who they are or what they hope to achieve. I believe I was targeted to suppress my research."

Anja's heart sank as she absorbed the gravity of Lucian's revelation. "So, you believe this group was responsible for the tragedy at your estate?" she asked.

Lucian nodded solemnly. "Yes, I do. My research apparently posed a threat to their agenda. They tried to strike to prevent me from discovering more before I could succeed."

Anja's mind was racing, connecting the dots and understanding the danger surrounding her. "And now they're after me too," she murmured, realization dawning upon her.

Anja offered a succinct version of her research into the Ashton Grimoire, a tome that held the promise of ancient knowledge and untold power. She shared warnings from the Ashton diary, recounting his ever-present sense of being watched and the diary's author eventually meeting a horrific end. Her discoveries hinted at a secret order that had spanned not just decades or centuries but possibly millennia.

Lucian's brow furrowed when Anja said she had mentioned her suspicions to Zoe about her new assignment and the potential danger. To Anja, he seemed to be troubled by the implications.

"She did find those unusual circumstances. She also assured me that you weren't responsible for their murders," Anja said, looking out the window at the city below.

Lucian just stared at her.

Anja, looking back at Lucian, nodded, seeing that he understood. They were both aware that the more they uncovered, the more dangerous the situation became. It was clear that they were treading on deadly ground.

"Anja," Lucian began, his tone serious, "I know the path we're on is filled with uncertainty and danger. But I can't help but feel that together, we have the potential to make a significant impact, to uncover truths that have been hidden for too long."

Anja met his gaze. "I believe that too, Lucian," she replied. "Whatever lies ahead, we'll need to face it together. We owe it to ourselves and those who came before us to seek the truth—to those who have died following such a path."

Lucian took her hand in his, offering her a reassuring squeeze. "I will do everything in my power to see this through, Anja," he said firmly. "You have my word."

Looking into Lucian's eyes, Anja felt a rush of emotions, both fear and gratitude. She knew that her life had changed irrevocably, and she was now caught in a tangle of secrets and dangers that she couldn't escape. But sitting there, hand in hand with Lucian, she also felt an inexplicable sense of trust and connection, a feeling that she was meant to be a part of this journey, no matter how perilous it may be.

Lucian continued. "You must come with me to England and attend the funeral. We'll be leaving tomorrow morning on my private jet."

Anja's stared at him for a moment.

"What?! No! I can't. There is more I need from the Grimoire. And I can't leave my job at the library. Lucian, I can't just abandon my research," Anja protested, her voice tinged with frustration. "The Grimoire holds so much knowledge, and I'm close to unraveling its mysteries. I can't walk away now."

Lucian leaned forward, his expression earnest. "We can find a way to continue your work."

Anja hesitated, torn between her passion for research, the attraction she felt toward Lucian, and the realization that her life was now at risk. She took a deep breath, trying to weigh the pros and cons of each choice.

Lucian added, sweetening the pot, "My uncle Howard will attend; I believe you have had a few conversations with him already. I think you two would get along brilliantly."

Anja raised her eyebrows but conceded, "Umm, yes, I would like to talk more with him—to meet him in person. I'll talk to my supervisor at the library," Anja finally said. "Maybe I can arrange a temporary leave of absence or something. But I can't promise anything."

Lucian nodded. "Thank you, Anja."

Anja glanced at Lucian, realizing that she had come to care for him in a short period. She knew the future with him would be filled with danger and uncertainty, but she couldn't deny the strong connection she felt anymore.

"I'll go to England with you," Anja said. "But on one condition—we work together to uncover the truth about these secrets. I want to be a part of this, Lucian, not just a bystander."

A soft smile formed on Lucian's lips. "I wouldn't have it any other way," he replied. "Oh, and by the way, can you convince your friend, Ms. Ananda, to join us?"

Anja's eyes twinkled with mischief and excitement as she thought about the dinner at the library with Zoe. They had joked about going on an adventure, but little had they known that the playful jests would turn into a very real and dangerous path.

"I think I can convince her," Anja replied with a grin.

Lucian chuckled, the sound sending a shiver of warmth through Anja. "Good," he said.

Excusing herself from Lucian, Anja stood up and left for her room.

She needed a moment to collect her thoughts and call Zoe. Entering the room, she noticed that it had been cleaned, the bed made, and a selection of clothes and shoes from her apartment had been brought over, including a long black dress and an overcoat. A hat box caught her eye. Rather than opening it, she turned, sighed, and sat back on the bed to make the call. Tapping Zoe's icon in her favorites list, she wondered what she would have to tell her to convince her.

The call rang a few times before Zoe answered, "Hey Anja, what's my favorite bookworm up to this morning?"

Anja took a deep breath and started nervously, "Umm, well...you won't believe this, and it may take some explaining. You see, I'm with Lucian now, in his penthouse apartment..."

"Wait, WHAT? Squee...girl! Spill! I knew he was HOT, but girlfriend, that was fast! Have you finally let loose? Did you...," Zoe went on in a rush.

Jumping in before Zoe could complete that line of questioning. "Zoe! Wait, slow down! Let me explain. I also need to ask a big favor." Anja scooted back and leaned against the bed's headboard, her hand on her forehead.

"A big favor? What do you need? Oh, wait, is he too much, and you need a third? I could be down for that!" Zoe added, laughing.

"NO! No... Oh, just listen, will you? Hussy!" Laughing at her word choice as hussy fit Zoe to a tee.

"Okay, okay, it figures you wouldn't want to share!" Zoe laughed.

Heaving a sigh, Anja tried again. "I'm going to England with Lucian for his family's funerals, and I need you to come with us. Please, could you get away for a few days? Maybe it might be good to observe him for your case or even others that may attend."

Zoe remained silent momentarily as Anja held her breath. "Um, I would be down for that too, maybe worm my way in as a third after all... No, just kidding...mostly. Well, sure, that could prove insightful, but the expense and getting authorization could be an issue."

Anja interjected. "Well, as for expenses, that would all be covered by Lucian. We'll be flying over tomorrow morning on his private jet and staying at his family's estate, well, his now, I suppose. All you need to do is dig out your passport, pack a bag, and meet us at the airport. I might even convince him to send a limo to pick you up. He's loaded if you hadn't noticed."

"Okay, keep twisting the knife. I'll see what I can wrangle. I guess I'll need to start making notes for that novel."

Another sigh escaped Anja's lips. "Yes, Zoe. We'll need to catch up on the flight over, but I need to get going. Today will be busy. I also need to let Mrs. Thompson know I'll be gone. Not looking forward to that…"

"I'll let you know, but I'm pretty sure the PTBs will authorize the trip. Mostly coming up empty on all the other avenues so far, so maybe this will move things along," Zoe replied. "I've been looking into other murders like Lucian's family. This is dangerous," Zoe added on a somber note.

"Yes, very. I hope I'm not dragging you into something you'll regret. But Zoe, we can't stop now."

"I know, I'll be careful. Okay, I'll let you know and hope to see you tomorrow. England, huh."

Hanging up, Anja sat back and closed her eyes. Images of hidden assassins and secrets buried in history flooded her mind, and something inside her stirred.

Twelve

Lucian sat in his office, engrossed in his thoughts, reviewing some documents on his laptop. The events of the day had been tumultuous, and he was grateful for the presence of his security team. Claire had been diligent in her duty. He knew he could rely on her expertise to keep Anja safe.

As the door to his office opened, Lucian glanced up to see Anja enter, accompanied by Claire. He smiled warmly at her, setting aside his laptop and standing up to greet her.

"Anja," he said, warmth filling his voice, "I'm glad you're back. And thank you, Claire. You can rest now and prepare for the flight to England in the morning."

Claire nodded and excused herself, leaving Lucian and Anja alone in the office.

Anja looked relieved to be back at the penthouse. Lucian could sense that the day's events had left her on edge. He motioned for her to sit, and she obliged, settling into one of the soft leather chairs. Watching Anja, he noted the weariness in her eyes. Her voice, steady, broke the silence of the room.

"I managed to secure time off from my duties at the library," Anja began, drawing Lucian's full attention. "I mentioned a family emergency to Mrs. Thompson, and while she wasn't exactly pleased, she understood. We have as much time as we need."

Lucian felt a wave of relief inside, though he kept his features composed. "Good," he remarked.

Anja's fingers grazed the edge of her messenger bag, her following words instilling further confidence in Lucian. "Also, I was able to gather more diagrams and notes from the Grimoire. Claire watched every corner, ensuring I could work in peace."

A hint of a smile threatened to break Lucian's otherwise stoic façade. "So, all went as planned?"

She nodded, her lips turning into a small, triumphant smile. "Exactly as we hoped."

Lucian couldn't help but feel a surge of satisfaction in their collective efforts and in the trust he'd placed in Anja.

"I spoke with Zoe," Anja said, her voice tinged with relief and excitement. "She received authorization to join us on the flight to England. Can you arrange for someone to pick her up?"

Lucian nodded with a smile. "Of course, I'll have Ava coordinate the arrangements. Zoe will be in good hands."

Anja let out a sigh of relief. "Thank you, Lucian. I'm glad she'll be able to come along."

Lucian leaned back in his chair, studying Anja's face. He could see the fatigue in her eyes and felt a sense of protectiveness over her. He knew that the situation was far from over, and many unanswered questions remained.

"Anja," he said gently, "you should also get some rest. Tomorrow will be a long day, and we'll need all our wits about us."

Anja nodded, acknowledging his concern. "You're right. I am a bit tired."

"Let me show you to your room," Lucian offered, standing up and gesturing for her to follow him.

Arriving at the guest room, Lucian opened the door and gestured for Anja to enter. "Your sanctuary," he said with a reassuring smile. "Rest, and we'll be off to England in the morning."

Anja smiled gratefully at him, her eyes lingering on his for a moment longer than she intended. "Thank you, Lucian."

"It's my pleasure, Anja," he said, maintaining his composure. "Get some rest, and I'll see you in the morning."

As he bid her goodnight, Lucian couldn't resist the temptation to drop some friendly banter and innuendo. "Sleep well and dream of our upcoming adventure," he said playfully.

Anja raised an eyebrow, clearly amused by his attempt to flirt. "You wish," she replied, a playful smile on her lips.

Lucian chuckled, feeling a sense of satisfaction at her response. She was still resisting his charms, but he could sense a hint of warmth in her demeanor.

As Anja closed the door to her room, Lucian couldn't help but smile to himself. He knew he had a lot to navigate in the days to come, and the dangers ahead were very real. But he was also excited about the prospects, the connection he felt with Anja, and the potential for something more.

Raven sat in her dimly lit apartment, her mind racing with frustration and anger. The recent turn of events had been less than favorable, and she couldn't shake the feeling that her once well-orchestrated plans were now spiraling out of control. The knowledge that someone was following her during her surveillance of Anja only added to her unease. Her bruised face and split lip didn't help. Pondering her next move, Raven glanced at the encrypted message from the controller. Anja and Lucian's potential alliance posed a grave threat to the Sodality's secrecy, and she had been tasked with finding a way to neutralize it.

However, it seemed like everything was going wrong. Anja was now under Lucian's protection, making any direct attack on her almost impossible. The fact that she was absent from her apartment and planning to be away from the library for an undetermined period complicated matters further. It was as if fate was conspiring against Raven, leaving her frustrated and out of options.

Raven's fingers flew across the keyboard as she composed an encrypted message to her controller; her frustration and determination were evident in every keystroke.

Subject: Urgent Situation

Controller,

I regret to inform you that the situation has taken an unexpected turn. Anja is now under Lucian's protection, which severely limits our options for a direct attack. Additionally, she is currently absent from her apartment and planning to be away from the library for an undetermined period. It seems like fate is conspiring against us.

However, I refuse to accept defeat. Be aware that they have plans to travel to England. Perhaps operatives there may be able to find other avenues of attack.

I will continue to develop the plans to drive Anja and Lucian apart. In addition to the leverage point you provided in Lucian's relationship with Vanessa Delacroix, I have started to gather information on Anja's past. There is very little to go on. So far, just rumors collected from her high school days might be sufficient if played correctly.

I can add additional pressure by strategically planting false, incriminating information to mislead Lucian or perhaps putting pressure on Anja at the Library.

I have begun to create compromising photographs, videos, and other litter that will cause Anja to fear and despise Lucian with the additional benefit of causing embarrassment for him.

I await your approval and further instructions.

Your loyal operative,

Raven.

She committed to the message with a final click of the send button. She knew it was now in the hands of her controller and could only hope they would approve of her strategy. Waiting for the reply, Raven felt the weight of the Sodality's future; it depended on her adaptability and resourcefulness. Setbacks wouldn't deter her; she prided herself on her deceptive skills and wouldn't rest until the mission was complete.

He sat back, his mind racing with the magnitude of the unexpected developments. Raven's report had jolted him, filling him with the unsettling realization that the situation was rapidly spiraling out of control. Nothing was going according to plan.

After sending a message to his counterpart in London, he pulled up the encrypted communication channel to the grandmaster. His hands trembled ever so slightly as he typed out the urgent message.

Subject: Code Red—Reassessment Required

Grandmaster,

I bring grave news. Our carefully crafted plan has hit an unforeseen snag. Anja is now under the protection of Lucian, making any direct attack on her nearly impossible. Our control over the situation appears to be slipping, and we must reassess our approach.

The unexpected absence of Anja from her apartment and her plans to be away from the library complicate matters further. We are facing an uphill battle, and I fear our secrets may be jeopardized.

I have also received a flight plan for Lucian's jet heading to England and a burial announcement for this Saturday. It seems that his family's tragedy is driving him, and we cannot ignore the potential implications.

I have already alerted the controller in London about the unfolding events, and they are prepared to take necessary action if required or if the opportunity arises.

As for Raven, she remains determined and resourceful. I have instructed her to continue her efforts to drive a wedge between Lucian and Anja. This option may still be viable, and we should not abandon it hastily.

I will continue to monitor the situation closely and take whatever actions are necessary to protect the Sodality and advance our goals.

I am confident we can overcome these challenges with your guidance and wisdom. We must adapt and be prepared for any eventuality.

Awaiting your orders,

USA/NE Controller.

With a deep breath, the controller sent the message to the grandmaster, knowing his response would dictate the course of action moving forward.

Richard couldn't help but feel a sense of unease as he waited for a reply. But he was resolute, even if it meant making difficult decisions and sacrifices.

PART TWO

Thirteen

Anja's eyes fluttered open as the soft knock on her door penetrated her dreams. Emma's voice came through, letting her know they would depart for the airport in an hour. Anja called out, "Okay, thanks."

Rolling out of bed, Anja stretched her limbs and yawned, residual tiredness from the previous day's events still lingering. A refreshing shower was just what she needed to invigorate herself for the trip ahead. Stepping into the bathroom, she turned on the water and let the warm spray wash away any weariness.

She double-checked her belongings, her fingers finding her favorite perfume she had retrieved from her apartment on the way back from the library yesterday. She spritzed it on her chest and forearms. Feeling rejuvenated, she dressed in the clothes laid out for her. Anja noted with appreciation that the bags were already packed and ready from last night.

With her thoughts swirling like the steam from her shower, Anja took a deep breath and focused on the present. As she took a moment to glance around the guest room, she realized how comfortable she felt in the penthouse. The previous day's events were still fresh in her mind, but being in Lucian's care offered a sense of security she hadn't expected. It was both comforting and unsettling at the same time.

As the time to depart neared, Anja made her way to the living room, where Lucian and the team had gathered. She exchanged nods with Claire and Emma, appreciating the silent reassurance of their presence.

Lucian greeted her with a warm smile, looking as dashing as ever. "Good morning, Anja. Ready for the flight?"

She nodded, excitement and worry churning inside her. "Yes, I am. It's just…I can't believe how quickly everything is happening."

"It can be overwhelming," Lucian acknowledged. "Let's head out."

His words resonated with her, solidifying the budding sense of camaraderie and trust between them.

Watching Lucian direct the team with such ease, she admired how each member seamlessly knew their role and followed his lead. Ava, his secretary, efficiently informed him of the limo's status, and Anja smiled at the thought of Zoe joining them for the trip.

Amidst the organized chaos, Ian, Carlos, Emma, and Claire swiftly gathered the luggage, their movements synchronized and purposeful. Anja was impressed by their seamless coordination.

As they made their way down to the underground garage, Lucian's driver, Thomas, was waiting; the Rolls sat next to an impressive black SUV. Ian took the front seat of the Rolls. Lucian held the back door open for Anja and slipped in after her. After the luggage was loaded, Carlos took the driver's seat in the SUV, and Ava, Claire, and Emma joined him. Following a quiet drive through the light traffic heading out of the city in the early morning, Anja marveled at the private airport. Lucian's sleek black Gulfstream G650 awaited them.

The tarmac buzzed with activity. The ground crew and security team, having arrived ahead of them, were loading the luggage from the SUV into the jet's cargo hold. Anja glanced around, taking in the scene. Remembering Lucian's penthouse, his team, and the private jet —it all felt like a world she had only read about in novels, and now she was a part of it.

Exiting the Rolls-Royce, her gaze immediately landed on an approaching limo. Her heart skipped a beat as the driver opened the door, and there, stepping out with wonder in her eyes, was Zoe.

"Anja!" Zoe exclaimed, a wide grin spreading across her face as she rushed up to her friend for a warm hug. "I can't believe we're really doing this! Thank you so much for inviting me."

Anja's heart swelled as she returned the embrace, thrilled to have her friend by her side. "I'm so glad you could make it," she said, her voice filled with genuine happiness.

As they neared the sleek jet, the hostess greeted them warmly. "Welcome back, Mr. Miller," she said with a friendly smile. "It's good to see you again."

"Thank you, Bella," he replied graciously. "I'm glad to be back and appreciate your efforts."

Bella nodded and then turned her attention to Anja and Zoe, offering them a welcoming nod. "Hello, ladies. It's a pleasure to have you onboard. I hope you have a comfortable and enjoyable flight."

"Thank you, Bella," Anja said.

As they stepped onto the jet, they were greeted by the first officer, who exuded a sense of calm and confidence. "Hello, Aaliyah. Is everything ready?" Lucian said in greeting.

"Yes, it is. Welcome aboard," Aaliyah said, gesturing to the plush seats. "Please make yourselves comfortable. We'll be taking off shortly once everyone is aboard. The weather looks good, so it should be a smooth flight."

Soon, everyone had boarded and settled in. Bella secured the cabin door and nodded to Aaliyah. Aaliyah joined the captain in the cockpit, leaving the door ajar. The jet's engine roared to life, and as Anja settled into her seat, a rush of excitement quickened her heartbeat. The jet taxied down the runway, gathering speed until it lifted off, climbing rapidly into the clear blue sky.

After reaching cruising altitude, Bella emerged from the galley in the back with a friendly smile, offering breakfast to the passengers. Anja and Zoe gratefully accepted the offerings, savoring the delicious flavors of the freshly prepared food. Anja couldn't help but appreciate the convenience and luxury of private jet travel.

Captain Alex Turner stepped out to greet the passengers as they enjoyed their breakfast.

"Good morning, Mr. Miller, and welcome onboard," Alex said with a nod to Lucian. "I trust you're finding the flight comfortable?"

Lucian returned the nod with a smile. "Yes, everything is excellent as always, Captain."

As the captain continued to chat with Lucian and the others, Zoe leaned over to Anja with a playful grin. "Well, Anja, it looks like we've entered a whole new realm of travel. No more cramped seats, stale pretzels, and crying babies. This is the life!"

Anja chuckled. "Indeed, it's quite a difference," she replied. "No doubt, we've been spoiled for regular commercial flights from now on."

Zoe raised her mimosa. "To private jets and the world of the elite!"

"To private jets," Anja echoed, clinking her glass with Zoe's. She felt a sense of camaraderie with her friend. BFF for sure now.

Zoe settled back, retrieving a folder from her worn canvas laptop bag. Anja recognized it as notes about the Miller family from the photos she could see. She then glanced up from her notebook to see Lucian approaching, asking Zoe to join him up front. Anja smiled at Zoe, her eyes crinkling at the corners in a playful grin.

"Looks like you've got some quality time with the man of the hour," she teased, giving Zoe a playful nudge.

Zoe gave a dramatic sigh. "Oh, I suppose someone has to keep him company," she replied, pretending to be exasperated. "But don't worry, I'll make sure he doesn't forget about you."

Anja chuckled in response. "Thanks, I appreciate it. I'll just be here with my notes and thoughts."

As Zoe headed to the front of the jet, Anja returned to her notebook, flipping through the pages filled with her research and musings. The familiar scrawls and diagrams comforted her, centering her amidst the whirlwind of events and discoveries. Anja found herself lost in thought. She knew the road ahead would be filled with unforeseen twists and turns, but she was ready. Anja relished the quiet moments, collecting her thoughts and emotions. As the hours passed, she knew they were getting closer to their destination—physically and metaphorically. The trip they were on was not just about reaching England but about uncovering the secrets that had been shrouded in darkness for centuries.

Zoe returned to her seat, and they exchanged playful banter as they stowed away their bags in preparation for the jet's landing. "I hope you didn't scare poor Lucian too much up there," Anja teased, a mischievous glint in her eyes.

"Oh, you know me, just keeping him on his toes," Zoe replied with a wink. "But don't worry, I made sure to put in a good word for you."

Anja chuckled. "Well, I hope it was convincing enough," she quipped. "I wouldn't want him to forget about me."

As the wheels touched the runway, a surge of adrenaline raced through her. Once the jet came to a stop, Lucian stood up from his seat, his expression composed and focused. "We've arrived," he announced, his voice carrying a sense of purpose.

Anja and Zoe followed Lucian off the jet, their eyes taking in the surroundings of the new destination. England—the land of ancient legends and wonders. It was a place steeped in history and tradition, and Anja could feel the weight of its significance. The weather struck her as dreary and overcast, with a palpable chill in the air. Aaliyah, the first officer, had collected their passports for processing. Meanwhile, Anja noticed the ground crew already loading their luggage into a waiting limo and SUV.

Zoe gave her a playful nudge as they walked. "Ready for this, partner-in-crime?" she asked with a grin.

Anja nodded, a smile forming at the corners of her lips. "You have no idea," she replied.

With its storied past as a fighter base during World War II, Biggin Hill Airport now stood as an emblem of luxury and convenience. Nestled amidst the rolling greenery of South East England, the airport's modern terminals seamlessly blended historical architecture with state-of-the-art facilities, catering to the world's elite travelers.

Private jets, like the one they had arrived in, were parked gracefully on the tarmac, their gleaming exteriors reflecting the moody gray skies overhead hinting at rain. The control tower, a relic from an era gone by, stood tall, overseeing the choreography of vehicles and personnel below.

Puddles, remnants of a prior shower, caught the shimmering overcast light, creating fleeting mirror images of the surroundings.

The limo driver, dressed impeccably in a black chauffeur's suit, polished the last rain droplets from the rear door. As they approached, he called out; his accent reminded Anja of BBC broadcasters she had heard, crisp and easily understandable.

"Mr. Miller?" His voice cut through the faint ambiance of distant aircraft engines and the rustling wind. He extended a gloved hand. "Pleasure to meet you, sir. I'm Geoffrey Barnes, your chauffeur for the duration of your stay. We're heading directly to the estate, I believe. The rest of your family will be arriving shortly after. It's best we get a move on; the skies have a temperament today."

Lucian nodded. To Anja, he looked serious, maybe even a bit fatigued. "Thank you, Geoffrey. We should indeed leave. Rain and these English roads aren't the best of friends."

As Lucian and Geoffrey exchanged pleasantries, ever-playful Zoe gave the limo an appreciative pat, her eyes twinkling with excitement.

With a more casual air about him, Ian headed to the front passenger seat, giving Geoffrey a friendly nod as he passed. Geoffrey returned the gesture and opened the limo's rear door for them. Lucian entered first, allowing Anja, Ava, and Zoe to step in after him. The plush leather seats and soft lighting of the limo's interior offered a stark contrast to the looming grayness outside. From the SUV, muffled conversations and the sound of doors shutting signaled that the other members of Lucian's entourage were settling in.

Anja noticed Geoffrey's skyward glance, perhaps wary of the impending rain, before sliding into the driver's seat on the right and closing the door. As the limo pulled away, the first sporadic droplets of rain began to hit its windows, gradually transforming into a steady downpour. The rhythmic sound of raindrops blended with the muted melodies of a classical piece playing on the limo's sound system. Outside, the landscape morphed into a watercolor painting as the rain smeared the picturesque scenery of South East England. Stone walls, ancient oaks, and rolling pastures whizzed by in a blur of greens, grays, and browns.

Anja heard Ian, sitting in the front, turn to chat with Geoffrey. The warmth from their conversation provided a contrast to the chilliness outside. "Bit of a dreary welcome for the guests, wouldn't you say?"

Ian remarked, nodding towards the increasing rain.

Geoffrey responded with a small smile, his eyes still focused on the road. "Typical British weather, sir. But I reckon it gives the country its charm."

Leaning into the plush seat, Zoe took a sip of water from the limo's minibar. "You know," she began, her voice soft and contemplative, "there's something almost magical about England in the rain. It's as if the past and present blur, and you're momentarily transported to another time."

Anja nodded in agreement. "It's as if the rain is trying to wash away the boundaries between the old and the new."

The limo continued along the road, moving through patches of fog that seemed to rise from the very earth itself. These ghostly mists rendered the world outside ephemeral, masking familiar landmarks and revealing them only as they came into close proximity.

Suddenly, through the thickening fog, the silhouette of Leeds Castle emerged, standing majestically on two islands in a lake formed by the River Len. Its reflection shimmered in the water, giving it an ethereal glow. Even from a distance, the sight of it invoked stories of knights, royalty, and age-old secrets.

Geoffrey cleared his throat gently to get the attention of the passengers. "Ladies and gentlemen, Leeds Castle," he announced with a hint of pride. "The estate isn't too far from here."

Zoe and Anja exchanged glances, their earlier conversations about history and wonder manifesting before them.

Ava, who had been silent for a while, finally spoke up. "Tomorrow's going to be a difficult day for all of us," she said softly.

Lucian cleared his throat, looking around at his companions. "I appreciate everyone being here for this. It means a lot to me."

Ian leaned over from the front seat, interjecting with a gentle reminder. "On that note, for those who might not be familiar with some British customs—it's considered respectful not to speak of the deceased in the past tense until after the funeral service. It's a way of honoring their presence and their impact on our lives, even if just for a little while longer."

Lucian looked grateful for the reminder. "Thank you, Ian. It's a beautiful tradition, keeping the memory of the departed fresh until the very end."

The Miller estate unfolded before Anja's eyes like a living tapestry of time and architectural evolution. The mansion seemed to whisper its history to her as the limo came to a complete stop alongside the SUV on the long gravel drive. She recognized the Tudor half timbering that stood proudly against the backdrop of the evening's dimming light, harmonizing with the richer red bricks of the Victorian era and the modern touch of expansive Palladian windows.

The engines of both vehicles fell silent. Mist, a lingering remnant of the day's rain, transformed the Victorian gardens into a dreamlike landscape. The light spilling from the mansion's windows bathed the grounds in a soft glow.

Lucian was the first to step out of the limo, his footsteps on the gravel breaking the twilight silence. Watching him, Anja sensed that the mansion evoked deep emotions within him. To her, it was clear that for Lucian, this was more than just a grand house.

Anja's experience as she stepped out into the fading light was unlike any other. To her librarian sensibilities, the estate was more than just an architectural marvel—it was a story unfolding. Ionic columns, discreet motifs of the East India Company, and perfectly sculpted terraces all spoke to her like chapters in a book. A stately portico grandly showcased the mansion's entrance. To the side, tiered gardens flowed gracefully down toward a serene lake. A bright Victorian conservatory whispered tales of opulence and far-off exotic places.

To Anja, the Miller estate was not merely a monument to one family's climb to wealth but a microcosm of Britain itself, reflecting the intricate interplay of trade, nobility, and global influences. She watched from a short distance as Lucian approached Geoff. The subtle glow from the mansion bathed the driveway, illuminating their exchange.

"Thank you, Geoff," Lucian said.

"Not a problem, sir. Your luggage will be taken to your rooms as designated by Mr. Edward," Geoff responded, his tone respectful.

Having parked the SUV alongside the limo, Claire stepped out and tossed the keys to Carlos, who, with a brief acknowledgment to Lucian, prepared to follow Geoff. The two vehicles, laden with bags and memories, would soon snake their way towards the servants' entrance, a more discreet section of the grand estate, where the luggage would be offloaded and transported to the respective rooms.

Anja's gaze shifted to a distinguished figure emerging from the portico's shadows onto the top landing—Edward, Lucian's uncle. He stood tall, radiating authority, but Anja could also sense a certain weariness in him, perhaps an emotional toll taken by the upcoming family funeral. His silver mane of hair and regal demeanor made it clear he was no stranger to power. Yet, something in his eyes, a flicker perhaps, led Anja to think there was more beneath the surface.

As Lucian walked towards Edward, Anja couldn't help but ponder the myriad emotions churning beneath the surface for both men. Tomorrow would be a day of reminiscing, saying goodbyes, and coming to terms with the cyclical nature of life.

"Lucian," Edward began. "It's unfortunate that our gathering is under such somber circumstances." There was a veneer of sympathy in his words, but Anja noted that the sentiment hardly reached his eyes.

Lucian nodded in acknowledgment, keeping his own emotions guarded.

Edward's gaze swept over the group, his sharp eyes assessing each individual before settling on the ladies. "Ladies," he said, emphasizing the word with a nod, "I've ensured everything is prepared for your comfort."

Anja noticed a man and two young women, presumably the butler and lady's maids, waiting attentively a few steps behind Edward. They both stood in stark contrast to Edward's dominating presence, their postures conveying a discreet readiness to serve.

"Lucian," Edward continued, gesturing to the butler, "James will show you to the master suite in the east wing—your father's on the second floor." He then looked at Anja and Zoe, "You both will be in one of the grand suites, next to Lucian and opposite my own. A strategic placement, I thought," he added with a knowing smile.

His mention of 'strategic' sent Anja's librarian instincts into overdrive. The placement of guests in a manor like this was never random and always spoke volumes about the host's intentions and perceptions of the guests.

Edward continued. "Howard is in the next suite down. The other family members will occupy the west wing."

Anja felt a momentary pang of curiosity. She looked forward to meeting the professor. It seemed he was being kept away from the other family members, most likely to avoid clashes.

Finally, Edward's gaze settled on Ava. "Miss Ava, you'll be sharing a suite on the third floor with my secretary," he informed, his tone courteous yet distant.

Ava simply nodded, her face betraying no emotion.

"Ian is the head of my security," Lucian said, indicating him. "Carlos, whom you saw earlier, is another key member. Then there are Claire and Emma."

Edward nodded at each introduction, but when his gaze landed on Claire, Anja noticed a barely perceptible pause. There was an unmistakable flash of recognition in Edward's eyes, quickly masked. Claire's response was subtle: slightly narrowing her eyes, a set to her jaw, and a wary nod—an unspoken acknowledgment of some shared past or event.

Zoe apparently caught the brief interaction as well, her eyebrows furrowing. Anja exchanged a quick glance with her, both silently questioning the history between the two.

As the introductions concluded, Edward, despite the tension, said, "Your security detail will be accommodated in the east wing as well. I'm sure all of you are tired after your long trip, so please feel free to freshen up. We'll be gathering in the ballroom in about an hour."

James and the lady's maids began guiding the guests, and as Anja followed, she couldn't shake off the feeling that this stay at the Miller estate would unravel more than just family secrets.

Anja wondered at the grand entrance as they stepped inside. The splendor was palpable, an opulent blend of history and architectural mastery. The high ceilings bore intricate frescoes, reminiscent of the family's trading ties with far-off lands. Majestic chandeliers hung low, their crystal prisms scattering light in a gentle play of colors. Large tapestries adorned the walls, each narrating a chapter from the Miller family's storied past. Directly ahead, a sweeping staircase curved upwards, its banisters gilded and carpeted in a plush deep red.

As they began their ascent, Anja's hand brushed against the smooth marble of the balustrade, its coolness contrasting with the warm ambiance of the space. Reaching the second floor, she noticed the lavishness didn't wane. The hallway was lined with portraits of Millers from generations gone by, each set in a gilded frame. Antique tables with vases of fresh flowers and ornate mirrors broke the continuity of the family gallery.

A maid dressed in a neatly pressed uniform gestured to Ava, Claire, and Emma. "If you'd follow me, please," she said, her voice soft yet assertive, pointing towards another staircase leading up to the third floor.

Meanwhile, Edward and James, the butler's posture ramrod straight, continued guiding the rest down the hallway and indicated the room Ian and Carlos would share. Anja couldn't help but notice the doors opening as they walked, revealing staff placing luggage inside the rooms, their movements deliberate and silent. The aroma of polished wood and fresh linen wafted through the corridor.

The maid pushed open a door opposite the one Edward had indicated was his own, revealing an expansive room adorned with plush furnishings and intricate draperies. Eager and inquisitive, Zoe stepped right in, her eyes darting around. Anja, however, remained just outside the room. She looked down the long, ornate hallway, seeking and finding Lucian. He stood a distance away. The weight of returning to his ancestral home was evident, especially under these circumstances. Even in this grand setting, amidst the hushed conversations and echoing footsteps, Lucian's silent contemplation spoke volumes to her.

Edward moved on to the last door with Lucian, indicating for James to open it. "Lucian, the master suite—yours now," he added somberly. "James, you already know, will assist you in whatever you need while in residence here." The door revealed a large room, lavishly furnished, a testament to the prestige of its occupants. Edward and Lucian stepped inside and closed the door. James then departed back out toward the stairs.

Anja watched as they disappeared into his rooms. A pang of sympathy threaded through her, tinged with longing, imagining the heavy mantle of family expectations and obligations Lucian must bear. Edward's polished charisma emanated an air of calculated design, making her feel cautious and a bit wary of him.

Releasing a quiet sigh, Anja turned her attention to the room she was about to enter. As she stepped in, the space opened up, revealing tastefully chosen pieces that hinted at the estate's storied past. The soft-spoken maid caught her attention from behind before she could contemplate more on the room.

"Miss, I be Emily," she said, her accent thick and distinctly rural. "I'll be seein' to yer needs whilst y'are here." Pointing to an ornate cord hanging delicately by the bedside, Emily added, "Just give that a tug, and I'll come runnin'."

"Thank you, Emily," Anja replied, touched by the young woman's sincerity.

With a final nod, Emily left, the door clicking softly behind her.

Having already begun exploring the room, Zoe glanced up with a playful glint in her eyes. "Well, Anja," she teased, "seems Lucian will be just next door tonight. Bit...convenient, ain't it?" Trying to pull off an accent of her own but failing.

Anja laughed, feeling a touch embarrassed, "Zoe! We aren't here on vacation. It's a serious time."

"Oh, I know," Zoe replied, a mischievous tilt to her lips. "But there isn't any harm in finding a bit of sunshine in the rain. Plus, I've seen how he gazes at you."

Anja tried to muster a comeback, but their meticulously unpacked luggage sidetracked her attention. Clothes are hung and folded precisely, and personal items are arranged thoughtfully.

"Blimey, they didn't dawdle, did they?" Anja remarked, eyeing her orderly belongings and doing a bit better at the accent.

"No, they sure didn't," Zoe chuckled. "But getting back to what I was saying, maybe later tonight, you might fancy a little wander. This place's got its fair share of...pleasant surprises." She added, trying again, bouncing her eyebrows.

Anja shook her head, a blend of amusement and affection for Zoe's relentless teasing. "We'll see, Zoe. We'll see. Now, time to get freshened up before more family drama."

Fourteen

THE SUN HAD dipped beyond the horizon, but the Miller estate was anything but dark. With its high ceilings and gilded chandeliers, the grand ballroom shone with a subdued brilliance, casting a warm, comforting glow over the somber gathering. Underneath the spender, Anja felt an undeniable weight in the air—the weight of loss.

Descending the ornate staircase leading to the ballroom with Zoe, Anja's eyes were drawn to the Dedicated Mourning Room adjacent. Draped in deep velvets and filled with photographs, memorabilia, and flowers, the room stood as a quiet tribute to the departed souls. The soft hum of grieving was a poignant testament to the love and respect the Millers commanded. Lucian, looking every bit the grief-stricken heir, stood next to Edward. To Anja, his countenance spoke of restrained pain, and she observed his stoic face occasionally breaking to offer condolences to well-wishers or to acknowledge them with a nod.

Anja's gaze lingered on Lucian for a while, but she was soon drawn into a whirlwind of introductions. Margaret Beaumont, Lucian's aunt, with her imperious air, scrutinized Anja with barely concealed disdain while her oil-baron husband, John, gave a curt nod. In stark contrast, Victoria Rothesay, another aunt with her restrained elegance, offered a gentle smile and a few words of gratitude for attending. Lord Alastair Rothesay, despite his regal bearing, exhibited genuine warmth.

The eccentric Howard Miller, with disheveled hair and distracted eyes, was lost in his own world, but he did manage to offer Anja a distracted nod. Now and then, he'd whisper something to a cluster of curious attendees, who seemed equally fascinated and horrified by whatever musings he was sharing. Lucian led Anja and Zoe towards Howard, who was now engrossed in a musty book he had fetched from one of the many bookcases lining the ballroom.

"Uncle Howard," Lucian began, clearing his throat to gain his uncle's attention. "I'd like to introduce you to Miss Anja Kinzey and her friend, Miss Zoe Ananda."

Howard looked up, blinking rapidly as if roused from a trance. "Ah, Miss Kinzey," he murmured, taking in Anja with an intense stare. "It's wonderful to meet you at last."

His eyes darted to Zoe, who shifted uncomfortably. "You're the FBI profiler, I presume?"

"Indeed," Zoe replied curtly.

Lucian, sensing the undercurrents, intervened. "We should catch up, Uncle. Perhaps after the funeral tomorrow?"

Howard nodded, his gaze lingering on Anja and Zoe. "Yes. There's much to discuss."

Standing near the grand windows draped with velvet curtains, Anja sipped her drink, inadvertently overhearing snippets of a juicy conversation between two well-dressed women. One had a string of pearls that caught the light, the other rhythmically fluttered her fan.

"You'd think on an occasion such as this, Philippa would at least make an appearance," the woman with the pearls remarked with a huff. "Her own family and she can't be bothered to show her face."

The fan-wielding lady replied with a scandalized whisper, "Did you hear about the latest escapade she's gotten herself into? Rumor has it she's taken up with some young Italian filmmaker, scandalously young!"

Pearls clutched her namesake necklace, her eyes widening. "No! But then again, that sounds just like Philippa. Always searching for the next escapade, always chasing youth."

Fan scoffed, "Well, it's one thing to chase after youthful endeavors and quite another to ignore your family in their time of need. Especially when tragedy strikes."

Pearls sighed, "It's a shame. The family could use her support now more than ever. But Philippa always was one to dance to the beat of her own drum."

Anja discreetly moved away from the duo, filing away the tidbit about Philippa. It was clear that the Miller family was rife with layers and complexities, and she was only just scratching the surface. She noticed Ian keeping a watchful eye on the entire room, apparently ensuring Lucian's security even amidst friends and family. Every so often, Anja observed him sharing a fleeting moment of camaraderie with a few other Scots present.

As the evening wore on, Anja found herself in the library, seeking refuge to escape the event's emotional weight. Lucian joined her. Their conversation was interrupted only by the soft steps of a maid bringing in a tray of drinks or by distant, muffled sounds of the wake from the adjoining rooms.

The evening, filled with whispered conversations, recollections, and subtle undercurrents of family dynamics, left Anja with much to ponder. As she retreated to her room, the intricate tapestry of the Miller family, with its bright threads of achievement like those hanging in the halls, hidden scandals, and dark strands of tragedy, was firmly etched in her mind.

The timid rays of the British sun peeked through the clouds but failed to pierce the heavy curtains of Anja and Zoe's shared suite. Anja was awakened by a soft rap at the door. Jet lag tugged at her eyelids, wrapping her in a blanket of drowsiness.

"Miss Anja, Miss Zoe," came the lilting voice from outside, "it's time t' get ready for the services."

Anja stirred first, pushing back the heavy duvet, her feet touching the cold hardwood floor. Zoe groaned, pulling the covers over her head, but soon gave in to the inevitability of the day.

The room was filled with a soft glow as their lady's maid, her face kind yet professional, entered. "Mornin'. I'm here t' assist ye both," Emily said gently, her eyes briefly settling on the ornate wardrobe that held their clothes, discreetly ignoring Zoe's undress.

Anja moved to freshen up, clearing the sleep from her eyes, as she noticed the maid begin her duties with the air of an old-time ladies' maid, which, in fact, she was.

Looking through the available clothes that Zoe had brought, Emily helped her into a conservative black dress that reached just past her knees. It had a high neckline, but a delicate lace overlay softened its austere appearance. Zoe paired it with a string of pearls and black patent leather heels.

Next, it was Anja's turn. After a brief contemplation, the maid selected a floor-length black dress with a draped cowl neckline. It flowed elegantly, hinting at her form without being overly tight. A silver brooch added a subtle touch of class to her ensemble.

Anja's eyes turned to the hat box the maid had opened. Ava purchased these for the funeral, according to the note inside. The box from a well-known New York millinery contained two options. Anja chose the pillbox hat with a birdcage veil, thinking it would provide some semblance of privacy during the somber event. On the other hand, Zoe was drawn to the wide-brimmed hat adorned with a black ribbon and a few feathers.

Looking at her reflection beside Zoe's, Anja understood how helpful Emily had been. Their dark and elegant outfits served as external representations of heavy hearts. With one last appreciative nod to their lady's maid, they took a deep breath and went to face the solemnity that awaited them. Arm-in-arm with Zoe for support, Anja began the descent down the grand staircase. The soft murmur of hushed conversations filled the air, giving the mansion an aura of subdued reverence.

Anja saw guests slowly converging in the grand entrance hall below her elevated vantage point. Many, like them, had stayed at the estate following the wake. But there were also new faces—well-wishers and mourners who had come from surrounding areas to pay their respects.

Men in sharp black suits nodded in acknowledgment as Anja and

Zoe made their way down. Adorned in their best mourning attire, women offered sympathetic smiles, their eyes glossy with unshed tears. She heard the occasional sound of a sob being suppressed, punctuating the low hum of voices.

Edward was near the entrance, greeting arriving guests with somber nods and handshakes. Lucian stood beside him, the weight of the last few days evident on his shoulders. He straightened up as he spotted Anja offering a tiny, appreciative smile, which she returned.

As Anja and Zoe approached the grand ballroom, the resplendence of the space, usually reserved for lavish parties and jubilant celebrations, was transformed. The large doors, crafted from rich mahogany, stood open, revealing a room bathed in soft, muted light. Gone were the glittering chandeliers, now dimmed to a gentle glow that cast ethereal shadows on the walls. The center of the room was dominated by a raised dais, upon which four ornate caskets adorned with simple, white roses and draped in black velvet rested. Portraits of Bartholomew IV, Eliza, Winston, and Abigail had been placed behind each casket, their faces frozen in happier times. The eyes of the deceased seemed to follow the mourners as if silently observing those who had come to bid farewell.

Rows of chairs, draped in black, were set up for the attendees. Most of them were occupied by somber faces, their hands either clenched in their laps or holding onto tissues, wiping away silent tears.

Flanking both sides of the ballroom were tall, elegant flower arrangements. White lilies, roses, and chrysanthemums formed a delicate lacework of grief, their fragrance filling the room with a sweet yet sad scent.

Upon entering with Zoe, Anja noticed several heads turning in their direction, offering nods of acknowledgment. They reached two vacant seats near the front, close to Lucian and Edward. Anja observed Victoria Rothesay, Lucian's aunt, sitting a few rows behind with impeccable posture, her husband, Lord Alastair Rothesay, by her side. She dabbed her eyes discreetly with a handkerchief while he offered a comforting arm around her shoulders. The Beaumonts, Margaret and John, were already engrossed in whispered conversations with a couple of high-society attendees.

Soft music began to play, courtesy of a string quartet positioned off to the side. The melancholy strains of the violin served as a moving reminder of the tragedy that had brought everyone together. Anja could feel the weight of the moment, the collective sadness pressing down on her. She took a deep breath, steadying herself, and reached for Zoe's hand, seeking and giving comfort simultaneously. Together, they waited for the memorial services to commence, surrounded by the haunting beauty of the ballroom.

Anja watched as Lucian stood first, taking his place before the portraits of his family. His voice, though steady, bore a heaviness, "My father, Bartholomew IV, was a titan in every sense: a visionary, a pillar of strength for our family and community. But more than that, he was my guide, my mentor. He taught me about business, life, and, most importantly, kindness. My mother, Eliza, had a heart that matched the vastness of the universe. Her laughter was contagious, her love unending. Winston...well, he had a zest for life. And Abigail...my precious sister. She was barely starting her life, yet her spirit was boundless. She dreamt big and loved even bigger."

There was a pause, a deep breath before he continued, "They may not be with us in body, but their essence, their teachings, and the love they poured into us will forever be embedded in our hearts."

Edward took the podium next, his politician's charisma displayed even in such times. "The Millers have always been leaders, builders, and visionaries. My brother was no exception. Together with Eliza, they formed a formidable pair. Their love story was one for the ages. Winston and Abigail—they were the future. We mourn today not just the loss of these four lives, but the loss of dreams, of potential, of futures that could have been."

Anja sensed Zoe looking around, perhaps taking stock of the room's reactions. She followed suit and noted how some leaned forward, hanging on every word, while others seemed lost in their own world of memories. Howard's eyes were fixed on the caskets, deep in thought. Margaret, the ever-snobbish socialite, looked almost disinterested, her gaze wandering, seemingly detached from the mourning around her.

As the speeches ended, Anja felt a melancholic hush again envelop the room, each attendee grappling with their memories, grief, and the harsh reality of the moment.

Outside, the gray clouds hung heavily, threatening more rain. The sporadic drizzle had left a sheen on the cobblestone paths that led to the family's private burial grounds. Umbrellas were being opened and shared, and as guests began to make their way, servants rushed forward, offering additional ones from a stand by the door.

Zoe leaned in to whisper to Anja, "I've always found something beautiful about rain during funerals. It's as if the heavens themselves are mourning, too."

Anja nodded, her fingers tightening around her friend's arm. "A shared sorrow," she whispered back.

As they stepped out into the cool, misty morning, a feeling of unity and collective grief washed over them. The Millers, despite their complexities and intricacies, had touched the lives of many. And today, in the heart of Kent, surrounded by centuries-old trees and the tranquil colors of nature, they would say their final goodbyes.

The grand ballroom's regality and the poignant speeches now behind them, Anja found herself among a somber procession, trailing behind Lucian and the immediate family following the pallbearers. The verdant path from the mansion to the cemetery was illuminated with tall candles, their flames flickering in a dance with the raindrops that tried to snuff them out.

In the distance, she heard the haunting wail of a bagpipe, its notes echoing through the misty morning like the cries of lost souls. Anja recalled Lucian mentioning a Scottish connection in their family, and she wondered if the tune was a tribute to that heritage.

Walking beside her, Ian leaned in and whispered, "It's the 'Floo'ers o' the Forest'. A traditional Scottish lament. Fitting, isn't it?" A hint of brogue in his words.

Anja nodded, appreciating the beauty woven into each note.

As they neared the cemetery, a sizable canopy emerged through the gentle drizzle, shielding the four elegant caskets from the rain. The attendees gathered around, forming a loose circle of unity and shared grief. The scent of fresh earth filled the air, mingling with the rain-soaked grass. Anja observed the whispered prayers, bowed heads, and freely flowing tears around her. A stoic priest, his robe sprinkled in droplets, began the graveside rites. His voice, though soft, resonated deeply.

When it was time, Anja watched as family members approached the caskets, each placing a single rose atop them.

With the final words spoken and the last rose placed, the caskets began their descent into the earth. One by one, attendees paid their final respects, the sound of rain providing a melancholic soundtrack to the farewell. Hand in hand with Zoe, Anja paused momentarily, looking at the four final resting places. The weight of the day, the gravity of the loss, and the burden of hidden threats settled deep within her, and she silently vowed to stand by Lucian, no matter what the future held.

The gravestones now wet from rain and tears, the mourners began their retreat from the burial grounds back to the Miller estate. The atmosphere was heavy with grief, but the impending reception offered a semblance of solace—a chance for everyone to come together, share stories, and find comfort in each other's presence.

As Anja entered the grand mansion, she noticed the drawing room and library doors open, inviting attendees in. Warm light spilled out from the rooms, starkly contrasting the gloomy gray of the outside world. From inside, she heard the soft hum of conversations that filled the air as a subtle reminder that life goes on despite its harsh blows. Feeling Zoe's gentle tug on her arm, Anja allowed herself to be led into the drawing room. The once silent spaces now buzzed with hushed conversations, reminiscent of times past and memories cherished. In every corner of the room, she saw small clusters of people, some laughing softly at a shared memory, others comforting one another in their mutual loss.

Elegant tables, draped in pristine white cloths, were laden with an array of finger foods. Sandwiches with various fillings, freshly baked pastries, and other treats were arranged meticulously. But what caught Anja's attention most were the silver tea urns and coffee pots, steam wafting from their spouts, signaling warmth and comfort. A server approached her, offering a choice of beverage. She opted for tea, the cup's warmth immediately seeping into her chilled fingers. Zoe chose coffee, inhaling its aroma deeply before taking a sip.

As they found a quiet corner, a distant relative approached them, sharing fond memories of Abigail's childhood antics. Anja listened intently, a smile on her lips to offer comfort.

The reception was at its height, the hum of conversations and the soft clinking of china creating a melodic background. Anja was momentarily lost in her thoughts when a familiar voice pulled her back to the present.

"Anja," Lucian said gently, touching her arm. His eyes held an intensity she couldn't quite decipher. "There's someone I'd like you to meet properly. I think you've had a few phone conversations with him already."

Anja nodded, memories of her exchanges with the enigmatic Howard coming to the forefront. "Professor Miller," she said, recalling their conversations filled with intriguing discussions on the occult and its historical significance.

"That's right," Lucian replied, a hint of a smile on his lips. "Come with me."

Following Lucian through a series of hallways, Anja sensed Ian trailing discreetly behind them. As they approached a heavy oak door, Anja could feel a distinct change in the atmosphere. The door seemed to shield a world apart from the rest of the house—a sanctuary of sorts. Lucian opened the door, revealing a well-appointed study. Walls lined with books of every size and subject surrounded a large mahogany desk, atop which sat an antique reading lamp. The faint scent of leather and old parchment filled the air, adding to the room's allure. Seated by the desk, engrossed in a particularly old book, was Howard. To Anja, his unkempt salt-and-pepper hair seemed even wilder than earlier. His eyes glinted with intelligence behind round spectacles.

As they entered, Lucian closed the door after exchanging a nod with Ian outside.

"Ah, Lucian! And Ms. Kinzey!" he exclaimed, marking his page with a ribbon and standing up. Anja sensed an air of excitement behind his scholarly demeanor.

Anja extended her hand. "Professor Miller, it's a pleasure to meet you in person."

Howard chuckled. "Ah, the formality! After our deep dives on the phone, I feel like we're old friends! Please, call me Howard."

Lucian cleared his throat, drawing their attention. "I thought it might be a good time for the two of you to connect properly," he said. "Howard has something of import to discuss."

Anja's curiosity was aroused. She took a seat opposite Howard, her mind racing with possibilities. What could the eccentric professor possibly want to share, especially on such a day? She was about to find out.

The room was heavy with expectation as Anja settled into the plush leather chair. She watched Howard carefully, noting his rather distinct habits. As he began speaking, his feet tapped softly, subtly, on the ornate rug beneath his desk.

"You know," he began, his voice low and reminiscing, "when Lucian was just a boy, I'd regale him with tales of the otherworldly – stories of magic, spirits, and the grand dance of energies that bind our world." As he spoke, he hummed a soft, indistinct tune, lost in memories between utterances. It was a habit Anja recalled from their phone conversations. It seemed to be an unconscious means for him to focus.

Lucian smiled fondly, a faraway look in his eyes. "I remember those stories. They'd fill my dreams with wonders and nightmares alike. You always did have a way with words, Uncle."

Howard, still lost in the past, bit his lower lip, a contemplative look in his eyes. "Ah, those were the days. Your unyielding curiosity, Lucian. How you'd sit and listen, taking in every word, every nuance."

Suddenly, his gaze locked onto Anja's, causing her to shift slightly in her seat. "But now," he said, drumming his fingers lightly on the wooden surface of the desk, "we have more pressing matters to discuss."

Anja felt a hint of impatience emanating from him as his eyes flitted momentarily to the antique clock on the wall. The action wasn't missed by Lucian either, who leaned forward, a sign he was anticipating what was to come.

"As much as I love reminiscing," Howard continued, crossing his legs and leaning back in his chair, "we're here for a reason."

Lucian nodded, his demeanor serious. "Anja, what Howard's about to share is something he has shared only with me. I thought it crucial for you to hear firsthand, especially given recent events and your inquiries to him recently."

Drawing a deep breath, Howard adjusted his sleeve, a hint of apprehension visible. "Very well," he said, his voice thick with gravitas, "let's begin."

Howard, lost in the world of the information he presented, didn't even notice as his feet began tapping restlessly against the carpet again. "The group you were trying to identify refer to themselves, I believe, as 'The Sodality of the Thorns.' The origin of this...Sodality," he began, tracing the line of his research with a methodical fervor, "is ancient, rooted in the dawn of Sumerian civilization. The group, even then, was marked by the 'Zu' cuneiform, a sign which denoted both 'knowledge' and, interestingly, 'tooth.' This organization, it seems, always had an appetite for hidden power."

Lucian listened intently, nodding at intervals. He seemed familiar with some of this, but Howard had apparently gone deeper since they had last talked. His humming became more pronounced, the resonance of his voice imbuing the room with an almost hypnotic feel.

"Their evolution," Howard continued, drumming his fingers in a rhythmic pattern against the desk, "has seen them weave in and out of history's shadowy corners. They've worn different names and faces, but the core ambition remained unchanged: domination of and via the unknown and the supernatural. I found an obscure reference to what I believe has evolved into their current incarnation. They seem to have solidified their current incarnation sometime in the early Middle Ages, taking up the moniker they use now."

As Howard elucidated the werewolf symbolism and how they'd

integrated themselves into notorious groups across history, Anja's mind raced. It was like something out of the gothic novels she had read, but this was all too real. She recalled her phone conversations with Howard, the pieces she'd provided him. Now, everything seemed to be coalescing into a disturbing mosaic.

Lucian's sharp intake of breath mirrored Anja's shock as Howard delved into the modern reincarnation of the group. "Corporate fronts, offshore companies…," Anja whispered, "It's all so calculated, so vast."

"And dangerous," Howard added, taking a moment to adjust his shirt collar, the weight of the information getting to him as well. "Their web of influence is far-reaching. They have eyes and ears everywhere. From governments to research centers, they exert control in the shadows, all in the name of keeping the human bloodline 'clean.' Look for rhetoric like that to find the more overt and nationalist elements or look behind those to find a hidden hand guiding them."

Anja noticed Lucian run a hand through his hair, his face visibly perturbed. "We have to stop them," he said, determination evident in his voice.

Howard leaned forward, his eyes leaving Lucian to lock onto hers. "That, my dear, is precisely why you're here."

Anja's mind raced to process the gravity of what Howard was suggesting. Her heart thudded loudly in her chest. It was no longer a matter of mere historical research or paranormal curiosities; this was personal, darkly so.

"You mean to say," Anja began slowly, trying to steady her voice, "that they were not after your brother, Eliza, or Abigail, but Lucian? Because he's a…potential threat? Because he might possess some inherent power or knowledge?"

Howard nodded gravely, "It's more than just potential, Anja. It's actual—an ancient force. For generations, our family has been interwoven with tales of unexplainable events, abilities, and strange occurrences. While most of us, including myself, only possess a mere touch of this power, Lucian, it seems, has the potential in abundance.

"You see, in recent times, our family has tried to hide from the past and shunned me as much as they can, but I am still family, and I knew there would be a time I would be needed for Lucian's sake."

Lucian looked troubled, his eyes distant as he processed his uncle's words. The implications were staggering. Anja could see the weight of it settling on his shoulders. He had told Zoe and herself that he first thought it was business-related or personal. It was becoming clear that was not the case—or at least not entirely.

"And, Anja," Howard continued, his gaze now fixed on her, "from our interactions and my senses, you have it too. It's dormant, perhaps. Yet, it's there. A latent force—but powerful. The occasional Scottish blood, as you mentioned, might be a catalyst, but it's not the only factor."

She felt a shiver. The implications were enormous, and if what Howard said was true, what did it mean for her future? For Lucian's? Anja realized he was to Lucian what Grandmother Madeline was to her.

Lucian's hand found hers, a comforting gesture that grounded her amidst the swirling revelations. "We're in this together now," he said firmly.

"But why now?" Anja asked. "Why act so overtly against the Miller family at this moment?"

Anja watched Howard lean back, his fingers drumming on the desk as he pondered her question. "The Sodality of the Thorns is methodical, yet perhaps not infallible. As their targets become scarcer, they grow more desperate to keep their successes. And perhaps, with Lucian's growing influence in the biotech world and his innate power, they saw a direct threat. It's a confluence of timing, power, and ambition.

"They've almost wiped out all traces of power from ancient bloodlines. They began by hunting and killing daevas in Sumerian times and influenced the development of Zoroastrianism in Persia. They also learned to covet power and eventually co-opted kingship through the Merodach-Baladan bloodline, setting the stage for neonatal King Nebuchadnezzar's future despotic reign."

Anja listened as Howard traced the Sodality's complex history—its roots in ancient Egypt, its associations with the Roman Empire, the

Teutonic Order, and even the Spanish and Portuguese Inquisitions. They worked in secrecy within the Nazi SS, using the wolfs-angel Z as a symbol—openly displaying it. Anja pondered as Howard suggested they might have a hidden influence on Russia's actions in Ukraine. She felt a chill, realizing the list was long and terrifying, especially considering its implications for the modern world.

The room went silent momentarily as Howard paused, the gravity of the situation sinking in. They were up against an ancient organization, deeply rooted, vastly influential, and ruthlessly dedicated to their cause.

"We must act," Lucian finally declared, his voice filled with determination. "They have taken from us. Now, we must ensure they can't harm anyone else."

Howard nodded in agreement, "This is the beginning, not the end. We must rally, strategize, and strike back."

Upon absorbing Howard's revelations, Lucian walked over to the door, opening it slightly to speak to Ian outside. "Can you have someone bring in some refreshments and a few nibbles?" he requested.

From his seat, Howard interjected, "How about some Guinness?"

Lucian glanced questioningly at Anja; she gave a subtle nod of approval. "Make that three stouts, Ian," Lucian added before shutting the door gently.

Anja could feel the weight of the revelations pressing down on her. The quiet intensity of the room was punctuated only by the ticking of a grand clock. Every shadow and whisper of the mansion felt like it held a secret now, and Anja found herself hyper-aware of her surroundings.

After sharing his years of research and personal insight, Howard seemed to relax slightly, as though a weight had been lifted from his shoulders. His fingers ceased their incessant drumming, and he looked at Anja, his eyes filled with worry and understanding.

The door opened a few minutes later to reveal Ian. In his arms, he held a tray filled with petite sandwiches, assorted pastries, and, as requested, three dark pints of Guinness. He handed out the pints, foam settling beautifully at the top, to each of them and nodded respectfully to Lucian. Anja took a moment to appreciate the rich aroma of the stout, noting the soothing, roasted notes wafting from the glass.

"Thank you, Ian," Lucian murmured as Ian left, taking a deep drink from his glass.

Raising her glass, Anja took a tentative sip, letting the malty flavor wash over her. The robust taste, combined with the creamy texture, was comforting amidst the day's chaos.

Howard picked up a sandwich, examining it for a moment. "You know, back in my early days, a pint of Guinness and a decent sandwich were all the sustenance I needed. Sometimes, it's the simple things that ground us when the world seems to be spiraling."

Lucian nodded in agreement, sipping his drink. "Here's to finding clarity and strength," he toasted, raising his glass.

Anja joined in. "To clarity and strength," she echoed.

The three drank deeply. Anja was lost in her thoughts, the dark liquid serving as a momentary balm in her emotional storm.

The momentary cheer from the toast settled, and the room again steeped in the gravity of their conversation. With a sudden spark of remembrance, Howard reached into the inner pocket of his coat and produced a small, pristine notebook, its cover yet untouched by time.

"This," he began, holding the notebook out for Anja to take, "is a distilled collection of my findings. After our conversations, Anja, I revisited my notes and conducted further research based on the clues you'd provided." He tapped the notebook lightly, "I decided to compile everything into this...for you."

Surprised, Anja carefully took the notebook. Its crisp, new pages were in stark contrast to the age-old secrets they contained. "You transcribed these just for me?" she asked, the weight of the gesture not lost on her.

Howard nodded, his habits manifesting as he bit his lip contemplatively. "Yes. It's essential that you have this knowledge. The original notes are, well, scattered and not very organized. This...," he gestured to the notebook, "...is concise, relevant, and perhaps, the key to understanding what we're up against."

Lucian watched the exchange, his respect for his uncle evident.

"Your dedication is unparalleled, Uncle. I can't thank you enough for this."

Howard gave a modest shrug. "It's what family does. We look out for one another. Especially in times like these."

He cleared his throat, shifting his attention to the aged book beside him on the table. The leather-bound book's exterior bore the signs of age with worn corners and an almost faded title; yet, it had an undeniable presence in the room.

"I've been immersed in this," Howard began, gently caressing the book's cover. "The *Ars Notoria* or, as it's sometimes referred to, the *Ars Nova*. A rather rare Renaissance grimoire and quite the find, if I may say so."

Anja's eyes widened slightly. She knew of the *Ars Notoria*, having come across mentions of it in her readings.

Howard took a moment before speaking again. "The *Ars Notoria* is particularly esteemed for its prayers, which share similarities with The Sworn Book of Honorius. These chants are believed to bestow upon the practitioner an impeccable memory and the capability of swift learning. The knowledge within could arm us against the Sodality and magnify our understanding. What's notably curious is that many versions of the *Lemegeton*, more comprehensively known as the *Lemegeton Clavicula Salomonis* or simply the Lesser Key of Solomon, dismiss the *Ars Notoria*. This omission lends an even greater aura of enigma to it."

Anja leaned in, her interest piqued. "The ability to gain knowledge quickly… Notorious art indeed."

"And beyond that," Howard added, "with it sharing a timeline with the Ashton Grimoire, there's potential for shared symbology and perhaps even ciphers."

Anja interjected, "It's always struck me how selective some of these grimoires can be in their dissemination, like certain knowledge was meant for only a select few. The fact that Waite and some versions of the *Lemegeton* overlook the *Ars Notoria* entirely… It's intriguing."

Howard nodded. "These old texts are like an insight into the very psyche of their time. Their omission or inclusion speaks volumes."

Feeling the weight of the text's potential, Anja replied, "Thank you,

Howard."

Howard took a deep breath, the weight of knowledge evident in his eyes again. "The Sworn Book of Honorius, also known as *Liber Juratus Honorii*, would undoubtedly be a valuable asset in this endeavor. It's one of the oldest medieval grimoires we know of, containing an extensive range of magical practices."

He paused to adjust his glasses and collect his thoughts. "I've sought that tome for years, but it's proven elusive. Rumors have hinted at its presence in various private collections over the decades. Some say it's hidden away in the catacombs of an old European monastery. Others believe it's held by a secretive order in Eastern Europe, guarded as one of their most prized possessions. The Sodality, perhaps? Then there are whispers about it being in the possession of an aristocratic family in Italy, hidden away from prying eyes and hands."

A hint of regret laced his voice as he continued, "All leads I've pursued have ended in dead ends or false trails. However, with our combined resources and connections, we might stand a better chance of locating it."

Anja caught the significance in his look, sensing his hope that her expertise combined with Lucian's resources might turn the tide. Leaning forward with keen interest, she ventured, "Do you think the Vatican Secret Archives might hold a copy or even the original?"

Howard's eyes widened momentarily before a thoughtful expression settled on his face. "Ah, the Vatican archives, a treasure trove of ancient manuscripts and hidden knowledge. There have been whispers, over the years, that they possess many rare grimoires, including The Sworn Book of Honorius."

He paused, seeming to choose his words carefully. "However, even if the Vatican does have a copy, procuring it would be an immense challenge. First, there's the matter of accessibility. The Vatican is notorious for its strict limitations on who can access its archives and for what purpose. Even if one were to gain access, finding such a specific manuscript in their vast collection would be akin to finding a needle in a haystack."

Howard sighed. "Moreover, given the nature of the text and the

Church's stance on certain esoteric matters, if they possess it, they would undoubtedly deem it too dangerous or heretical for anyone outside their highest echelons of the papacy to access. And then there's the matter of security. The Vatican is one of the most fortified places on Earth, both physically and spiritually."

Lucian nodded in agreement. "Indeed, if it resides there, the challenges are manifold. But we should never underestimate what's achievable when the right motivations and resources align."

Howard glanced at Lucian and Anja, a hint of a smile on his lips. "True, and while the Vatican is a long shot, it's a lead worth considering, even if just for the sake of thoroughness."

His eyes twinkled as he glanced at Lucian, then refocused on Anja. "Now, Anja," he began with a wry smile, "given your profession as a librarian and researcher, you might just have an edge. With the right sponsor backing you and a well-crafted research project, you could potentially gain access to the archives."

He leaned in slightly, lowering his voice, "It would undoubtedly be a challenge to organize and one filled with bureaucratic hurdles. However, should you manage to secure an audience within those hallowed walls, even just confirming the existence of the text would be a triumph. And who knows?" He winked, "With your skills and a touch of cunning, you might just manage to steal more than just a look."

Lucian chuckled lightly, "Always one to consider every angle, aren't you, Uncle?"

Howard shrugged, the corners of his mouth lifting in amusement. "It's served me well so far."

Anja noticed Lucian's expression change, his playful demeanor replaced by earnest concern. He took a deep breath, steadying himself. "Howard's revelations about the Sodality are deeply troubling. Their history, their reach...it's more extensive than I ever imagined." He paused and glanced at Howard. Anja noticed Howard drumming his fingers on the armrest, seemingly lost in thought.

Anja bit her lower lip, her mind racing. "If what Howard says is true, and they've been purging potent bloodlines, then it isn't just you, Lucian, who could be at risk. Howard, you, too, have the same lineage. They might come after any member of the Miller family with these…abilities."

Howard nodded slowly, taking a moment before speaking. "That's what concerns me as well. I've been careful, always staying under the radar, but if they've linked Lucian to recent events…then they could be aware of my research and involvement."

Lucian's gaze settled on Anja. "What worries me is that they didn't just go after me. They targeted my family—innocent lives. They were targeting you, Anja. If they believe I, or any of us, have these powers or knowledge they so desperately want to control or eliminate, they might be relentless."

"We need a plan," Anja said, determination evident in her tone. "We need to protect ourselves and find a way to counteract them."

Lucian reached out, taking her hand in his. The warmth of his touch was a slight comfort amidst the looming threats. "We'll face this. The first step is gathering all the information we can. Your ideas, Anja, combined with Howard's research, might just give us a chance."

He paused, his gaze sweeping over the documents and notes strewn across the table. Anja sensed the heaviness that seemed to settle over him, the palpable tension emanating from the pages before him. When he turned to Howard, his eyes, at least to Anja, carried a wary look. "Howard, considering the potential target on our backs, you might want to consider taking a sabbatical and lying low for a while," Lucian suggested.

Howard, ever the scholar, adjusted his glasses and leaned back in his chair. "A sabbatical, you say? It's been years since I took any extended time away from the school. But given the circumstances, you might be right. Disappearing from the public eye for a while could be wise."

He pondered for a moment, tapping his fingers thoughtfully on the armrest. "I could perhaps use the time to conduct research in more remote archives and libraries. Places the Sodality wouldn't think to look. Perhaps somewhere in the Far East or even South America. Some off-the-grid locations where ancient texts and artifacts are rumored to be."

Lucian nodded. "That's a start. Keeping mobile and unpredictable would be an advantage. You can also use this as an opportunity to gather more knowledge, maybe even find allies in unexpected places."

Howard smirked, "Turn the tables on them, so to speak. Instead of them hunting us, I could be gathering more tools and allies to counter them. Not a bad strategy, nephew."

Lucian smiled, "Stay safe, Howard. We need you."

He looked contemplative for a moment. "Someone else might be able to help us, especially with piecing together more tangible evidence." He looked at Anja. "Zoe."

Anja's eyebrows raised in mild surprise. "Do you think she can handle this?"

Lucian stood up and opened the door slightly, signaling Ian. "Can you fetch Zoe for us? It's important."

Ian nodded and disappeared to fetch Zoe. Lucian closed the door and returned to the room. "It's true, Zoe might not be well-versed in the occult or the supernatural, but she's sharp, observant, and has resources in the investigative department. We just need to approach the subject carefully."

Anja nodded in agreement, "We should keep the details to a minimum, focusing more on the 'purity' angle. The ties to white supremacy are real and tangible. Zoe can use that in her investigation without delving into the occult."

Howard added, "The history of the Sodality and its associations with historical power structures can be presented as an extreme form of radicalism linked to racial purity. There's enough in the history books to make that a convincing narrative with the added benefit of being true."

Just as they aligned their approach, there was a soft knock on the door. Ian ushered Zoe in, who looked a tad curious but also alert.

"Zoe," Lucian began, guiding her to a seat. "We've found some information that might be pertinent to your investigation into the murders. It's...complex, and some might seem outlandish, but bear with us."

Over the next hour, they carefully laid out the modified narrative, weaving a story that painted the Sodality as a powerful group with a long history of seeking racial purity, connections to past power structures, and possible motivations related to eliminating anyone they saw as a threat to that agenda.

Zoe took notes and asked pointed questions. Her sharp mind was already drawing connections and considering potential avenues of investigation. She might not have the complete picture yet, but she was getting new information that she could act upon, and that was a start. She tapped the notes in front of her and cleared her throat, catching the attention of everyone in the room.

"Based on my observations, the Miller family murders were most certainly a contract hit of some sort," she began, locking eyes with Lucian. "And I'm not just talking about some hired thug. This was the work of a professional."

Howard adjusted his glasses, "How can you be so certain?"

Zoe replied, "The meticulous planning, the efficiency of the execution, and most importantly, the almost spotless forensic scene. This isn't the work of an amateur. This person, or perhaps persons, knew what they were doing, down to the finest detail."

Lucian leaned forward, "So, you're saying someone wanted my family out of the picture? But why? For financial gain? Power?"

Zoe nodded, "Potentially. The motives could range from those to even more sinister agendas, such as suppressing dangerous secrets. However," she added, focusing on Anja, "given the strange circumstances in Abigail's room, there might be another layer to this."

Anja's eyes narrowed, "You mean the way they mutilated Thomas? The symbolic removal of his heart?"

"Yes," Zoe agreed. "It's a deviation from the clinical nature of the other killings. This had personal or ideological undertones. And given the details you've shared about the Sodality and their motivations…"

Lucian interrupted, "You think they are involved?"

Zoe shrugged, "It's likely—almost a certainty. The brutality towards Thomas, who they seem to have believed was you, Lucian, indicates that you were possibly the primary target. There seems to be a symbolic element to the heart removal."

Howard looked thoughtful, "This aligns with the Sodality's modus operandi. They've always used symbols in their actions."

Anja said, "And if we consider their history of purging bloodlines or perceived threats, it fits."

Zoe added, "Also, given the Miller's connections, the depth and breadth of your family's dealings could have created many enemies. This was more than just a contract killing, though. This seems like an orchestration by a well-established organization."

Lucian exhaled deeply, "The Sodality of the Thorns. Then, we need to step carefully. They've shown what they're capable of."

Howard agreed, "Indeed. And if they believe there are loose ends, they'll be back."

Zoe concluded, "Our best bet is to continue digging, to find out more about this organization, and to stay vigilant. We're dealing with shadows here, and they won't be easy to pin down. But with any luck, we can shine a bit of light into those shadows."

Zoe's brow creased, her usually composed demeanor giving way to a hint of concern. "Lucian, your family's vast network is both an advantage and a potential weakness. Corporate fronts, offshore accounts, and possible government ties make it difficult to determine who's friend and foe. But the one thing that unnerves me the most is the potential for puppeteers operating from hiding."

Howard tilted his head, "Puppeteers?"

She continued, "Someone, or some group, pulling the strings from a distance. This would line up with how you described the Sodality, Howard. And with that, there's a risk that our investigation could be compromised from within."

Lucian's eyes narrowed, a deep-seated concern evident. "Do you think we might have a mole in our midst? Perhaps even more than one? I've already initiated a review within the corporate sphere of our operations. The timing of my travel announcement and the attack on my family feels too closely intertwined. It was an opportunity that had me away from the security of my corporate offices and at a secluded estate. If my suspicions are confirmed and a leak is found, I'll give you another lead you can chase."

Zoe replied with a serious nod, "Your instincts might be right,

Lucian. It wouldn't be far-fetched to consider one or more insiders. We need to be judicious about whom we let into our circle of trust. Even for me, within the FBI. I hate to consider that, but I should be very judicious with this information. I don't want to have this shut down on me."

Anja looked at Lucian, her expression serious, "Zoe's right. We should be cautious. With such deep connections and resources, it wouldn't be surprising if the Sodality tries to steer the investigation away from them."

Howard took a sip from his glass, "And if they have ties in the government or law enforcement, they could obstruct or misdirect our efforts." He pointed out. "This isn't just about finding a killer anymore; it's about uncovering a potential web of deceit, centuries in the making, perhaps even millennia."

Zoe nodded, "Exactly. We need irrefutable evidence, allies we can trust implicitly, and a strategy to reveal them without exposing ourselves to further danger."

Anja interjected, "And we need to move quickly. The longer we take, the more opportunity they have to try again or to disappear for a while. I can't see them letting go, though."

As the night had grown deeper, Anja was wrapped in a cocoon of thoughts and restless contemplation. The weight of the revelations shared during their intense discussions weighed heavily on her mind. The Sodality's history, their sinister motivations, the danger that loomed—it was a tangle that had taken root in her thoughts, refusing to let go.

After their conversation had ended, Anja and Zoe retreated to their shared room, the dim glow of a bedside lamp casting soft shadows on the walls. She had paced back and forth, replaying the words that had been spoken and the implications of their discoveries echoing in her mind. Sitting on the edge of the bed, Zoe watched her with a knowing gaze. She could see the turmoil in Anja's expression and how her thoughts consumed her. "You're thinking too hard, Anja," Zoe finally said, breaking the silence.

Anja looked up, her thoughts momentarily interrupted. She sighed, ran a hand through her hair, and sat on the bed next to Zoe. "It's just… It's a lot to process, Zoe. The Sodality, their aims, the danger. I can't help but wonder if we're getting in over our heads."

Zoe shifted closer, resting a comforting hand on Anja's shoulder. "We're in this together, you know. I'm your sidekick, remember? You're strong, Anja, stronger than you give yourself credit for."

Anja offered a small, appreciative smile. "I know. It's just that this is different. The stakes are higher, and the enemy is more formidable than anything I've ever imagined."

Zoe nodded in understanding. "I get it. But you know it is worth it, and you would regret not following through."

Anja's gaze softened as she looked at Zoe. "Thank you, Zoe. Your words mean a lot." She paused, a hint of curiosity in her eyes. "Speaking of Lucian, what do you *really* think of him after all of your recent exposure to him?"

Zoe leaned back, a playful glint in her eyes. "Ah, Lucian Miller, the enigmatic heir with a hint of danger and a lot of charm. He's intriguing, that's for sure."

Anja raised an eyebrow. "Intriguing?"

Zoe chuckled. "Yeah, intriguing. There's more to him than meets the eye, don't you think? He's not just a wealthy aristocrat—there's a depth to him, a resolve to pick apart this web to find the spiders. And I have to admit, he's not hard on the eyes either."

Anja felt a warmth rise to her cheeks. "Zoe, are you teasing me?"

Zoe laughed, a light and carefree sound. "Oh, come on, Anja. A little harmless ribbing never hurt anyone. Besides, it's a good distraction from all the talk about the Sodality and their plans."

Anja couldn't help but smile, feeling the tension ease slightly. "You're right, Zoe. We could all use a bit of lightheartedness in the midst of all this…this…whatever it is."

Zoe winked. "Exactly. And who knows, maybe your scholarly mind and his determination could make a formidable team…in more ways than one."

Anja rolled her eyes playfully. "Let's not get ahead of ourselves,

Zoe."

Zoe stood up, stretched her arms above her head, then stripped. "Just planting a seed, Anja, but you need to water it, get it all wet, if you know what I mean. Now, get some rest. Tomorrow is another day, and I'm still trying to catch up on sleep."

Anja nodded, comforted in Zoe's presence but trying not to look at her friend. As they settled into their beds and switched off their bedside lamps, Anja's thoughts were still consumed by what lay ahead, but the talk with Zoe had taken the edge off, even if just for a moment. But then, now, she had images of Lucian in her head. Again.

The next morning arrived with the soft golden rays of the sun peeking through the curtains; the rain had finally given up its hold. Anja blinked her eyes open, the remnants of her dreams fading away. The sound of a gentle knock on the door drew her attention, and she exchanged a groggy look with Zoe before they both moved to answer. The maid stood there, her face illuminated by the soft morning light filtering through the corridor.

'Mornin', ladies,' she greeted with a kindly smile, her eyes flicking only briefly over Zoe's total lack of attire, a small, knowing smile playing at her lips. The household staff seemed accustomed to the idiosyncrasies of their guests, and Zoe's carefree nature was no exception.

Anja exchanged a knowing look with Zoe before nodding at the maid. "Thank you. We'll be down shortly."

The maid curtsied before leaving, and Anja let out a soft sigh as she turned back to Zoe. "Well, I suppose we should get *dressed*."

Zoe stretched and yawned, then giggled. "Definitely. I could use some coffee to jumpstart my brain. I guess they are not shocked by much around here."

Anja exchanged a glance with Zoe, the familiarity of their shared history as college roommates evident. To Anja, Zoe's complete lack of modesty was a trait she had once found slightly embarrassing but had grown to be both amusing and endearing. As they prepared to get dressed, Zoe couldn't resist teasing Anja.

"Come on, Anja," Zoe chided, rummaging through her wardrobe. "You're not at the library now. Let's give Lord Charming a little something to appreciate." They had been able to borrow each other's clothes while living together.

Anja rolled her eyes. "Zoe, this isn't the time or place for that kind of attention."

Zoe grinned mischievously, holding up a dress of hers that was definitely more on the provocative side. The dress's deep maroon hue seemed to complement Anja's hair, but its plunging neckline and form-fitting silhouette were a far cry from Anja's usual style.

"Oh, come on! A little peek won't hurt. Live!"

Anja sighed, her lips twitching with a hint of a smile. "Hah, I don't need to dress provocatively to make an impression, Zoe."

"True, but it wouldn't hurt to have a little fun. Besides, Lucian might…no…would appreciate the effort. This is the profiler in me speaking, so you better listen up."

Anja raised an eyebrow. "Are you still trying to hook us up?"

Zoe shrugged, all feigned innocence. "I'm just saying you two have a lot in common. I've seen the way he looks at you. And keeps looking at you. And yes, actually, I am, and I will keep it up until you finally give in. You need to go for it sometime, so who with and when better than now?"

Anja's cheeks warmed slightly, and she was about to respond when Zoe finally settled on their outfits. Zoe's ensemble was a fusion of styles, combining her Indian heritage with a modern, cosmopolitan flair. Her outfit's bold colors and intricate patterns showcased her confidence and vibrant personality.

For Anja, on the other hand, she had chosen a dress that struck a balance between sophistication and understated elegance. The deep green fabric complemented her burgundy hair and fair complexion; its flowing lines accentuated her natural grace. The dress hinted at her curves without being too overt, which she paired with a delicate necklace. With final touches of light makeup and her perfume, Anja felt ready to face the day.

As they made their way downstairs to the dining room, the aroma of breakfast met them. Lucian was already there, seated at the head of the table. His attention was drawn away from his phone as they entered, his eyes immediately finding hers.

Fifteen

As THE EARLY morning sunlight filtered through the grand windows of the estate's dining room, Lucian sat at the head of the long wooden table. Upon hearing the soft shuffle of footsteps, he looked up from his phone. Anja and Zoe entered the room, and his gaze instinctively locked onto Anja's. He couldn't help the tightness in his chest as their eyes met; her presence was magnetic.

"Good morning," Lucian greeted warmly, a subtle hint of playfulness in his tone. "You both look stunning this morning. I trust the night treated you well?"

Zoe beamed, taking the compliment effortlessly. "Thank you, Lord Charming."

He saw Anja rolling her eyes at Zoe's playfulness. As they took their seats, Lucian gestured to the spread of food. Anja's response was more reserved, a thoughtful look in her eyes. "Thank you, Lucian. Let's just say the night provided much to ponder."

Zoe chimed in with her twist, "I'm starting to suspect the sheets here have some sort of enchantment."

Lucian chuckled, his gaze flickering to Zoe for a moment. He appreciated her seeming ability to add a touch of levity to even the most serious of situations. Turning his attention back to Anja, he found himself studying her more closely, noticing how her eyes held a glint that matched his own. Maybe even a matching attraction. He had looked forward to this breakfast, eager to have another opportunity to talk with Anja. The circumstances were far from ideal for discussing the Sodality's sinister history, but the moments they shared were undeniably charged.

"Help yourselves," Lucian invited. Gesturing toward the array of food on the table. "I've always found that delicate matters are easier to tackle with a full stomach."

He leaned back in his chair, satiated; for now, his gaze lingered on Anja. He realized that his curiosity about her had evolved into something more. The attraction he felt wasn't just based on her expertise or beauty. It was something more profound, a connection that defied the circumstances they found themselves in.

After they finished eating breakfast and as Zoe continued to savor her coffee, Lucian turned his attention to laying out their plans for the day.

"Anja, I'd like you to work with Howard today," he said, his voice firm yet thoughtful. "There's much to be explored in the library, and I believe you and Howard will make excellent progress together. Your insights so far have been invaluable, and I trust you'll continue to uncover the secrets that may lie within our family's history."

Anja nodded, fixing her eyes on his. "I understand, Lucian. I do need to have a deeper conversation with Howard and figure out what may be possible."

Lucian then turned to Zoe, a mischievous glint in his eye. "Zoe, I'd like you to take a more...social approach. I don't think you should have any issues with that. Mingle with the remaining relatives and guests, engage in light banter as you seem so adept, and see what you can uncover about the recent incidents. Your ability to get people talking is a skill that should come in handy today."

Zoe grinned. "You mean to play the part of the gossiping guest? I think I can handle that."

"And I," Lucian continued, his tone shifting to a more serious note, "will be meeting with Edward and the acting CEO of our family business. There's much to discuss regarding future arrangements and the ongoing probate actions concerning the estate. I must align plans with them to keep things moving smoothly.

"We'll reconvene here in the afternoon to compare notes and plan our next moves," Lucian said, finalizing the arrangements.

Soon, they dispersed, each heading off to tackle their respective assignments. As Lucian made his way to his meeting in the study, he couldn't help but reflect on the complexity of their situation. The blend of investigative work, estate management, and the undeniable undercurrent of attraction between him and Anja added layers to his day. Leaving the dining room, thinking still about Anja, Lucian couldn't help but wonder if there was a chance for something more between them. He had always been pragmatic, guided by logic and strategy, but now he found himself drawn to the possibility of a connection that went beyond that. Amid uncertainty and danger, Lucian's thoughts were consumed by a question he had never truly considered. Could there be room for romance amidst the chaos? In the past, he had turned to no-strings-attached relationships, like with Vanessa, for his sexual needs. But this seemed different. The answer remained unclear, however, one thing was certain—Anja had captured his attention in a way that no one had and that he couldn't easily dismiss.

The morning business discussions went as expected. Edward retained his position as CEO, and other than some interesting byplay between him and his secretary, everything seemed to be on track. He had hardly even noticed lunch coming and going.

Outside the door, Ian stood ready to escort Lucian to the library. The afternoon had brought with it a sense of purpose and direction, and there was work to be done. Lucian's mind was already shifting to Anja and Howard, the next steps in their investigation, and the convoluted paths that lay ahead. With a last glance back at the study, the door closing behind him, Lucian stepped into the corridor, his thoughts focused. His footsteps echoed in the grand corridor as he went to the estate's library, Ian following just a step behind. Leaving Ian outside, he opened the mahogany door. He was immediately greeted by the usual musty scent, lightened by Anja. At a massive wooden table at the far end of the room, Anja and Howard were deep in discussion, their heads bowed over scattered notes and open books. The *Ars Notoria* lay open in front of them and highlighted by several place markers. Howard's intense gaze was focused on the ancient text, his hand moving to trace a particularly curious passage. Anja, her expression thoughtful, was taking notes in her notebook, her brows furrowing as she attempted to decipher the layered meanings.

Lucian noticed they were so engrossed in their work that they seemed oblivious to his presence. He cleared his throat softly, announcing his presence, and they both looked up, their faces brightening with renewed awareness of their surroundings. The dynamic of the room shifted as he approached the table, ready to join them in discussion. Lucian listened intently as Anja and Howard took turns relating their discoveries.

"I must admit," Howard continued, his voice imbued with enthusiasm and frustration, "the more we dig, the more questions we uncover. It's as though we're circling the truth without quite reaching it."

Anja's eyes gleamed as she nodded in agreement. "I feel the same, Howard. But some of Lucian's thoughts on genetics," she glances at Lucian with a knowing smile, "could be what we need to push forward—to break through, so to speak."

Lucian raised an eyebrow. "You think that might lead somewhere with this?"

Anja's excitement was palpable as she responded, "I do. There's something about your approach that feels right as if it's tapping into something fundamental in the very nature of human potential. You have felt that all along but have almost reached the limit with science. You admitted that and asked for my help in this."

Howard leaned back, stroking his chin thoughtfully. "There are interesting Scottish bloodlines interwoven in the Miller family tree," he mused, turning to Anja. "Do you think that could be significant?"

Anja's face lit up. "I do believe so. I've noticed something similar in my own lineage. It's as if certain capabilities were passed down through my maternal grandmother's line but seem to skip every other generation. My grandmother had gifts and said I carried the same potential, perhaps even more than she had. That I only needed to embrace myself fully to achieve it. I have been endeavoring to do that and have begun to accept it."

Lucian's interest deepened, the implications of their words settling in. "So you are saying it's a combination of heritage, science, and… magic?" He paused for a while to consider the implications of what he had just said aloud, almost ready to believe but still needing some form of proof—or, at least, more convincing evidence.

Anja nodded eagerly, her eyes bright with passion. "Yes, that's exactly what we think. Your ideas, Lucian, may hold the key to unlocking that potential. Real magic, not just parlor tricks or illusions."

Howard interjected, flipping through the Miller family tree, "And don't forget these bloodlines. They must be significant. If we accept that the Sodality had been working on 'weeding out' problematic bloodlines, then certain characteristics of some of the Scottish clans may have played a role in shielding some from their purges."

In lecture mode now, Howard continued. "There were certainly clans known for their strong sense of loyalty and community. These clans often resided in remote and rugged terrains, contributing to their insularity. This could have made it more difficult, or even impossible, for the Sodality to infiltrate or exert influence over them. They would have jealously protected their Duine Sònraichte, their 'Gifted ones.'"

"The key might lie in how we combine our approaches," Anja suggested after a momentary loss in thought, her eyes distant.

"I agree," Howard concurred, his tone serious. "It would redefine everything we know."

Lucian felt the pull of something more significant, the promise of profound understanding. "Then let's continue. Together, we might achieve the extraordinary." He paused for a while to consider the implications. "I was planning to learn more from my research center in Switzerland. Anja, would you accompany me there? I need to share more information with you and show you what I've already accomplished there."

Anja's eyes widened, surprise mingling with excitement.

"Switzerland? Are you serious?" she asked, looking between him and Howard, who both nodded at her.

"Um, what about Zoe?" she asked.

Lucian reassured her. "After the jet drops us off at Cointrin Airport just outside of Lake Geneva, it will take Ava and Zoe back to the States, then return to Switzerland to be on hand for us."

Just then, Zoe entered the room as if summoned, prompting Anja's quip, "Speak of the devil," generating smiles.

Zoe retorted, gesturing around her, "Well, I couldn't find you all in the dining room like we agreed, so I had to track Anja down to her natural habitat." Grins spread across their faces, and Howard even let out a choked laugh.

Lucian turned to Zoe, his expression curious. "How was your day, Zoe? Did you discover anything of note in your investigation?"

Zoe leaned back, a mischievous smile playing on her lips. "Nothing new on that front; the staff and relatives seem loyal. All the staff are longtime retainers except for Geoffrey, the driver. He's new but carefully vetted by Edward." She paused, raising an eyebrow. "After Bartholomew and Eliza passed, the former driver and senior ladies' maid chose to retire. It seems they had a thing going and have gone off together."

Anja chimed in, her tone teasing. "A love story blossoming in the downstairs of the estate? How romantic!"

Zoe chuckled, her eyes sparkling with amusement. "Oh, it gets better. On other fronts, I did have fun gossiping with the downstairs servants. They are well-treated and have a genuine fondness for the estate. I couldn't imagine why..." She trailed off, her voice dripping with sarcasm.

Lucian grinned, recognizing Zoe's flair for the dramatic. "And what else did you uncover in your gossip sessions?"

Zoe leaned closer, her voice dropping to a conspiratorial whisper. "Well, I did hear about several downstairs romances and had it confirmed that Edward is indeed sleeping with his secretary."

Lucian heard Anja gasp. "Really, now?" he asked, his sarcastic tone betraying no surprise.

Zoe nodded, her eyes twinkling. "Oh yes, the secrets of the estate are deep and delicious. But don't worry Lucian, your secrets are safe with me."

Lucian's laughter filled the room, the sound rich and warm. "I'm glad to hear it. I wouldn't want my intrigue to become common gossip."

The three of them shared a laugh, the camaraderie between them evident.

Lucian stood, stretching slightly as he surveyed the room. "It's been an eventful day," he mused, his voice tinged with satisfaction. "I think I'd like to take a walk out around the grounds. Clear my head a bit before tomorrow. We'll be leaving sometime around noon."

He turned to Anja, his gaze softening. "Would you care to join me?" he asked, the invitation in his eyes.

Lucian noted Anja's hesitation and saw Zoe giving her a challenging and encouraging look. A smile tugged at the corners of Zoe's mouth, silently egging Anja to accept. Anja looked back at Lucian, a slow smile spreading across her face. "I'd like that," she said, her voice warm.

Lucian's face lit up, and he extended his arm to her. "Shall we?"

Moving toward the door, Lucian caught Zoe's eyes twinkling with unspoken mischief. She turned to Howard, who was still immersed in his notes. "Well, this should be interesting," she murmured.

The well-kept grounds of the Miller estate spread out before Lucian and Anja, a lush space maintained with care and artistry. The pathways meandered through the garden, bordered by meticulously pruned hedges, creating a sense of intimacy and wonder. Lucian guided Anja along, his stride confident and relaxed. The air was filled with the delicate fragrance of blooming flowers, a symphony of colors and scents that caressed the senses. Verdant lawns stretched out to where the dark line of forest created a beautiful contrast. Lucian watched Anja's eyes widen as she gazed around, filled with curiosity and delight.

"This place is incredible, Lucian," she exclaimed, gesturing at a nearby pond, where the soft murmur of a fountain mingled with the gentle quacking of ducks. "How long has this garden been here?"

Following her gesture with his eyes, Lucian smiled. "Oh, for several centuries, at least. This part," he motioned toward an elaborate rose garden, "was designed by a famed landscaper in the Victorian era. My family has always taken great pride in maintaining the estate's beauty."

Anja's eyes sparkled as she took in the beauty of the roses, their petals like delicate pieces of art, tinged with shades of pink, red, and white. "And what's that building over there?" she asked, pointing to a charming gazebo nestled among towering trees.

"That's a summerhouse," Lucian explained, leading her toward it. "It's a peaceful place where one can enjoy a quiet moment, read, or even have a small gathering. We've had many family picnics there. I believe the staff and their children had an Easter Egg Hunt this morning."

"Oh, Easter! It completely slipped my mind with so much happening. I wish I had a chance to watch the kids." Surprise and regret flickered across her face.

They continued to wander, each step revealing another facet of the garden's beauty. They passed statues of Greek gods, intricately carved benches, and trellises heavy with the fragrance of blooming jasmine, much to the delight of Anja, the scent so familiar and comforting. Anja's questions flowed easily, her curiosity a delightful match to Lucian's knowledge of the estate. Their conversation ranged from the history of the estate to the variety of plants and even his favorite spots to enjoy the outdoors. They paused upon reaching a small hill overlooking the entire garden, taking in the breathtaking view. The sun was beginning to dip toward the horizon, casting a golden glow over everything.

"It's stunning," Anja whispered, her voice filled with awe.

Lucian looked at her, his eyes reflecting the beauty of the scene before them. "It is," he agreed, his voice soft. "Especially when shared."

The sun continued its descent, casting a soft, warm glow over the garden as Lucian and Anja made their way back toward the mansion.

Now bathed in the setting sun's golden light, the pathways gently led them back to reality, but the garden's magic lingered in their shared glances and easy conversation. From the corner of his eye, Lucian saw Ian following discreetly at a distance. His presence was subtle, unobtrusive, a reminder of his vigilance, yet he maintained enough distance to afford Lucian and Anja their privacy.

"I must confess," Lucian began, his voice tinged with a touch of weariness, "today's events have left me in need of solitude, save for the company I find most pleasing at present."

"Lucian," Anja began. "This must have been hard for you. Losing your close family. You have been keeping it in."

"I know, Anja, it is still sinking in. I was never that close to them. I was always more solitary and focused. But their sudden loss has hit harder than I would have expected. The anger about it has pulled my attention more, and I have needed to control it. I think controlling and focusing on finding justice for them have kept the other feelings from surfacing. Maybe after dealing with the threat and finding solace in that justice, I can be more at ease to handle it all."

She reached out and touched his arm gently. "If you need to talk about it, please know I'll be there for you."

"Thank you. This stroll through the gardens has helped, and just being with you lightens the burden," he said quietly. He glanced at Anja, his eyes conveying an invitation. "Would you join me for a light meal and wine in my chambers? I assure you, it will be a relaxed affair, free from the day's burdens."

"I'd like that, Lucian," she replied, a smile playing at the corners of her lips.

They continued their walk, the mansion growing larger as they approached, its grandeur a fitting backdrop to the elegance of the garden. Lucian's hand brushed against Anja's, a casual yet intentional touch that spoke of their mutual comfort. As they reached the entrance, Lucian guided her upstairs, their footsteps echoing softly in the opulent hallways. The walk to his chambers was filled with shared glances and an unspoken understanding that they were venturing into a space reserved for trust and intimacy.

Lucian escorted Anja to a plush seating area, the furniture adorned with intricate woodwork and fine fabric. With practiced ease, he pulled the cord to summon the butler before turning to Anja, a mischievous glint in his eye. "I hope you enjoy red wine, my dear. Or would you prefer white? Perhaps something sparkling to match our conversation?"

Anja laughed, her eyes dancing with amusement. "Oh, I think red will do just fine. It's rich, full-bodied, much like our stroll through the garden today."

Lucian's lips twitched, a smile threatening to break free as he leaned in closer. "I must say, your appreciation for the finer things is quite intoxicating. It makes me wonder what other tastes you might have."

A knock at the door cut through their playful banter, and Lucian called out, "Enter!"

The butler, James, a man of stoic demeanor, entered the room, followed by a serving maid. Together, they pushed a cart laden with covered dishes and wine.

"Ah, dinner is served," Lucian announced, rising from his seat to assist with the arrangements. He uncovered the dishes, revealing an elegant spread. "I hope you're as hungry for this meal as I am for our continued conversation."

Anja's gaze met Lucian's, a knowing smile playing at the corners of her lips. "Oh, I'm quite famished, Lucian. But I must warn you, I'm a woman who enjoys taking her time to savor each bite."

Lucian's eyes narrowed playfully, and he responded, his voice dripping with suggestion, "In that case, my dear, we are well-matched. I believe in savoring every delightful morsel, ensuring nothing is rushed or overlooked."

The butler and maid finished arranging the table, lit candles around the room, and exited, leaving Lucian and Anja to enjoy their meal. As they settled in, their connection deepened, and the conversation flowed as easily as the wine, each word and glance a shared secret, a dance that led them further into the uncharted territory of desire and trust.

Moving aside the dinner plates, Lucian unveiled the final course: a stunning Kentish Berry Trifle, the layers of sponge, cream, and fruit artfully arranged in a crystal bowl. Beside each dessert plate was a small glass of chilled cordial, its deep purple hue glinting invitingly in the candlelight. Anja's eyes widened at the sight, and she couldn't help but let out a soft gasp of delight. "Oh, Lucian, this looks incredible."

Lucian's smile was warm, his eyes on Anja, "I thought you might enjoy something sweet and refreshing to end our meal. The tartness of the blackcurrant cordial should complement the trifle beautifully."

They each took a spoonful, the flavors dancing on their tongues, a harmonious blend of richness and zest. The cordial added a refreshing twist, enhancing the sweetness. Anja leaned back in her chair, a contented smile on her lips. "Lucian, this has been wonderful, but I must confess, after such a long day, I could really use a shower and some time to settle into my room."

Lucian's eyes met hers, a hint of a proposal in his gaze. "Well, Anja, if it's a shower or maybe a bath you're after, I assure you that the facilities here are quite luxurious. I'd be happy to accommodate your needs."

Anja's expression changed slightly, and she looked down, her hands nervously playing with her napkin. Now attuned to her emotions, Lucian sensed something was on her mind.

"Anja?" he prompted gently.

She took a deep breath, and her voice trembled as she confessed. "Lucian, I have another admission to make. I...I've never been with a man before. I want to, very much, but right now...it just doesn't feel right, and I'm fighting myself."

Lucian's eyes softened, and he reached across the table, taking her hand. "Anja, there's no need to rush anything. We have all the time in the world. I want you to feel comfortable with me."

Anja's eyes lifted to meet his, gratitude and relief evident in her gaze. "Thank you, Lucian. Your understanding means a lot to me."

He smiled, squeezing her hand reassuringly. "It's my pleasure, Anja. Now, let me show you to your room."

As they reached her door, conveniently located next door to his chambers, Lucian paused and turned to face her. The air between them was charged with anticipation and unspoken desire. They stood close, their eyes locked, a silent understanding passing between them. Slowly, Lucian leaned in, his lips meeting Anja's in a soft, lingering kiss. She returned it, tentatively at first, but then with growing confidence, her body responding to the warmth of the kiss. They broke the kiss, and he found himself slightly breathless, his eyes still locked with hers. Lucian could feel her desire, the undeniable pull between them, but he knew this was not the moment to pursue it further. With a gentle smile, he reached for the doorknob, opened her door, and stepped back.

"Until tomorrow," he whispered, his voice tinged with promise.

Anja nodded, her eyes shining. "Until tomorrow, Lucian."

With a final lingering glance, he turned and walked back to his chambers, consumed by a whirlwind of thoughts and emotions. He sank into a chair with his mind replaying the evening's events. He contemplated the unexpected connection he'd discovered with the intriguing librarian. Anja was so beautiful, her allure going beyond mere appearance. He sensed so much hidden beneath the surface, waiting to be understood and freed. He pondered the subtle looks and clues she'd given him. Her eyes filled with longing, hinting at unfulfilled desires. Being her first held a particular appeal, an intoxicating power. Lucian had always been the one in control, always the one dictating the terms. But he wondered if he could withstand Anja once she captivated his heart completely. And then the question arose: *does he even want to resist?*

The potential of their connection could be spectacular, but Lucian understood it might also come with sacrifices. For the first time, he felt his treasured independence could be at risk. Was he prepared to pay that price? He also recognized Anja's pivotal role in his ambitions to unlock the hidden potential of their bloodlines. His discussions with Howard have only confirmed her significance. The spark between them has deepened into something more profound, something he found irresistible. With a sigh, he leaned back, his gaze drawn to the window and the moonlit garden where they had strolled earlier, carefree and content. He reflected on the difference between the tranquility of that garden path and the path ahead of him, no...of them, one teeming with both potential and danger. Lucian knew his choices now would shape not only his future but Anja's, and he felt the weight of that responsibility like never before.

The first light of dawn filtered through the heavy curtains, finding Lucian awake and alone in his large, ornate bed. He'd been tossing and turning, his mind abuzz with thoughts of Anja. Sitting up, he ran a hand through his unruly hair, a frown creasing his forehead. The feelings welling inside him were unfamiliar and confusing. Desire, yes, but also something deeper, more profound. It scared and excited him simultaneously. It was not a feeling he was familiar with, but one that made him feel alive like never before.

He reached for his phone on the nightstand, his fingers tapping out messages to Ian and Ava. His mind was made up; they must leave the estate quickly and move on to the next phase. Perhaps distance would give him clarity, allowing him to regain control over emotions threatening to unbalance him. As he coordinated the return to the airport and the packing of their belongings, he couldn't shake the image of Anja's eyes. They were filled with curiosity, longing, and innocence that tugged at something deep within him. He recalled the soft press and taste of her lips, the warmth of her hand in his, and the sound of her laughter. The realization hit him with a jolt. He had fallen for her, truly and deeply. And for a man who had always been in control, always one step ahead, this was both thrilling and terrifying. With a heavy sigh, he set the phone down and rose from the bed, his movements mechanical as he prepared for the day. The path ahead was no longer clear, no longer simple. Anja had changed everything, and Lucian knew he couldn't just walk away. What that meant for their future and his plans was something he still couldn't quite grasp. He only knew for certain that he was stepping into the unknown, guided by a force more powerful than anything he'd ever known. With a final, determined glance out the window at the estate's well-kept grounds, he turned away, ready to leave.

Lucian strode down the ornate hallway, pausing momentarily to glance at Anja's door before reaching Edward's. He knocked firmly, waiting for the muffled response from within before turning the handle.

Edward greeted him at the door. "Lucian, good morning. Is everything alright?" he asked, a hint of concern in his eyes.

"We're leaving sooner than expected, Edward," Lucian explained, his voice carrying an urgency that reflected his inner turmoil. "I know it's sudden, but I trust you to handle the family's affairs competently. You've always been there."

Edward nodded, accepting the information without protest. "Of course, Lucian."

"Thank you for all you've done and will continue to do," Lucian replied, his gaze steady. He clapped Edward on the shoulder and moved on.

Next, he arrived at Howard's door, knocking again and entering after hearing a muttered response. Howard, quite disheveled and evidently still waking up, looked up as Lucian closed the door behind him.

"Lucian, what's the matter?" Howard asked as if sensing something unusual in Lucian's demeanor.

"We're leaving now, Howard," Lucian said, getting straight to the point. "I want to ensure you have all the resources you need and contact numbers for me and Ava."

Howard's eyes widened, but he quickly recovered, reaching for his spectacles and a notepad from his desk. "Alright, Lucian. I'll take care of things on my end. Just let me know what you need. Sabbatical it is —no need to worry about me. I have a few thoughts I'll be tracking down, and I'll let you and Anja know what else I can uncover. But, Lucian…take care of Anja—she's a treasure beyond price."

"I intend to, Howard, and thank you."

Lucian proceeded to provide Howard with the necessary details, his mind still on Anja but knowing these practical matters must be addressed. He thanked Howard for his help and headed back down the hallway.

The house was stirring to life now, the staff moving efficiently, preparing for the sudden departure. Lucian's mind was a whirl of emotions and thoughts, but he pushed them aside, focusing on the tasks at hand. The next steps were crucial, and he must be ready to face them, even as his heart ached with the desire to understand what was happening within him. The connection with Anja had awakened something new, something powerful.

The convoy, consisting of a sleek limousine and a spacious SUV, glided onto the road from the gravel drive as they began their drive back to Biggin Hill through the ethereal morning mists. The world outside was wrapped in a delicate shroud of fog, the sun striving to pierce through, casting a mystical quality over the countryside again.

Geoffrey, his hands firm on the steering wheel, navigated the winding roads with practiced ease, his eyes attentive to the shifting landscape. In the back, Lucian, Anja, and Zoe occupied themselves in quiet contemplation. Gone was the banter of their last ride—lost to thoughts.

Lucian saw Anja's attention focused out the window next to her, eyes lost in the misty fields and undulating hills of the Kent countryside—the fog danced and twirled around the ancient trees and over the lush meadows. Time seemed to stretch and blend for him, the outside world ever-changing, until finally, they approached the tarmac at Biggin Hill. The sight of his jet gleaming under the growing light of the day brought him back to reality. The transition from the limousine and SUV to the jet was carried out with seamless efficiency. Guards and ground crew attended to the luggage, swiftly loading it into the cargo hold as the passengers boarded. Once everyone settled in the luxurious cabin, buckled into plush leather seats, and surrounded by modern amenities, the doors closed, and the engines began to purr. The ground crew gave the final clearances, and the jet gracefully taxied toward the runway. Lucian glanced out the window, watching the tarmac slide past, his mind turning to the destination ahead—Lake Geneva—a relatively short flight.

The jet took off smoothly, ascending through the thinning mist, leaving the green fields and rolling hills of Kent behind. In the cabin, the occupants settled in for the journey, some lost in thought, others engaging in soft conversation. As the jet soared above the English Channel, the view from the windows presented a breathtaking transition. The English countryside's patchwork fields and quaint villages gave way to the expansive blue waters below. Sunlight danced on the waves, casting shimmering reflections that created a mesmerizing and constantly shifting pattern. Lucian gazed out at the spectacle, the interplay of light and water a soothing contrast to the intensity of his thoughts. The flight continued over France, offering glimpses of historic cities, meandering rivers, and, eventually, the majestic peaks of the Alps. The mountains rose in grandeur, their snow-capped peaks standing sentinel over lush valleys and alpine meadows.

As they neared Lake Geneva, the panorama became even more stunning. The lake unfolded like a crescent-shaped sapphire gem, its deep blue waters nestled between the surrounding mountains and hills. The terrain was dotted with picturesque towns and vineyards, their orderly rows stretching toward the water's edge.

The jet began its descent, and the details of the landscape became more apparent. The city itself was a blend of traditional Swiss architecture and modern urban design. Geneva's historic districts, with their charming rooftops and narrow streets, contrasted against the sleek lines of contemporary buildings. Green spaces were abundant, with carefully maintained parks adding a touch of freshness and tranquility to the urban fabric. Aaliyah's professional announcement brought a momentary focus on the upcoming customs and immigration procedures, but the atmosphere remained relaxed. She collected passports and documents from the passengers and exited when the door opened. The interaction between Anja and Zoe captured Lucian's attention. The warmth and understanding in their gestures, the shared smiles, and the intimate touch of hands and hugs suggest a reconciliation of sorts. Their connection appeared genuine and deep, hinting at shared experiences and emotions beyond mere friendship.

Anja looked at Zoe, her eyes seemingly filled with regret and understanding. "Zoe, I need to apologize for last night. I snapped at you, and I didn't mean to. Everything was just so overwhelming, and I let my frustration get the best of me."

Zoe reached out to take Anja's hands, her smile gentle. "Bit my head off more like… Hey, it's okay. I understand. I'm the one who should be sorry. I kept pushing you about Lucian, and that wasn't fair. When you're ready, it will be easier. Don't stress about it."

Tears welled in Anja's eyes as she squeezed Zoe's hands. "I know, and I appreciate your concern. But I do need to figure things out at my own pace. Promise me you'll be safe."

Zoe pulled Anja into a hug, her voice soft. "I promise, Anja. And I'll be there for you whenever you need to talk or anything. You have my number. Just take care of yourself, okay?"

Anja nodded, her face buried in Zoe's shoulder, a few tears escaping. "I will. And you, too. Thank you, Zoe."

Aaliyah stepped back onto the jet with an air of efficiency, distributing passports back to everyone. "Everything's cleared, and the limo is being loaded. You're all set to go."

As the passengers gathered their belongings, Lucian, having caught the tail end of Anja and Zoe's conversation, turned to Zoe and Ava, his expression warm and sincere. "Safe travels, Zoe, Ava. We'll be in touch soon."

The bodyguards filed out of the plane, leaving the intimate group to say their final goodbyes. Lucian's gaze shifted to Anja, and he extended his hand toward her. His voice was both determined and inviting. "Let's do this, Anja."

Anja took his hand with a firm grasp. She turned back to Zoe, her smile relaxed. Zoe met her gaze and responded with a smile and thumbs-up, her eyes twinkling with encouragement.

Carlos sat attentively with the driver as the limo glided smoothly along the road, leaving Lucian to address those in the back. His tone was both earnest and commanding as he laid out the plan.

"We'll be heading to NexGen headquarters first," Lucian informed them, his eyes scanning their faces. "The hotel will come later. I need to ask a favor of all the guards, as well. I'd like you to volunteer for some blood tests. I promise the results will be kept private and only shared within the group if you agree after discussing them. Until then, I can't share more."

The request sparked a flurry of questions and curious glances. Lucian held up his hand to quiet them. His eyes were intense but reassuring as he continued.

"I know this may seem strange, but it's about performance enhancements," he explained, choosing his words carefully. "But it's not what you might think. We're not talking about steroids or other experimental drugs. This is something on another level entirely."

"Lucian, are you saying that this could enhance our natural abilities? Without any harmful side effects?" Claire asked.

Lucian nodded, a confident smile playing at the corner of his mouth. "Exactly, Claire. But it's still experimental, and I want to be upfront about it. That's why I'm asking for volunteers, not demanding compliance."

The others exchanged glances, clearly considering his proposal. The air was thick with uncertainty and a sense of opportunity, a chance to be part of something groundbreaking.

Finally, Ian spoke up, his voice steady. "If it's as you say, Lucian, and there are no risks, I'm in."

The words seemed to break the tension, and others began to agree. Lucian's smile broadened.

"Thank you," he said, sincerity ringing in his voice. "I appreciate your trust and willingness to be part of this."

Lucian's expression turned more serious as he continued to address the guards in the limo, his words carefully measured.

"I want to clarify something important," he began, his gaze steady. "While the testing poses no risks, if your test results show certain indicators, you may be invited to participate in some trials. There could be risks associated with those, but they would also be explained in detail, and participation would, of course, be entirely voluntary. I believe, however, that your histories and performance have demonstrated exceptional capabilities, and I anticipate positive outcomes for all of you."

He turned to Carlos, instructing him, "You'll be staying with the driver, and I'll fill in more details after Emma gives a blood sample and replaces you."

With a nod of understanding, Carlos shifted in his seat, and Lucian raised the divider, cutting off the back of the limo from the front. The change in the atmosphere was tangible as he leaned closer to Anja and the other guards, his voice dropping to a more confidential tone.

"I have something else to report," he said, his words heavy with significance. "We have likely identified the organization responsible for my family's murders and the continued threat we face. They're likely attempting to suppress exactly what I'm trying to accomplish now. The threat will only increase because of this. This is just so you can be aware of the threat. This information is to go no further than those here."

His revelation was met with silence, the weight of his words settling over the limo's occupants. Ian broke the silence, his voice filled with defiance and determination. "Okay then, let them come at us. They don't seem to realize who they are messing with."

Lucian's face broke into a rare grin, his eyes glinting with resolve. "Exactly, Ian. We'll be cautious, but we won't back down. We're on the cusp of something extraordinary and won't let them stop us."

The limo glided smoothly to a halt in front of a sleek, modern building, its mirrored glass reflecting the vivid blues of the nearby lake and the rugged peaks of the Alps in the distance. There was an air of cutting-edge innovation about the place that lent it a unique character. One by one, the limo's occupants exited the vehicle, each wearing an expression of anticipation. Ian was the first to step out, scanning the area, followed by Emma and Claire. Lucian emerged next, extending a hand to help Anja out.

Upon entering the building, they were greeted by a receptionist, her professional smile broadening as she recognized Lucian. She retrieved lanyards with badges and photos courtesy of Ava, handing them out to each group member.

"Welcome back, Dr. Miller," the receptionist said with genuine warmth. "It's wonderful to see you again. If you'll follow me, I'll escort you to the elevator. Dr. Sinclair is expecting you."

They followed her lead. The soft click of their shoes on the polished floor was the only noise as they made their way to the elevator. With a soft chime, the doors opened, and they stepped inside, the receptionist pressing the button for the top floor. After a brief ascent, the doors slid open to reveal the floor where Dr. Isabelle Sinclair awaited them. She greeted Lucian with a welcoming smile as they exited the elevator.

"Lucian, it's wonderful to see you again! I trust your journey was pleasant. Please, come this way; we can head to my office and adjoining conference room."

Lucian nodded appreciatively, and his confident voice filled the corridor. "Thank you, Isabelle. It's good to be back. Before we settle in, though, I'd like to get blood samples all around. If we can also have Emma replace Carlos with the limo to have him tested, that would be ideal."

Hesitating a moment before adding, "On second thought, Ian, do you think it would be possible to secure our luggage and the team's more sensitive belongings or have some brought in and stored temporarily in here? Maybe also putting a tracker on the limo as well? I may have been hasty in my rush to get started. I would like to have Carlos available here to participate fully."

"I think that can be arranged. I'll work it out with Carlos before we start the blood tests."

"Of course," Isabelle replied, her eyes reflecting understanding. "I'll make sure everything is arranged."

As Ian headed down to the limo while Emma and Claire were guided away to have their blood drawn, Lucian and Anja followed Isabelle to her office. A long, polished conference table sat in the adjoining room, surrounded by ergonomic chairs.

Sixteen

Lucian began, "Before we get into details, Isabelle, can we get a technician to take blood samples for Anja and me? A full epigenetic workup for both."

Isabelle nodded at Lucian's request, her eyes moving to Anja. "Certainly, Lucian."

Anja's eyebrows rose slightly. "Epigenetic workup? What exactly does that entail?"

Isabelle leaned back in her chair, her voice taking on a gentle, explanatory tone. "An epigenetic workup examines how the genes in your DNA are expressed. It doesn't just look at the genetic code but the markers that control how the body uses those genes. These markers can be influenced by various environmental factors, lifestyles, and even thoughts and emotions. Understanding them can give us unique insights into your physical and mental well-being."

Lucian added, "It can also reveal certain hidden potentials or predispositions within your genetic makeup. In our particular area of research, understanding these epigenetic factors could be instrumental in unlocking capabilities that might otherwise remain dormant."

Anja listened intently, her intelligent eyes reflecting comprehension. "I see. It's like looking beyond the basic blueprint to see how the building is actually constructed and functions. What doors are open or closed even."

"Exactly," Isabelle confirmed. "It's a rather complex process but fast and automated these days, and the insights we can gain from it are invaluable. A cheek swab would do for a regular DNA genetic sequencing, but for this, it is much more accurate and complete to use a very fresh blood draw."

Anja's expression settled into one of trust and acceptance. "I understand. I'm ready whenever you are."

Isabelle reached for her phone and dialed an extension. "I'll have a technician come in right away to take the samples. It won't take long, and then we can continue our discussions."

Shortly, the door opened and a technician entered, carrying a tray filled with sterile vials, needles, and other equipment necessary for drawing blood. Clad in a white lab coat, her demeanor was professional and efficient.

"Good afternoon," she greeted them, setting up the tray on a nearby table. "I'll be taking your blood samples today. We'll get started if you could both roll up your sleeves."

Lucian and Anja complied. She deftly tied a tourniquet around Lucian's arm, finding a suitable vein with practiced ease. A quick swab with an alcohol pad and a gentle insertion of a thin-tube needle attached to a port. With a deft insertion of a vial, Lucian's blood began to flow. The process was repeated with Anja, her eyes taking in the needle and the bright red blood flowing.

As the technician finished, Isabelle watched closely, her instructions clear and authoritative. "Make sure to label the samples for priority analysis. I want a comprehensive epigenetic workup on both. The results should be encrypted and stored securely. I'll be the only one to access them, so please notify me as soon as they are ready."

The technician nodded. "Understood, Dr. Sinclair."

The blood samples were labeled within minutes, and the technician packed up. With a final nod, she exited the room, leaving them to continue their discussions.

Lucian turned to Isabelle and asked, "Could you give Anja an overview of our work to date?"

Isabelle gave Lucian a questioning look; her concern was evident.

"Yes, Isabelle, full disclosure. She is a part of this now and a vital one at that."

"Certainly, Lucian." Isabelle turned to Anja, her eyes reflecting seriousness and excitement about what she was to explain.

"Anja, welcome to NexGen. Our work here is groundbreaking, to say the least. As I mentioned earlier, we're focused on unlocking human potential through a complex understanding of genetics and epigenetics.

"We're investigating how certain environmental and chemical triggers can activate or suppress gene expression. Many methods can be used, but I won't go into those details. The point is that this can lead to the enhancement of certain abilities or characteristics. It's about tapping into hidden potentials that lie within our DNA."

Lucian interjected, his voice filled with conviction, "And we believe, Anja, that you possess some of these unique genetic traits. Traits that might be the missing link to fully understanding how to control and direct these enhancements."

Anja looked taken aback, her mind racing to process the information. "Me?"

"Remember our discussions with Howard? What the Sodality is trying to suppress—desperately, it seems. I once admonished Isabelle for mentioning the 'magic' ingredient we seemed to be missing. It seems I was hasty in that assessment. Real magic, Anja. Not just parlor tricks, didn't you say? A combination of heritage, science, and...magic."

Anja nodded in acceptance.

"Yes, Anja," Lucian's look and voice were gentle but firm.

Isabelle smiled, her voice reassuring. "That's what makes this all so unexpected. Your expertise and interests might be linked to something deeper, something encoded in your very genes. It's not just about biology; it's about a connection to something greater, a connection that transcends time and place."

Lucian reached out, placing a hand on Anja's shoulder. "We need you, Anja. Not just for your genetic potential, but for your insight, your knowledge."

Anja's eyes met Lucian's, and a new understanding formed between them at that moment—a connection deeper than mere attraction, a connection that spoke of destiny and purpose. Finally, she nodded, her voice steady and determined. "Alright, I'm in. Let's see where this goes."

With a serious expression, Isabelle recounted a previous discussion with Lucian to Anja, explaining the two experimental techniques they had been exploring. She gestured to screens showing images and graphs, illustrating their successes and limitations.

"Now, don't worry too much about the technical terminology or diagrams; it will probably be confusing for the most part," Isabelle assured her.

"First, we've worked with the amplification of Flux Receptors using the EpiPhase CRISPR technique that Lucian pioneered. By amplifying the expression of specific receptors attuned to the Genoformatic Flux, we've enhanced some subjects' sensory perceptions and physical abilities significantly." She paused before continuing. "These receptors act like molecular antennae, allowing the cells to detect and respond to even subtle environmental fluctuations. We also use these reactions to tag or identify locations on the genome with that potential—another insight provided by Lucian."

Anja asked, "But what are the limits of this technique? Why isn't it enough? And what is this 'flux ' you mentioned?"

"This flux, in its simplest terms, is like a large-scale quantum entanglement at a molecular scale. This scale of entanglement has been generally considered impossible, but recent experiments have shown it to be attainable under certain circumstances or conditions. That, tied to a catalyst of some sort, could enable rapid changes at a vast scale. Advanced science that appears to be magic. Perhaps it even is…"

Isabelle continued, "It's like tuning into a radio frequency. The receptors can detect and use the flux when not suppressed, but we don't have complete control over how they respond. It's inconsistent and varies greatly between subjects. We've been on the brink of something incredible, but there's a missing piece we can't quite grasp."

Reflecting on his change of stance regarding magic, Lucian added,

"That's where another option comes in, and it's where I believe your abilities, Anja, may provide a catalyst."

Anja leaned in, her eyes wide, absorbing the possibilities.

He continued, "We've been experimenting with flux-stabilizing implants. I would still like to find a more natural alternative. Something where the body can generate and store a stable supply of the flux, ideally by expressing the proper genes to manufacture it consistently. The complexity involved has limited what we have been able to understand."

Lucian turned to Anja, his eyes filled with fiery determination. "Your expertise in medieval and occult texts, your connection to something ancient and magical, could be the key to unlocking this mystery, Anja. We've pushed the boundaries of science, but now we may need to delve into the realms of the unexplained."

Anja's mind raced. She said, her voice barely above a whisper, "So you're saying that the blend of science and something mystical might be the key?"

Lucian nodded, his voice soft yet filled with conviction. "Exactly. Your unique insights could bridge the realms of the known and unknown. Together, we could forge a new path, uncovering secrets that have been hidden for centuries."

Anja's eyes sparked with an idea as she shared her thoughts with Lucian and Isabelle. Her voice was animated, reflecting the excitement of a new possibility.

"You know, in many of the ancient texts I've studied, rituals are described as powerful transformative experiences. They're not just symbolic; they're said to have real, tangible effects on the practitioners. It's not so different from how intensive study or training can alter neural pathways, enhancing cognitive and physical abilities."

She leaned forward, her words flowing with growing confidence. "What if there's more to it? What if certain rituals or practices, combined with these advanced genetic techniques, could unlock this suppressed epigenetic coding? We might find the bridge needed to achieve these additional capabilities by fusing the old wisdom with modern science."

Lucian prompted her to continue, "Go on, Anja."

Anja took a moment to gather her thoughts. "Consider this: perhaps the ancient rituals were not merely symbolic or spiritual exercises. Maybe they evolved as specific tools to tap into the human genome's potential. A sort of coded instruction in thought patterns to awaken dormant genes and unlock those abilities. They may not have known what a genome was, but they could see the results. It could be that earlier, these abilities were not as suppressed or hidden as they are now."

Isabelle's eyes widened, clearly intrigued by the concept. "It's a bold idea, Anja. Unconventional, but it aligns with our current challenges. The fusion of ritualistic practice with our genetic engineering could indeed provide a new avenue to explore."

Lucian nodded. "It's a compelling direction, one that bridges the mystical with the empirical."

Isabelle's phone beeped, interrupting the flow of the conversation. She glanced at the notification. "Some preliminary results are in," she announced, her voice betraying a hint of excitement.

Lucian held up a hand. "Could you have the others brought back in? They should be here too."

"Certainly." Isabelle dialed an extension and passed on the request.

Lucian gestured for her to bring the results up, and the room fell into silence as they turned to the screen. The data appeared seemingly incomprehensible to Anja, but Lucian and Isabelle appeared at home, scanning through the information with knowing eyes. The door to the conference room opened, and Anja noticed Claire and Emma walking in. Following close behind were Ian and Carlos, who seemed to have sorted out the details that allowed everyone to be present.

Lucian, sitting across the table, looked up as they settled in. "Ah, perfect timing. We've just received some data suggesting that all of us, including you four, have the potential to be more than we currently are."

Claire's eyebrow arched in curiosity. "How common is this?"

Isabelle replied, "It's fairly rare, which makes the situation even more intriguing."

Ian leaned forward, the skepticism evident in his voice. "If it's so rare, then why do we all have whatever this is?"

Anja watched as Isabelle hesitated, clearly grappling with the weight of Ian's question. "If you had asked me that a few months ago, I would have said the odds were astronomical against it. As to why…?"

A heavy silence draped the room. Then Anja spoke, breaking the tension. "This might not be a coincidence or a statistical anomaly. We may have been brought together because we all have this…potential. Destiny, perhaps?"

Lucian met her gaze and then looked at the others as he spoke. "You were all chosen for your skills and expertise. The fact that you are already so capable is a testament to your potential and the drive you all have to excel. Perhaps your heritage played a larger role than you would have thought."

"So what do we do now? How do we unlock this 'more' within us?" Claire asked.

Anja followed Isabella's gaze as the attention shifted back to the data on her screen. "That's what we're going to find out."

Isabelle continued, still partially looking at her screen. "The markers Lucian and Anja have are unusual. They don't correspond to any of the standard genetic markers for therianthropy we've been studying."

Anja felt her curiosity aroused. "The Otherkin… Could these unusual markers in our genetic codes be a key to understanding this phenomenon further?"

Lucian turned to her, eyebrows raised. "Otherkin?"

She took a deep breath before explaining. "They're individuals who feel a deep kinship to animals or even mythical beings. Some claim memories or sensations connected to their non-human aspect."

As she continued, Anja could feel the weight of the room's attention on her. "In essence, otherkin is the idea that a person's essence or soul is not entirely human. But with Lucian and Isabella's approach, these feelings or beliefs might manifest in more tangible ways."

Emma's voice brought her back to the present. "But how does that apply to us?"

"In a manner of speaking," Anja replied carefully, "these otherkin aspects could manifest tangibly in all of us."

Ian leaned in, "That is a lot to take in."

She nodded. "Yes, it is."

After a slight pause, Isabelle spoke up, excitement clear in her voice. "Anja, your particular genetic makeup might provide insights we've been missing. It's uncharted territory, but one that holds incredible promise."

Lucian looked at Anja, a shared understanding passing between them. He then pushed his chair back, stretching. "Well, might as well think big, right? Anyway, I think it is time for a break. How about lunch? I skipped breakfast, and I'm starving."

After finishing a simple lunch of sandwiches, ice water, and some red wine, the tension in the room grew as the weight of their discoveries sank in. Anja's eyes were alight, and her mind was racing with the possibilities.

"I don't want to wait any longer," Anja declared, her voice filled with conviction. "Is there a quiet room somewhere? I want to try an incantation or ritual. Something tells me it's the right thing to do."

Isabelle looked thoughtfully at Anja before nodding. "We have a relaxation room that might be suitable. And there's a serum formulation we've been working on," she explained, her voice measured and professional. "It's comprised of chromatin remodeling proteins targeting flux receptors in general. It's been found safe in our previous experiments but seemingly not very effective, although those trials were aimed at therianthropy, not what you would be attempting. For you, it may be more effective when combined with your esoteric methods."

Lucian's brows furrowed and he started to object. "Anja, we don't need to rush into this. We can take our time and..."

But she shook her head, cutting him off. "No, Lucian, I need to do this. I can feel it, deep down, like it's calling to me. I know it's the right thing."

The intensity in her eyes silenced any further objections. She was driven by something beyond reason, a connection to her heritage and something else inside. Lucian and Isabelle exchanged a glance. She led Anja to the room, a serene space filled with soft lighting and comfortable furniture. The serum was drawn from a small vial, and Isabelle injected it with a steady hand. Lucian watched them, his expression showing deep concern. Anja sensed his worry and offered him a reassuring smile.

"Trust me," she whispered.

Anja's mind whirled with the possibilities as she settled in. Isabelle had explained that it was a room intended as a break from overwork, bright laboratory lights, and sterile medical smells. The weight of their discoveries, her connection to the flux-sensitive markers, and the potential for breakthroughs all convinced her to take this next step. Her instinct, combined with her innate curiosity, drove her to put theory into practice.

After Lucian and Isabelle departed, she opened her messenger bag and took out her notes, opening them to the sketches she took from the Ashton Grimoire. She also took out the copy of the *Ars Notoria* Howard had entrusted to her. The ancient text contained rituals and formulas, and the diagrams suggested a pathway to unlocking untapped potential. Perhaps her heritage held the key.

When Isabelle administered the injection, Anja felt the cool liquid coursing through her veins. It was a leap of faith, guided by science and driven by intuition. As she waited now, feeling the subtle shift within her, a tingling sensation assured her that the serum was taking effect. She turned her attention to the ritual for eidetic memory and fast learning. Her eyes traced the intricate symbols and her mind absorbed the ancient words. The room was filled with stillness, as if time itself was holding its breath, waiting for her to bridge the gap between the known and the unknown.

With a pounding heart, Anja began to recite the angelic names specified for the incantations, her voice steady and confident. The words resonated within her, vibrating at a frequency that felt foreign yet familiar. The symbols on the pages seemed to come alive as she traced the words with her eyes in spirals toward the center of one diagram, now seeming to glow with a soft, ethereal light. She felt a connection, linking her mind with something vast and unexplored. The world around her faded, and she was transported to a realm of pure thought, where knowledge flowed like a river and memories crystallized into flawless gems; she no longer felt her body.

The ritual continued, each word and gesture building upon the last, weaving a tapestry of understanding that bound her mind to the fabric of her existence, unlocking the potential hidden within her genetics. She opened herself to accepting all of what she was and could be. Her mind expanded, absorbing details at an astonishing rate, retaining every detail with perfect clarity. Slowly, the ritual came to an end, and Anja was brought back to the physical world. Her body was trembling with the aftershocks of the experience; the only word she could find to describe it was...orgasmic. She felt different, changed in a way that was both profound and subtle. She also felt very aroused and needy. She would deal with that later—hopefully not that much later. She felt that attempting to pleasure herself would not relieve the need but only amplify it.

She knew she'd succeeded, that the combination of the serum and the ritual had unlocked a door within her. The eidetic memory and the fast learning were now a part of her, gifts from her unique heritage and the daring exploration of science and magic. And more. She felt like she had awakened to a new reality.

She settled herself into a soft recliner and closed her eyes. Her mind traced her ritual experience. She saw that tapestry of understanding again in her mind's eye. Overlaying that with research on Otherkin and the virtually limitless hybrids possible, she cataloged them from memory and compared them to herself. Animals? No, nothing lined up. Mythical beasts, dragons, unicorns, others...nothing resonated. Okay, angels? No, definitely not any of them. Demons? Well, there were a lot of possibilities there, but she didn't feel evil. She may not be a demon, but a part demon? Were demons inherently evil, or was that just one frame of reference?

It seemed as if her life flashed before her eyes, playing in fast snippets. She saw pages from her studies in the esoteric medieval history turning, showing her diagrams and drawings of demons; their names and types flashed by.

She replayed conversations with her grandmother, Madeline. Hints were there, but she was probably too young to understand at the time. Madeline had not explained explicitly, but Anja felt her grandmother must have known. She reviewed Madeline's tales from old times in the highland and the clans passed down to her by her grandmother: a story of a traveler accepted into the clan who was hunted and persecuted for her gifts. She had seduced the clan's chieftain. She was renowned for her beauty and ability to influence the other leaders. Her grandmother had gifts, but it seemed like time and the weakening of bloodlines had diluted her ability to use them. It was obvious in hindsight that it was still present, at least a little bit.

Flashing back to the night when she had pleasured herself so profoundly, imagining the scenes in the books Raymond had loaned to her, she felt the echoes of that night coursing through her body. She could feel that need rising now but needed another for completion. Lucian.

Anja realized now what she was. She had done as her grandmother encouraged her to do. Madeline had told Anja she had a destiny to fulfill if only she could embrace herself. To accept what lived in her. Yes, Madeline had known what she was, but also that she needed to discover it for herself. She had and now was ready to accept it— embrace it. Succubus. Although she was not too sure whether she should share that insight with the others just yet. With that realization, she considered all she had read about succubi. Much of it didn't seem to directly apply to her as more of a half or partial breed, at least not yet. Could she project into dreams? Daydreams? Maybe read other's desires? Influence or seduce others at will? She would need to be careful, but it opened a whole realm of possibilities.

With a newfound sense of herself and a determination to explore further, Anja gathered her notes and headed back to Lucian and Isabelle. She opened the door, her eyes still aglow with the thrill of success, only to be met by Claire. With a smile and nod to Claire, they walked back to Isabella's office together. Upon arrival, they found the others deep in discussion over the preliminary findings from the guards' tests. Anja was taken aback to find that many hours had passed. It was late afternoon.

"Anja," Isabelle said, her voice tinged with curiosity and concern. "How did it go? If it's alright with you, I'd like to request another blood sample."

Anja nodded, still smiling, and the sample was quickly taken. Her excitement was palpable, and she couldn't help but share her success with the others.

"It worked," she exclaimed, her voice filled with joy and triumph. "Better than I had hoped! But I must admit, I'm tired and...and would like to go to the hotel to recover."

Lucian, watching her closely. "That's a good idea," he said, his voice gentle and supportive. "We've made incredible progress today, and there's no need to push ourselves further. We can continue in the morning."

At the hotel, Anja watched as the group settled into a well-practiced routine. Claire took her position as the on-duty guard, her eyes sharp and vigilant, scanning the surroundings. The other guards assisted the bellhop with the luggage, retaining a few bags for themselves while maintaining their professional demeanor. Lucian gracefully released the limo driver, ensuring he would be available again in the morning. He then approached the front desk, where he was immediately recognized from previous stays. Ava's meticulous planning has secured them the presidential suites, and everything seemed in order.

Then, from beside him, Anja's soft voice broke through the hotel's muted ambiance. "I'll be staying with you," she whispered to Lucian, her voice filled with a quiet certainty.

Lucian's response was a totally out-of-character double take of surprise. But as quickly as it appeared, the surprise vanished, replaced by an understanding smile as he looked down at Anja. He simply nodded.

They were escorted to the top-floor suites, the elevator doors opening to reveal an elegant corridor that led to their rooms. The suites were luxurious and well-appointed, offering a sense of comfort and refinement. The manager, a professional-looking man with a practiced smile, swung open the doors to the presidential suite, giving way to a breathtaking expanse of luxury. Their bags were already in place, neatly arranged by a bellhop, who received a generous tip from Lucian on his way out.

"Mr. Miller, I trust everything is to your satisfaction?" the manager asked, his eyes flicking to Anja, then back to Lucian.

"Everything looks perfect, thank you," Lucian replied, shaking the manager's hand.

After the manager's departure, the sense of formality in the room eased, and the team went into action. Emma and Claire headed straight for the guards' quarters, their trained eyes scanning for anything out of place. Carlos moved to the assistant's room while Ian approached the guest suite.

Ian glanced at Lucian, a knowing look in his eyes. "I suppose this one is mine then," he said.

"That's right," Lucian confirmed, a touch of warmth in his voice. "Anja and I will be in the master suite."

The team secured the area, conducting a meticulous sweep for hidden devices or potential threats in all the rooms. Once the search was complete and security measures were in place, Lucian addressed the group, his tone more relaxed. "You're free to use room service or venture out, but only two at a time, and you must stay together. Be vigilant. We're in a delicate situation, and the threat is very real."

Everyone nodded, their faces reflecting the seriousness of their circumstances.

Lucian turned to Anja, a gentle smile playing on his lips. "Are you ready?" he asked.

She looked into his eyes, her confidence clear, and said. "More than ready."

In the master suite, the door closed behind them, and they were alone at last. Anja knew what she wanted. Needed. Craved. With the door closed, the outside world seemed to fade away, leaving only the two of them in a cocoon of intimacy and anticipation. The room was softly lit, with elegant furnishings creating an ambiance of subtle luxury, but she didn't pay much attention to her surroundings. Her focus was now solely on Lucian.

He approached her, his eyes dark and intense, filled with a passion that seemed to pull her in. She met his gaze, her body responding to his nearness with a thrill of excitement...and a deep hunger. He reached out, brushing a stray strand of hair from her face. Her breath caught, and she leaned into his hand, her eyes closing briefly as she savored the sensation.

"Anja," he whispered, his voice low and filled with emotion. "I've never felt this way before. Something about you draws me in, something I can't quite explain."

He pulled her closer, his lips finding hers in a kiss that was gentle at first, then deepened, becoming more urgent, more demanding. She responded, her body melting into his, her mind lost in the sensation. They broke apart, both breathing heavily, their eyes locked. The world had narrowed down to this moment, this place, this incredible connection that seemed to transcend the ordinary. Looking into his eyes, she gave him a small mental push. Without waiting any longer, Anja stepped back and watched as Lucian's eyes gauged her. She slipped her dress from her shoulders, let it pool at her feet, and gently kicked it aside. Next, she reached back to undo her bra and held up her hand, stopping him as Lucian started to come to her. She wanted to feel this power. She wanted to look into his eyes as she revealed herself to him.

As he stopped, eyes still watching her, she unclasped her bra and tossed it to her side. Her nipples hardened; she pinched one and then the other. Lucian's eyes locked on them; she could sense his need building. Standing only in her thin thong panties, she trailed one hand slowly down her belly, the other cupping a breast. Her hand continued down into her thong, teasing him with the view of her bare skin. She reached down and slowly pulled the thong to the side, revealing herself to him for the first time. She could see the heat in his eyes as he looked at her. He stepped closer to her, his hands almost shaking with anticipation.

"You're so beautiful," he said, touching her.

She moaned softly as his fingers grazed her skin, sending shivers down her body. He slowly pulled the thong down; she stepped out of it and stood before him, fully nude. He stared at her; she could sense his desire for her growing stronger with every passing moment. She looked at him with a smoldering gaze, telling him with her eyes that she wanted him just as badly. Without a word, he reached out and drew her into his embrace. Their bodies melded together perfectly, each curve and contour complementing the other. The scent of his cologne mingled with her perfume. She could feel his heart beating against her breasts. She stepped back and tugged at his shirt.

"Your turn," she said.

He nodded and reached for the buttons on his shirt, only managing a few before he pulled it over his head impatiently. She knelt before him, looking up at him with a seductive smile. As Anja settled in front of Lucian, her long, curly red hair cascaded down her back like a fiery waterfall. She looked up at him with a sultry gaze that set fire to his blood, all his reactions laid bare to her now.

Her hands moved over his hips, and she reached for the button on his pants. As soon as she had got it undone, she slid the zipper down and took hold of his erection through the silk of his boxers. She ran her fingers lightly over the bulge, feeling his pulse as he moaned softly. She reached behind him and tugged the boxers down, then pushed him backward so that he could sit on the edge of the bed. Now free, his erection stood proud. Next, she pulled his pants and boxers down his legs, getting them stuck on his shoes. She drew each of his shoes and socks off, tossing them all behind her along with the rest.

She leaned back on her heels, still kneeling in front of him, and took in the sight of him as he rested back on his elbows, now completely nude. His erection was large, long, and thick but not huge. She came in and pushed his knees apart enough to get closer. Her face was just inches away, and she wanted to feel, explore, and taste it. Reaching up, she lightly touched the tip where a glistening drop had formed. She felt the slickness as her finger traced along the darker skin down the front, feeling the silkiness she had only imagined before. Under the silkiness, she felt the hardness and the ridge running down his length. She lightly cupped his balls as they began to tighten up to his body. He stared down at her, fire in his eyes, but letting her take the lead.

She stood, then spread her legs slightly to give him a good look at her. She took another drop of moisture from his tip and touched herself with it, spreading her folds with her other hand.

"Anja! You will be my ruin…," in a breathy voice.

She just smiled and crawled slowly up beside him on the bed. She leaned over his erection and blew softly before tentatively licking his tip, circling his length with her fingers. She looked up into his eyes as she began to stroke him. Taking him in her mouth, she tasted the slightly salty and sweet of him.

"I won't be able to hold back; that feels just too good ." He watched her mouth take him in. Deeper and deeper.

She relaxed her throat, her nature taking over perhaps, and took him all the way in. She was unable to breathe for a moment, but it was just too incredible to stop, feeling him so deep down her throat. She backed off to just take in the sensitive areas around the head. Now able to breathe again, she moaned in pleasure, one hand stroking herself, feeling her own wetness and arousal. Bobbing shallowly and faster, she picked up the pace as he added his moans to hers. She knew he was about to come and didn't stop, wanting to taste him, drink him down. He tensed and jerked forward with her movements. He watched for a moment longer before throwing his head back and exclaiming, "Oh, fuck Anja!"

She felt it as he exploded into her mouth. A wave of energy followed, sending her over the edge, too, as she felt his orgasm mixed with hers. Her orgasm was intense as she tasted him. Pulse after pulse of semen filled her mouth, too much to swallow all at once. A little escaped down her chin and dripped down onto his length, which she greedily licked up, savoring the taste. She was smiling up at him as his eyes opened to find her.

"Damn, Anja, that was not how it was supposed to be for your first time."

"Oh, but I think it was just what I needed. Don't worry," fingers still around him, "I'm not done yet, and neither are you!"

Anja moaned softly as Lucian's fingers grazed over her bare thighs, sending shivers up and down her spine. With a seductive smile, she took hold of his erection once more and began to stroke it in earnest, willing it to full harness again. Lucian groaned deeply and shivered as Anja's hand worked over his cock, bringing him fully erect again, still sensitive from just coming. As she continued to pleasure him, he reached out to touch her breasts, feeling the firm flesh under his hands and reaching down between her legs to feel her wetness. Anja moaned even louder at the added stimulation, her hips bucking forward. She could feel the slickness surrounding his fingers. She could feel his surge of desire as he reached down to stroke her clit in time with the movements of her hand on his cock.

She stopped stroking his cock for a moment, then climbed up to straddle him. Eyes locked together, she lowered herself so that his cock rested just at her entrance. With one last look into his eyes, she leaned her head back and sank in one sudden motion with a gasp, crying out with the bite of pain, which quickly merged with pure pleasure. She felt him seated deep inside her. He leaned up to catch one breast in his mouth and sucked on a nipple. Starting to move, she picked up the pace and began to meet his thrusts from below. She reached down and felt his cock under her fingers going in and out as she rubbed her clit, her fingers searching for more wetness. She brought her fingers to her mouth and tasted herself and their joining on them, savoring it on her tongue, licking them to add more moisture. She then returned her hand to her sex, using her now slick fingers to rub her clit once more. Looking down, she could see him burying himself in her. She watched in fascination at the sight of his cock sliding in and out, hardly believing it had finally happened. As she neared the edge, she locked eyes with Lucian again. She pushed him, and as they reached their peak together, Anja felt waves of pleasure wash over her body. She moaned, feeling Lucian's erection pulse, again and again, shooting into her, filling her. Energy—magic flowing along with his seed.

Her hunger was finally sated. For now.

As their breathing settled back to a more normal pace, Lucian couldn't help but feel wholly ruined for any other woman. Her ability to read emotions and intentions informed her, and she reveled in it.

With a sense of intimacy still hanging in the air, Lucian placed a call to room service. The atmosphere was light yet potent, as though the room was conscious of the magnitude of what transpired between them. When the meal arrived, accompanied by a bottle of wine, the staff discreetly set it up and departed, leaving them in their private sanctuary. They sat down to dine, but it was evident that the sustenance they craved couldn't be found on their plates. As Lucian poured the wine, Anja looked into his eyes, sensing it was time to reveal a significant piece of her newly discovered self.

"Lucian, there's something I need to share with you," she began cautiously. "What has happened to me, the change you've sensed, is more profound than even I initially understood."

Lucian met her eyes. She could sense he was intrigued but prepared for whatever revelation she might offer.

"I've awakened a part of myself that's been dormant. Another piece of my soul, you might say," she continued. "It's of Otherkin or, more significantly, demonkin. Specifically, a succubus. Passed down, most likely, from one of Naamah's lines."

The weight of her words settled in the space between them, but Lucian didn't flinch. Instead, his eyes searched hers, trying to comprehend the full scope of what she was saying.

"That explains the intensity," he murmured, "the magnetism that I've found so irresistibly attractive."

Anja nodded, relieved by his reaction yet equally excited about what this meant for them. "I've always felt different, even before I knew what it was—what I am. But now, I've not only recognized it but embraced it. And it changes everything."

"Changes?" Lucian asked, finally taking a sip of his wine.

"It amplifies my abilities, my senses, even my influence over emotions and physical well-being. And," she paused for a moment, choosing her words carefully, "it may mean that our connection can be deeper, more intense, than a typical relationship."

He set down his wine glass, capturing her eyes with an electrifying gaze. "I can't say I'm opposed to exploring the depths of what that might mean. So you're saying I have my own sex fiend now?" he said, leaning closer and grinning.

"Lucian! Well, yes, I suppose that is kind of true. And we will explore it in much more depth," Anja assured him, her eyes twinkling in a way that left no room for doubt. "This is only the start for us."

They toasted to new beginnings and boundless possibilities, each fully aware that they were venturing into uncharted territory.

Anja looked deeply into Lucian's eyes as they sat on the plush sofa, savoring the last sips of their wine. "Lucian, there are more things about me that I've awakened." Her gaze remained unwavering. "I can sense thoughts and desires in others. It's not mind reading per se, but I understand their motivations and wishes."

"Interesting," he murmured.

"There's more," she continued. "I believe I can also persuade people, my words carrying an influence that's hard for them to resist. Combined with sensing their feelings, I could probably convince someone of just about anything."

"So, you're saying you could affect what they believe or want?" he remarked, a hint of amusement in his voice. "Like seducing someone in a hotel room?"

"Something like that," she grinned. "Additionally, my capabilities as a seer have amplified. It used to be vague feelings, but now it's becoming clearer and more specific. It's a lineage gift, something my grandmother Madeline had and her grandmother before her."

Lucian felt tensed. The powers she described were both intriguing and daunting.

"Also, I can see auras now. It's conditional, dependent on my focus and the environment, but I can see them. I can see yours. It's faint still. And it's akin to mine—demonkin. I have a feeling I know which you're related to, but we'll try to awaken that part of you tomorrow. For now, let's just sleep and dream."

With that, they rose from the sofa, their hands lightly touching as they made their way to the bed. Slipping under the covers, they found themselves enveloped in the comfort and warmth of each other's presence.

Seventeen

The following morning, the sun bathed the suite's common area in a warm, gentle glow. Lucian had ordered an impressive breakfast spread that covered the entire length of the dining table. Croissants, cheeses, fresh fruits, strong coffee, and a variety of other treats filled the room with irresistible aromas. The platter of fish, however, sat mostly untouched. Everyone had gathered around the table, their moods noticeably lighter than the day before. The team had settled into a comfortable camaraderie, with teasing exchanges and laughter punctuating the meal.

"Fish for breakfast?" Ian raised an eyebrow, casting a dubious glance at the smoked salmon. "That's not quite my taste."

"More for me, then," Emma grinned, scooping a generous helping onto her plate. "Don't knock it till you've tried it."

Claire made a playful face. "I'll pass, thank you."

Lucian's announcement that soon they would have the complete DNA and epigenetic profiles brought an immediate focus to the room. All eyes turned to him, the previous lightheartedness giving way to anticipation and curiosity. Anja, however, seemed different. Her eyes were sharpened as though she was seeing things in a way she never had before. Her perception had shifted, and her understanding of the situation seemed to have deepened. Lucian noticed the change in her, sensing she held new insights.

"I have some answers," she said quietly, her voice carrying an air of confidence and determination. "But I'll share them at NexGen. There are some things I would like to see there first."

Everyone exchanged glances. Anja's transformation was palpable; they were all eager to learn what she had discovered.

Lucian continued, "Now that our belongings are securely stored here, we'll all travel together. But I have to ask: is anyone having second thoughts about participating in some experiments?"

The room was silent for a moment before Emma quipped, "As long as I don't end up howling at the moon, I'm in."

The tension broke, and they all joined in, speculating about possible wereanimals and the wild possibilities awaiting them. The energy in the room was electric, fueled by a shared sense of purpose and adventure. Finally, Lucian brought them back to the task at hand.

"Alright, everyone, let's head out. Isabelle is waiting."

They gathered their things, leaving behind the elegant suite and the remnants of breakfast. A sense of unity and determination filled the air as they headed to the limo. Driving toward NexGen, with the scenery passing by the windows, Lucian and Anja shared a look, and their connection deepened. They were on the edge of something profound. The world of science, magic, and human potential beckoned, and they were ready to answer the call.

At NexGen, the group was met by Isabelle, who excitedly informed them that all the results were in. Her eyes were wide with astonishment and curiosity as she explained the unprecedented findings.

"What's most surprising," Isabelle began, her voice filled with wonder, "is that in the second run for Anja, there was no return to inhibited flux receptors. This has never happened before in any previous tests."

She turned to Anja, a question in her eyes. "Your state of mind, the meditation, or the rituals seem to have unlocked or awakened permanent changes. This is an extraordinary discovery!"

Anja nodded, her face calm, but her eyes alight with the knowledge that something powerful had taken place within her. She then turned to Lucian, her voice determined.

"I think we should try another use of the serum for you, Lucian," she said, guided by her intuition. "But I want to wait on trying this on the others until we see how you respond. I believe you might have more insights for fine-tuning the process once you can. What do you think?"

Lucian looked thoughtful, then nodded, trusting Anja's judgment. "I agree. Let's see what the results show for them first. There may be unique patterns that we can leverage."

They gathered around the display as Isabelle brought up the results for the guards. While analyzing the data, Anja surprised Lucian and Isabelle again by pointing out specific patterns and connections they hadn't noticed. Isabelle looked up from the screen, her eyes meeting Anja's. "Anja, your grasp on this subject matter is remarkable. Genetics isn't an easy field to navigate, especially not this quickly. How did you manage to pick it up so fast?"

Anja paused. "Let's just say that my gifts have expanded recently. I now have an eidetic memory and can learn new things quickly. That's helping me absorb the complex information easily."

Isabella's eyebrows lifted, impressed. "Well, your new gifts have provided us with a new lens to look through."

"Look here," Anja continued, tracing a particular sequence on the screen. "This seems to correlate with specific essential genetic markers. It could be the key to understanding how the flux receptors interact with different individuals."

Lucian and Isabelle stared at the screen, realization dawning on their faces. Anja's insight opened up a new path of exploration that could have profound implications for their research.

"You're right," Lucian said, his voice filled with respect and admiration. "This could change everything."

As the day progressed, they explored and theorized. Their drive for discovery pushed them forward, blurring the lines between science and the supernatural.

After reviewing the data, Anja's attention shifted to the guards. She looked deeply at each one in turn, her eyes probing and discerning, filled with newly awakened wisdom and knowledge.

First up, Emma. Anja's eyes softened as she started with a gentle quip. "No, Emma, I don't think you have to worry about howling at the moon."

A ripple of laughter passed through the room, but Anja's gaze moved to Claire, and the atmosphere shifted. "Though Claire may need to," she said, her voice serious.

Claire sucked in a breath, starting to shake her head but then locked her amber eyes on Anja. The room fell into a tense silence as Anja simply nodded.

"You have suspected, haven't you?" Anja asked, her voice gentle but filled with certainty. "Tales from your family? Secrets passed down?"

Claire closed her eyes and nodded, her face a mask of mixed emotions. The revelation hung heavy in the room; others looked on, awe in their eyes.

"I can see things now so much clearer than before. Little signs or tells, if you will, coupled with observations of the past few days," she explained, not revealing the entire depth of her newly discovered talent. "Yesterday, with the aid of science and ritual, I accepted what I am, and with it came new abilities that I hadn't imagined possible but now are a part of me. If you are willing to try, you could be more, too."

Anja's attention returned to Emma, whose eyes were now wide, a touch of defiance in their green depths. The room seemed to hold its breath as Anja studied her, a new understanding dawning in her eyes.

"Emma," she began, her voice soft and probing, "look at your phone. What do you see? You thought it might be a striking picture that you could relate to. Look again. See a reflection of your inner self. I noticed the picture a few days ago, and it was interesting. I can see the way you move and stand ready, the way you observe your surroundings missing nothing, and the way you can blend into the background."

Emma's hand trembled slightly as she held up her phone, and the room went still. The lock screen picture displayed a large black cat, its eyes a stunning green, eerily mirroring Emma's eyes. The silence stretched out, charged with meaning and revelation. The black cat, a symbol of intuition, mystery, and transformation, seems to have chosen Emma, or perhaps she has chosen it. The connection ran deeper than mere coincidence; it was a reflection of something intrinsic, something that resonated with her very soul.

The others in the room watched, a sense of awe and wonder growing. Their world had shifted again, unveiling yet another layer of the hidden and the extraordinary.

Anja's eyes lingered on Emma's for a moment longer, a knowing smile on her lips. She could also sense a desire forming in Emma's thoughts, an attraction she tried to suppress. Anja paused a moment before turning away, ready to explore the next revelation.

Anja's piercing gaze turned next to Carlos, and the room could sense a slight change in the air as she focused on him. The much larger man seemed somehow unnerved by Anja's attention, his eyes flicking away as he unconsciously touched his left shoulder with his hand. Anja's slender hand reached out and rested over his, her touch gentle yet firm.

"You have tales in your family, too, don't you?" she asked softly, her voice resonating with something ancient and knowing. "Out in the field, you have seen them circling, flying by, or watching out for you? What is it, Carlos? What do you dream of? Flying? While at the funeral, I noticed you looking at one in the trees as it watched over us in the rain."

The room waited, the silence filled with anticipation and a palpable tension. Carlos's eyes met Anja's, and something unspoken passed between them. When he finally spoke, his voice was low but filled with conviction.

"Falcon," he said, the word heavy with meaning.

Anja nodded in acceptance, her eyes gleaming with insight. The connection between Carlos and the falcon was more than a family tale; it was a spiritual link, a part of his essence that reflected his inner strength, agility, and freedom.

The others watched, realizing these revelations were not mere chance or coincidence. Anja's abilities to see into each individual's core and uncover hidden truths and connections were both mesmerizing and humbling. And, a little scary.

Anja looked at Ian, her eyes filled with understanding. Her hand reached out to rest gently on his chest, and her voice showed profound reverence while speaking to him.

"Ian of Clan MacGregor," she said, her words resonating with the weight of history and legacy. "You have also heard tales and have been sworn to secrecy. I think that secrecy should still be kept for all outside this room, but it is your choice for us. Yours is a wise and noble heritage, jealously guarded. I will leave it to you to reveal, but you can claim it, make it more than a talisman. Again, at the funeral, I watched as you held your hand to it as it rested under your shirt as the bagpipes played."

Though speaking, her eyes never left Ian's. There was a sense of connection, of deep knowing that passed between them. Ian's expression changed, becoming one of acceptance and determination. Slowly, he reached around his neck and extracted an etched and worn bone hanging from a simple leather thong. Roughly the size of a human thumb, the talisman had an organic, asymmetrical shape. Its curves and contours fit naturally in Ian's hand as though it were an extension of himself.

"This talisman has been in my family for many generations," he said, holding it up for the others to see. "It's more than a mere object; it's a symbol of our heritage, our lineage. One that traces back to something…ancient."

His voice carried a note of pride, and his eyes shone with the knowledge of something powerful. The room was filled with anticipation as he continued to speak of his family's legacy, the secrets they have guarded, and the potential that lay within—the wisdom and strength of a bear.

Isabelle made preparations to inject Lucian with a dose of the serum. Eyes followed them as Isabelle, Lucian, and Anja departed for the relaxation room. The room seemed to hum with a subtle energy as Anja and Lucian prepared for the ritual. The atmosphere was charged with anticipation and connection, the boundaries of the conventional world dissolving as they stepped into the room.

"Lucian, since you have not had extensive occult training, I can guide you and help your mind accept what it needs. Your deep understanding of Quantum Chemistry fills in its place. Our connection from last night also builds on a bond of intimacy. For me, the connection to you is sexual at its heart, so to amplify that, I want to be naked with you for this. To feel the skin-to-skin connection. I can use that to help guide you into yourself."

"And besides," she added with a smile, "I am part sex demon after all."

Lucian started to smile and say something, but Anja placed a finger over his lips and let it linger momentarily. They both disrobed; the shedding of clothing was a symbolic shedding of constraints and expectations. Their bodies would become canvases for ritual symbols and movements, weaving together science, magic, mind, and soul.

As Lucian sat crosslegged on the soft carpet, Anja guided Lucian with a gentle touch, her voice a soft melody as she led him through ancient words and gestures picked from her memories, a complex symphony of sounds and movements. They moved together, their bodies harmonizing in a dance that transcended physicality, reaching into the very essence of their beings. Lucian's eyes locked onto Anja's, and he saw her glowing, an ethereal light emanating from her very core. He fell into her eyes, lost in their depths, feeling a connection beyond mere attraction, touching something primal and profound.

Anja straddled him, getting close, touching her breasts to his chest as she raised up and then slid down onto his erection and stilled, taking him all the way in, wet and ready for him inside her. She continued to chant and drew him along pathways his eyes couldn't see, but his mind was now following.

The ritual built intensity, the energy in the room swirling around them, enveloping them in a cocoon of warmth and connection. Anja moved up and down in time with the chants, feeling him slide in and out. Time lost its meaning as they moved together, their bodies and minds intertwining, reaching for something that lay just beyond the veil of the ordinary world. And then, in a moment that felt both infinite and fleeting, it happened. A new door unlocked within Lucian, a gateway to a realm of understanding and ability that he had never before accessed. His mind opened, his memory expanded, and knowledge flowed into him with a clarity and speed that was both exhilarating and humbling. At that moment, they both climaxed together, their orgasms intense. Anja felt the spurts deep in her, and as she did, she took and fed on the energy and sent it back to Lucian, which she drew back, intensifying it even more.

They returned to themselves slowly, the room settling around them, the glow fading but leaving a lingering warmth behind. They remained locked together but changed in ways words couldn't fully capture. Lucian pulled her in and held her close, his eyes reflecting his wonder.

"I see it now, Anja. Feel it."

She smiled at him, her eyes sparkling with shared joy and connection. "We've only just begun, Lucian. Together, we can explore so much more."

Lucian smiled. "I don't know if I can stand much more...or even stand at all right now."

"Lucian, have you ever considered that your talents in quantum biology or chemistry might be, let's say, otherworldly?"

Lucian paused, his brow furrowing as if wrestling with the weight of her words. "You mean like a gift?"

Anja nodded, a half smile curving her lips. "More like a legacy. I believe your lineage traces back to Marbas—an entity associated with healing and hidden wisdom. You're not just scientifically gifted; you're gifted, gifted."

Leaning back, Lucian took a moment to process the information. "So, you're telling me that my affinity with understanding biological systems down to their quantum mechanics...is because I have demonkin blood?"

"Yes," Anja confirmed, her eyes locking onto his with a sense of earnestness. "It's why you're so uncannily good at what you do. But the gift isn't just scientific, Lucian. It's far more...comprehensive."

Lucian looked intrigued, perhaps even a bit incredulous. "How so?"

Anja leaned in, her eyes suddenly serious. "Well, Marbas is known for the ability to heal, among other things. Could it be possible that you can actually 'tune' quantum states in biological tissues? Imagine mending damaged cells or even shifting your genetic makeup."

He started to speak, "Shapeshifting? That's rather..."

Anja cut him off, her eyes holding a gravity that told him she was not jesting. "Don't underestimate the power of your legacy, Lucian. It's not mere folklore or fantasy; it's a part of who you are now."

The words hung in the air. Lucian's eyes met hers again, this time carrying a hint of newfound understanding as if a curtain had been lifted or a door had opened.

Framing her next words carefully. "There are other cultures that speak of shapeshifting abilities like that, you know. Native American lore, for example, speaks of skin-walkers—beings with the ability to turn into animals or even other people. Their powers may have been derived from the same line as yours. I would guess that not all of Marbas' lines manifest exactly the same. It may have to do with culture, learning, experience, or many other factors."

Lucian listened intently, the gears in his scientific mind visibly turning as he tried to mesh folklore with genetics.

"Could it be that these stories of skin-walkers also hint at some sort of quantum-level process? We don't know how these abilities would work exactly, but it's fascinating to consider the possibilities," she continued.

Lucian nodded, taking it all in. "So, you're suggesting that I could aid Claire or Emma in awakening their potential and, perhaps, with enough mastery, I might be able to unlock those abilities in myself as well?"

Her lips twitched as if suppressing a knowing smile. "Yes, Lucian, but more as well for you. You may not be limited to just one form, but perhaps any that you can internalize from DNA patterns.

"The serum you're working on is not just a triumph of modern biology. If tailored correctly to their unique genetics, it should serve as the catalyst the others need. Think of it as a...key, if you will, unlocking their dormant abilities. It could be transformative in more ways than one."

The implication of Anja's words resonated with Lucian. His gaze sharpened, eyes alight.

"Relax for a bit, and then we can head back and see what you can sense from them and review their testing results."

After relaxing and languidly touching and kissing some more, they get dressed again and head back to the office.

Back in the familiar surroundings of Isabella's office, Lucian's excitement and anticipation were palpable. The ritual's success had opened up new avenues of exploration, and Lucian's mind was rife with possibilities. He eagerly outlined his ideas for specific serum enhancements for the guards, each tailored to their unique attributes. Isabelle listened intently and took notes, her eyes holding intrigue and admiration for the depth of Lucian's insights and the innovation of his approach. She quickly agreed to start on the formulations and prepare additional doses of the serum used by Lucian and Anja. Her scientific curiosity had been supercharged, and she recognized the potential for more groundbreaking discoveries.

Lucian's decision to relocate the experiments to his estate in New York was met with acceptance. The need for privacy and space was clear, especially as they delved into more ambitious and complex trials. Isabelle ensured that all necessary supplies, including blood sample taking equipment, would be arranged and promised to work closely with Lucian and Anja on the ongoing analysis.

The team's energy was infectious, and the room hummed with the excitement of innovation and the unknown. The boundaries of science and magic had been stretched, and they were standing on the brink of a new frontier. The six of them headed out with a few last instructions from Lucian to Isabelle. They settled quietly in the limo on their way back to the hotel. The guards were quiet and contemplative but with an undertone of eagerness as well.

As Lucian and Anja sat together in the back of the limo, the world around them seemed to pulse with potential, the very fabric of reality tinged with a new kind of magic. Their connection deepened, not just as lovers but as pioneers of a path that was as heady as it was uncertain. They shared knowing glances, understanding they were stepping into the unknown together. But they were doing so confidently, guided by their instincts, intellect, and a connection that transcended the mundane.

The urgency in Lucian's voice left no room for delay. Momentum was building, and everyone could feel it. They packed their belongings in haste and returned to the limo, the atmosphere charged with purpose. The flight back was a blur of activity, with Lucian orchestrating ground preparations from the air. His fingers flew over his phone, making arrangements and ensuring that everything would be ready at the estate. The sense of expectation grew as they touched down at Teterboro Airport and swiftly checked in. Another flight took them upstate. The scenery changed, giving way to lush countryside and the serene beauty of upstate New York.

As the private jet touched down on the tarmac, the door soon opened to reveal Mark, standing a respectful distance away but waiting for their arrival. He was a man in his late forties; his salt-and-pepper hair cut in a military fashion highlighted his stern yet welcoming demeanor.

Lucian descended the steps and extended his hand. "Mark, it's good to see you, especially under these circumstances."

Mark shook his hand firmly. "Likewise, Mr. Miller. Despite the recent events, we've been doing everything we can to ensure the estate is ready for you. How are you holding up?"

"It's been a challenging time, to say the least," Lucian said, his eyes momentarily clouding. "But we are hanging in there. How about the staff? How are they coping?"

"We're all doing our best, sir. Keeping busy has been a good distraction for most," Mark replied, his tone solemn yet steadfast.

"That's good to hear. Let me introduce you to my team," Lucian turned back to the jet's staircase as his entourage began to make their way down. "First, this is Anja."

Anja stepped forward and extended her hand, her gaze meeting Mark's. "Nice to meet you, Mark."

After a round of introductions, Mark added, "Just so you are all aware, I am armed and would like to avoid misunderstandings. I have training and additional weapons available."

Ian looked at Mark and said, "I appreciate your candor and concern. I think you could be handy to have around. We'll need to discuss this further once we settle in."

Lucian gestured toward the white limo waiting nearby. "Shall we?"

"Of course, sir," Mark nodded, stepping aside to let everyone proceed.

The estate loomed majestic, framed by centuries-old trees and a well-cared-for landscape. For a moment, Lucian paused, absorbing the view as if it could fortify him for what lay ahead. Then, with a nod to himself, he led the way towards the entrance.

The grand doors swung open almost ceremoniously, revealing an equally impressive foyer adorned with intricately carved wood and works of art that spanned centuries. Standing at the entrance was Victor, the butler, who radiated the same kind of timelessness as the estate itself.

"Welcome back, Mr. Miller," Victor greeted with an inclined head. His deep-set eyes took in the entourage following Lucian. "I trust your journey was smooth?"

"As smooth as it could be, Victor," Lucian replied. "Thank you for gathering the staff. It will be good to meet everyone together."

"Of course, sir. If you would kindly follow me," Victor beckoned as he turned on his heels, leading the way to a spacious receiving area where the rest of the household staff had assembled.

Anja and the bodyguards followed Lucian closely, their eyes taking in the interior while their senses remained keenly alert, attuned to the nuances of this new environment.

Lucian stepped into the receiving area, where various faces, young and old, met his gaze with apprehension and anticipation. Each person stood with a sense of duty, clearly committed to their respective roles within the grand estate.

"As you know, these are trying times for all of us," Lucian began, sweeping his gaze across the room. "I appreciate your dedication and your service. I'd like you to meet some important people joining our efforts."

He introduced Anja, Ian, Carlos, Emma, and Claire to the staff, each nodding or shaking hands as appropriate when their name was called.

"Thank you, everyone," Lucian concluded. "We have much to do, and I have every confidence that we will achieve great things together. For now, let's get everyone settled in. There will be time for more detailed briefings soon."

"Certainly, Mr. Miller," Elena, the chef, replied with a warm smile. "Any preferences for tonight's menu?"

Lucian pondered briefly, glancing over at Anja and his team. "Something comforting would be perfect. We've all had a rather intense period of travel and change."

"I understand," Elena nodded. "I can do that. It will be ready in a few hours, giving everyone ample time to settle in and refresh themselves."

"Thank you, Elena. That sounds perfect," Lucian confirmed, appreciative of her keen understanding of the group's needs.

Elena nodded, returning to the kitchen. Lucian could almost see her mind was already buzzing with ideas for a dinner that would balance comfort and sophistication.

Lucian looked around at his assembled team. "Everyone, please make yourselves at home. Victor will show you to your living quarters. Get settled, rest up. We've got a big evening ahead, and it starts with getting to know each other a little better over Elena's excellent cooking."

Lucian then turned his attention to Ian and the other bodyguards. "I've had security upgraded throughout the estate. A monitoring room downstairs is equipped with cameras and sensors covering the entire grounds. Mark Harrison also has security and weapons training and can help augment the team as needed."

Victor stepped forward, his demeanor both welcoming and professional. "If you would kindly follow me, I'll take you to your rooms. Please don't hesitate to let me know if you need anything."

Anja exchanged a knowing look with Lucian. Indeed, as inviting as the estate was, it was clear that it would be the stage for pivotal events in the days to come. For now, though, it was a sanctuary, a place for them to gather their strength.

Eighteen

DINNER IN THE lavish dining room was nothing short of extravagant. Elena, the gifted chef, had prepared a three-course meal that made even the most elite restaurants pale in comparison. The table was adorned with white linen, gleaming silverware, and porcelain plates; the centerpiece, a modest yet elegant bouquet of fresh flowers from the gardens, brought a smile to Anja.

The first course was a delicate lobster bisque enriched with a dollop of crème fraîche and a hint of saffron. There were perfectly cooked filet mignons for the main course, set atop a bed of sautéed wild mushrooms and a side of truffled mashed potatoes. Dessert was a delightful raspberry mousse accented with a mint sprig and a drizzle of dark chocolate sauce.

As they ate, a comfortable camaraderie settled over the room. Ian, Carlos, Emma, and Claire had blended seamlessly into roles that were more than just bodyguards; they were partners in an unfolding tale of extraordinary events. Each member at the table was integral, a spoke in a wheel of intricate dynamics and unique capabilities.

With the completion of the meal, Lucian graciously thanked Elena and dismissed her and the other staff to their quarters, located in a separate building on the estate's vast grounds. Once the door closed behind the departing staff, Lucian turned his attention back to the table.

"Firstly, I thank you all for being here with me," he began, making eye contact with each individual. "Your presence, skills, and dedication are invaluable to me, Anja, and the cause we're undertaking."

Anja felt a warmth flush through her at Lucian's words, her eyes meeting his with gratitude and affection. She sensed a deep-seated respect for every person in the room, not just Lucian. They were a team, a unit, a microcosm of a greater unknown future.

"As you know," Lucian continued, "we have the potential to unlock abilities and skills that extend beyond the ordinary. Anja and I have already begun this process, but it's essential that we also explore this potential in each of you."

He then opened the floor for discussion, "We need to be smart about this, weigh the risks and benefits. Any suggestions on how to proceed?"

"I think," Anja added, "that part of the process is awakening the otherkin aspects within each of you. Here, we have a safe, controlled environment to do this."

The discussions continued with everyone contributing suggestions and ideas ranging from baseline testing to record keeping and consultations with Isabelle at NexGen. Anja listened intently to everyone's suggestions, nodding her agreement. As the conversation lulled momentarily, she leaned forward, her gaze capturing everyone's attention.

"I've been thinking about the order in which we should awaken these otherkin aspects," she began, her voice steady. "Perhaps it might be best to first start with the smaller, less formidable variants and move upward from there. This could give us a better understanding of how the process affects us mentally and physically."

"Meaning?" Carlos inquired, intrigued by her proposal.

"Well," Anja elaborated, "I suggest we start with you, Carlos. Your falcon, or bird of prey aspect, could be our initial focus. Next would be Emma, awakening her feline side. Claire, you would follow, and if all goes as expected, Ian would be last."

Lucian considered Anja's suggestion before nodding thoughtfully. "That sounds like a logical approach. By starting with less intimidating forms, we can minimize risks while gaining invaluable insights. Ian," he turned to the man in question, "given that you'll be the last in this initial round, it might be beneficial for you to familiarize yourself further with the estate and our new security enhancements in the meantime."

Ian nodded. "I can start on that first thing tomorrow. Familiarity with the grounds and preparedness for any scenario is crucial."

The room resonated with a collective agreement. The plans were becoming more concrete, and though the road ahead was uncharted, the sense of unity and shared resolve made it seem more attainable.

"So, it's settled then," Lucian concluded. "Carlos, you'll be up first. We'll establish baseline tests for each of you before we start the awakening process. Emma, Claire, you'll follow. And Ian, you'll take point on the estate and security measures."

He added, "We'll start setting things up in the morning. For tonight, rest well. We have a monumental set of tasks ahead."

As the meeting adjourned and they began to leave the room, Anja felt a surge of hope tempered by the weight of their collective responsibilities. Yet at that moment, looking around at those she'd come to regard as more than allies—indeed, as her newfound family —she knew they were ready, as ready as they'd ever be.

He read the message from the grandmaster carefully, absorbing the gravity of the situation and the trust vested in him.

Subject: Re: Code Red—Reassessment Required

USA/NE Controller,

Your vigilance is commendable. I share your urgency and appreciate your loyalty to the Sodality in these times of high tension and uncertainty.

We face a myriad of challenges on multiple fronts. Our assets in the UK and Europe were regrettably limited in their abilities to intervene. Lucian Miller, Anja Kinzey, and their team of bodyguards have proven to be elusive, a concern we must not underestimate. The sudden disappearance of Howard Miller further complicates matters. His absence is disquieting and warrants investigation.

Given that Lucian Miller appears to have retreated to his upstate mansion in New York, we must use this as an opportunity. Plans must be devised with utmost discretion and efficacy for my review. I hereby authorize the mobilization of all resources at your disposal.

We must be prepared to act swiftly and decisively. We may need to make sacrifices, but remember, the longevity of the Sodality and our clandestine objectives remain paramount.

Awaiting your detailed proposals,

Grandmaster.

His fingers hovered over the keyboard as he began to draft plans that would align with the grandmaster's directives. Time was of the essence, but so was meticulous planning. He was determined to take any actions necessary, whatever the personal cost. With the grandmaster's approval to utilize all resources, the stakes had escalated, but so had the tools at his disposal. He remained a sentinel, ready to bring to bear the full weight of the Sodality's network to secure their aims. Crafting a new message, Richard began to type.

Subject: Re: Urgent Situation

Raven,

Your situation analysis and the subtle approach outlined are apt under the current circumstances. Your plan to drive a wedge between Lucian and Anja shows promise. I approve of the strategy of planting false, incriminating information to create doubt and discord between them. Make sure the planted information appears convincing and blends seamlessly with actual events to ensure credibility.

The utilization of Vanessa Delacroix's relationship with Lucian also remains advantageous. Creating compromising photographs and other materials is a good tactic, but it must be executed with the highest level of precision.

I recommend you extend your efforts to include seeding discord at Anja's workplace, the Morgan Library. Leverage the incident from her high school years to create a narrative that questions her character. This could involve generating images or creating rumors that place her credibility under scrutiny. The idea here is to weaken her professional standing and add further stressors to her relationship with Lucian.

I authorize you to put these actions in motion as soon as feasible. Time is of the essence, but the risk of exposure remains our greatest threat. Therefore, every move must be calculated and each action meticulously executed.

Continue to keep me updated on your progress. Your loyalty and dedication to the Sodality are highly valued.

Proceed with caution, but do proceed.

Controller,

USA/NE

With the controller's approval, Raven felt a surge of anticipation. The controller's added suggestion regarding the Morgan Library gave Raven an additional point of attack, a way to extend the discord. The plan was complex and multi-pronged, but Raven was well-versed in the art of deception and subterfuge. The game had evolved, and the stakes had skyrocketed, but Raven was prepared for the intricate dance ahead.

Anja lay beside Lucian, the morning sunlight filtering through the curtains and casting soft, golden rays across the bed. The atmosphere was serene, yet Anja felt a knot of tension pondering the delicate subject she needed to broach.

"Lucian," she began cautiously, "there's something I need to discuss with you, something a little sensitive."

Lucian turned toward her, his eyes meeting hers. "What's on your mind?"

She exhaled softly, choosing her words carefully. "You know how we've been talking about awakening the others—starting with Carlos?"

He nodded. "Yes?"

Anja continued, "Well, the awakening process can be deeply personal, intimate even. Given that each of us might have different triggers or catalysts to tap into our otherkin sides, it could be that for some, a...a more sensual or even sexual approach may be necessary. It may not come up, but rather than wait and have the issue be an awkward surprise, I would rather address it upfront."

Understanding dawned on Lucian's face, but Anja sensed no judgment there. "You're saying that for Carlos or others, that connection may be needed for awakening?"

"Yes," she confirmed. "How would you feel if that were the case?"

Lucian paused, weighing his words. "Anja, I trust you. And I trust that whatever methods you choose will be in the best interest of helping Carlos or the others awaken. I remember what you did for me quite well, so I understand what you are saying. Our goal is to understand ourselves better and harness the potential within us. If that requires crossing some boundaries, then I'm okay with it. I know it's for the right reasons."

Anja felt a wave of relief wash over her. "Thank you, Lucian. I just didn't want to proceed without having this conversation first."

Lucian pulled her close, sealing his words with a tender kiss. "I couldn't agree more. As long as we're clear and honest with each other, we can navigate any...awkward situations that may come up."

Lucian and Anja, now dressed and refreshed, descended the grand staircase and headed toward the dining room. As they stepped in, they found a breakfast spread waiting for them. Elena had prepared an array of classic American breakfast items: fluffy scrambled eggs, crisp bacon, stacks of buttermilk pancakes with maple syrup, and fresh fruits. Carlos, Emma, Claire, and Ian were already seated, animatedly discussing the day's plans over cups of coffee.

"Morning, everyone," Lucian greeted as he sat at the head of the table, Anja beside him. "Elena seems to have outdone herself today."

"Good morning," the group echoed back, welcoming them into the discussion.

"So, what's the game plan for today?" Ian asked, looking between Anja and Lucian.

"We were planning on starting the awakening process, beginning with Carlos," Anja shared, glancing thoughtfully at Carlos. "In terms of falcon traits or characteristics we might be looking to awaken, I've made a list. These are general baseline tests for before and after the process."

Going from memory, she went through the list. "Enhanced visual acuity, speed and agility, precision, instinctual awareness, and strength. Perhaps even the ability to attract various local raptors or projections like the ability to command actions or see through their eyes."

Almost as an afterthought, she added. "Shifting. Due to the mass disparity, I think it would be best not to attempt that until we know more."

Carlos looked intrigued, clearly fascinated by the possibilities. "This sounds incredible. A little overwhelming, maybe, but exciting for sure."

"I think the awakening will be a multi-step process," Lucian added. "It's not something that will happen all at once. We'll take it slowly, methodically, making sure we're all comfortable at each step."

Anja interjected, "And we'll keep an open dialogue throughout the process. If, at any point, anyone feels uncomfortable, we will pause and reassess."

Nods of agreement circled the table.

"Then it's settled," Lucian concluded. "We'll prepare to begin Carlos' awakening process after breakfast. The rest of you should think about testing each other and recording baselines. Some of the same basic concepts as for Carlos."

Anja took a bite of her scrambled eggs, feeling the weight of the responsibility and an exhilarating sense of potential. Today was a new beginning for all of them, and she couldn't help but wonder what incredible transformations awaited them on the horizon.

In the lush openness of the estate's extensive grounds, a series of testing stations were set up, each designed to measure and evaluate the specific traits Anja and Lucian had identified as indicative of falcon-like abilities. Their team worked diligently, ensuring each station had the necessary equipment and safety measures. Once the baseline tests were completed, results were gathered to compare initial metrics with any observable changes post-awakening. For now, they had a snapshot—a starting point, a benchmark that would help them quantify and understand any changes.

Carlos and Anja found a secluded spot by the lake, the gentle rippling of the water mirroring the nervous anticipation that filled the air between them. Lucian had administered the serum designed for Carlos just moments ago before retreating up the path to the estate, and now the two awaited its effects.

Carlos looked contemplative, "I do feel a tingling sensation, like electricity running through my veins."

Anja looked into his eyes, fully aware of the significance of the moment ahead. "Before we go any further, I want to talk about intimacy. This process might require us to cross some boundaries. Do you have any reservations or specific limits you want to set?"

Carlos paused, considering the weight of the question. His eyes met Anja's, the seriousness of the situation reflected in them.

"I trust you, Anja. But I'd say, let's take it step by step. If at any point something feels wrong or uncomfortable for either of us, we'll stop."

Anja nodded, touched by the trust Carlos was placing in her. "Absolutely, communication is key. If you're uncomfortable or need a break, just say the word."

Carlos smiled. "Sounds like a plan."

Anja took a deep breath, grounding herself. The shimmering lake in front of them seemed to reflect not just the trees and sky but also the emotional complexities of what lay ahead. She knew her abilities could influence Carlos' boundaries and desires, but she also had the power to read his innermost feelings and sense his comfort zones. She felt a responsibility to respect those boundaries, even as she held the power to transcend them.

Focusing on Carlos, she saw a mix of commitment and trust that reassured her. "Close your eyes," she instructed, her voice both soft and authoritative.

Carlos obeyed, his eyes shutting as if he were about to enter a deep meditation. Anja took this moment to recall a chant she had learned from her grandmother, one that had been passed down through her lineage. The words were old, predating most modern languages, yet their power seemed timeless. Her voice became almost melodic as she began to chant, each word perfectly articulated. As the chant echoed between them, she reached out with her mind, gently touching the periphery of Carlos' thoughts. She sensed his heightened awareness, the tingling he had described amplified. Guiding him, she encouraged his mind along the pathways that would awaken falcon traits within him. Her chant acted as a guide, directing his consciousness to merge with the latent instincts that had been dormant.

Carlos' face was serene, his breaths coming out in a slow, rhythmic pattern. Anja felt him relax under her mental touch, his trust and openness allowing her to delve deeper, to push gently against his mental boundaries just enough to nudge him into a new realm of awareness.

Finally, Anja felt it, a shift, subtle but definite. As if a door had been unlocked, Carlos' mind seemed to expand, and his essence reaching out beyond its human limitations. The traits that had been dormant now stirred to life, rising to the surface of his consciousness. She stopped chanting, and a few moments of silence filled the air. Then she whispered, "Open your eyes, Carlos."

Carlos did so, and for a moment, Anja thought she saw a gleam in them, an almost avian sharpness that hadn't been there before. Both realized something profound had changed, and yet, his essence as an individual remained, magnified and united by this unique, shared experience.

Carlos looked up to see a falcon perched on a branch high above them. Its eyes seemed to lock onto his as if recognizing a kindred spirit. Anja nodded encouragingly.

"See if you can call it down," she suggested.

A bit hesitantly, Carlos lifted his arm and made a soft whistling sound, like a call. The falcon launched itself off the branch, circled once above them, and then gently landed on his outstretched arm. Even without a falconer's glove, the bird's talons settled gently as if aware of the fragile human skin it perched upon. The connection was immediate and intense. He could sense the bird's thoughts and feel its sharp focus and boundless freedom. It was like looking into a mirror reflecting his physical self and his newfound spirit.

"Name it," Anja said, breaking into his reverie. "It will strengthen the bond."

Carlos looked into the falcon's eyes. "Her. Aria," he said softly, feeling that the name fit this majestic creature. The falcon seemed to approve, tightening her grip on his arm ever so slightly as if to acknowledge her new name.

Anja stood up, her eyes meeting Carlos'. "I'll leave you two to get to know each other. Explore your connection. See if you can look through Aria's eyes and feel what she feels."

Carlos nodded, his eyes never leaving the falcon. Anja turned to go, but not before she sensed Carlos' gratitude flooding through her, as palpable as a warm breeze. She returned to the mansion, leaving him to explore this newfound facet of himself.

Alone with Aria, Carlos focused on the deep connection he felt with the raptor. As he concentrated, his vision seemed to blur and shift. Suddenly, he found himself seeing from a vantage point high above, taking in the panoramic view of the estate, the lake shimmering like a jewel below him. He realized he was seeing through Aria's eyes. Amazed and a bit overwhelmed, he relaxed the connection, returning to his own perspective. Aria ruffled her feathers as if to confirm their newfound link. A sense of awe washed over Carlos. He felt a unity, not just with Aria, but with something much larger—nature, life, and the intricate connections that bind them all.

Sitting there, marveling at this newfound bond, Carlos knew he had crossed an irrevocable line. Life would never be the same again, which was more than okay. It was as if he had tapped into a primal force, an ancient energy, and he couldn't wait to explore it further.

At the dinner table that night, the atmosphere was electric. Elena had outdone herself once more, preparing a grand spread featuring roasted lamb, various colorful vegetables, and an apple pie that filled the room with its comforting aroma. Carlos was visibly elated as he recounted his afternoon experience with Aria, his newfound falcon companion.

"It was like we were two parts of the same whole. I saw through her eyes and sensed the world as she did. It's an indescribable feeling."

Equipped with a tablet, Emma added that she had recorded some initial baseline data for Carlos before the awakening. "Your visual acuity and reflexes are already above average. It will be fascinating to see how they have improved."

Lucian, listening intently, put down his fork and looked at Carlos. "Would you mind if I took a blood sample later? We should send the results to Isabelle for further analysis. Besides, it'd be good to compare your genetic markers before and after the awakening."

Carlos nodded in agreement, intrigued to learn about the potential scientific aspects of his transformation.

Anja, quietly observing the conversations, turned her gaze toward Emma. "What about you? Would you like to try awakening tonight? Do you feel ready?"

Emma looked thoughtful for a moment, her eyes meeting Anja's. "I think so," she finally said, her voice tinged with a mix of eagerness and a touch of apprehension. "I've been looking forward to this, and after hearing Carlos' experience, I think I would like to."

Anja nodded approvingly. "Good. Then let's make preparations for tonight. This is only the beginning, and each step we take brings us closer to understanding who we are and what we can become."

Nineteen

UNDER THE CLOAK of night, the trio made their way down to the lake, the beams of their flashlights slicing through the darkness. Reaching the lake's edge, Anja unfurled a thick, comfortable blanket on the grassy ground while Lucian prepared the serum tailored specifically for Emma. With a nod of mutual understanding, he injected the serum into Emma's arm. A brief moment of silence hung in the air before Lucian broke it.

"I'll leave you both to it," he said, his voice tinged with solemnity and respect for the ritual about to unfold. He turned and made his way back up the path, his flashlight gradually diminishing into the distance until it was just a pinprick of light.

Now alone in the moonlit forest, sitting comfortably and relaxing on the blanket, Anja turned her attention to Emma. "How are you feeling?" she inquired softly, her gaze searching Emma's face for any sign of discomfort.

Emma took a moment, feeling a subtle warmth radiating from the injection site. "It's strange; I feel a tingling sensation, but it's not unpleasant."

Anja nodded, pleased with Emma's response. "Good. Now, we should discuss the next part of the awakening. Intimacy can play a role in fully unlocking your otherkin self." She paused, wanting to tread delicately. "Are there any reservations or boundaries you'd like to establish before we proceed?"

Emma looked into Anja's eyes, sensing the genuine concern and respect there. "I trust you, Anja. I can't say I have a definitive list of reservations or boundaries. But I trust you'll be attuned to how I feel."

Anja felt grateful for Emma's trust. "Alright. Then let's begin."

Anja took a deep breath and re-established eye contact, her focus narrowing while trying to read Emma's emotional state once more. Despite Emma's words of readiness, the resistance remained tangible. Perhaps it was tied to the desire and attraction she had sensed before. Anja released her breath slowly, carefully weighing her words. "Emma, I'm sensing there's still some resistance within you. It's completely alright, but I think we might need a bolder, more intimate approach to help you break through. How do you feel about that?"

Emma hesitated before speaking, her eyes dropping momentarily. "You're asking about intimacy with another woman, aren't you?"

Anja nodded. "Yes, I am. I sense that you're attracted to women, including me."

There was a pause, and then Emma looked up, locking eyes with Anja once more. "You're not mistaken. I'm bisexual. I have experienced both, though I do tend to enjoy women more. But I've never explored that side of myself in a context like this, something so…spiritual, transformational."

"Intimacy can be a powerful catalyst for personal and spiritual change; don't think of it in a separate context, just be yourself," Anja said softly, her gaze still fixed on Emma. "If you're comfortable, this could be the key to unlocking the part of you we're trying to awaken."

Emma took a deep breath, her eyes searching Anja's. Finally, she nodded. "Alright, let's try it. I have to say the prospect is arousing, and I do find you very attractive."

"Emma, I should be honest with you," Anja began, choosing her words carefully. "I've never been with another woman intimately. However, I've always been curious about it, and I can certainly appreciate the beauty of women…your beauty."

Emma looked pleased at the compliment. "Thanks. That's fair. I can guide the sensual aspects since you'll lead us through the ritual and chants."

Anja nodded, smiling. "That sounds good. Before we begin, is there anything else you would like to know?"

"Well, yes, actually," Emma paused, a glint of curiosity lighting up her eyes. "I've been wondering what type of otherkin you are. I just realized that I don't actually know."

A soft laugh escaped Anja. "You know, I think I've been so focused on others' awakenings that I've suppressed everyone's curiosity about me. I didn't feel comfortable sharing that with everyone just yet. Lucian is aware of my abilities. My talents…they derive from sexual energy, from intimate connections, from sex. I haven't had a lot of experience with it yet."

Emma looked at her, surprised. "That's…intriguing. So, in a way, this is an exploration for both of us, tapping into aspects of ourselves that have yet to be fully discovered."

"Yes, very much so." Anja agreed, her eyes meeting Emma's. "Are you ready to take this next step?" She could sense her desire rising.

Emma nodded. "Yes, I am."

Anja transferred a little more energy to Emma, looking into her eyes, and felt it settle. She added another little push to relax the remaining remnants of hesitation or inhibitions in them both. She found that the succubus in her was eager, but she was still who she was, and the walls she had built around herself were still there—but they were beginning to crumble. They each took a deep breath, steadying themselves for the ritual and the intimacy that would follow, wondering how this experience would unfold. Turning off the flashlights and setting them aside, they sat for a little while, letting their eyes adjust to the night. The waxing moon shining in a nearly cloudless sky added a silvery glow with colors just barely discernible —enough for them to see but adding a touch of mystique as well.

After a few minutes and with a quiet nod, Emma reached for the hem of Anja's shirt, lifting it over her head smoothly. The two women locked eyes as if to say, "This is the moment." Emma leaned in, planting a series of soft kisses along Anja's collarbone, each one a feathery touch. They took turns removing pieces of clothing. Anja unbuttoned Emma's shirt and slid it off her shoulders, letting her hands glide down her arms to reveal a black bra. Emma moved closer and embraced Anja, looking into her eyes as she unfastened her bra and pulled it slowly forward and off, freeing her breasts. Their hands traced unspoken stories across each other's skin, lines of affection, need, and possibility. The rest of their clothes were soon removed, leaving them naked in the night air. A slight chill was in the air, but that would quickly be forgotten. Emma's fingertips brushed Anja's arms as if she were reading her through touch, her eyes following that same path. The touches were exploratory but sure.

Looking into Emma's eyes, Anja could feel the need building—in both. She leaned in and kissed Emma deeply, cupped her breasts, feet the softness and weight of them, and thumbed her nipples, feeling them tight and hard. Emma reached down between Anja's legs, spreading them more, then cupped her and started to rub across her clit. A moan escaped Anja as she leaned in to do the same to Emma.

Emma gently leaned over Anja, laying her back onto the blanket and moving so that one of her legs was raised to give Anja access. Soon, they were exploring the depths of each other, both slick and intensely aroused.

Feeling the electricity building between them, Anja began to murmur the chant, her voice rising and falling in melodic cadences, somehow able to focus despite the feeling of having Emma's fingers deep inside her, stroking in and out. Each syllable seemed to harmonize with the beat of their hearts, the flow of their blood, and the movements of their bodies. Anja timed the actions of her fingers to the rhythm of her voice, thrumming across Emma's clit on the rising elements and slipping back inside and slower on the lower ones.

Anja felt the power of the ritual swell around them, the energy between them glowing in the moonlight. A final chant, and she sensed a breaking point, a metaphysical shudder that seemed to emanate from Emma. A look of pure wonder filled Emma's eyes before she closed them to let go, signaling an internal change, an awakening as she came, spasming tightly around Anja's fingers. Anja's orgasm was just as intense, a new doorway opening for her as well. She could feel Emma's pleasure overlaying and amplifying her own.

As they lay together, wrapped in a blanket and each other's arms, it was clear that something profound had happened. Emma was different—her presence stronger, a newfound vitality in her gaze.

"Emma," Anja finally spoke, her voice still tinged with awe. "Do you feel it? The awakening?"

"Yes," Emma breathed, almost in disbelief. "I feel...remade. Like I've tapped into something primal and powerful within me. Everything is so bright, so vivid, almost like daylight, but different. I can hear your heartbeat steady and strong. The forest is alive with sound and smells. It's like my senses have all blossomed."

Anja leaned in to kiss her gently, sealing their unspoken bond. "Welcome to your new self," she whispered, her lips near Emma's ear.

"I can feel you almost ready to shift, but I suggest holding off for a bit and letting Lucian and I figure out how to best guide you through that first time. He has that power, but it is untrained and untested."

"Okay." Emma relaxed in to cuddle more, Anja gently stroking her hair. "You are incredible, Anja. I'm not sure if I should bring this up, but I would not object to exploring more with you."

Anja leaned in and kissed Emma, allowing herself to bask in the afterglow of their intimate moment. It was beautiful, in a fresh and exhilarating way. "I think I'd like that, Emma. We'll be busy for a while, but I think we may need a repeat performance soon. I want to try this again, without distractions, in a more intimate setting where we can take our time and fully appreciate each other."

Emma returned the smile, her expression dreamy yet tinged with anticipation. "God, Anja, That could be intense—count me in."

After a little while, they reluctantly dressed and headed back up the trail to the mansion hand in hand. Flashlights were no longer needed as Emma could now guide them back easily, even through the trees' deep shadows. She also noticed her night vision had also improved.

As Anja closed the door behind her, she found Lucian sitting on the edge of their bed, his gaze distant, as if he were turning over many thoughts at once. The room, dimly lit by a single lamp, seemed to hold its breath, waiting for her to speak.

"Emma's awakening went well," she began, meeting his gaze squarely. "She succeeded, and it was an incredibly intense experience. Different from Carlos, but significant in its own right."

Lucian looked up at her, his eyes searching hers. "And how are you, after all of this?"

Anja took a deep breath, feeling the depletion of her energies. "I'm running a bit low on…might as well call it magic. Transferring that kind of energy is no small feat."

He nodded, gesturing for her to come closer. As she sat next to him, their hands instinctively entwined, grounding each other in a reality that seemed to shift with each passing day.

"I sensed a different energy in you when you returned tonight," Lucian said, carefully choosing his words. "Something related to your encounter with Emma. How was it?"

"It was umm…beautiful," Anja admitted, looking into his eyes. "Intimacy was necessary for the ritual's success, and I can't say it was just a part of the process. There was a connection there."

She felt him tighten his grip slightly, but his face remained impassive. "And how do you feel about that connection?"

Anja sighed, weighing her words. "It was necessary, but it also felt…natural, if that makes sense. My abilities needed that closeness to work, and Emma was receptive. It was mutual and achieved what we intended it to…and more."

Finally, Lucian spoke, his voice tinged with understanding. "If your involvement with Emma, or anyone else we're awakening, serves our larger purpose, then I can accept that. However, I want us always to be open about these experiences with each other. No secrets. I think it could also be stimulating to hear all about it."

"Okay," Anja said, feeling relief and a deepening love for the man beside her. "It's a delicate balance we're striking here, Lucian. But how do you feel about it all?"

Considering her, he reached over and pushed a strand of hair behind her ear, his touch lingering on her cheek. "I can't be jealous of this. It's your nature, and it calls to you."

"It does. I really appreciate your understanding. It could also open up other possibilities for us. I love that we can be this way and understand each other."

Lucian leaned in and kissed her gently. "So am I. And now, you said you're running low on power?"

A small smile spread across Anja's face. "Indeed, I am."

"Then let's focus on replenishing that," Lucian said, his eyes glinting with desire.

As they lay down together, the room seemed to breathe again, enveloped in the complexities and simplicities of their ever-evolving relationship.

Lucian stirred from his slumber, his eyes gradually adjusting to the ambient morning light that seeped through the curtain gaps. He sat up, taking a moment to collect his thoughts. Beside him, Anja remained in peaceful repose, a hint of a smile on her lips and her breasts exposed, the covers not quite reaching them. He allowed himself to admire her before slipping out of bed, careful not to disturb her.

He contemplated the day ahead, dressing in a tailored shirt and trousers. Descending the staircase, he found Ian in the conference room, intently studying the security blueprints of the estate. Carlos and Emma soon joined, discussing plans to rerun some of their earlier tests to measure any improvement post-awakening.

After a round of morning greetings, Anja entered, her presence shifting the room's dynamics like a tide under a full moon. She sat beside Lucian, her eyes meeting his momentarily—a silent communication shared between them.

"So, I've been thinking," Anja began, "Claire's awakening could benefit from the lunar cycle, which peaks next week. If we could combine that natural boost with our ritual, we might have a unique opportunity."

Lucian nodded in agreement. "It's a solid plan. But before that, we have some days ahead filled with additional testing. Ian, you're next for baseline tests. Are you prepared?"

Ian looked up from his blueprints. "As ready as I'll ever be."

"We'll conduct assessments to determine your baseline attributes, as discussed. For Emma and Carlos, we need to rerun some tests to measure improvements and changes post-awakening. Sound good?" Lucian asked.

The room filled with nods and affirmations. Lucian and Anja shared another look as they dispersed to prepare for the day's activities.

Twenty

A s   w i t h   E m m a, they prepared the same way: Lucian injected Claire with the serum designed for her and retreated. Bathed in the moonlight that spilled across the forest clearing at the shore of the lake, Anja and Claire stood facing each other. The weight of the ritual and the energy of the full moon seemed to heighten their senses. They each disrobed as agreed: Claire in a simple pullover dress and Anja in a wrap dress, both easy to remove. The atmosphere seemed thick with expectation and held a hint of nervousness from Claire.

"Claire, I don't want to cross any boundaries," Anja said softly. "We can go as far as you're comfortable with."

Claire nodded. "I appreciate that. I think I'd like to stay at this point without diving into deeper waters. I can handle the nudity, but any more may be too much for me."

"Understood," Anja replied, locking eyes with Claire as if to anchor them both in the moment. "Then let's just settle on the blanket and sit quietly. With the light from the full moon, we can also turn off the flashlights. Perhaps that will help you to relax."

Sensing the pull of the moon, Anja began the chant, her voice a soft, soothing cadence. She guided Claire's mind through pathways and thoughts of tales from her past, the serum opening the way. The energy built, curling and coiling around them like invisible smoke. She could sense that the serum had accomplished what it was meant to do, and the chants had opened new doorways, yet resistance, an unyielding tension, remained in Claire.

Anja paused the chant and asked, "Is everything okay? You seem… restrained."

Claire's eyes were clouded, her expression one of inner turmoil. "It's pulling at me, Anja. The moon—it wants me to change, and I'm fighting it. I don't want to shift, not here, not now."

Anja reached out to hold Claire's hands, trying to pour her focus into the ritual to stave off the transformation. "Hold on, just hold on. I'll try to contain it."

But the energy she was pushing into her just seemed to amplify that need to change. Despite her best efforts, Anja could feel Claire slipping away from her, the moon's energy too strong, too insistent. With a shudder that seemed to ripple through the very air around them, Claire transformed. Her form elongated, her body becoming leaner and more muscular. Fur, the color of her golden brown hair, sprouted all over, darker areas mixing in, and when she looked up, her eyes were a luminous amber, almost seeming to glow. What stood before Anja was a wolf of striking beauty and immense presence. For a few heart-stopping moments, they simply regarded each other. Claire's wolf eyes held depths of intelligence and emotion, and Anja found herself awestruck by the creature she had become.

"Amazing," Anja whispered, almost to herself. She approached cautiously, offering her body for Claire to sniff. The wolf moved closer. It was an overwhelming feeling, knowing that this magnificent being was still Claire, yet so much more. Even though the ritual didn't go as intended, it was rather obvious that they had succeeded—a transformation on the most primal level. It might not have been the original outcome they intended, but it was a powerful one nonetheless.

Claire padded down to the water's edge with a grace that seemed innate to her new form. She lifted her head toward the sky and let out a long and joyous howl before looking back at Anja. She turned and leaned down to the water, and her tongue lapped up the cool liquid; each taste stirred a reflection of the moonlight on the lake's surface. After quenching her thirst, she turned back toward Anja, nudging her gently with her nose. The touch was soft but purposeful, and Anja immediately understood.

"You want to go back, don't you?" Although she sensed Claire's intentions, Anja spoke as if asking for confirmation.

Her amber eyes met Anja's, glowing softly in agreement. Anja wrapped herself in her dress, its fabric rustling in the quiet of the night. After folding the blanket, she picked it up along with Claire's dress. She glanced at the wolf again before starting up the trail that led back to the estate. Claire moved effortlessly beside her as they walked, her four-legged gait a natural counterpoint to Anja's bipedal stride. The wolf's fur shimmered in the muted light filtering through the canopy of leaves, her presence both ethereal and very real. They proceeded in a silence that wasn't awkward but intimate, each wrapped up in their thoughts yet profoundly connected.

Anja couldn't help but marvel at how comfortable they seemed. It was as if Claire had always been this magnificent creature of the night. Yet, she also knew this was new territory for both of them—unmapped and intriguing. It wasn't the outcome they'd anticipated for the evening, but as they neared the estate, Anja felt a swell of gratitude and awe. Claire had awakened in a way that was unexpected but entirely her own, and that in itself was something to be cherished.

Emerging from the tree-lined trail onto the lawn adjacent to the mansion, Claire, in her wolf form, seemed to catch sight of the obstacle course that had been set up earlier for testing. Without hesitation, she bolted, launching herself into a full run. Anja watched, captivated, as Claire dashed through the obstacles with astonishing grace and agility. She darted through tight gaps, navigated sharp turns, and leaped over hurdles as if propelled by some internal joy. After completing the course, Claire trotted back toward Anja, her tongue lolling happily and her tail held high in what could only be interpreted as a sign of triumphant exhilaration.

Just then, Lucian emerged from the mansion, followed by Ian and Emma. They paused, eyes widening as they took in the sight before them—a large, majestic wolf, her amber eyes twinkling and fur glistening in the moonlight.

Emma broke the silence, her eyes twinkling mischievously. "Well, I guess some of us really do feel the urge to howl at the moon," she jested, her tone light yet filled with awe.

Lucian caught Anja's eye, and for a moment, no words were needed. The atmosphere was thick with wonder, curiosity, and an undercurrent of something more—a sense that each unfolding event was a step closer to unraveling all of their potential. As they all headed inside, the atmosphere remained charged, imbued with the unbelievable occurrences of the evening. Lucian led the way, his gaze lingering on Claire, who, upon entering, shimmered briefly before resuming her human form. She looked momentarily disoriented but also exhilarated, her eyes meeting each of theirs as if for the first time.

Once they were all in the spacious living room, Lucian turned to address the group. "This has been a significant evening. Claire, your transformation was nothing short of miraculous. How are you feeling?"

"I fought it at first; I didn't want it to go this far, too afraid of the consequences and what it would mean. There came a point when I just couldn't fight it off anymore, and then…I just accepted it. Just let go. Now I feel alive like never before—and hungry." Claire answered. "As if layers of myself have been peeled back to reveal something… primal. Oh, and I guess rather naked, but I don't seem to be bothered by it."

There were a few nervous chuckles and a cough by Ian trying to hide his grin behind his hand.

Anja stepped over and handed Claire her dress. "I'm sorry, I was still so in awe with it all."

She took her dress and pulled it on, "Thanks, it's okay, Anja, really."

Lucian interjected. "With awakening comes an entire spectrum of new experiences and sensations. It's crucial for us to understand them, not just for our well-being, but for understanding the process."

Anja, settling into an armchair, looked at Emma. "Emma, you also went through an incredible experience. What are your thoughts?"

Emma sat down opposite Anja, her expression reflective. "It's like becoming attuned to a part of yourself you never knew existed, yet feels intensely familiar. I'm still trying to process it. But I guess now there will be a whole new meaning when I call Claire a bitch."

"Watch it, kitty!" Claire replied with a glare, trying not to smile.

Ian, who had been quietly absorbing the conversation, finally spoke. "It appears we're moving in a direction that could change not just us but possibly the world's understanding of human capabilities. I've been studying the estate's security measures and preparing for my eventual awakening. It's crucial we keep these developments under wraps until we fully understand them. Probably longer."

Lucian looked appreciative. "Well said, Ian. We have much to explore, individually and collectively. Given what we've discovered so far, our next steps will be equally, if not more, challenging. We need to prepare, train, and—most importantly—understand the implications of our awakenings."

Anja interjected, "And we still have to proceed with Ian's awakening, which will complete the circle for us, at least for now."

Lucian caught Anja's gaze, holding it momentarily before addressing the group. "Tomorrow, we reconvene to share findings and plan the next stages. But for tonight, I think we've all earned some rest. And maybe a steak for Claire. I'll call Elena and have her fix something, and there is some dessert left from dinner. "

Carlos joined them as they headed for the dining room. "Well, Claire, that was astonishing. I was watching the monitors downstairs and didn't get to see you up close, but it was still glorious."

The night was far from ordinary, but then again, so were they.

The morning sun streamed through the large windows of the mansion's conference room, casting its warm glow over a long, polished table. They all gathered around it, laptops and notebooks open, reviewing their recent observations and findings. A laptop at the end of the table was set up for a video call, ready to connect them with Isabelle for their update.

Lucian cleared his throat and initiated the video call. The screen flickered for a moment before Isabella's face appeared. "Good morning, everyone. I trust you've all been busy?"

"We have," Lucian replied, glancing at his assembled team. "We've made significant progress in the awakenings, and we're prepared to discuss the details and what we've observed." He gave an overview of events and related the progress they have made.

The changes in each of them were evident and beyond expectations. Anja talked briefly about Claire's full moon transformation into a wolf, describing her agility and strength, the rich color of her fur, and the deep, amber hue of her eyes. "In performing her awakening under the full moon, we probably overstepped and created added risks, but fortunately, it worked out okay. It could have gone badly, but Claire's instincts for protection played a role. We will need to determine how much control she has over shifting and whether it will be limited to the lunar cycle, but we can only speculate at this point."

Isabelle smiled. "Impressive work, all of you. I'm keen to see the data. And what's next?"

Lucian leaned forward. "Next, we'll focus on Ian. Given his military background, we're curious to see how his abilities will manifest."

Isabelle nodded. "Very well. We're entering uncharted territory here, and each piece of data is a step forward."

After lunch, in the dim light of the study, surrounded by books and artifacts of Miller's history, Anja, Lucian, and Ian convened. Anja leaned back in the leather chair she had chosen, thinking of Ian's bone talisman.

"Ian, you've been wearing that charm for as long as we've known you. I remember you mentioned it's a family heirloom. Have you ever heard tales within your family about its significance? Do you think that talisman might be more than just a symbol?"

Sitting across from Anja, Ian pulled the talisman free from his shirt and glanced down at it hanging from his neck. He removed it and placed it on the table, running his fingers over the intricate carvings. "It's been in my family for many generations. There are stories, more like myths. They talk about unlocking the 'true self,' but the details are scarce, often abstract."

"Abstract how?" Lucian asked, interested.

Ian took a moment to gather his thoughts. "Symbols, metaphors... Grandfather used to tell me about the 'key to our essence' but never elaborated. It was supposed to guide or protect us somehow, especially during life-altering changes. But he was never clear on the specifics."

Anja leaned forward, elbows on the table. "The term 'life-altering changes' seems quite appropriate for what we're going through. Do you feel comfortable incorporating it into your awakening ritual? It could be a powerful conduit, but we need to proceed with caution considering Claire's experience."

Ian looked between Anja and Lucian, sensing the gravity in their eyes. "I've thought about it, especially since watching the rest of you go through your awakenings. To be honest, I've felt a different... resonance with this periapt lately. Like it's been more active, it could just be psychological, but I'm open to exploring its potential impact."

"Alright," Anja added. "We will try to tread carefully but be aware that its power will likely be significant. Each of us has found unique keys to our awakenings; perhaps this is yours, Ian."

She leaned back in her chair and twisted a finger through her hair. "Ian, adding some intimacy to your ritual may also be necessary. Seeing as how a shift may also be possible, as demonstrated by Claire, you should be prepared and not be wearing anything. Are you comfortable with that?"

Ian looked from Anja to Lucian as the topic changed to intimacy. "Well, as for nudity, I don't have any reservations. It's a natural state; if shifting is involved, it only makes sense. But what about further intimacy? What do you mean? How do you, Lucian, feel about that?"

Lucian considered the question carefully, his eyes meeting Anja's before answering. "Intimacy, let's just say it—sex is part and parcel of Anja's abilities, her essence. I'm not just accepting of it; I fully understand its importance. Her powers are derived from sex and from that connection. It's elemental to who she is."

Turning to Anja, he asked, "And you, Anja, is this really true? This is a...stimulating, if uncertain, possibility."

Anja smiled, a touch of arousal coloring her words. "I will look forward to it if it becomes necessary, and to tell you the truth...I rather hope it does. Each person's path to discovering their true self is unique. If sex turns out to be a useful component for you, Ian, then it aligns perfectly with my nature. It would be a pleasure, and I'd be more than willing to facilitate that part of the process."

The arousal Anja felt at the prospect of sex with Ian is something that she noticed was growing. Not just with Ian but with anyone, really. *Is this me, or is this something that will take over my life?* She asked herself. *Can I control it? Do I want to? Questions for another time, I guess...*

Lucian nodded, his eyes filled with trust and something else unreadable. "Then it's settled. We proceed as needed, with openness and the recognition that this is part of the journey, part of who we are."

Ian nodded, picking up the talisman and putting it back around his neck, leaving it out for all to see. "Then let's do it. Let's find out what 'life-altering changes' await me."

Lucian added, "Tomorrow, we will do it. Perhaps after lunch to give us all time to consider and prepare."

The room fell quiet, but the atmosphere had shifted. There was a sense of resolve, a mutual agreement that they were stepping into uncharted territory together.

Twenty-One

ANJA, LUCIAN, AND Ian moved through the woods, the scent of damp earth and leaves filling the air. Ian wore black sweats, comfortable and easy to remove—a necessary practicality given what was about to occur. Adorned in her now favorite flowing wrap dress, Anja carried a soft, comfortable blanket over her arm. She was already attuned to the energy of the space.

As they walked, Anja felt attracted to a patch of land up ahead. It was a clearing ringed with trees, their branches seemingly stretching toward the sky in both a plea and a welcome. The ground was soft, carpeted in a layer of leaves that had turned to rich mulch over the years. A circle of unexplained lushness marked the center of the clearing, like a green island in a sea of past autumnal decay. Anja glanced at Ian, catching the subtle shift in his posture. His eyes were assessing as they stepped into the space, and she could tell he felt it too—this place was special.

"Here," she said softly, "this is where we should do it."

Ian nodded, already transfixed by the natural space before him. It was as if the forest itself had conspired to offer this spot as the venue for his rebirth—or perhaps his revelation.

"Feels right. I had spotted this place on my explorations of the grounds, and it felt special." Ian agreed, his voice tinged with a reverence Anja hadn't heard before.

She unfurled the blanket in the clearing's center, smoothing its wrinkles. She felt a new sense of solemnity settling around them; this was a sacred ground, and they were about to venture deeply into the mysteries of Ian's soul.

In the bright afternoon sun filtering through the trees, Lucian approached with a small glass vial and syringe. "Are you ready?" he directed the question at Ian with a hand on his shoulder, who nodded affirmatively. Anja stepped back, observing the momentary exchange between them. Lucian skillfully filled the syringe with the slightly luminescent liquid and administered the injection into Ian's upper arm, his touch lingering momentarily in a supportive squeeze.

"With that, I'll leave you to it," Lucian commented, glancing briefly at Anja—a silent exchange conveying trust and assurance. He turned and returned the way they had come, leaving Ian and Anja in the isolated, sun-dappled clearing.

Lucian's departure seemed to alter the atmosphere, charging it with a sense of expectation. "How are you feeling?" Anja inquired, directing Ian to sit on the blanket she had spread on the ground. Ian complied, discarding his black sweats until he was clad only in his boxers.

"Comfortable, thanks," Ian replied. "And you, any boundaries I should be aware of?"

Anja shook her head. "No, but the boxers need to come off too. Today is about you. I'm here as a guide to help you unlock something extraordinary within. Just stay open."

Ian hesitated only for a moment before removing them and adding them to the pile of his sweats just off the blanket before sitting cross-legged. Anja removed her dress to stand completely naked, having not worn anything underneath. As Ian looked up at her to admire her form and beauty—he could not suppress his body's reaction, and his erection started to rise.

Anja sat cross-legged in front of him, close enough to reach out and take his hands in hers, their knees barely touching and leaving nothing to the imagination. Glancing at his now full-fledged erection, she noticed that he was quite well-equipped. Taking a deep breath and locking eyes, Anja commenced the chant. Her voice wove around the clearing, the notes shimmering in the warm air. Each word seemed to hang briefly before dispersing as if it had physical weight. She sensed Ian's energy reacting, a subtle humming that grew stronger with each uttered syllable. Finally, she leaned forward, her lips inches from Ian's ear. "Surrender, Ian. Allow your innate self to rise to the surface."

At that moment, a distinct shift occurred. The blockages seemed to lessen, and energy flowed more freely. Anja leaned back, meeting Ian's gaze once more. Something had changed; a new fire danced in his eyes. It was a point of no return, a barrier crossed, and both knew it. Ian maintained eye contact with Anja, sensing the depth unfurling between them, almost as if they were standing at the edge of a cliff, staring into a space filled with both promise and mystery. Anja could see Ian's apprehension wane, replaced by an eagerness to leap into the unknown.

"Keep your eyes on mine," Anja murmured, her voice soft yet full of urgency. "You're close, so close to the edge. Let yourself be guided."

The atmosphere grew heavy with expectation, their energies mingling like two converging currents. Anja sensed that Ian was on the cusp, his latent power churning, yearning to burst forth. It felt like a door within him was trembling, keys in the lock, just one turn away from opening. However, a final, stubborn barrier remained despite the potency of their eye contact, the ritual, and the serum working in synergy; that last wall seemed resistant to collapse. Ian was almost there, yet not letting go.

Anja leaned back slightly, her brows knitting in contemplation. They were so close. A voice inside her whispered, *Don't think, feel, just let go...* She took a deep breath, knowing what would be needed to shatter that remaining barrier. The forest around them seemed to hold its breath as if acknowledging the critical juncture at which they found themselves. Both sensed the urgency; they were on the edge of something transformative, yet still a step away. Anja leaned closer to Ian, her lips hovering just a breath away from his ear. "This last barrier," she whispered, "let's dissolve it together."

She felt his pulse quicken, the vibrations of his arousal resonating with her own. Sliding her hand to the small of his back, she pulled him toward her as she laid back on the blanket, spreading her legs to accommodate him.

He hesitated. "Anja, you are so seductive, so beautiful. I can't believe this is happening."

"Don't think, Ian, just feel, let yourself go." She said as she reached down to stroke herself, to open herself up to him.

His eyes, drawn to Anja's hand and what she was doing, spreading her lips and then moving to circle her clit, banished the last of his hesitation. As Ian settled himself between her legs, his tip pausing just against her opening, resting on his arms, his height making it easy to kiss her, tentatively at first but with a light mental push from Anja, turning into much more.

Anja felt him push into her slightly, stretching her, but she was slick and ready. She moved her body to meet him and took more of him in. Ian soon lost any remaining hesitation and began to move in earnest. Pumping in and out harder, faster and deeper with each stroke and picking up an unremitting rhythm.

As their lips met again in a kiss imbued with the weight of their joining, Anja broke the kiss and laid her head back on the blanket as he filled her. Anja resumed her chant and intensified the cadence, the melodic phrases imbued with the essence of long-forgotten rites in rhythm with Ian's thrusts. Her connection to his thoughts and mental pathways was clear. This was the moment the catalyst needed to tip the scales. She felt the culmination of energies stirring within them, a culmination of desire and will. Anja could sense Ian ready to climax and locked eyes with him once more, the chant and all preparations complete; only the last element was needed, and it was immanent, his rhythm now fraying.

With one last thrust, he came deep inside her. Anja felt the spasms and heat filling her, driving her to her orgasm, clenching spasms around him as she felt his seed spill inside. She pulled energy and power and shoved it back into him, amplifying their sensations even more. Ian's eyes flickered for a moment, a brief shadow passing over them, and then they were alight with a new kind of fire, a manifestation of the awakening they both had been striving for. The barrier crumbled like a dam breaking, allowing the pent-up energies to flood through him akin to his orgasm. The key had been found to unlock the door shut for generations. It sprang open now with ease.

Anja found his eyes again, both equally awed by the sensation of something profound and irrevocable that had just transpired. Ian's frame trembled slightly, both a reaction to his release and an echo of the resonance of his newfound self. Anja felt a surge of satisfaction to go along with the aftershocks of her orgasm and the sharing of power.

Gently, Ian rolled off and lay next to Anja on his side, admiring the sight of her spread out on the blanket with a blissful smile and her chest flushed and mottled pink, red hair in disarray around her. He reached out to cup a breast to stoke a still-hard nipple gently.

"That was incredible, Anja, no…more than that…I have no words."

"No words are needed, Ian. It was truly, in all senses, my pleasure."

Anja looked into Ian's eyes, now dancing with new opportunities. She sensed the internal struggle within him, the hesitation tempered with curiosity and wonder. Still maintaining eye contact, Anja took a deep breath and let it out slowly, releasing the last remnants of tension from the air around them.

"You've crossed a threshold, Ian. Do you feel it? The power, the… possibilities?"

Ian nodded, his eyes now holding a different kind of intensity, one infused with newfound understanding. "It's like I've been blind, and now I can see in colors I didn't know existed."

Anja smiled, her eyes twinkling. "The question is, are you ready to explore this new spectrum? Do you want to attempt to shift? To become that bear that you've just awakened to?"

Ian hesitated, his gaze drifting off into the space around them as if trying to read the very air for guidance. Finally, his eyes met hers again, a clarity settling within them.

"I think I can. But it's like standing at the edge of a cliff and not knowing what's at the bottom," he admitted.

Anja nodded, her eyes full of understanding. "This is your choice to make. But know that whatever happens, you've already achieved a major milestone today."

Ian took a deep breath as if gathering the courage and strength from the earth beneath his feet. "I want to try. I feel like if I don't, I'll wonder."

"Then let's take that step together," Anja said, reaching over to pick up the talisman and handing it to Ian. "Your ancestors knew this would guide you to find their true self. Use it. Feel it. Focus on it.

As Ian closed his eyes, Anja could see him internalizing her advice. His body started to shudder slightly, an indication of the transformation he was about to undergo. She held her breath, knowing this was right, her eyes never leaving him, ready to assist, guide, witness, and provide a last push of power. And then, with a rush, the moment they had both been waiting for arrived.

With a deep concentration on his face, Ian's form began to shudder more intensely. His muscles twitched, and then his body started to morph. Anja watched as his limbs broadened, his physique expanding, and his hair sprouted and darkened until it was a lustrous dark brown. His face elongated, becoming a snout, while his eyes, still holding that human intensity, changed shape but retained their original color. In moments, where Ian had stood, now sat a majestic and very imposing brown bear, its coat so rich and dark it almost appeared black.

Anja's breath caught at the awe-inspiring sight before her. She felt the energy in the clearing shift, now charged with primal, untamed power. Cautiously, she approached the bear. Ian, now in his ursine form, sniffed her cautiously. Recognizing her scent, his eyes softened, and he let out a gentle huff as if in acknowledgment.

Anja couldn't help but smile, her hand trembling as she touched the deep, thick fur on his shoulder, feeling the immense strength that lay beneath. It was an exhilarating and humbling experience to stand in the presence of such raw, untamed power yet feel such a deep connection and mutual understanding. With one last look into his eyes, holding a mix of the primal and the sentient, Anja took a step back to allow Ian to explore his new form. He rose and ambled around the clearing, testing out his newfound strength and senses. Anja watched as he sniffed the air, his ears pricking at the sounds of the forest, and she realized that they had crossed into a realm as ancient as it was wondrous. Standing on his hind legs, he towered over her, taller by over two feet, his presence immense. Finally, Ian returned to her side, his eyes meeting hers in a silent but potent exchange. And for that brief, magical moment, all was right with the world.

Anja bent down to gather her dress, pulling it on, tying the wrap, and letting the fabric fall into place. She took a moment to collect Ian's clothes, folding them neatly and placing them on top of the blanket she had brought. Reaching for Ian's talisman, she looped it carefully around her neck, sensing warmth from the bone against her skin. With one final glance toward Ian, she saw acknowledgment in his eyes and started toward the estate. Ian ambled beside her, his large paws leaving impressions on the forest floor.

As they reached the edge of the manicured lawn, the contrast between the domesticated grounds and the wild forest was stark. Anja turned to face Ian, looking into his eyes as she had so many times before, but now they told a different story.

"Would you like to change back, or would you prefer to stay like this and explore the woods some more?" she asked.

The bear seemed to ponder the question, his gaze lingering on the sprawling mansion and drifting back to the wilderness behind them. Then, his eyes met Anja's, communicating his choice in that silent language they had come to understand. With a low rumble that seemed like a bearish version of a satisfied sigh, Ian turned back toward the wilderness. Anja nodded and unhooked the talisman from around her neck, holding it out in her palm toward him.

In an awe-inspiring transformation, Ian's large form began to contract, fur receding as his bear shape morphed back into human form. Standing before her, naked and unabashed, he reached for the talisman and placed it around his neck.

"Seems I have a lot to explore," Ian said, his voice tinged with a newfound depth that made Anja wonder just how much the awakening had changed him.

"Take all the time you need," Anja said, handing him his clothes. "The forest should be a good teacher for you."

With that, Ian dressed quickly and, casting one last meaningful glance her way, walked back into the forest, each step taking him deeper into his new identity and further along the path of self-discovery.

Anja watched until he disappeared, contemplating the profound changes they had all undergone. Then, clutching the blanket to her chest, she turned and headed back to the mansion. For now, she felt content in the knowledge that another soul had found its proper form. She sensed that their group was not yet complete, that more awakenings would come. She didn't know who yet, but that was a concern for another day. It was time to regroup, share stories, and plan their next steps. Lucian would be waiting, and she was eager to share this new experience with him.

Twenty-Two

ANJA FOUND LUCIAN deeply engrossed in some new research papers, his eyes lifting as she entered the study. The room was bathed in the golden glow of the afternoon sun, casting intricate patterns of light and shadow on the bookshelves that adorned the walls.

"How did it go?" Lucian asked as she sat in the leather armchair across from him.

"It was a success. Ian has a lot to explore in himself and how it all unfolded, but he should be back in time to join everybody for dinner. He went off into the forest to reflect."

"Unfolded? What happened?"

Anja paused a moment before responding. "The ritual that I had planned came close to working. He was on the cusp of unlocking that door inside himself, but unlike Claire, who had the moon calling so strongly to her, something else was needed to push past the last barrier."

"That's incredible," Lucian said. "Um, intimacy…did it come into play?"

Looking into his eyes, she added, "It did, but you don't need to be so delicate with me, Lucian. I had to take him beyond his inhibitions —all of them. The initial ritual took us to the line but not across it. I sensed an inhibition and a lack of sufficient power; my nature was calling, and to be blunt, the power I was able to gather from our orgasms helped greatly. I used that energy to push through the last barriers and lock his changes in place. I seem to be able to draw more power each time I have sex—as I gain experience. Practice makes perfect, as they say."

"I guess we will have to practice more," he replied with a grin.

"Oh, I intend to. I'm glad you can accept that part of me so easily," she said with her own smile.

Lucian sat back in his chair. "It's not always easy, but it is who you are, and I wouldn't want to change that. Besides, the fringe benefits for me are…enticing. I just miss not being able to be with you during those times. Not jealous, really, but just…"

"You know, I'm not sure how it would work with more than two involved, though it might provide even more power. If you were willing, I would like to explore that possibility with you sometime," she said, looking up expectantly.

Appraising her and noting that the idea clearly aroused her, as evidenced by her nipples now outlined through her thin dress. "I think you could convince me to try something like that. Even just watching would be…stimulating."

Anja, almost purring, responded, "Hmmm, I can see your point. Let's put that on our list then."

Lucian nodded, his gaze meeting hers. "But back to the subject of awakenings. It's amazing what you can do, Anja. Your abilities have added a dimension to them that I don't think anyone else could have accomplished."

Flattered but wanting to steer the conversation to their next steps, Anja changed the subject. "What else has been happening here while I was off playing?"

"Playing?" he mused, chucking, then stood. "A package arrived from Howard today. He sent some texts that might interest you."

He moved to a corner of the room and returned with a package, carefully unwrapping it to reveal a set of books. "Here, take a look," he said, handing her the books.

Anja skimmed the titles: "The Book of Liminal Spaces," "Twilight Mysteries: A Guide to the In-Between," and "Water's Edge: Thresholds to Other Realms."

"These could be useful," she said. "I've been considering an attempt to access another plane to gain more power or knowledge. I've read that it might be possible under the right conditions, and now that we seem to be able to tap into at least some forms of magic, I might finally succeed. I have tried before and was never able to do it. I still can barely believe we have come this far in such a short time."

"Yes, and speaking of time, he suggested that certain boundary moments like twilight or particular physical locations like water's edge could be crucial in accessing other planes."

"The undrentide or the fairy hour," Anja mused. "Moments or places where the barrier between worlds is thin enough to breach."

"Would you want to try it?"

Anja considered for a moment before answering. "I would. But succeeding would be unlike anything we've tried so far. There could be risks."

Lucian leaned forward, eyes locking onto hers. "All the more reason for us to do it together, don't you think?"

Anja felt a surge of warmth at his words. With Lucian at her side, she thought they could conquer any challenge and breach any barrier. "Yes, together, but maybe not in the way you might think. Let me read over the texts that Howard sent. I have a sense that I could use an anchor here—You. A way to find my way back."

"I see, but how would that work?"

"I'm not sure yet, but these books may hold the key to doing so safely or at least reducing the risks."

Lucian looked at her, his gaze serious yet filled with a certain curiosity. "I'll support you in any way I can. Let's plan to make it happen if you're ready to expand your understanding and dive into the unknown."

"Okay, let me read through these and see what I can find. Let me know when dinner is ready, please," she said, clearly intent on the new arrivals.

She moved the books to the soft leather couch by the windows and settled in. Pulling out her notebook and pen, she also wanted the familiar routine of organizing her thoughts on paper. She no longer needed the notes with memories so clearly etched in her mind, but it was a comforting routine that she treasured.

Before dawn and after an intense bout of morning sex, Anja established a close mental link with Lucian. "The Book of Liminal Spaces" suggested such a link, but the method was not specified. She had improvised, guided by her growing awareness of her powers and the ability to draw energy from sex. The process left Lucian drained and in a near dreamlike state. She found that she could influence his dreams much like lucid dreaming. He was the dreamer with her in control. Mostly. She looked forward to experimenting with that more when she had the chance. The possibilities were…enticing.

Leaving Lucian naked in bed, she went down to the estate's lake to the eastern edge down a rocky slope a distance from where she had come with Emma. She could still feel her connection with Lucian from here. Taking off her sandals, she approached the edge, that division of spaces—where the shore met water.

The forest was dark and silent now. She stood on the lake's edge amidst the rocky pebbles that lined the shore. She looked across the still water, which acted as a mirror reflecting the stars and the moon that was just slipping down through the trees on the far side of the lake. Dawn was approaching, the stars fading away with the brightening of the sky. Everything was still with not even a hint of wind. It seemed like the world was holding its breath. Waiting. Waiting for her, perhaps.

Anja stood before a large stone thrust up from the shore, her back almost touching it. The stone was sharp and tall. She was concentrating, focusing on her desire to break through the bindings holding her back. Her mind followed a ritual to open the way. It felt like the stone's strength was biting into her back, propelling her toward the still waters. She had tried this before but had never felt so close. Letting her mind drift, seeking that place deep in her being that had always pulled at her but never as strongly as now.

She felt a shifting, almost as if something in her had changed. A pulse followed with a faint reverberation. Her pulse quickened, her heart beating strongly in her chest. A flush spread up her body and heat spread lower. Her arousal surprised her as her nipples tightened. A feeling of elation flowed through her.

That's interesting, she thought, contemplating her arousal. She had done it, which was surprising after so many prior failures.

A rift stood shimmering in the reflection of the last of the moon as it slipped from sight, colors of dawn just starting to streak against the sky, only one star remaining. Maybe this rift was even real, physical, this time. She stepped toward the shimmering rift and felt a frosty chill. It was colder now than it had been moments before on this warmer-than-usual spring morning. The dress she had chosen was not helping. Her breath was fogging in front of her.

As she pressed into and through the rift, she found herself... somewhere. Her bare feet were just at the water's edge; she felt the cold and the pebbles biting into her feet. The stone still looming behind but now somehow different. The moon had dipped too low to see, and a fog had sprung up low over the lake's surface.

There is power here. Her heart was still beating fast. Fear? Yes, but that arousal, too. Would she be able to find her way back? To the world or herself? She wasn't sure. She felt the thread leading back to Lucian and hoped it didn't fray. Anja knew that she was in the right place. This was the place she needed to find—was always meant to find.

Fear coursed through her, crawling up the back of her neck—the tang of adrenaline providing a boost of energy and a heightened awareness of her body. She walked along the lake's edge until it became impassable from brambles, rocks, and fallen trees stretching out into the water. Her bare feet were painful from the abuse, and fearful that she wouldn't be able to return, she retraced her path back to her starting point. The light of dawn had not changed, the sky still a mournful grey. She realized where she started was not the rocky slope with the sharp jutting rock but an imposing cliff face standing atop a slight rise near the shore. The stone still stood sentinel but now in front of a rocky path leading up to the mouth of a dark cave opening in the rock face.

Unable to help herself, she approached that foreboding entrance through tendrils of mist drifting up from the lake. She took a deep breath. *No light, no shoes, only a too-small knife...crap.* Peering in, she could see rough-hewn steps leading downward in the dim light from outside, disappearing into the darkness. Was that a faint flickering around a bend? Drips of water could be heard faintly echoing as the drops plunked into what had to be a pool of some sort.

A hand grabbed her throat from behind, an arm wrapped around her waist, lifting her against a solid body at her back—an obviously male body.

"Oh, fuck!"

Lucian's voice cut through the atmosphere like a hot knife through butter. "That sounds like a wonderful idea," he said, his voice close to her ear.

Anja felt the arm around her waist, solid and familiar. She turned her head slightly, confirming what she already knew in her gut. Lucian was here, but not just as a mere vision; he looked solid, felt very solid—and very naked. As if reading her thoughts, he tightened his embrace momentarily.

"Incredible," Lucian murmured, taking in their surroundings. "Where are we?"

"I think," Anja hesitated, "this might be what could be called my soul place or home. I've read about such things, though I never thought I'd have one to visit, let alone bring someone with me. 'Nexus' seems to be a name better suited to me, though, rather than soul home."

Unable to resist, Lucian queried, "Lair?"

"Yeah, okay, but rather cliché, don't you think?"

Lucian looked deeply into her eyes. "Whatever you call it, it's as mystical and captivating as you are, Anja."

Being here was one thing, but having Lucian here felt like a whole new layer of connection that was both exhilarating and intimidating. She wondered what his presence here could mean. In literature, the soul home was considered the most intimate realm of an individual, a sanctuary where their essence was at its purest. Could his presence signify that their souls were intertwined in ways beyond the physical realm?

Anja turned to Lucian, her eyes intent as she spoke. "The dreamlike state you were in and the quality of this place, combined with the connection we established earlier, may have acted as a beacon. My earlier fear, in particular, might have amplified that signal, bringing you into this space with me. I have no idea how that worked."

He nodded, letting out a breath he seemed to have been holding. "Then let's explore this place together."

As Lucian spoke, Anja couldn't help but feel that the environment around them responded. The gray skies seemed to lighten a shade, and a gentle wind began to whisper through the brambles and trees as though the very world they were in was acknowledging their presence. Anja and Lucian stood before the cave entrance, silently contemplating the dark void that beckoned them. With mutual acceptance, they descended, the flickering light growing brighter as they moved further down the steps. The air grew warmer, and the atmosphere shifted from one of foreboding to one of promise.

Finally, they reached a chamber, its outline softly lit by glowing stones embedded in the walls. As they stepped inside, Anja couldn't help but gasp. There, at the center of the chamber, was an invitingly plush couch surrounded by bookshelves lining the walls. The bookcases were filled with titles she recognized—texts she had read or browsed. Astonishingly, even the Ashton Grimoire found a home here.

"This place…," Anja trailed off, her eyes scanning the room. "It's like a sanctuary for all the knowledge I've absorbed or perhaps for what I'm still meant to understand. A manifestation of what I carry inside of me."

Feeling an invisible pull, they moved to another chamber. This one was more intimate—a bedroom adorned in intricate details. When they entered, a fire sprang to life in the fireplace, casting a warm, flickering glow that danced across curtain-lined walls. Mirrors were strategically placed opposite a large bed, its four posts draped in layers of soft, gossamer fabric.

Lucian whistled softly. "I must say, your soul home is turning out to be an incredibly layered place. Sensual, academic, a little mysterious."

"It reflects parts of me, my essence, and perhaps even my future," Anja responded, captivated by the room and the moment.

"Then the mirrors here might symbolize more than vanity," Lucian ventured, his eyes locking with hers in the glass. "They could be about introspection, self-awareness."

"Or just for watching," Anja added as a smile crept to her lips, enticed by the notion.

"The relationship we have," Lucian said, turning to face her fully, "is unlike anything I've ever experienced. Being here, in your…nexus, solidifies that perception for me."

Anja took in the chamber, the bed, and the inviting fire. Then her eyes found Lucian's, and she felt a subtle but undeniable pulse of desire course through her. The realm they were in might be symbolic or even metaphorical, but the emotions she was experiencing were tangibly real.

"Then let's not rush to leave," she suggested softly. "Perhaps we should see what else we can learn about ourselves, about this unique bond, while we're here."

Lucian took her hand with an appreciative smile and led her to the bed. The fire seemed to blaze a little brighter as they sat, filling the room with light and warmth. Anja felt the soft fabric of the bed yield under her weight as she sat, and Lucian joined her, their hands still interlaced. The chamber seemed to envelop them in an ambiance of unspoken promises, each flicker of the fire casting a soft glow on their faces. The room was like a manifestation of the intimacy that had been burning between them, a physical space where the abstract and the tangible met.

With Lucian's hand gently resting on her knee, Anja looked around the chamber. She was struck by the thought that this space—existing somewhere between fantasy and reality—was an extension of her innermost self. And here was Lucian, not just an observer but a participant.

As Lucian leaned in, his lips lightly grazed hers, igniting a gentle warmth that resonated with the crackling fire. His touch was like a catalyst, and the room seemed to respond, its atmosphere thickening with a palpable tension.

Lucian broke the kiss, and his eyes sought hers. "Are you okay?"

"More than okay," she whispered, her eyes heavy with a desire that was new yet profoundly familiar. "It's as if this place was waiting for a moment like this, waiting for us."

Her words hung in the air as they came together once more, this time in a kiss that was less tentative, much more assertive.

Lucian's hands traced the contours of her back through the thin fabric of her dress, eliciting a pleasurable shiver. His lips moved from her mouth to the nape of her neck, each kiss leaving a tiny blaze in its wake. She felt as if her very soul was awakening, spreading its wings for the first time. In that time-suspended moment, Anja understood something profound. This place, her nexus, had layers still unseen, depths yet to be explored. But for now, it was enough to know she didn't have to navigate its labyrinthine chambers alone.

Lucian lay back, pulling her to him into a soft embrace. As they reclined on the bed, draped in the gossamer that adorned it, Anja felt an overwhelming sense of completeness wash over her. And so, enveloped in warmth and lost in each other, they existed in a reality entirely of their own making—a place where the boundaries of this plane and the real world blurred, where questions were answered with a touch, a glance, a sigh.

Unconsciously, she banished her dress and realized that capabilities like that would be very convenient. Lucian's eyes seemed to devour her, exploring every inch of her body. Following the same path his eyes had followed, he began to explore her body with his hands, lips, and tongue. He was listening to the sounds she made and feeling her writhe.

"Lucian, I can feel your desires. I'm not fragile—take me the way you want."

Anja stood before the large mirror, her reflection capturing the soft, dim light of the chamber. She scrutinized every facet of her image in the stillness of the moment. It was a contemplation, not of vanity but of existence—her place within the intricate tapestry of reality and illusion.

As her gaze remained fixed, her reflection began to flicker and transform. She looked mostly the same—her eyes, her hair. Still, new elements blended into her silhouette: red, almost burgundy-colored bat wings unfolded gracefully behind her, complementing her hair, their membranes stretching to full span. Through her deep burgundy hair, two slender horns poked through, delicate yet assertive, and a tail—a tail—sleek with a wide, spade-shaped spear-tip at the end, wound around one of her legs. As she continued to watch, her form continued to shift subtly—she appeared taller, her breasts fuller and nipples rosier, all of her body hair completely gone, imparting an imposing yet erotic presence. This confirmed, rather than revealed, her nature.

Feeling his presence, she glanced over her shoulder to find Lucian leaning against a bedpost, his eyes locked onto her. "Lucian, come look. What do you see?"

Lucian stepped away from the bed and slowly approached, standing beside her before the mirror. His eyes met hers in the reflection before dropping to take in the full image. "I see you, Anja," he began cautiously, "but I also see more. The wings, the horns—they're as much a part of you as anything else. And they're beautiful."

His words, sincere and without a trace of alarm, brought a sense of ease. Lucian's acceptance, so openly given, rendered the moment extraordinary. "This is me, a fuller expression of my being," Anja said, her voice soft but unwavering. "It's something I've sensed but never fully appreciated until now."

Lucian's eyes met hers once more in the mirror's reflection. "Understanding is a process, not an endpoint," he said. "And I'd like to be there for every step, every discovery you make about yourself."

"Lucian…I don't want to lose myself to it, though. I don't want it to be just the sex. Don't get me wrong, it's wonderful, and I can finally let down my guard with those I trust, but…I don't want it to take over everything. But with you here, I can feel you anchor me to myself. Does that make sense?"

Looking thoughtful, Lucian replied, "It does. No matter what happens, I'll be with you."

Standing before her reflection, Lucian beside her, Anja felt a profound sense of unity. Here, in this chamber, she'd revealed another layer of her essence—more complex yet whole. And in Lucian's eyes, she found not just acceptance but a deep, abiding resonance.

Anja's eyes shifted from her transformed reflection to Lucian's image in the mirror. There was something inherently potent about his aura similar to her own yet distinct, magnified, and radiant in this mirrored view. It beckoned questions and teased at limitless possibilities.

"Lucian, look into the mirror. Look deeply into yourself," she instructed, her voice tinged with intimacy and guidance. "Your heritage carries Marbas' essence. There's potential for change within you too—to take on another form, perhaps the form of a lion—it was one of his favorite forms and thus may be easier for you."

Lucian nodded, his eyes meeting hers briefly before their gazes returned to the mirror. Lucian's gaze met his own in the mirror. His eyes seemed to search, to dig into the reflected layers of his being. He focused intently, his brows knitting together in concentration and hidden memories. Anja watched as the air around him seemed to shimmer, a tactile tension building. His body seemed to waver in the mirror and beside her as if made of liquid rather than flesh and bone. Gradually, his facial features elongated, his hair merging into a dark mane that framed his face with regal elegance. His ears shifted position, becoming more prominent and pointed, and fangs elongated from his upper jaw. Within moments, Lucian's reflection had transformed into a majestic lion, still bipedal and distinctly him but with the attributes of the great beast.

The air in the room felt thicker, charged with the power of the transformation. Anja watched in awe as Lucian gradually shifted back to his original form, his eyes meeting hers in the mirror again.

"How do you feel?" Anja asked.

"Empowered," he said. "It was as if I reached into an untapped reservoir within myself. It felt natural, as though this had been a part of me all along, waiting for the right moment to emerge. It's as if another facet of my being has been revealed, as yours was to you."

Anja stepped closer, her eyes meeting his. "We're both discovering more about our natures, aren't we?" She said softly, almost rhetorically. "Our powers, our possibilities are just extensions of who we've always been."

Lucian nodded, his eyes glowing with an inner fire. "Yes, but not just extensions. They're revelations. And I can't help but feel that something led us to this moment."

As they stood before the mirror, their reflections still vibrant with untapped potential, Anja couldn't help but feel they were on the cusp of something monumental—personal evolutions. They had ventured into the depths of their identities and found not just individual power but something that spoke of an even greater union.

Twenty-Three

ANJA'S EYES MET Lucian's one final time before she focused her will on sending him back. "I'll be back soon," she whispered.

With a thought, Lucian's form dissolved into mist, dissipating like a memory. The character of her space—the power of her dominion—lay thick around her. Seizing the moment to explore further, she started to wander. Each chamber she discovered seemed to expand upon the last, adding layers of complexity and potential to her sanctuary. She marveled at a lavish bathing chamber where pools of varying temperatures beckoned, from icy cold to luxuriously hot. One shallow pool under the cascade of a shimmering waterfall, glowing rocks behind the cascade cast sparkles through the spay and mist. The space had an ethereal quality, as if not just her body but her very soul could be cleansed here.

Further exploration revealed a wardrobe chamber, rows and rows of garments for every conceivable occasion. There, amidst silks and velvets, her eyes fell upon her familiar wrap-around dress, hanging as if it had always been there.

Feeling curious, her eyes darted toward the unexplored chamber entrances. She peered into one that hinted at darker possibilities—a dungeon, its purpose and utility not yet clear but certainly imbued with significance. It gave her pause, a moment to acknowledge that complexities and contradictions resided in the core of her being.

Various implements adorned the walls, hanging from pegs—whips, floggers, paddles, and other implements. A large X-shaped stand was in one corner: a Saint Andrew's Cross. Tales from gothic novels sprang to mind, bringing an arousal she couldn't deny.

Feeling almost overwhelmed by the revelations of her explorations, Anja decided it was time to return. She traced her way back through the intimate labyrinth to the bedroom. Approaching the mirror again, she took one last look at her reflection before assuming her original form. With a thought, she called back her dress, wrapping up her body somewhat reluctantly. As she walked through her reading room, fingers trailing along the spines of the books, she felt at home. With a sigh, she climbed up the dark stone steps. She reached the entrance and went down the path until she stood again before the gate near the rock. She reached out mentally, feeling for the tether that connected her to Lucian and, through him, to the tangible world she had momentarily left behind. With a focused thought, she stepped through the gateway, finding herself by the estate's lake, her feet touching the natural ground, her face kissed by actual sunbeams.

Even after returning to the physical realm, she realized something profound: her power was more alive than ever. As if emboldened by the sojourn into her deepest self, her abilities felt magnified, resonating with the very fibers of her being. It was another awakening, not just of power, but of the seemingly infinite possibilities ahead.

Slipping on her sandals, Anja took a deep breath and started walking up the rocky slope. The air, laced with the earthy scent of the forest, seemed to greet her with a whispered acknowledgment of her newfound power. She moved through the trees effortlessly, their leaves forming a rustling chorus, until she reached the sprawling estate. For all its grandeur, the imposing structure felt like a different kind of sanctuary. Stepping inside, the lively hum of conversation and the clatter of cutlery reached her ears. A breakfast gathering was in full swing in the dining room. Carlos and Claire were talking together, plates already empty. Lucian looked up as Anja entered, and their eyes met. It was a silent but eloquent exchange. She greeted him with a kiss and a radiant smile, a secret shared.

As she passed along the table, her touch lingered on Emma's arm, a soft acknowledgment of their unique friendship. Ian caught her eye, the lingering look between them charged with the experience they had shared. Anja nodded toward Carlos and Claire and proceeded to fill her plate. Bacon cooked to crispy perfection, fluffy eggs, and a colorful section of fresh fruits made their way onto her plate. And more bacon. As she settled into her seat, Lucian resumed outlining plans.

"Given our recent awakenings, it's imperative for us to understand our new capabilities fully. Regular physical testing and training will continue for all, including Anja and myself."

"The Sodality threat looms large," he added, shifting the atmosphere subtly. "So combat training is also on the agenda for Anja and me. The rest of you should continue to adapt and incorporate your new strengths and abilities."

Anja set down her fork, the remnants of her breakfast pushed to the side of her plate. Turning her attention to Ian, she asked, "Combat training? I have absolutely zero experience in that." She glanced briefly at Lucian, whose eyes met hers with a mix of understanding and reassurance.

She added, "Though, I can sense a sort of excitement at the idea of violence. I seem to have a darker side."

The room quieted, the mood shifting subtly as everyone at the table tuned in to listen. Ian leaned back in his chair, his face taking on a serious expression. "Well, all of us guards are proficient in various combat styles. They could certainly assist and maybe even alternate depending on the skills that need to be honed," he began.

"While in the service, I had occasions where I was called on to instruct various combat skills and have received extensive training in various types. I will probably lead most of your sessions," Ian continued. "We'll start with the basics—hand-to-hand combat, knife training, and some pistol exercises. This will help us gauge where you both are skill wise."

He paused, looking around the table to gauge reactions before adding, "Once we have a baseline, we can tailor the training further. Given our unique abilities, it would be beneficial to incorporate some unconventional tactics. We each have new capabilities and need to try them out to leverage them. We should all explore and practice to adjust to our new strengths."

Raven was happy with how the photos of Lucian with Vanessa had turned out. Vanessa's escort profile and a few leaked videos provided suitable graphic material for training the deepfakes. There were plenty of publicity photos of Lucian as well. Combining them with a few porn videos that had good matches for Vanessa and Lucian's general appearance and hair would set the media alight. The kinky scenes of hardcore bondage should be enough to scare away the meek librarian.

She had been able to gather more rumors from Anja's high school, but they tended to be exaggerated and wild. They didn't seem to fit Anja's personality, but perhaps they were useable anyway. There were virtually no images of Anja online. No social media profiles. Nothing. Not enough to work with unless she could take some photos herself, which now seemed unlikely. The only viable plan would be to plant rumors with some of the library's patrons along the lines of gathered rumors. She had been reclusive and apparently squeaky clean, so rumors would have to do.

Now, she only had to decide on how to get the photos and videos in front of Anja for her to see. Maybe leak them online to one of the porn streaming sites and point the tabloids to them, then get the library to tip her off—leak rumors about a 'secret' romance between Anja and Lucian to the same tabloids. Select a few library patrons, researchers, or even the head librarian and pass on some juicy rumors about Anja. She might even be terminated as an employee. That seemed promising.

Raven sat in the dim light of her secured workspace, the glow of multiple screens illuminating her face. After double-checking her encryption protocols, she typed her report to the US/NE Controller. She attached the files carefully, each one a calculated strike designed to maximize damage.

Subject: Proceeding as planned

USA/NE Controller,

Enclosed are videos and images of Lucian with Vanessa. The deepfakes are convincing enough to pass most scrutiny. The objective is twofold: to embarrass Lucian and Vanessa publicly and to cause a rift between Lucian and Anja. The emotional fallout should give the Sodality new inroads.

Once the files are uploaded, I'll alert my contacts in various New York and the UK tabloids. They're known for their lack of discretion and should jump on this. It will spread like wildfire, discrediting them both in the public eye.

Simultaneously, I will disseminate rumors among selected patrons of the Morgan Library regarding Anja's relationship with Lucian and her questionable conduct. The intent is to put her employment in jeopardy. If my sources are accurate, she's particularly vulnerable to this form of attack.

After the tabloid articles hit the stands, I'll ensure that the head librarian at the Morgan Library receives a 'concerned tip,' accompanied by hard copies. The insinuation will be clear: Anja's continued employment is a liability they can't afford.

Your loyal operative,

Raven.

Raven reviewed her report one last time. Satisfied, she hit 'send,' the message and its toxic attachments whisking off into the digital ether. Her plan would be set into motion. The Sodality would have its openings; it was only a matter of time.

Richard sat back in his leather chair, the air in his hidden location humming with tension. After decrypting and reading Raven's message, a glint of satisfaction flickered in his eyes. The plan was proceeding well, almost too well.

He opened a new encrypted message window and began typing:

Subject: Re: Proceeding as planned

Raven,

Your efforts should produce the desired effects. I've reviewed the files, and they meet the quality and verisimilitude we need to implement our plan. Deploy them as you have detailed.

I am activating several additional operatives to be on standby. These resources will provide further depth and reach for our endeavors. They'll be prepared to move as soon as the situation unfolds and opportunities arise. You should likewise be prepared to assist them. More details, including their contact information, will be forthcoming.

Proceed with your part of the operation. Once the fissures appear, we'll expand them into chasms impossible for our targets to bridge.

Your Controller,

USA/NE.

His fingers hovered over the mouse, contemplating briefly, then clicked "send." The wheels were now in motion; soon enough, they would have their opportunity. And when that moment came, they would strike swiftly, mercilessly. Like vipers striking from the tall grass, they would make their move.

Raven sat before her computer, her fingers dancing across the keyboard with practiced ease. She had meticulously scrubbed any metadata or digital fingerprints that could link her to the uploaded files. Once satisfied, she navigated to several different streaming porn sites, uploading the deepfakes of Lucian and Vanessa and titling them to be easy to find. Her software routed her connection through a labyrinthine series of virtual private networks and proxy servers, effectively rendering her untraceable. With the files uploaded, she paused momentarily, a sense of anticipation tingling through her. Soon, the world would bear witness to her crafty manipulations, and the resulting fallout would wreak havoc in the lives of her targets.

Next, she prepared a series of anonymous tips, cloaking her digital missives in layers of anonymity. These she sent to the selected tabloid contacts in New York and the UK, 'journalists' who had a knack for sensationalism and a reputation for not looking too closely at their sources. Feeling the buzz of adrenaline, she took a step back. Now, it was a waiting game. The tabloids would soon bite, and the scandal would erupt when they did. In the coming hours, she would check and recheck the sites, bask in the spreading chaos, and prepare herself for the next phase.

While Raven harbored no illusions about the morality of her actions, it would further their plans. The sheer excitement of setting multiple wheels in motion and anticipating their inevitable collision was intoxicating. Reclining in her chair, her thoughts drifted toward the next phase, where she would be called upon to assist in what promised to be a dramatic and potent execution of their long-term goals.

PART THREE

Twenty-Four

By LATE AFTERNOON of their first intensive training day, sweat glistened on everyone's brow. The week had been a constant flurry of activity, each day revealing new layers of their enhanced abilities. Tensions and spirits ran high; a clear sense of purpose united them all.

Standing before the assorted group, Ian wiped his brow and surveyed the faces before him. They had been at it since morning, interspersing standard combat drills with attempts to harness their newfound gifts. Each member had shown surprising aptitude, but the physical toll was evident, even considering their improved stamina. They had a picnic lunch delivered by Elena, but they were beginning to flag even after that replenishment.

"So far, we've tested the limits of our bodies and our newly awakened abilities. It's time to combine them. Let's move into knife training," Ian announced, his voice unwavering but tinged with exhaustion.

He paired everyone up for the next drill, his eyes lingering on each pair as he gauged their readiness. "Anja, you're with me: Lucian, team up with Carlos. Emma, you'll work with Claire. We'll start with basic moves and proceed to something more advanced."

They began with simple knife-handling techniques; each pair focused intently on their blades and movements. Soon, the air was thick with concentration and the scent of physical exertion. Anja initially felt awkward; her grip on the knife was not as assured as she would have liked. Ian noticed and adjusted her hand gently. "Remember, it's an extension of you. Don't fight it; flow with it."

After several minutes, they switched to defensive stances and light sparring. During this exchange, Anja felt a surge of something... different. Buried instincts cascading to the surface, she summoned a long, single-tailed whip from her nexus. With a flick of her wrist, the whip snaked out, entangling Ian's hand and pulling the knife from his grasp. Enmeshed in the fight and the sudden thrill of instinctual violence, she didn't stop there; the whip looped around, catching Ian on his forearm with a crack, leaving a deep cut. He winced but looked more surprised than hurt.

"Sorry! I didn't mean..."

"It's alright, Anja. That was...impressive," Ian said, holding his bleeding arm. "I think a knife might not be your best option in situations like this. You with a whip is rather intimidating. Whatever you did to call it will be quite useful, to say the least."

Before anyone could reach for a first-aid kit, Lucian stepped in, his eyes locked onto Ian's wound, and lightly touched the cut. A gentle glow emanated from his fingers, and when he pulled his hand away, the cut had vanished, leaving only unblemished skin. Ian looked at his arm, then at Lucian, and then at Anja. "Well, that was convenient, too. Um...it looks like there is more to learn, and anyone that comes after us is in for a few surprises."

Anja exhaled, visibly relieved. "Thank you, Lucian."

Lucian nodded, his face unreadable, but his eyes gleamed with pride and curiosity. "We're all learning here. And it seems we have much to discover about ourselves. Some of the most powerful talents seem to be instinctual, and I'm not sure how we can draw those out in a controlled manner—we'll need to think about that. I'm feeling more drained now after that expenditure. I hope we can call it a day."

Lucian's words lingered in the air, marking the end of an intense day. "Agreed," Ian said, picking up his training knife. "We'll reconvene tomorrow; let's eat and rest for now. We've earned it."

The group dispersed, their auras mixing as they made their way indoors. The atmosphere was a blend of accomplishment and lingering questions, like puzzle pieces waiting to fit together. Dinner was a quiet affair; the day's revelations provided much to chew on mentally as well as physically. After a hearty meal, they retired for the evening, bodies tired but minds racing. Sleep, however, came surprisingly easy, as if their inner selves were also exhausted from the day's revelations.

Over the next few days, each individual focused on honing specific skills. Ian, leveraging his newfound strength, practiced MMA techniques against multiple partners. His advanced training in the service proved invaluable, and he was able to adapt quickly to his enhanced strength and awareness.

Carlos, meanwhile, found that his newfound abilities afforded him an uncanny accuracy with weapons. He trained relentlessly on sniping and other firearms skills, his eyes sharp and his hands steady. He spent hours in seclusion, honing his abilities to blend into his environment. His gift for stealth was becoming remarkable, and his skills with long-range weaponry reached new levels. When he wasn't practicing his sniping, he was working on perfecting aerial commands with his falcon, Aria, who had also seemed to gain sharper instincts. The ability to watch and scout through her incredibly sharp eyes high in the air would be valuable.

Lucian excelled in handgun accuracy, his shots hitting the bullseye with near-perfect consistency. His healing abilities were also tested on the occasional training injury, and the limits of his energy and focus were observed and recorded. Each healing session left him a bit drained, but he was undeterred, knowing the importance of mastering this skill and building a reservoir of what could only be described as magic. They found that Anja could also lend him power.

Anja devoted time to her newly discovered whip, that form of combat proving both intimidating and rewarding. She also practiced defensive maneuvers, focusing on evasion and distractions. Her movements became increasingly fluid as if she were dancing on the edge of reality itself. She developed an uncanny ability to direct her opponents' attention where she wanted it, often leaving them bewildered long enough for her to gain the upper hand.

Emma and Claire honed their unique skills as well. Emma's agility came to the forefront as she trained. Her movements became increasingly fluid, her reactions lightning-fast. On the other hand, Claire found that her instinctual urge to protect could manifest in tangible ways, giving her an edge in defensive postures and maneuvers, constantly aware of her surroundings.

Each day, they met to cross-train, sharing their progress and teaching one another what they had learned. During these moments of unity, the group felt almost invincible, a perfect synergy of strength, skill, and supernatural capabilities.

But as they discovered the extent of their new abilities, they couldn't shake off the sense of impending danger that hovered over them like a gathering storm. They were getting stronger, but would they be ready for whatever was coming their way? And so, day by day, they pushed their limits, determined to face whatever lay ahead, known or unknown.

Just when Anja felt like she was making strides—mastering her new skills, embracing her newfound abilities—the world came crashing down. She was in the middle of a quiet morning, reviewing some of her notes, when her phone buzzed. Seeing Mrs. Thompson's name on the caller ID made her stomach churn. An uncomfortable premonition settled over her.

"Anja, I'm afraid we have a very serious issue at hand," Mrs. Thompson's voice was formal, tinged with an emotion Anja couldn't quite place. "Pictures and stories are circulating online that make it difficult for you to continue in your role at the library."

Anja's heart plummeted. "May I ask what these stories are specifically?" she queried.

Mrs. Thompson hesitated before continuing. "I believe it would be best if you see for yourself. They involve you and Mr. Lucian Miller, and it seems a call girl, and the content is…compromising."

Anja knew she had to tread carefully. "Could you please send me these allegations? I assure you there must be some mistake."

"I will email you the links," Mrs. Thompson agreed. "However, the board is alarmed, and I must tell you, your employment is now terminated."

Anja felt her cheeks flush with both humiliation and anger. She closed her eyes for a moment and focused. She knew Mrs. Thompson had always had a soft spot for her. She tapped into this, her new abilities humming under her skin. "Mrs. Thompson, are you sure you can't reconsider? Could you at least entertain the possibility that these images and stories are fabricated?"

There was a pause, longer than Anja was comfortable with, before Mrs. Thompson finally spoke. "Fine, I'll consider the possibility. But understand, Anja, the board won't be easy to convince. I will need solid proof."

"Thank you, Mrs. Thompson," Anja breathed, a sliver of hope piercing through the fog of her emotions.

After ending the call, Anja stared at the space in front of her. A mixture of feelings—betrayal, confusion, anger—competed for her attention. But she couldn't afford to lose focus. With or without her job, she still had a role to play, skills to master, and, quite likely, enemies to fight. She couldn't allow this setback to define her. It was a painful reminder of how precarious her new life might be.

Anja braced herself as she opened her laptop, a sense of foreboding enveloping her. She found the email from Mrs. Thompson right at the top of her inbox. Navigating through it, her eyes widened as she read the disturbing allegations about her—rumors that she had been caught in a compromising position within the sacred spaces of the library. The sting of the accusations hit her hard, especially with what had happened in high school. She felt the walls she had built tremble and try to close in, at war with herself and her new identity. This was a low blow.

Anja's hands hovered over the laptop's trackpad momentarily, her eyes narrowing at the incriminating email before her. She took another steadying breath, steeling herself for whatever lay beyond those hyperlinks. Her fingers moved almost of their own accord, clicking on the first link. Her eyes scanned the lurid headline and the scathing text that followed, laying bare the details of an alleged relationship between Lucian and a known high-priced escort, Vanessa Delacroix. But what caught her attention—and twisted the knife deeper—was the speculation in such a public manner that she, Anja, might have taken Vanessa's place in Lucian's life as his paid companion.

For a moment, Anja was paralyzed, her mind racing. Questions flooded her thoughts. How had this happened? Who had orchestrated this elaborate sham? It had to be someone with resources and a motive to damage not just her but Lucian. No—she knew who was behind it—the Sodality. The article was a jumble of insinuations and images. Pictures of this Vanessa and Lucian, manipulated to look compromising, appeared alongside scathing text that painted Anja as a whore. Her face flushed with indignation and a wave of dark anger as she scrolled through the article.

She returned to the email and clicked the second link, then the third. Each article was more audacious than the last. Still, all spun the same narrative: Anja was a scandalous figure who had ensnared Lucian Miller, using her charms for immoral purposes even though there were no pictures of her, only lurid descriptions.

She shook off the initial shock, her resolve hardening within her. Whatever was going on, those behind this had just made it personal. And while she might be new to this strange, newfound life—with its powers and threats—she was no longer a stranger to fighting.

After reading the articles, she dug deeper, noting several references to unnamed sources and videos with enough clues to provide search terms that would likely lead her to them. Gathering herself once again, she started her searches and quickly found the links. Unable to stop herself, she followed the links to the porn sites. What she saw was beyond belief—so realistic they would convince anyone who didn't know Lucian as intimately as she did. These were videos of what appeared to be Lucian and Vanessa engaged in full-on hardcore BDSM sex with nothing left to the imagination. It was this that spoiled the effect. She knew Lucian's body intimately, and whoever had created them must not have considered that. She might have been fooled if she didn't realize that it was not Lucian's body she was seeing.

She didn't feel jealous so much as strangely turned on. She knew she would need to unravel those feelings more to understand them, but for now, she continued to view what she had found. One was a slideshow of images of the couple going into a familiar restaurant but also included still photographs of Vanessa nude and one of them getting into his Rolls. These images were the source of the photos used by the tabloids. She closed the laptop with a snap, her hands trembling. Anger and confusion waged a battle within her, but beneath it all simmered a powerful determination.

First, she would need to talk to Lucian. And together, they'd need to formulate a plan. This storm was far from over; if she was in its eye, she had to be prepared. She picked up her phone with a newfound sense of urgency. Dialing Lucian's number, she listened to its ring before going to voice mail. Hanging up without leaving a message, she decided to wait and think.

Lucian's phone buzzed insistently on the glass coffee table. The screen displayed "Uncle Edward," and he sighed before picking it up. Edward had a knack for calling at inconvenient times, but today, his timing couldn't be worse—or better, depending on one's point of view.

"Lucian, have you seen the tabloids?" Edward's voice crackled with urgency.

"I haven't, and I can't even guess what they're about," Lucian replied, a sinking feeling settling in his stomach.

"I suggest you look into it. Your name is being dragged through the mud along with a Vanessa Delacroix, and Anja is also getting slandered."

Edward had faced his share of public scrutiny, and Lucian knew he was speaking from experience. "I appreciate the heads-up, Uncle. I'll deal with it."

"As you should. Try to get ahead before it spirals too far out of control.”

Hanging up, Lucian immediately dialed his corporate lawyer, Charles. The conversation was quick and to the point. “Charles, we’ve got a situation—a scandal. I need you to see what you can find and to prioritize damage control. Issue take-down orders and retractions to every outlet that’s run this garbage about me and Anja.”

He heard the beep of an incoming call but ignored it for the moment, sure that it was also related to this situation.

“Got it. I’ll also contact Jonas Richter, your head of security. We’ll start looking into the origins of whatever is out there.”

“Good,” Lucian said curtly. “I want to know who’s behind this. And I want them stopped.”

As he set the phone back on the table, Lucian couldn’t help but think about the chaos erupting. This malicious, calculated move had been designed to destabilize, distract, and divide. Whoever was orchestrating this had underestimated him. He felt a sharp jolt of anticipation. This was a fight, and he was ready to take it on.

He leaned back in his chair, his eyes narrowing. Someone had just made a very dangerous enemy. Whoever was responsible was about to discover that some storms didn’t just pass—they ravaged. And this storm was just getting started.

He looked at his phone again to see who had called and what message they may have left. *Anja!* “Fuck,” he muttered to himself. No message. His anger resurfaced.

Lucian’s footsteps were quick and purposeful as he navigated the corridors of the mansion, his senses zeroing in on Anja’s location. The library. It was her sanctuary, a place she’d go for solitude and thought, but today, it seemed like a chamber of reckoning. As he entered the room, he found her staring at her closed laptop. He could feel the tension radiating off her. Before he spoke, his heart tightened at the thought of losing her over falsehoods and manipulated truths.

“Anja, have you…seen it?” His words hung in the air, heavy and loaded. She didn’t need clarification. They both knew what ‘it’ was.

She looked up, locking eyes with him, and it was as if time had slowed and each second stretched out, filled with the unspoken thoughts and fears that passed between them. Finally, she spoke, her voice low but steady. "Yes, Lucian, I have. Much of it is not real, but some of it is. Vanessa? She's real, isn't she?"

Lucian exhaled, not realizing he had been holding his breath. "Yes, she's real, but the context—it's twisted, manipulative."

Anja's gaze never wavered, searching for the depths of his sincerity. "I know… I believe you, Lucian."

She leaned back in the chair, her eyes narrowing in thought. "This was a targeted attack to drive a wedge between us. But in that, they have failed. This has the Sodality's fingerprints all over it."

Lucian nodded, pacing a few steps before stopping to face her. "Agreed. But if they're resorting to such underhanded tactics, it means they're desperate. They're trying to unbalance us."

Anja slowly smiled. "Then let's use it to our advantage. They're underestimating us and won't know they failed to create a rift between us, so let them think they succeeded. They have no idea of our new capabilities."

Lucian paused, weighing her words. "It would be a risky play, but it's not without merit. Their strategy is to divide and conquer. They'd expect us to be weaker apart."

"Exactly," Anja said, "and we can make it look like their plan is working. That should draw them out into the open. I can go to my grandmother's estate. It's not too far from here, and I've felt a pull to go there anyway."

"And I'll return to the City," Lucian mused. "But I'm not letting you go alone. I'll send Carlos with you. I don't like us being apart at all, but it seems to be our best option."

Anja considered for a moment before speaking. "And Emma, if you don't mind. She and I have a bond that might be useful."

Lucian nodded, the gears turning in his mind. "Yes. That's a good idea. She was an undercover agent and has been in tight situations before."

They both knew the weight of their decision—stepping directly into danger, each going their separate ways, yet bound by a plan that was as dangerous as it was daring.

Anja stood up, crossing the distance between them. "Then it's settled. We make it look like they've succeeded in tearing us apart, but we'll be more united than ever."

Lucian took her hands in his, his eyes meeting hers with unwavering intensity. "They'll soon find out that they've gravely underestimated us. We're not just pawns in their game."

Anja looked at Lucian, a sly expression curling the corners of her lips. "So, about this Vanessa. Care to enlighten me? Shall we review the videos together?"

Lucian grimaced at the suggestion. "I'd rather not at the moment. But to clarify, Vanessa is a paid companion. Our relationship was never deep—more of a business arrangement, really. She's submissive by nature, appealing to a darker facet of me that I like to indulge."

Anja nodded, her eyes probing into his. "I see. Like in the videos? Well, as long as we're being honest, you should know that it doesn't affect how I feel about you. In fact, I think I might like watching the two of you together but with the real you, perhaps learn something from a different perspective. Would you be up for something like that?"

"Um, you're serious about that, aren't you?" Seeing her nod, he continued, at least one part of him 'up' for it, "I think we could consider that sometime, but let's come back to that later."

Anja leaned closer to him. "Then, let's use every weapon in our arsenal, both dark and light, against them. And let's ensure that anyone who tries to come between us regrets it."

In the mansion's private conference room, all key members assembled around the elegant mahogany table: Lucian at the head, with Anja to his right, followed by Emma, Carlos, Claire, and Ian. Maps, electronic devices, and a few laptops were scattered around, tools easily at hand.

"We need to adapt," Lucian began, glancing around the table. "Given the recent tabloid revelations, our original plan needs modification."

Anja chimed in. "Correct. The Sodality thinks they've devided us, backed us into a corner, so we use that. Make them believe they've succeeded in separating us."

Ian nodded, "I understand. Misdirection. But it does raise a logistical concern for security. With each of you going to different locations, the guards will need to switch to twelve-hour shifts with no days off. It's not ideal, but it's necessary, and we can deal with it."

Carlos looked at Ian and nodded solemnly. "It's a tough schedule, but these are unique circumstances."

Lucian continued, "Emma and Carlos, you'll accompany Anja to her grandmother's estate. Ian and Claire, you come with me back to New York."

Turning his gaze to Anja, he added, "And we'll have to make our separation convincing. Anja, you and your team should leave first and make it look like you're doing so in a fit of indignation."

"Yes," Anja confirmed, her eyes meeting Lucian's. "I can do 'indignant' pretty well, I think."

Ian said, "Right after Anja leaves, we'll follow suit, Lucian. That should give the impression that we're urgently tackling the tabloid fiasco, lending more credibility to the separation."

"Exactly," Lucian said. "Before we go, I'll send our updated results and observations to Isabelle, keeping her informed."

"Alright," he concluded, "let's move out. Remember, everyone, this is a game of perception as much as action. Let's use the Sodality's arrogance against them."

A shared understanding hung in the air as they rose from their seats. It was time to put their plan into action. And whether together or apart, they were a formidable force.

Lucian moved swiftly to make the necessary arrangements. He dialed Ava's number, "I need an SUV ready for Anja and delivered here at the estate." Once that was arranged, he made another call to his private jet service to pick them up as soon as possible. Lastly, he sent a comprehensive email to Isabelle detailing their latest results and the data they'd gathered so far.

Lucian watched as Anja took out her phone and made her call. Her face softened when she began speaking, a look he interpreted as relief mixed with nostalgia.

"I'm well, Carl, thank you. And it has been too long, hasn't it?" She paused, her eyes momentarily lost in thought before refocusing. "I've wanted to visit the estate for some time now."

Lucian noticed her lips press into a thin line at the silence from the other end, signaling concern from Carl, perhaps.

"Yes, it is, in a way. Carl, I'll be coming to the estate and won't be alone. There'll be three of us in total. Can you prepare for our arrival and let Anna know? I'd like for everything to be ready when we get there."

Another pause, this one shorter. Anja looked slightly apprehensive but not overly so, a subtle clue that she had navigated whatever concern Carl might have voiced.

"I'll explain everything when I arrive. It's a bit complicated, and I think it's best discussed face to face. But don't worry, we're all okay. I'm looking forward to this visit."

One more short pause as she relaxed.

"Thank you, Carl. I can't tell you how much I appreciate this and look forward to seeing you and Anna."

Anja ended the call, her shoulders subtly lowering as if letting go of a burden. They were clearly people Anja trusted, people who could offer her a sanctuary. In the current turmoil, that seemed more precious than ever.

Carlos was busy as well, assembling a collection of falconry supplies —hood, perch, and cage—that had been delivered earlier. He had been preparing Aria for eventual travel, familiarizing her with the equipment. Today, that training would prove its worth.

Soon, a black SUV pulled up to the mansion, followed by another to take its driver back. Anja walked up to Lucian, and their lips met in a deep, lingering kiss. "See you on the other side," she whispered, her voice tinged with longing.

When they were ready to depart, bags at the ready, Carlos stepped outside, letting out a sharp whistle. Aria descended from her perch high in the trees like a feathered arrow and landed gracefully on his arm. With practiced ease, he placed a hood over her head and situated her on the perch inside her cage. He then secured the cage in the back seat of the SUV.

From a second-story window, Lucian watched as the trio got into the vehicle. Carlos settled into the driver's seat, Emma beside him as co-pilot and Anja in the back, her fingers lightly resting on Aria's cage.

As the SUV pulled away, Lucian felt a swirl of emotions: hope, worry, but most of all, determination. It was a high-stakes endeavor they were embarking on, but with the skills and the resolve they each possessed, he had every reason to believe they would pull through.

His phone buzzed; a message from Ian signaled that all would be ready for their departure in about an hour. Lucian took one last look out the window, then turned, ready to leave.

Twenty-Five

The SUV glided along the winding roads. Carlos was at the wheel, eyes focused on the road, but his demeanor relaxed. Emma occupied the front passenger seat, swiveling occasionally to converse with Anja, who was in the back seat next to the caged Aria.

"So, your grandmother's estate," Emma initiated, "I assume it's the kind of place where you can forget the world for a while?"

"Exactly," Anja replied, a wistful smile gracing her lips. "It's a sanctuary, a place where we can recalibrate. And believe me, we all need it right now."

Emma chuckled, "Recalibrate? Is that a fancy term for forgetting your worries with copious amounts of wine?"

Anja grinned, "Among other things, yes."

Carlos interjected, "Well, if it's a sanctuary for you, Anja, then I suppose we'll find Emma in a sunny corner, chasing a beam of light."

Emma playfully swatted at him. "Oh, stop it, you! Just because you all call me 'Kitty' doesn't mean I do feline things."

Carlos chuckled, "Right." Drawing the word out. "I'm just glad to have some distance between you and my bird. The way you eye Aria sometimes makes me wonder if you see her as a cat toy."

"Oh, Carlos, if I wanted a toy, it wouldn't be that bird," Emma shot back, laughter in her eyes.

As the banter continued, Anja felt her shoulders finally start to relax. The knot of tension in her stomach began to loosen. Even amid chaos, her friends, her newfound family, had a way of creating a haven of normalcy. It was one of the things she cherished most about them.

The SUV was now driving through terrain that was becoming increasingly wooded, a serene atmosphere settling over its passengers. Feeling the comforting nostalgia of the landscape, Anja decided it was a good time to share more about her roots.

"Since we're headed there, I should tell you a bit about the estate and its caretakers, Anna and Carl," Anja began, her voice tinged with sentimentality. "They've been with my family for decades since my grandparents moved there. My grandfather Patrick had the place built especially for my grandmother Madeline; he was devoted to her. She stayed there after he passed away. Carl and Anna were so devoted to her that she left them the cottage they lived in on the estate grounds."

Carlos glanced in the rearview mirror, catching Anja's eye. "That's a beautiful gesture," he remarked.

"It was," Anja agreed. "She set up a trust fund to take care of them, too. They're more like family than employees, really."

Emma was intrigued. "Your grandmother sounds like a remarkable woman."

"Oh, she was," Anja confirmed, her gaze distant as if visualizing Madeline's face. "She had what some would call 'second sight,' an intuitive understanding of things that went beyond the physical world."

"Ah, so that's where you get it from," Emma commented lightly.

Anja nodded, "She sensed that I had inherited the 'gift' as well and believed it to be because our family traces back to ancient bloodlines. She was the first person I confided in about feeling different, about sensing things that others couldn't."

"And what did she teach you?" Carlos asked, intrigued by the spiritual lineage similar but distinct from his own.

"She guided me through old chants to focus my energies and thoughts," Anja explained. "She taught ancient rituals and how to trust my feelings. I was using some of them for you two during your rituals. She taught me about goodness and love, too. I think she knew more of me than she let on, possibly seeing I needed to discover it for myself. Maybe she felt I was too young or not ready yet. Both were probably true. She saw potential in me, telling me I had a significant destiny if I could embrace myself and accept what lived within me."

With a smile and a significant look, Emma responded. "Well, that almost seems like an understatement now. I, for one, am really happy for that embrace." The double entendre was clear.

Her words lingered in the air, reverberating with unspoken possibilities. The SUV's interior was quiet for a few moments, except for the gentle hum of the engine and Aria's occasional ruffling sounds from her cage.

Finally, Carlos broke the silence. "Well, it sounds like we're headed somewhere special, a place that's been steeped in wisdom and love. I can't think of a better place for us right now."

"Me neither," Anja said softly, her eyes bright with gratitude for her past and hope for their collective future.

Lucian and Claire found themselves in the backseat of the green Rolls sedan and Ian up front with Mark, the engine's hum filling the air as they made their way to the airfield. Each lost in their thoughts, they glance out at the passing landscape—rolling hills and small towns giving way to the more industrial outlines of the airport. The car finally stopped, and they stepped out, greeted by the sleek lines of Lucian's private jet waiting on the tarmac.

Aaliyah welcomed them aboard. The cabin's plush seats and understated luxury served as a subtle reminder of the world Lucian came from—a world that, until recently, had seemed far less complicated.

The jet engines roared to life and soon soared above the clouds. The flight to Teterboro was quick, the skyline of Manhattan drawing closer until the plane touched down with a soft screech of tires. After a short taxi, the doors opened, and they disembarked, met by the familiar face of Thomas, Lucian's NYC driver.

"Welcome back, Mr. Miller," Thomas said, nodding respectfully to

Ian and Claire. "The car is ready whenever you are."

The trio slipped into the back of the Lucian's Rolls, the tinted windows enveloping them in a cocoon of privacy—the traffic as light as it could be for this time of late morning. The sounds of horns and the rumble of traffic were muted in the comfort of the Rolls. They pulled up to Lucian's penthouse in Manhattan, hoping to be observed as they returned. Ian stepped out and scanned their surrounding with a critical eye. Thomas opened the car door for them after getting a 'clear' signal from Ian. "Will you be needing anything else, sir?" he asked as they stepped out of the car.

"No, Thomas. That'll be all for now, thank you," Lucian replied, nodding.

They entered the building, the doorman offering a courteous greeting as they headed up to the penthouse. The elevator doors slid open, revealing the expansive, elegantly designed space that Lucian called home.

"We're here," Lucian stated, his voice tinged with relief and concern as they exited the elevator. "Now, let's figure out our next move."

Lucian stepped into his Manhattan penthouse, greeted by the familiar face of Ava, his supremely competent personal secretary and assistant. He noticed a faint blush coloring her cheeks as he caught her eye. "You've seen it too, haven't you?" he inquired gently.

Ava's eyes dropped, and her blush deepened; she nodded almost imperceptibly.

Lucian chuckled softly, a sound devoid of mockery. "It was convincing but faked," he assured her. "I'm sorry you had to be exposed to that, but it is what it is."

"It's good to see you, Ava," he added, his voice imbued with a comforting warmth. "Could you arrange a late lunch for us, please? Something light but satisfying. Also, I'll need a meeting with Jonas Richter, Charles from legal, and Dan Reynolds. Let's schedule it right after the lunch."

Regaining some semblance of composure, Ava met his eyes again. "Understood, Lucian. I'll set everything up."

As the clock neared the end of the lunch hour, Lucian's guests began to arrive. They exchanged brief greetings and small talk before heading toward the conference room adjacent to Lucian's office.

"Thank you all for coming on such short notice," Lucian began, locking eyes with each of the men who've played key roles in various aspects of his life and business. "We have urgent matters to discuss."

Jonas, Charles, and Dan shared a quick, knowing look. The urgency in Lucian's tone wasn't one they'd heard often.

"Let's start with the immediate concern: the scandal and the ongoing smear campaign against me—and Anja. Charles, what's the legal status? Have we been successful in issuing take-down orders?"

Charles cleared his throat before speaking. "We've issued cease-and-desist letters to the media outlets, if you can call them that, running these stories. Most have complied, but a few are holding out. It's proving a battle, but we're fighting it on every front."

"Good. And Jonas, what about tracking the source?"

Jonas Richter, head of security, leaned forward. "They're covering their tracks well—proxies, multiple IP addresses, the works. It's complex but not necessarily untraceable. We'll get to the bottom of it eventually, but it's taking time."

Lucian nodded before turning to Dan Reynolds, the private investigator. "Dan, what do you have on the rumors circulating around the Morgan Library concerning Anja?"

Dan flipped open his notebook. "Still in the early stages, but I've got a contact in there. I'm also trying to look at the security footage as I think it likely that the woman following Anja from the library obviously knew she worked there. It's almost certain that she was the source of the rumors there, if not all of the other materials. If I can identify that woman or spot her there, it could be a valuable lead. So far, nothing concrete."

"Good, Dan, keep at it." Lucian pursed his lips thoughtfully. "Ava, I assume you've been in touch with PR?"

"Yes," Ava chimed in. "We're working on a statement and some media coverage focusing on your philanthropic work and your business achievements. A redirection of sorts."

Lucian considered that before making his next point. "I want us to make it seem like the scandal has caused a rift between Anja and myself. Leak that to the rumor mill. Our enemies believe they can weaken us by driving a wedge between us; let's use that belief against them. Feed them the illusion of success. I want to see if they can be drawn out of hiding."

"Interesting strategy," Charles mused, clearly intrigued. "It's risky but could be effective. Redirect the scandal, so to speak."

"Yes," Lucian affirmed. "Let's proceed swiftly. This situation is delicate, and we have much at stake."

Before the meeting wrapped up, and just as Dan was about to leave, Lucian gestured for him to stay behind momentarily. As the others filtered out, Lucian leaned against the conference table and locked eyes with Dan.

"Dan, I need you to initiate some rumors. Make it known that I'm searching for Anja," Lucian started, watching Dan's expression closely for any signs of hesitance.

Dan nodded, jotting down notes. "Alright, I can do that."

"And," Lucian continued, "perhaps stir up some trouble around her former employment at the Morgan Library. But make sure it doesn't trace back to you."

"Create some noise about her being terminated, you mean?" Dan clarified, his eyes narrowing slightly.

"Exactly, but not by you. Get someone else to do that part. Don't blow your contacts there. I'm probably not very welcome there at the moment." Lucian affirmed. "Also, consider staging a break-in at Anja's apartment. Try to make sure it's observed but not too conspicuous. People know you're affiliated with me, and I want them to make the connection that I'm looking for her."

Dan paused, considering the implications. "This is all pretty high stakes. You sure you want to go this far?"

"I am," Lucian said, his voice firm.

Dan rubbed his chin, contemplating the assignment. "Got any other thoughts on how to sell this? It's delicate work, spreading rumors without them tracing back to you."

Lucian contemplated for a moment. "Oh, I want them traced back to me. I need them to believe I'm desperate to find her. Any other suggestions you might have would be welcome."

After a beat, Dan grins, "Alright, I've got a few ideas that could add authenticity to the situation. I'll get on it."

Lucian nodded, satisfied. "Good, make it happen."

As Dan left the room, Lucian couldn't help but feel the gravity of the complex web they were weaving. It was a gamble, but they needed every advantage they could get right now.

Lucian turned to Claire, "Go get some rest. You've earned it."

Claire nodded, a flash of gratitude crossing her eyes before exiting, leaving Lucian and Ian alone in the room.

Lucian took a deep breath, his eyes meeting Ian's. "I don't like putting Anja in a potentially dangerous situation, but given the circumstances, I believe it's our best option."

Ian leaned back, crossing his arms as he studied Lucian. "Are there truly no other options? The risk is considerable."

"Between Carlos, Emma, and Anja herself, they should be able to handle anything that comes their way," Lucian assured him, yet the weight of the decision hung heavy on his shoulders.

Ian pressed, "Anja is special, Lucian. It doesn't sit well with me, risking her like this."

Lucian looked at Ian, his expression softening yet resolute. "She is very special—more than you know. But trust me, Ian, she can handle it."

Ian locked eyes with Lucian for a moment longer, searching for something—perhaps reassurance or a sign of doubt. He nodded, seemingly placated yet still on edge. Both men knew the gravity of the decisions being made, and both were keenly aware that in their world, even the best-laid plans could unravel in the blink of an eye.

Lucian instructed Ian to step out to the reception area with Ava, a request he acknowledged without question. Alone in the room, Lucian sank into his leather chair and stared at his phone. He scrolled through his contacts until he reached the one he'd been avoiding. His finger hovered over the call button momentarily before he finally pressed it.

The line rang twice before a voice answered in French, "Allo?"

"Vanessa…," Lucian's voice trailed off, the tension palpable even through the phone.

There was a weighty pause on the other end. "Lucian," she said, dragging out his name as if searching for meaning in the syllables.

"You've seen it then," Lucian finally stated, cutting through the layers of awkward silence.

"Oui," she replied, her voice laced with anger and confusion. "What is all this about? Why? What's going on, Lucian?"

He exhaled deeply. "It's complicated, Vanessa. This isn't something I can discuss openly. Not over the phone. Not in public, given the circumstances. Can you come see me? Discreetly."

Another pause filled the line before Vanessa spoke, "Fine. I've been taking some time off. I'll come over this evening."

"Thank you," Lucian said, a mixture of relief and regret coating his words.

"À ce soir," she said, signaling the end of their conversation.

Lucian hung up, placing his phone back on the desk. The night would undoubtedly be complex, fraught with difficult conversations and awkward explanations. Yet, it was a necessary step in this intricate dance he'd found himself in. And with that thought, he summoned Ian back into the room.

Ian closed the door behind him and sat across from Lucian, who leaned forward, elbows on the desk, eyes locked on Ian's. "We need to discuss Anja's situation. She's at her grandmother's estate, and we need to think strategically."

Ian nodded, considering the variables. "Anja is in a vulnerable, geographically isolated position, making her an attractive target where we are not. We should assume they'll go after her first."

"Exactly," Lucian interjected. "They might think capturing her will give them leverage over me. It's a typical move, go after someone who seems less protected to get to the real target."

"Then we need to make them think they're right, that she's unprotected," Ian suggested, his eyes narrowing. "Use it as a bait-and-switch. Make them believe they've gained the upper hand, only to trap them in the act."

Lucian rubbed his chin, pondering the idea. "And once we have one, we can use that individual to trace back to their leaders—cut off the head of the snake, so to speak."

"Exactly. We could set up some hidden surveillance around the estate and even plant misinformation—leaked schedules, fake security lapses. Once they take the bait, we close the net," Ian elaborated.

Ian leaned back, a bit deflated, when Lucian raised his objection. "No tech surveillance. They are too easy to spot, and we can't afford to tip them off. They're more cunning than that. Also, we must try to keep Emma and Carlos' presence hidden. Make it seem like she is on her own and vulnerable."

Lucian paused, letting the words settle. "Carlos is there and has eyes in the sky with Aria. Emma is competent and skilled. As for Anja, she has quite a few surprises up her sleeve that would catch them off guard."

Ian grinned, appreciating that thought. "Like the whip, you mean?"

Lucian chuckled, an edge of admiration coloring his voice. "Yes, that, and much more. Anja is a force, not easily subdued—and she has been taking it easy on you in practice, just so you know. They will underestimate her, and it'll be their downfall."

"She has, huh? That's kind of scary if true. So, we let the Sodality find them on their own?" Ian asked, catching on to the subtlety of Lucian's plan.

"Exactly," Lucian confirmed. "No bread crumbs, no trails. Let them take their time finding her, thinking they've found a weak link. It will buy us more time to prepare. And when the Sodality makes their move, they'll walk into a situation they can't control."

Ian nodded, fully aligned with the plan now.

Lucian closed his computer, finishing his conversation with Ian. "Keep me posted on any new developments with Anja," he instructed as Ian gave a curt nod in agreement.

At that moment, Claire came in from her room. "I'm ready to take over for the night," she said, looking first at Lucian and then Ian.

Lucian announced. "Just so you know, I'm expecting company tonight. Vanessa will be coming over for dinner. The meal will be delivered shortly before she arrives."

Claire and Ian fixed their eyes on Lucian, a 'look' that demanded an explanation.

"She was involved in the scandal as well. We need to discuss those matters, and it can't be in public or over the phone. Too impersonal and too many risks," Lucian clarified, his palm out in a 'hold on' motion. "It's not the best, but it may also lend veracity to the situation we are trying to portray."

"All right. If you're sure you need to do this, I'll leave you to it. I'll see you in the morning," Ian said, heading for his room for the night.

Claire had already been alerted about a visitor from building security below. When the elevator doors swung open, Vanessa stepped in, her eyes first meeting Claire's professional but courteous gaze and then shifting to Lucian's. There was an awkward silence, a room filled with unspoken words and lingering questions. Lucian stepped forward, an implicit invitation for Vanessa to enter further into the penthouse and the complexity that awaited them.

"Come in, Vanessa," Lucian finally said.

With Ava having already gone home, Claire sat behind her desk as Lucian guided Vanessa back to the living spaces and into the dining room. The room was subtly lit, and a meal had been carefully arranged on the dining table. The atmosphere was designed to help cut through the awkwardness. Lucian poured two glasses of red wine from a decanter set to breathe, then started to uncover the dishes set out and still warm.

"So why, Lucian? Why would someone do this? And who?" Pain and anger were both evident in her voice.

"There is a group; I won't go into details. They were the ones who killed my parents, brother, sister, and her lover." His tone grew angrier, "They were after me but failed. They want to stop what I'm trying to accomplish."

His voice softened. "Since you have been noticed, there is the possibility you could be used as leverage to get to me. I don't think it is likely, but please be careful. More careful than you already are."

They sat, the air still thick with tension. Vanessa picked up her fork but hesitated, her eyes finally locking onto Lucian's.

"So, this Anja person," she began cautiously. "You two are an item now—or were?"

Lucian nodded, swirling a glass of his wine before taking a sip. "Yes, we are. But for appearances, we want to maintain the illusion that she's left me. This scandal has added...complexities."

Vanessa put down her fork, leaning back in her chair. "And what about us?" she asked. "What does this mean for our...arrangement?"

Lucian set his glass down, his gaze steady. "I've been working diligently to bury this scandal. For both of us. Rest assured, I'm using every resource at my disposal."

"But the question remains," she persisted.

Lucian sighed, weighing his words carefully. "I think it's likely that I won't be requiring your services anymore, Vanessa."

"I can't say that does not sadden me," she admitted, her eyes meeting his once again as a mixture of acknowledgment and sadness washed over her face. After all, she enjoyed their time together in a way that went beyond the professional.

"We've had our moments," Lucian conceded, "and for what it's worth, I've genuinely enjoyed our time together. But yes, circumstances have changed."

Vanessa nodded, her eyes slightly misty but composed. "Then let's make the best of now," she said, lifting her wine glass.

Lucian followed suit, and their glasses clinked, then added hesitantly. "But..."

She raised an eyebrow—waiting.

"Well, Anja has expressed an interest in learning...watching...and maybe more. She brought up that topic after watching those fake videos of us. She could immediately tell it was not me but only my face. She knew they were fake."

"She sounds like an interesting woman."

Lucian grinned, "Oh, you have no idea..."

Vanessa considered him for a few moments before responding. "As a couple, you say. I have entertained that way, but usually, I'm the one to arrange for the extra company. It is uncommon for a dedicated couple to seek my services, though not unheard of. But, yes, I would be willing as long as that is what you both want."

"It won't be anytime soon, as too much is happening. Let's just keep it in mind for the future as a possibility."

The tension that initially gripped the room dissipated, replaced by a nostalgic warmth as they engaged in a more casual conversation. They reminisced and laughed, and it felt like old times for a brief moment. Eventually, the clock ticked its way into the late evening, signaling it was time for Vanessa to leave. Lucian stood and escorted her to the door. As they reached it, she turned to him, her eyes reflecting a complex blend of emotions—gratitude, sorrow, and a hint of wistful longing.

"Au revoir, Lucian," she said softly, her words tinged with a hopeful note. "J'espère que nous aurons l'occasion de nous revoir."

He looked into her eyes and nodded. "Goodbye, Vanessa," he replied.

With a soft, lingering touch, she reached up to give him a gentle kiss on the cheek. Then she turned and stepped into the elevator, disappearing into the night. Lucian stood there for a moment longer, contemplating the weight of farewells and the passage of time before finally closing the door behind her. Regretting not having Anja with him even more, he headed back to his rooms.

Twenty-Six

ANJA FELT A wave of nostalgia as Carlos guided the car down the winding driveway of the estate. Lush rhododendrons and towering sugar maples, evidence of Carl's attentive care, flanked the path. When the car pulled to a gentle stop in front of the main entrance, Carl and Anna came out to greet them. As Anja stepped out of the vehicle, her eyes met Carl's warm, earthy gaze. The corners of his eyes crinkled as he offered a quiet smile. A similar warmth emanated from Anna, her green eyes twinkling.

"Anja," Carl exclaimed softly, moving toward her. Their hug was like an embrace from the earth itself—solid, genuine, and comforting. Anna was next, her embrace like a warm hearth, bringing an immediate sense of home.

"Carl, Anna," Anja said, pulling away, "I'd like you to meet some special people. This is Emma, a dear friend of mine."

Emma offered a charming smile, met with welcoming nods from Carl and Anna.

"And this," Anja continued, gesturing to Carlos, "is Carlos."

Carlos stepped forward, offering Carl a firm but courteous handshake and then Anna. Aria, his majestic falcon, perched gently on his other arm, whose keen eyes seemed to take in her new surroundings with measured curiosity. He had already taken her out and removed her hood from the drive.

"It's a pleasure to meet you both finally. Anja has told me so much about you," Carlos said.

"And this fine creature?" Carl asked, looking at Aria.

"This is Aria. I think she's ready for a bit of exploration."

With a graceful motion, Carlos extended his arm, releasing Aria into the sky. She circled once above them before venturing into the canopy of trees.

"Aria, stay near," Carlos called out, watching as the falcon soared but stayed within sight.

Carl and Anna looked at each other, then back at their visitors. "Welcome to your home, Anja," Carl said softly. "And welcome to all of you. Let's head inside. Anna's prepared something special for dinner."

Once inside, the comforting aroma of home-cooked food filled the air, mingling with the scent of freshly polished wood and floral arrangements. Anna guided everyone into the dining room, where a large table awaited, impeccably set with fine china and silverware. Crystal glasses gleamed in the soft lighting, reflecting the intricate patterns of the tablecloth.

As they took their seats, Anja caught Carlos' eye and smiled, a sense of contentment settling over her. "Carl and Anna have been like parents to me," she said softly, her eyes drifting to the couple who had just seated themselves at the opposite end. "Their love and support have always been a constant."

Carl and Anna exchanged glances, smiles pulling at the corners of their mouths. "It's been our joy to watch you grow, Anja," Anna said. "And a pleasure to meet your friends."

Dinner commenced with a series of delectable dishes, all expertly prepared by Anna, each telling a story of the estate's history and the people who had called it home. Laughter and conversation flowed as freely as the wine, the room infused with camaraderie and genuine affection. During the meal, Carl and Anna couldn't resist sharing a few anecdotes from Anja's childhood—times she had tried to plant her own "garden" consisting of wildflowers and weeds, or the Christmas where she'd insisted on cooking the dinner herself, which ended up being more of a lesson in fire safety than culinary arts.

Carlos and Emma joined in the laughter.

After dessert, Anna grew somewhat contemplative, her eyes meeting Anja's. "There's something I need to give you, Anja. Something from Madeline."

Anja felt a momentary ripple of surprise but nodded. "Of course."

Anna rose from her chair, her movements graceful and purposeful. "If you would come with me," she said, her eyes briefly meeting her husband's. Carl nodded, a quiet understanding passing between them.

As Anja stood, she noticed Carlos subtly rise, as if compelled to follow but not wanting to intrude. She offered him an encouraging glance, granting silent permission.

Anna led Anja through the main house and out the back door, walking the short distance to the quaint cottage that she and Carl now called home. As they entered the cottage, Anna finally spoke. "Madeline told me years ago that a day would come when you'd visit with mysterious guests," she said softly, moving toward an antique cabinet. "She felt that would be the right time for you to have this."

She opened the cabinet door and carefully pulled out what appeared to be a fair-sized keepsake box wrapped in a cloth tied with a red ribbon. With reverent hands, she passed it to Anja.

"She said you should have this. She told me that she wished she could pass this on to you herself, but it was not to be. She knew you would not be ready yet."

Anja took the box, its weight surprising for its size, and looked up to meet Anna's eyes. "Thank you, Anna. This means more than you can imagine."

Anna simply nodded, her eyes moist. "She loved you very much, Anja. We all do."

As they returned to the main house, Carlos' eyes met Anja's, questions in his gaze. She smiled, her grip tightening around the bundle. Now wasn't the time for answers, but she felt in her heart that the day would come soon when the mysteries of the past would blend into the promises of the future.

Carl had prepared a tray of tea and an assortment of biscuits, a warm pot steaming gently amidst the fine china cups. The array sat invitingly on the coffee table in the living room, a soft glow from the chandelier overhead casting a serene ambiance.

"Ah, perfect timing," Carl said, his eyes catching Anja's as she entered with the cloth-wrapped treasure still firmly in her grasp.

They settled into the plush armchairs and sofas that encircled the room, each person selecting their tea and accompanying biscuit. The air grew quiet, an unusual gravity settling over them as they sipped their drinks. Anja was the first to break the silence.

"There's something you should know," she began, her eyes glancing between Carl and Anna. "There may be trouble coming—dangerous individuals who intend to come for me."

To her surprise, Carl and Anna exchanged a look, not of shock or alarm, but of expectation—as if they had been waiting for this news.

"We had a feeling that this day would come, didn't we, Anna? Madeline hinted at something like this." Carl remarked, his voice steady as he looked over at his wife.

"Yes," Anna confirmed, her expression unchanged, but her eyes now deeply focused on Anja.

"We'll be making preparations over the next few days," Anja continued, reassured by their unflappable composure. "It's important that we're all ready."

Carlos leaned forward, setting down his tea cup. "I think it would be wise for me to explore the grounds with Carl. I need to get to know the surroundings as thoroughly as possible."

Anna caught on instantly. "And Emma should acquaint herself with the cottage and the manor. I can show her around—point out the little details that could be important."

As they dispersed, Anja felt a mix of emotions. The comfort and strength she drew from Carl and Anna's steady presence were like anchors, yet the looming threat turned her thoughts inward. With the mysterious box in hand, she went upstairs to her bedroom—once Madeline's sanctuary—gently closing the door behind her.

The room was, as she remembered it, tasteful and elegant. The light of sunset filtered through the curtains, casting soft patterns on the furnishings. She sat on the bed, her eyes finally settling on the bundle. It felt both alien and familiar—its origins rooted in the past, yet its presence seemingly a key to her future. Anja focused on the gift before her. She gently untied the ribbon and unwrapped the plain cloth, revealing the box within. Its exterior was unassuming but smooth from wear and weathered by the ages.

A sense of nervousness washed over her. This was no ordinary box; it held secrets passed down from generations that might have been deliberately kept hidden—or saved for a moment like this. Her fingers traced the box's smooth wood surface as if searching for an invitation, a clue, or perhaps even a whisper from the past. For a moment, Anja simply stared at it before opening the lid, absorbing the gravity of what lay before her. Inside, she found an assortment of items carefully arranged: diaries, trinkets, notes, and tokens. The diaries were leather-bound and aged, their pages yellowed but well-preserved. A couple of them had Madeline's name elegantly scripted on the first page, while one bore the name of Anja's great-great-grandmother, Elspeth Black.

Scattered among the diaries were various notes and tokens—small artifacts that seemed inconspicuous but carried the weight of generational narratives. Under it all was a piece of tartan fabric with fringed ends—a sash—its pattern a vivid dance of green, blue, and a streak of crimson, with interspersed threads of gold. It was an ancient design, hailing from the McGregor clan of the Scottish Highlands, a tangible relic of a history that reached across both geography and time.

As Anja unfolded the tartan and laid it out on the bed in half, she felt a connection snap into place—like a circuit completing its loop. The fabric seemed to embody a legacy of resilience and lore, and as she touched it, her thoughts circled back to Madeline and her hidden lineage. She carefully laid out the contents of the box on the tartan. With a sense of urgency mixed with reverence, Anja reached for the oldest diary, eager to connect the dots of her complicated legacy. As she opened it, the pages seemed eager to divulge their secrets. She felt as though Madeline and the generations before her were granting her access to collective wisdom, urging her to use it in navigating her life.

She felt a pulse of recognition upon touching them as if some part of her already knew their contents. This was her legacy, spelled out in ink and penned in the hands of the women who had come before her. The entries spoke of their experiences, challenges, and even vaguely of a lineage traced back to Naamah's line. Madeline's entries were particularly intriguing; she wrote of a "sight" that allowed her glimpses into realms others couldn't perceive, a diluted but undeniable gift from her heritage. Anja felt a burgeoning sense of empowerment; her lineage was not just a history but a tapestry of strength, choices, and potential. And she, with this newfound knowledge, was the latest weaver of its ongoing design.

Alongside the diaries, she found notes filled with ancestral tales, the stories undoubtedly warped and changed as they passed from generation to generation but still holding grains of truth. There were other items: a bronze brooch and pin cast with knot work, a worn stone carving, and other items she would need to examine and understand later.

Sitting there, the diaries and tokens surrounding her, Anja felt a connection unlike any other. It was as if she were finally plugging into a network that had always been dormant and waiting. The box was a treasure trove. With these newfound insights, Anja felt supported by the silent but potent strength of the women who had walked this path before her.

Emma's knock on the door came as a soft, rhythmic tapping— enough to alert Anja but not startle her from her introspective state. "Come in," Anja called, and the door swung open to reveal Emma's face, tinged with curiosity and concern. Darkness had fallen long ago.

"Would you like to stay with me tonight?" Anja suggested, her voice softer now yet tinged with a fatigue that reached beyond physical exhaustion. "The bed is large enough, and I think it would be good for both of us. I have grown to like having someone next to me."

Emma nodded, her eyes meeting Anja's in silent agreement. "I'll go get my things," she said before stepping out.

Left alone, Anja placed each diary, note, and token back into the box with the same care one might use to handle heirlooms, which, in essence, they were. She placed the box on her bedside table, its presence a silent sentinel of her lineage and legacy. By the time Emma returned, Anja had undressed and was pulling back the bed's luxurious covers. Emma soon followed, and both settled into bed, their movements becoming comfortable familiarity. Anja felt an almost magnetic pull towards Lucian. Closing her eyes, she extended her senses, tapping into their unique connection. She found him in dreams, his consciousness adrift in slumber. Anja entered those dreams like a gentle breeze, offering a sense of comfort and presence. She sensed Lucian's momentary awareness, a soft ripple in the landscape of his dreamscape, before pulling away. While she wished to linger, to provide a deeper level of reassurance, the weight of her fatigue and the need for rest nudged her back into her own mind.

With a final sigh, Anja let herself sink into the comfort of the bed and the soothing warmth of Emma, her mind still tingling from the evening's revelations. As her thoughts drifted and her body relaxed, she felt as though she was settling into a deeper understanding of herself—an understanding enriched by her past and emboldening her for the challenges of the future.

The morning light streamed through the dining room windows, casting dappled patterns on the elegant table setting. Anna had prepared breakfast—a spread of fluffy pancakes with real maple syrup, harvested and prepared by Carl, crisp bacon, freshly baked pastries, and seasonal fruits, with Carl pitching in by pressing fresh orange juice, brewing a fresh pot of coffee, and arranging a colorful bouquet of flowers from the estate's garden.

As everyone settled in and filled their plates, Carlos initiated the conversation, cutting through the pleasant morning haze. "I've been in touch with some of the local raptors. There's an owl I've particularly connected with. I'll be out in the woods for the next few days, keeping watch on the grounds with my friends. It'll be like old times, just...more comfortable."

He flashed a half smile, and Anja couldn't help but admire his ease in adapting to their current circumstances.

"I'll make sure to leave your supplies at the spots we found last evening," Carl interjected, his voice steady and supportive. "You'll have everything you need."

"Emma should stay inside, out of sight," Anja added, casting a glance towards her friend, who nodded in acknowledgment.

Anna set down her teacup, giving Anja a focused look. "We'll carry on as usual, then. Pretend you are our only guest; make things look ordinary."

"Thank you, all of you," Anja said, her voice tinged with a sincerity that needed no embellishment. "I couldn't ask for more."

The room settled into a momentary silence. Then, with the clatter of cutlery and the soft murmur of conversation, breakfast continued, a veneer of normalcy that couldn't quite mask the undercurrent of worry.

Shortly after they had dispersed from the table, a call came in; Zoe's voice was like a swirl of colors against the estate's muted tones —a reminder of another life, another reality. The conversation was a flurry of worry and indignation on Zoe's part and cautious reservation on Anja's. When Zoe insisted on coming to see her, Anja had to quell an instinctive urge to keep her world secret. Yet, there was something comforting about the intrusion of an old friend, especially one like Zoe.

"Look, if you don't tell me where you are, I'll track you down and find you anyway!"

"Alright, Zoe, I'll text you the address and directions, but please have a taxi or someone drop you off; um…no space for other cars."

Zoe could immediately tell something else was going on but didn't press. "I'll be there as soon as I can."

"I can tell you more when you get here. I really am looking forward to seeing you again."

As the sun dipped toward the horizon, casting long shadows on the estate grounds, a car rolled up the gravel drive. Zoe stepped out, her eyes widening as she took in her surroundings. She had already paid the driver, and he left after she grabbed her bag. The moment Anja saw her, she felt relief and worry. Both women stood still for a moment. Then, as if pulled by an invisible cord, they moved toward each other and embraced, clinging to the tactile reassurance of an old friendship.

"You look well," Zoe said, studying Anja's face. "Considering the madness that's consuming every media outlet."

"I'm managing," Anja replied, her eyes not quite meeting Zoe's. "It's complicated."

They made their way inside the manor; Anja was aware that Zoe's presence added another layer of intricacy to their precarious situation. Anna greeted them warmly, bringing in a tray of iced tea and pastries, ever the impeccable hostess. After a brief introduction, Anja and Zoe retreated to the more private sitting room.

"Okay," Zoe began, sipping her tea and setting it down. "Start talking. Because right now, all I can think about is the hellfire that's raining down on you and Lucian, and I can't reconcile it with…this," she gestured broadly, indicating the tranquility of the estate.

Anja took a deep breath, fortified and unsettled by Zoe's frankness. How much could she reveal? How much did she dare? And yet, despite the risks, the thought of confiding in someone from her 'former' life was deeply appealing.

"I suppose you could say I'm in a sanctuary," Anja began cautiously. "And I'm not alone. There are others here, good people, helping me get through this."

Zoe scrutinized her as if sensing the words left unsaid. "That sounds evasive, even for you."

Anja sighed, her fingers closing around her cup for comfort. "There's much more, Zoe, perhaps more than you're ready to hear. But for now, know this: I'm safe, and we're preparing for some uncertainties."

It was a half answer, a partial truth, but it was all Anja could offer just now. And, as she looked at Zoe, she saw her friend process it, weigh it—then reject it.

"No, Anja, Spill!"

Before Anja could respond, Emma entered the room, the door softly clicking behind her. At the sight of Zoe, her eyes narrowed for a fraction of a second before widening in recognition.

"Zoe? I remember you from our trip." Emma said, taking a seat and cutting through the awkward tension. "You're armed, I assume?"

"Yes, as always," Zoe answered, her eyes darting between Anja and

Emma. "But what's going on here that would make you ask?"

Emma glanced at Anja, silently seeking permission to proceed. Anja nodded, accepting that it was time to fold Zoe into their patchwork of allies and confidantes. Emma spoke briefly about their current situation and preparations for the unwelcome visitors who might soon arrive.

With a sigh and a promise from Zoe that what she was about to hear was to remain their absolute secret, Anja began her tale. "What I'm about to tell you will strain your credulity."

Anja provided the highlights to update Zoe—from when they separated in Switzerland. She related the awakening experiences of the group, leaving out explicit details. She continued her narrative and finished with their plan to draw the Sodality out and what they had been doing to prepare.

"Things have escalated," Anja concluded, her eyes locking with Zoe's. "I know this is difficult to wrap your mind around. Hell, I'm living it, and there are days I can barely believe it."

As Anja finished her tale, Zoe's eyes were wide, taking it all in. Then, after looking back and forth between them, finally settling on Anja, she said, "What. The. Fuck. Anja… I know I was pushing you to let go and live a little—but a succubus? Really?"

"You have no idea, Zoe… No idea, but yes. Really."

The room seemed to absorb their words as Zoe and Emma discussed their situation. Zoe took another sip from her glass before swirling it, ice tinkling.

"I've had experts look at those videos. They're deepfakes, sophisticated but fake. I suppose that's not news to you?"

Anja shook her head. "No, it's not. Lucian and I orchestrated the public breakup to mislead the Sodality. They're a more immediate danger than anyone realizes, especially after what happened at Lucian's estate. It's crucial we maintain the narrative of our separation."

Zoe's eyes went sharp at this admission as if filing away the implications of this decision for later scrutiny.

"So, let me get this straight," Zoe began. "You and Lucian have been playing 4D chess with these people, blaming them for your scandal while planning to take them down? That's quite the gambit."

Anja nodded, her eyes meeting Emma's momentarily, registering a flicker of approval. "That's correct, and it's not just about us. We believe they have been suppressing—killing—those they suspect with 'superhuman' or 'paranormal' capabilities or even just the potential."

"Those rumors about me at the library in the tabloids and getting me fired from the Morgan?" Anja began shifting topics.

Both Emma and Zoe nodded, listening.

"Those rumors weren't random. They were deliberate and intended to sabotage my reputation. Leave me more vulnerable. They seem to have dug up an incident from my past to base them on—to twist the knife."

Anja hesitated momentarily, her gaze dropping to her hands, clasped tightly on her lap. She felt the weight of Emma's and Zoe's eyes on her, filled with expectation and concern. She took a steadying breath before looking up, making eye contact with them.

"Back in high school, there was an incident that...well, it shaped how I viewed myself, how I perceived intimacy and trust," Anja began, her voice soft but steady.

Zoe and Emma exchanged a brief look before returning their gaze to Anja but said nothing, silently encouraging her to continue.

"I used to hide in a small, secluded nook in the school library. It was a quiet place tucked behind tall bookshelves. It was my sanctuary. One afternoon, I was there, and I was...exploring myself. It was private, or so I thought."

Anja took another deep breath. The next part was harder to say.

"Two classmates found me. Instead of leaving or pretending they saw nothing, they lingered, whispering and giggling. By the next day, the entire school seemed to know an exaggerated version of what happened. I was the talk of the rumor mill."

Emma's eyes tightened, anger flaring briefly. Zoe's expression was unreadable, but her eyes were hard.

"The aftermath was unbearable. Whispers, laughter, notes with inappropriate drawings in my locker. That event changed how I related to intimacy and how I viewed trust. I built walls, thick and high, around myself."

Anja paused, looking at each of them to measure their reaction.

"It's why for years, even as I might have wanted to be physically close to someone, I couldn't. There was always a part of me on guard, wary of judgment, of betrayal."

Silence filled the room as Anja's words hung in the air. It was Zoe who broke it first.

"Anja, that's...I don't even know what to say. Those kids were horrible."

Emma nodded, her voice tinged with a combination of sympathy and fury. "The cruelty of youth is staggering, but it shouldn't define us as adults. And it certainly doesn't define you, Anja."

Anja felt a warmth spread through her at their words, their acceptance. "Thank you, both of you. It's the first time I've ever spoken about it, and it feels...cathartic, in a way."

Zoe reached across the table, placing her hand on Anja's. "Well, secrets have a way of losing their power when they're brought into the light. And remember, you're not that young girl in the library anymore. You're a strong, intelligent woman. Don't let those ghosts define you. And besides—succubus, remember?"

Anja chuckled and nodded, feeling a semblance of release as if voicing her long-suppressed memories had lightened her load. "I'm working on it, and it helps to have people I can trust. Not to mention a new appreciation for sex. Even now, I'm still struggling to find a balance though. Sometimes, I think I have an inner demon pushing me into it—to jump into the sensations and pleasure with no restraint. The hunger for it builds, and if I don't feed it, I'm afraid it will take control of me."

"I don't think you should worry about losing control, but I can relate to that feeling. Like I said, you are strong, and everything I know about you tells me you will come out on top, no pun intended." Zoe said before leaning back in her chair. Her eyes lost focus as she seemed to drift into another mental space. Anja had seen this look before, the 'Profiler Mode' as they called it, where Zoe would analyze a situation, event, or person, peeling back layers to reveal the unspoken or unseen. But this time, as Anja watched, her newly awakened senses picked up something new—a particular aura emanating from Zoe, an energy reminiscent of what she sensed in Lucian. Anja made no comment.

Finally, Zoe's eyes snapped back into focus, meeting Anja's gaze. "You know, those two classmates didn't just stumble upon you by accident. They were in that part of the library for their own reasons, probably looking for a place to make out or more. They weren't just being cruel to you out of spite. They likely wanted to claim that space for themselves."

The notion had never occurred to Anja. She'd been so focused on her humiliation, her sense of betrayal, that she'd never considered the motives of the two who'd disrupted her privacy.

"I've never thought about why they were there in the first place," Anja admitted.

Emma said, "Well, that's the difference between you and Zoe, and even me to some extent. We're always considering the plots, the motivations, looking for the underlying game."

Zoe nodded. "Exactly. And speaking of underlying games, this adds another layer to my thoughts on the Sodality. Yes, that is probably where the rumors of behavior in the library came from. Someone has been digging deep, looking for things to use against you and Lucian. That clearly speaks of an organized and directed effort pointing back to the Sodality. They're a problem that has entangled itself deep into the roots of many lives, including yours, Anja. That's a weed that needs to be pulled out completely."

Anja nodded, her eyes meeting those of both women. "Then we'll have to get to those roots, won't we? And pull this weed out once and for all. That's why we are here now. Waiting for them to expose themselves."

Twenty-Seven

THE CONTROLLER SCANNED through Raven's report, taking in each detail with a seasoned eye. She had provided details of the scandal and fallout, the culmination of what she had planned meticulously for weeks. She had also highlighted the successful separation of Lucian and Anja. Her research has led her to a property upstate owned by Anja. The inference was clear: it would be a likely sanctuary for the woman in question.

Nodding in approval, he quickly drafted a reply, instructing her to maintain her surveillance of Lucian and gather additional intelligence. Pausing for a moment, Richard turned his attention to another matter. Smoke, a previously sidelined operative, has resurfaced, reporting in after a period of inactivity. Remembering Smoke's past mistakes and shortcomings, the controller considered the risks and decided he deserved another chance, albeit a final one.

With a sense of gravitas, the controller typed out a secondary directive aimed at Smoke. "Your task is to prepare for a mission targeting Anja's estate upstate," he wrote, emphasizing the caution that must accompany this undertaking. "Failure is not an option. I will also send others; Nomad will oversee the operation. You will follow his directives without question. Consider this your last chance."

The controller sat for a moment, contemplating his available resources. He had few operatives in the region, but the gravity of the situation demanded additional support. Deciding on a course of action, he opened a new file and began typing directives. First, he activated Nomad, having already decided to use him, a seasoned and highly reliable operative known for his surgical precision in executing missions. "You are to oversee the operation targeting Anja's upstate estate," he wrote. "The objective is to use Anja as leverage to get to Lucian Miller. Ensure there are no witnesses. Your experience and judgment are paramount. You will have two other assets at your complete disposal: Smoke and Viper. Communications protocols and profiles are attached, as well as the estate's location data."

Next, he activated Viper, another operative similar in profile to Smoke, although less experienced. "You are to assist in the mission targeting Anja's estate," the message read. "Your primary contact and the leader of the operation will be Nomad. Use extreme caution; we cannot afford errors."

He didn't like exposing them to each other, allowing every asset to coordinate their efforts directly. Typically, he preferred to keep his operatives compartmentalized, but the current circumstances necessitated a more collaborative approach.

With a few keystrokes, he sent the encrypted messages on their way, realizing he has just set into motion a complex game where the stakes couldn't be higher. For a moment, he considered the weight of his decisions and the risks involved. Then, pushing away any doubt, he turned to his next task. He opened another encrypted channel, reserved for communications with the grandmaster. He outlined the recent developments and the newly initiated plans, conveying the urgency and the calculated risks involved. "Will keep you updated," he typed before encrypting and sending the message.

Sitting back, he reflected on the only meeting he had with the grandmaster. It was during his elevation to the position of controller in a ceremony that was compelling yet austere. The grandmaster was an imposing figure, exuding an air of command that was almost palpable. His presence was unnerving, like a weight you couldn't shake off. The memory served as a potent reminder that failure was not an option. With the weight of this lingering thought, he pivoted his chair back to his multiple screens.

In the peaceful quarters of his penthouse, Lucian stared out at the city skyline. The labyrinth of the illuminated windows reflected his complex thoughts—the peace only external, inside, Lucian was in turmoil. Beside him, Ian paced the room as if he could somehow walk off the restless tension that gripped them both. Claire sat at a computer, typing rapidly and sporadically, pausing to read the information on multiple screens. The atmosphere was thick with a sense of urgency, barely held in check by their need for secrecy and strategy. They'd managed some damage control, issuing take-down orders for the falsified videos and misinformation. Still, the digital footprints seemed to vanish into the ether, making it frustratingly difficult to pinpoint the source.

Lucian had gone to extreme lengths to maintain the illusion of his rift with Anja. A carefully leaked story to the tabloids depicted him in a state of deep depression, haunted by the scandal and the supposed end of their relationship. They'd even hired actors resembling Carlos and Emma, directing them to make visible entrances and exits from his apartment building. The paparazzi had lapped it up, oblivious to the ruse.

"Days like these make me miss fieldwork," Ian muttered, halting his pacing to glance at Lucian. "At least then, the sense of doing something, anything, was tangible. This waiting in silence is driving me up the wall."

"You and me both," Lucian replied, his eyes not leaving the sprawling city below. "I would imagine that in the field, your next move is often clear, even if dangerous. Here, it's like we're playing chess in the dark. We know there's a board and pieces, but we can't see them. It's unnerving."

Claire swiveled in her chair to face them. "The lack of a clear enemy makes this more complicated. We know the Sodality is behind this, but they've covered their tracks so meticulously that even our best efforts haven't broken through yet."

Lucian finally tore his gaze from the window and looked at his allies. "That may be true, but we have one advantage—they don't know we're onto them. They still believe their deception is working. It's a thin silver lining, but it's something to hold on to."

"It's frustratingly little," Ian countered, "especially when there's so much at stake."

Lucian nodded, his thoughts drifting to Anja. He felt her absence like a phantom limb, an integral part of him that was missing. His connection to her offered him snippets—mere fragments of her emotional state—but it wasn't enough.

"We'll need to stay patient," Lucian finally said, his voice tinged with a resolve he struggled to embrace fully. "The moment will come when we can act decisively, and we'll need to be ready. For now, all we can do is wait and prepare."

The heaviness of the waiting settled further into the room as Lucian picked up his phone, quickly relaying instructions to his private jet service. "Have the crew on standby. We may need to be airborne within the hour as soon as we get the word," he commanded, his tone brooking no room for misunderstanding.

He turned to Ian, his gaze unwavering. "Make sure we're fully kitted out. Weapons, supplies, attire—anything we might need. I want it all prepped and on the jet. We can't afford any delays when the time comes."

Ian nodded, understanding the necessity of the preparation. "Will do. By the time we get the signal, we'll be ready to move."

"Everything's in motion," Lucian murmured, more to himself than to Ian or Claire. "We've done what we can. Now all that's left is to wait, but damn, this waiting gnaws at the soul."

Ian and Claire nodded; no words were needed to convey the shared sentiment. They were a triad of restless energy, each battling their internal tempests while a quiet storm brewed in the world outside, its impending arrival felt but not yet seen.

Nomad sat on the edge of a worn motel bed, the fabric scratchy and faded, as if worn out from years of providing temporary comfort to transient souls. The room was minimal, just bare essentials—a strategy designed to leave as little trace of their presence as possible. Smoke and Viper sat across from him, all eyes on the laptop screen displaying the satellite layout of the estate.

"We need a low-profile approach," Nomad said, his eyes tracing the boundaries of the property on the screen. "Have we mapped out all the entry and exit points?"

Smoke nodded, manipulating the screen to highlight the possible access points. "Best routes are from the west or east perimeters. More cover. We could easily move in and out."

Nomad looked at Viper. "And the drone?"

Viper sighed. "Well, it was working just fine until it got too close to that damn bird. Must have been a hawk or something. Anyhow, the drone's toast, but before it went down, it did give us some useful intel."

He paused, refocusing the image on the screen to display a series of photos captured by the drone. Anja could be seen walking in the garden with two servants. "We've got Anja, a man, and a woman who appear to be domestic staff. No sign of anyone else. The two servants stay in a cottage nearby at night, so she is alone at night."

Nomad leaned back, taking a moment to process the information. His mind calculated risks, weighed options, and sifted through a myriad of scenarios before speaking. "If they have minimal staff and no security, we can make our move tonight. We wait until they're asleep. I want a silent entry—no mistakes, no traces. We extract Anja and leave as though we were never there."

Smoke and Viper exchanged a glance. There was no room for error, and they both knew it.

"Do we have everything we need?" Nomad asked, breaking the brief silence.

Smoke began listing the inventory: "Three sets of night-vision goggles, tranquilizer darts, rope, and untraceable disposable phones. Plus, I've secured a van with black, tinted windows and stolen plates."

Nomad nodded. "Good. Tonight, we go in. I don't want to waste any more time. Remember, we're like ghosts—seen by no one."

As the sun dipped below the horizon, plunging the world into darkness, Nomad felt a coil of anticipation tightening inside. It was a feeling he'd come to rely on, a razor-sharp focus that cut through the fog of variables and unknowns, leaving the path ahead clear, uncomplicated, and inevitable. Tonight, they would claim their prize.

Nomad picked up an encrypted phone from the small wooden table next to the bed. He dialed a number, waiting for the line to connect. After a few rings, he was greeted by the gravelly voice of the controller.

"Nomad, what's the status?"

"We're proceeding as planned. The location has been scouted; Anja and two others on-site, no visible security. We'll move tonight under the cover of darkness."

The controller paused before responding, "Good. Raven sent an update. All four of Lucian's bodyguards are accounted for in New York City; none have been dispatched to the estate. Our little media circus seems to have done the trick. Lucian and Anja are as good as done."

A ghost of a smile crossed Nomad's face. "Excellent. Then it's even more imperative we strike now while the iron's hot. It will only be a matter of time before someone gets wind of the truth."

"You have the green light. Execute the operation, Nomad. No slip-ups."

"Understood," Nomad replied, ending the call. He looked at Smoke and Viper, who had been attentively following the conversation. "It's a go. We've got a few hours before mobilizing. I suggest you both get some rest. We need to be at our best."

They nodded in agreement, dispersing to their respective corners of the room to grab whatever rest they could. Nomad sat for a moment longer, pondering the intricacies of the night ahead. Then he, too, reclined, letting his eyes close, but his mind continued to whirl, meticulously reviewing each element of the operation in his head. There was no room for error, no margin for oversight. Tonight was the night. And everything was in place.

Twenty-Eight

IN THE ELEGANT confines of the manor, Anja and Emma tried to make the best of their waiting game. The comfortable setting did little to mitigate the tension that seemed to grow thicker with every passing hour. After spending a night together in sapphic delights in an attempt to alleviate some of the stress, the two women found only temporary respite; as pleasurable as it was, the underlying unease remained palpable. Zoe was also increasingly restless, doing remote research on her laptop and following the few leads she could find. She had taken the room originally intended for Emma.

Anja flipped through tabloid photos on her phone, casting them onto the large TV screen. Grainy images of people resembling Emma and Carlos entering and exiting a New York City building filled the screen.

"You're quite the traveler, it seems," Anja said, looking at Emma with a wry smile. "Being in New York and here at the same time."

Emma chuckled. "I always knew I was talented, but I didn't think I was that gifted."

Carl had been instrumental in keeping the lines of communication open between the manor and Carlos, who was stationed in the woods. They exchanged critical information through a network of handwritten notes delivered by Aria. Carlos' brief but pointed notes reported suspicious activity around the property—two individuals had been spotted doing recon, a clear indicator that the Sodality was closing in. He also noted that Aria had learned to take down new prey, a not-very-tasty surveillance drone.

During one such exchange, with Carl arriving from his latest rendezvous, Anja and Emma reviewed the emergency signals they had established. Mock attacking one of them if they were outside during the day or a window at night to indicate it was time to enact their prearranged plans and that an attack was imminent. The conversations had a serious undertone, yet they tried to lighten the mood when they could. Despite their attempts at levity, both knew the pending confrontation was no laughing matter. The Sodality had already shown its fangs, and they all braced themselves for what would undoubtedly be a dangerous encounter.

While Emma might be growing restless in the confines of the manor, and Anja, too, felt the weight of waiting, they knew that the stakes were higher than their personal comfort. The pieces were in motion, and the endgame was nearing. There was no turning back now.

With the tension ever-increasing, dinner was a subdued affair. Anja's intuition was screaming that the night ahead would be pivotal. She shared her feelings with Zoe, who had grown to trust Anja's hunches. On Zoe's recommendation, Carl and Anna retreated to their cottage, locking up securely and turning in early. Emma insisted that Anja and Zoe should also lock themselves in. She, however, would remain downstairs, concealed in the shadows, prepared for whatever might unfold. The women agreed, and each took to their rooms, a thick layer of anticipation settling over them like a heavy blanket.

Hours later, in the dead of night, a commotion at Anja's window roused her. She'd barely closed her eyes, attuned to any disturbance, however slight. An owl—a creature not foreign to these woods—scratched at the window before pecking at it three times. The sequence was repeated before the bird took off into the night. Anja was out of bed in a flash. Sliding open her bedroom door just a sliver, she whispered into the dark hallway, "They're approaching. Three of them." Three taps echoed back, a prearranged signal from Emma confirming she'd heard and understood.

Retreating to her room, leaving the door an inch ajar, Anja moved to the shared wall with Zoe and knocked three times. After a few moments, hearing the signal echoed back, she knew they were ready. Anja took the necessary steps to prepare herself for what was coming. Her eyes, adjusted to the darkness, darted around the room one last time; deciding to add one final rather cliché touch, she stuffed some pillows under the covers. She took a deep breath, steeling herself. This was it, the confrontation they'd been preparing for, the culmination of countless hours of planning, subterfuge, and strained nerves. Now, the waiting was over; it was time to act.

Drawing from a wellspring of internal strength, Anja summoned the memory of her reflection in the nexus mirror. Her time here with Emma had generated a reservoir of power, a potent blend of instinct, emotion, and spiritual energy that she could now tap into. As she focused, she felt an invigorating transformation within her, as though each cell in her body was buzzing with life, aligning to some ancient, unspoken rhythm and shape. Her hand grasped the handle of her whip, fingers curling around it with a practiced ease. The whip seemed to hum as if recognizing the electric charge in the air, eager to be an extension of her will.

Anja positioned herself beside the door so that she would be hidden behind it when opened, her stance grounded, her eyes alert. Every sense was heightened; she could hear the night creatures outside, sense the movements of those nearing the manor, and even perceive Emma's guarded readiness from below and Zoe nearby. Her body was a coiled spring, her mind focused. She was no longer just Anja; she was something more—a synthesis of her experiences, her newfound powers, and her unyielding resolve to protect those she loved and others she had yet to meet—and revenge for those already lost.

And so she waited, whip at the ready, all her senses focused, and every fiber of her being prepared.

Zoe's heartbeat thrummed in her ears as she stood, back pressed to the wall next to the cracked open door. Her senses were on high alert;

she could feel the weight of the Glock 17 in her hands, its textured grip melding with her skin. Her bulletproof vest felt like a second skin, a tactile reminder of stakes that could not be ignored. Every part of her was coiled for action, adrenaline humming through her veins. Her eyes, as adjusted as they could be to the dimness, darted around, focusing primarily on Anja's room near the top of the stairs. Shadows cast by the low light stretched long and dark across the floors and walls, turning benign objects into questionable figures. Images of her shoot house training at Quantico flickered in her mind like an old film reel. The instructors' voices, laden with stern advice and tactical wisdom, echoed in her head. "Stay focused. Don't hesitate. Trust your instincts."

Zoe had aced every simulation, every drill, but this was no drill. This was the untested field, where theory met reality, and despite her extensive training, she had never had to translate those skills into real-life action. The potential cost of any misstep weighed heavy on her, adding to the tension that had already filled the air. Yet, underneath the nerves was a baseline of unyielding resolve. She trusted her training, instincts, and the woman Anja had become. She also trusted Emma's experience as a former agent herself. She tightened her grip on her Glock, her finger resting just outside the trigger guard, prepared to move immediately.

As the minutes stretched on, turning elastic in the heavy stillness, Zoe's attention remained laser-focused on Anja's door and the expanse of shadowy space beyond it. They had left the doors unlocked while securing the windows to steer any intruders to two entryways. Zoe's eyes narrowed as she watched the shadowy figure ease through the front door, his form momentarily outlined by the faint glow of the nightlight. The gear was what one would expect from someone operating under the cloak of darkness: night-vision goggles, all-black attire, a small backpack, and a firearm held at low ready. His movements were deliberate and practiced, each step calculated to make as little noise as possible.

Zoe felt a surge of adrenaline at the sight of the intruder. Here was tangible, concrete proof that the threat was real. This was no drill, no simulation; the man creeping through the lower level of the home was there with dark intentions, and the thought heightened her senses even more.

She watched as he paused in the doorway, scanning the room before making a subtle hand signal toward the door he'd just entered. She didn't know what it meant, but it clearly indicated that at least one other was within sight. Leaving the front door wide open, he began to approach the base of the staircase crossing the room, pausing once more to assess the situation at the bottom. The man's actions betrayed extensive training—a professional.

Every instinct she had trained into her came to the fore. She was one with her firearm, her thoughts crystalline, each option running through her mind with sharp precision. The man had not seen her, and her position provided a tactical advantage. But she was also aware of the others in the house—Anja, Emma, Carlos outside, and Anna and Carl in the separate cottage. One wrong move could jeopardize them all.

It was a critical moment, a delicate balance of action and consequence, and Zoe hated even more the plan for her to wait. Her fingers tightened ever so slightly on her Glock, prepared for what would come next. There was no turning back now; the real test had arrived. With her heart pounding a relentless rhythm in her chest, she steadied her breath and waited for her moment to strike.

Zoe felt her senses heighten as the intruder ascended the stairs. Each cautious footstep on the staircase seemed to resonate with her pulse, a thumping echo that matched her heightened awareness. He stayed close to the wall, likely aware that stairs can creak.

As he reached the top of the stairs, Zoe shifted back into the shadows of her room, her eyes never leaving the sliver of her doorway through which she watched. Her ears caught the subtle sounds of his boots brushing against the carpet of the landing, almost drowned out by the tension that filled the air. Then she heard the soft, almost imperceptible creak of Anja's door. Zoe moved back to her vantage point, peering through the narrow opening of her door just in time to see the man stepping into Anja's room.

It was the moment of decision, a fleeting instant that could tip the scales one way or the other. Her fingers were tense around her Glock, and her breath seemed to hang in the air as if time itself was holding its breath along with her. With her mind crystal clear and focused, Zoe knew that it was time to act. Her door opened with a whisper as she tiptoed out onto the landing, gripping the Glock firmly in her hands. Trusting Emma to handle any threats from below, she focused on the room ahead. Every step seemed calibrated, a perfect balance of speed and silence, as she closed the distance to Anja's room.

Then, the room erupted in a cacophony of unexpected sounds. First came the sharp crack of a whip, almost like a gunshot in the quiet of the night, followed by a pained and surprised grunt from the intruder. Zoe's ears then heard a thump—hopefully, the man's weapon falling to the floor. As she reached Anja's doorway, she heard another swish and crack, this one culminating in a bloodcurdling scream from the intruder. The sound of heavy footfalls came pounding up from the kitchen, signaling another approach. Adrenaline spiked through her veins, urging her to act. Her fingers found the light switch just inside the door and flicked it on.

The sight that met her eyes was not one she could have adequately prepared for, despite all the words of warning she had received. The vision before her was so extraordinary, so far beyond the realm of her previous experience, that she froze in the doorway, unable to move. Zoe's eyes widened as they darted from the intruder, his hands frantically clawing at the whip coiled around his neck, to Anja, an otherworldly figure. Anja stood nude, red hair streamed behind her like a living flame, her eyes ablaze with a fierce red light. Two horns adorned her head, but what arrested Zoe's gaze were the wings! Wings that slowly unfurled behind Anja, dark in the soft light of the room. And as if that wasn't enough, a tail swished back and forth, punctuating the scene before her.

Just as she was trying to process this extraordinary tableau, the chilling sound of gunfire snapped her back to reality. Two shots echoed almost simultaneously, and Zoe felt a hot, searing pain in her shoulder blade, strong enough to knock her sideways.

Another shot sounded, this one distinctly louder and coming from outside the manor. A scream followed, pitched with the finality of dire consequences. The urgency of the situation reclaimed Zoe's focus;

she braced herself against the door frame, her Glock aimed and ready, her senses heightened despite the pain radiating from her shoulder.

She found herself enveloped by the timbre of Anja's voice, deep and resonant, saying, "Handcuffs, Zoe." With practiced skill, Zoe pulled one of the intruder's limp wrists behind his back, then secured the other, rendering him immobilized while he continued to fixate on Anja.

The urge to give in to her fascination with Anja's transformation was powerful, but Zoe suppressed it, focusing instead on securing the captive. When Anja handed her a ball gag, materializing it as if from thin air, Zoe applied it, effectively stifling any potential outcries from the man. Only then did she allow herself a moment to fully take in Anja's altered form, a spectacle that was as captivating as it was unbelievable.

Anja, unselfconscious in her newfound guise, turned her gaze just as Emma strode into the room. "The one downstairs is dead, and Carlos has apprehended the other," Emma reported, her voice tinged with the adrenaline of the night's events.

Anja smiled, the tension that had gripped her face relaxing slightly. "Call Lucian," she said, "let him know that we've secured them."

As Emma pulled out her phone to relay the message, Zoe couldn't help but think about the confluence of events that led to this moment: the waiting, the planning, and the raw display of abilities she had just witnessed. And though many questions still lingered, one thing was clear—their immediate threats were neutralized, and it was a victory worth savoring, however briefly.

Now safe from any immediate danger, Zoe and Emma briefly paused to marvel at Anja's awe-inspiring form. Radiant and fierce, her red hair billowed as if it had a life of its own, her wings unfurled in a display of power and elegance, and her tail moved with an autonomous grace that complemented the whole. It was a glorious and alluring sight, capturing the essence of the extraordinary.

Carlos' voice broke through the hushed reverence. "Where are you?"

Zoe responded, "Up here."

When Carlos arrived, even he, usually stoic and unflappable, was captivated by Anja's transformation. Zoe, sensing the tension in the room, lightened the atmosphere with a few playful remarks. "Well, I see someone's been keeping secrets," she said, nodding toward Anja's tail. "Think of all the multitasking possibilities!"

Carlos then reported that the third intruder was outside, critically wounded, despite his intention to only incapacitate him as he approached the manor.

Upon hearing this, Anja's form began to shift. Her wings retracted, her tail disappeared, and her fiery hair settled as she returned to her 'human' form. This gave everyone a momentary reprieve, allowing them to refocus on the situation at hand.

"So, we have at least one fatality and possibly a multitude of other complications," Zoe said, pragmatism reclaiming her voice.

Emma picked up her phone again and dialed Lucian, putting him on speaker as the call connected. Their mission was not yet over, and many questions loomed, but for now, they all shared a quiet sense of accomplishment, standing together in the light of the room, each person changed in their way by the night's extraordinary events.

In the dim glow of his office, Lucian stood in pensive thought. Ian and Claire had joined him swiftly after the first call, their faces etched with concern and anticipation. Lucian's phone buzzed on the desk, Emma's name lighting up the screen. He swiftly connected it to the room's speaker system.

"We're all here," Lucian announced.

Emma's voice filled the room. "Everyone's fine. Zoe has a nasty bruise, but we're all okay. We've got one captive, relatively unharmed. Another is dead, and the last one might not make it."

Carlos chimed in, "We also know where their van is. Could be useful for evidence or transporting the captives."

As Carlos finished his report, Zoe's voice took on an authoritative tone, "I need to report this..."

Lucian interrupted, his voice tinged with incredulity. "Report this, Zoe? To whom? What would you say? A red-haired succubus with wings and a tail intervened? They'd have you committed before the ink dried on your statement."

Caught in her tracks, Zoe faltered. Her duty as an agent, her training, all screamed at her to report, to document, to uphold the law. But faced with the implausibility of the night's events and the incredulous eye of a skeptical public, her words failed her. Lucian's question hung in the air, a sobering call to the reality of their extraordinary circumstances. It was a world unprepared to believe the unbelievable, even when the proof was standing right before them.

"Wait, we didn't say anything about Anja; how did you know how she looked?"

Lucian paused momentarily, absorbing Zoe's question. "I know Anja well. I figured she'd seize the opportunity to startle those…less enlightened individuals," Lucian replied, his voice laced with a sense of wry approval. "I gather it was effective.

"Regardless, we need to act fast. Time's of the essence," Lucian asserted, pivoting back to the matter at hand. His tone became crisp, assuming the form of a man accustomed to giving orders. "Zoe, Emma, inspect that van immediately. Look for any tracking devices or electronics and neutralize them. Carlos, once they give you the all-clear, load and blindfold any surviving captives. Put the body in the van as well; we'll deal with it later. Emma, you'll drive the van back to my estate. Carlos and everyone else, return here as soon as you can. Move the van into the estate's garage upon arrival."

He paused, his voice softening for just a moment. "Anja, I look forward to holding you again. To all of you, you were truly magnificent tonight."

Lucian closed the call with one final note. "We're on our way; the jet is already warming up. We'll likely be waiting for you by the time you arrive. Get moving, and be safe." His finger lifted off the end call button, and he immediately met the gazes of Ian and Claire.

"All set?" he asked, though it was more a rhetorical question; their faces were etched with readiness.

"Everything is on the jet, Lucian. We're good to go," Claire confirmed.

Ian simply nodded, already jingling keys to the Rolls-Royce, the final part of their fast-approaching journey to the airport. The air between them was filled with an electric tension, a unifying energy connecting them in the mission. Within moments, they would be on the road, then in the air, and finally reunited with those who had successfully navigated the night's perils.

The SUV rumbled softly as it cut through the night, headlights piercing the darkness ahead. Carlos gripped the wheel firmly, his eyes focused on the road. Beside him, Aria dozed peacefully in her cage, seemingly unaffected by the evening's tumultuous events. In the back seat, Anja and Zoe sat side by side, their bodies tense even as they tried to unwind. Anja couldn't shake the concern about leaving her place in such a state, but she found comfort in Anna and Carl's gracious acceptance of the situation. They were more understanding than she had expected, and it lifted a weight off her shoulders.

However, another weight seemed to be settling in, particularly on Zoe. She finally broke the silence. "I've been trained to handle situations methodically, to go by the book. What we're doing...it's unsettling," Zoe confessed, her fingers nervously drumming on her knee. "I've devoted myself to upholding the law. I can't shake the feeling that we're crossing some serious lines here."

Anja turned to look at her, her eyes filled with a wisdom that seemed to stretch beyond her years. "Zoe, the world you're stepping into, the world you've already witnessed, operates on a different set of rules. Your training and oaths were designed for a world that doesn't account for those complexities. You're in new territory now, and the map you've been using won't help you navigate it."

Zoe looked skeptical but also hopeful as if Anja was trying to draw her a new map.

"You also have hidden layers, Zoe. If you choose to explore that side of yourself, understand that you can't revert to ignorance. The path doesn't go back the way it came. You've seen too much already, and even now, reverting to your previous life would be challenging, to say the least."

Zoe seemed to ponder Anja's words, her gaze turning inward as she wrestled with this new perspective. The silence enveloped the car once again, but it was a different kind of silence this time—filled with contemplation, laden with choices to be made.

As the car sped on, they sat wrapped in their own thoughts, aware that their lives were irreversibly altered, whatever path Zoe chose now. Anja had already made her choices and embraced them. Seemingly, they were pulling in at their destination all too soon, then briskly went inside.

Lucian's arms enveloped Anja in a warm embrace, a haven of familiarity and safety amidst the chaos. When their lips met, it was as if the world paused for a moment, allowing them this brief respite before throwing them back into the fray. They parted, their faces still close, as if tethered by an unseen force.

Turning his attention to the group, Lucian gestured towards the sitting room, where an array of sandwiches, a carafe of ice water, and a pot of hot coffee were laid out on a side table, and mugs and glasses lined up. "Please, make yourselves comfortable. We have much to discuss."

As everyone settled, Ian walked in, closing the door behind him. Lucian sat, leaning forward to capture everyone's attention. "We need to act swiftly. We need to identify any controlling structures through interrogation to understand their hierarchy and objectives. We also need to consider the possibility of planting false information as bait to draw more of them out."

Zoe looked uneasy, still grappling with the rules of this new world she had stepped into. "We're dealing with illegal detainment now, not to mention what might be construed as torture depending on the interrogation methods. Maybe even murder, obstruction, and the list goes on. How do we proceed without further breaking the law?"

Lucian's eyes met Zoe's, unwavering and calm. "Sometimes the law fails to account for shades of gray. What we're dealing with here surpasses legal technicalities. We're confronting a threat that the law, as it stands, is ill-equipped to handle. If we adhere strictly to the conventional rule book, we risk letting them slip through the cracks. Let them continue to operate in the shadows and continue to murder and who knows what else. They are the ones responsible for my family's murders. Don't lose sight of that. I haven't!" His anger rose to the surface.

Carlos said, "There's another operative out there, a female. We need to factor that into our plans as well."

Anja sipped her coffee, her eyes never leaving Lucian's face. "Do we have leads on her? She's the one who approached me in the library, followed me, and attacked and injured Dan, isn't she? And where do we stand on confirming identities for the ones we have now?"

Ian replied, "We don't have anything on her yet. She remains a ghost. The three who came after you only had false IDs, another dead end. Emma reported that they did have electronics in the van, an encrypted phone and a laptop—hard drive encrypted. We may need more from our captive to access them. Once we have more information, we may have some strings to pull on, but until then…"

The room went quiet for a moment as everyone absorbed the weight of the tasks that lay ahead. Plans had to be made, actions taken, and the unknown navigated cautiously. Yet, despite the challenges that awaited them, a sense of resolve filled the room. Lucian finally broke the silence.

"We each have our roles to play. Let's use this time to prepare and get a plan in place. We can reconvene in an hour to review any other ideas for a strategy. Emma should arrive by then. Until then, eat, rest, and gather your thoughts. We have a long night ahead."

With that, they dispersed for individual discussions or to eat, each aware that the quiet before the storm had ended and they were nearing its eye. Their choices now would set the course for events yet to unfold, and the risks, though high, were dwarfed by the consequences of inaction.

Lucian motioned towards a door upstairs, hinting at a well-appointed guest suite. "Zoe, you can use that room. Try to get some rest or clean up; we have much to do."

She nodded, then turned to catch Anja's eye. "Could we talk? In private?"

Anja felt concern pull at her; she couldn't say no. "Sure."

Twenty-Nine

ONCE INSIDE THE room, Zoe closed the door and flopped onto the bed. She exhaled loudly, a turbulent mix of emotions roiling through her. "Fuck, Anja. What am I supposed to do? Everything has changed. Is changing. It's overwhelming."

Anja took a seat across from her. "You're right. Life has taken an unexpected turn for both of us. But life is about adaptation, Zoe. We can be part of something much larger than ourselves."

Zoe ran her hands through her hair as if trying to extract answers from her head. "But look at you, Anja. You fit in this new world like a glove. What about me?"

Anja's smile was understanding yet tinged with amusement. "Fit in? Zoe, you're seeing only the surface. It's more than that. Complicated."

Zoe let out a strangled laugh. "Yeah, 'complicated' that includes whips, wings, even a tail—and absolutely gorgeous tits. How do you expect me to compete with that?"

Anja leaned in, her voice a touch more stern. "First, it's not a competition. Second, whether you accept it or not, you're already a part of this world. Third, my tits don't define me any more than yours define you. You know we're both more than that."

Zoe blinked, processing Anja's words.

"Exactly," Anja affirmed. "You're grappling with a sense of loss but not seeing the gain. Now, you know a world few are aware of. That's power, Zoe. And your skills, even as they are now, are special—unique. We could use your help."

"Unique or not, I feel like I've been thrust into a life I didn't sign up for. I was comfortable being an FBI agent, upholding the law. It's all I ever wanted. And now here I am, part of some underground group dealing with things I never even thought were real. And you? You've changed, too. How do I fit into this new world, Anja?"

Anja took a deep breath, the weight of Zoe's words settling over her. "Zoe, the only constant in life is change. We either adapt, or we get left behind. The world is much bigger and maybe even more dangerous than you thought."

Zoe sighed, the weight of her thoughts slowly lifting. "And what about us? Where does our friendship stand amidst all these changes?"

"Friendship isn't about staying the same; it's about growing and changing together," Anja said, her eyes softening. "So, whatever you decide to do, know I'll always be here as your friend, ally, or whatever you need me to be. You are my oldest and best friend, Zoe."

Zoe nodded, a small smile creeping onto her face. "Thanks, Anja. I think I needed to hear that."

"Anytime," Anja said, standing up to leave. "You have a lot to think about, but whatever we choose, let's promise to support each other, okay?"

"Deal," Zoe said, her eyes meeting Anja's. A flicker of light seemed to pass over Zoe's eyes. "You make it sound so simple, so easy."

"It's not simple or easy. It's just a perspective. The sooner you embrace the complexity, the easier it'll be to navigate."

Zoe looked up at Anja, vulnerability etched on her face. "I pushed you, Anja, into this…and now I'm not sure I can handle it."

Anja held Zoe's gaze, a smile pulling at her lips. "No, you didn't push me. I made my own choices, just as you will make yours. But whatever you decide, know that you're not alone. You've got me, Lucian, the others, and a whole new world that's just as baffling for me as it is for you. We'll figure it out together."

It wasn't a resolution, but for the first time since this whirlwind began, Zoe seemed to take a breath that reached deep into her lungs, filling her with something that felt a lot like hope.

As Anja moved to exit the room, Zoe rolled onto her side with a groan. "Ugh, my back hurts. The vest did its job, but...ouch."

"Hold on, don't move. I'll be right back."

"If laughing didn't hurt, I'd chuckle at that," Zoe replied, wincing.

Stepping out briefly, Anja caught Lucian's eye and gestured for him to come up. They returned, and Anja closed the door behind them.

"Lucian, could you take a look at Zoe's back?"

Gently, Lucian prompted, "Could you remove your shirt so I can take a look?"

"Now he asks..." Zoe had to interject before shrugging off her T-shirt and laying her face on the covers. "Owww!"

Lucian sat next to her on the bed, his eyes widening as he took in the severity of the bruise. "This looks bad—bone-deep. Here..." He unclasped her bra with delicate fingers and lightly touched the damaged skin. A soft glow emanated from his fingertips, dancing over the darkened area the size of a grapefruit.

In seconds, the bruise's discoloration began to fade. Zoe let out a soft moan. "Oh, God, that felt...that is...amazing. What did you do? How?" In a swift motion and with her usual lack of modesty, she sat up to look directly at Lucian.

Anja stepped closer to the bed, her gaze shifting between Lucian and Zoe. "Healing is one of Lucian's abilities. He's like me—otherkin or, more specifically, demonkin. As I told you before, we've been able to unlock our innate talents with the right blend of science and ritual."

She looked at Zoe intently, gauging her reaction. "You could unlock your own unique abilities, too, if you choose to. I see it in you as well. Think about it, Zoe. Join us."

Standing, Zoe stared at the spot where her bruise had been in the mirror on the dresser, her fingers tracing the now unblemished skin. The air in the room felt heavy with opportunity, tension, and temptation woven tightly together.

After a moment, her eyes met Anja's in the mirror. "Well, if you guys are handing out party tricks like that, how could I say no?"

"Trust me, it's not a party trick," Anja replied, smiling. "It's a commitment—a new perspective on life."

"Yeah, well, any life that includes miraculous healing sounds wonderful to me," Zoe joked, her eyes betraying the struggle she still felt. "Guess you all have the secret handshake down, huh?"

Lucian chuckled. "A secret handshake would be the least of it."

"So what's the initiation like? I have to ask—are there goats involved? Or chickens? I've heard stories," Zoe teased, despite the gravity of the decision hanging over her.

"No goats, I promise. It's more like an awakening than an initiation," Anja reassured, her eyes twinkling. "But, knowing you, I think you would find it rather pleasurable. I guess I glossed over some details when I gave you the highlights."

Zoe sighed, her posture softening as if leaning into a new reality. "Alright, count me as interested. But you'll have to give me more than miraculous healing and promises of no livestock to make this official."

Anja nodded. "More we can do. We'll discuss it—when you're ready."

Lucian adjusted his cufflinks as he walked into the sitting room, where the assembled group waited in the pre-dawn hush. His eyes briefly scanned the room—Anja, Emma, Zoe, Carlos, Claire, and Ian—all weary but alert. The weight of the night's events pressed down on them, but there was no time for rest.

"We need to extract information from our captives," Lucian began.

Emma interrupted, "Captive, singular. The other one didn't survive the trip."

Lucian nodded, registering the information without allowing it to derail his focus. "Very well. Ian, Anja, Emma, Zoe—you're coming with me to the garage. Zoe, you should witness this too."

With a nod from the others, they filed out of the room. The air was thick with anticipation as they moved past grand portraits and opulent furnishings through the hallway to the utilitarian steel door leading to the garage. Lucian punched in the security code, and the door unsealed with a faint hiss, revealing a dimly lit garage that contrasted sharply with the rest of the mansion's elegance.

As they stepped in, their eyes adjusted to the murky light, and soon, the van became visible, shrouded in an aura of menace. Emma had parked it meticulously, ensuring its dark silhouette blended into the surrounding shadows. Ian approached the van's back door, gripping the handle tightly before swinging it open. Bound, gagged, and blindfolded, the captive inside was a pitiful sight, yet no one in the group felt any sympathy. This was a man with intent to harm, maybe even kill. Lucian gestured for Ian to remove the blindfold, and as he did, the captive squinted against the sudden flood of light, taking in the stern faces around him.

"Let's begin," Lucian said, his voice calm but laced with an undercurrent of undeniable authority.

This was a crossroads, for the captive certainly, but also for Zoe and perhaps others in the room. What they learned in the next few moments could define their paths moving forward, cementing alliances and revealing capabilities both light and dark. Lucian held the gaze of each of his companions, reminding them—silently but unequivocally—of the gravity of the choices they would make.

He gave a slight nod to Anja, who approached the bound captive. The atmosphere was tense, the air thick with unspoken questions and the scent of machine oil from the garage. As her form came into his view, the captive's eyes widened, his body convulsed against his restraints, his muffled screams echoing around the ball gag in his mouth.

Anja moved closer, her approach slow and calculated but not without a touch of empathy. Her fingers grazed his cheek, and as they did, his muscles tensed as if electricity had passed through him. And then, perhaps to the surprise of everyone but Anja, he relaxed slightly. A tear, incongruous in such a setting, escaped from the corner of his eye as he turned his head away from her.

Anja removed the gag from his mouth with a swift, seemingly practiced motion. The captive inhaled deeply and then locked eyes with her, his gaze imbued with fear and wonder.

"You are a demon. I saw it—you," he said, his voice hoarse.

Anja leaned in closer, her eyes unwavering. "We may not fit into your narrow definitions of good and evil, but consider this: the ones you follow, the ones who've sent you here—they are the ones twisted and truly evil. They've taught you to kill, to perpetuate a cycle of violence and hatred. Think on that," she concluded.

The room fell quiet, the tension palpable, yet somehow different now. It was as if the scales of moral ambiguity had tilted ever so slightly, compelling those present to reassess their positions. Lucian observed all of this with a scrutinizing eye, mentally scribing the unfolding dynamics in their expressions as each person grappled with the implications of Anja's words. The captive's response, whatever it might be, would set the stage for the subsequent decisions they had to make.

Anja stepped closer again. This time, she placed her hand firmly over the captive's heart. He flinched initially as if expecting some form of pain or betrayal. But as her hand maintained contact, his body seemed to ease into a state of reluctant tranquility; his eyes closed as if surrendering to the inevitable. A very faint glow traced the outline of her hand. With a measured tone, Anja began her questioning. As if guided by her touch, he answered. Names, operations, key locations— every confession felt like a piece in a grotesque puzzle finally falling into place. It was apparent her powers of persuasion were very effective.

The captive, now more pliant, disclosed that a man named Smoke —the one who died during transport—was the perpetrator behind the recent Miller murders. Viper, another of their companions, had been the one killed at the house.

Emma searched Smoke's body, finding a ring adorned with a large sparkling sapphire. As it was held up for everyone to see, Lucian recognized it instantly, and he could see by her reaction that Zoe did as well. It was the ring Lucian had given to his mother on the eve of her birthday—the night she was murdered.

The atmosphere in the room turned leaden, heavy with implications that suddenly became personal for Lucian. It was a moment that intertwined the complexities of fate, justice, and vengeance. Anja withdrew her hand from the captive's heart, her expression one of complicated emotions, and looked at Lucian. They had just unearthed a new layer of darkness that tangled past traumas with present dilemmas. Lucian clenched his fist, feeling the weight of the ring and the past it invoked resonate through him. The road ahead promised more obstacles but also the possibility of closure and justice.

Here was absolute confirmation of the Sodality's existence. And threat.

Lucian's gaze met Anja's as they continued to extract information from Nomad. The captive seemed genuinely invested in aiding them now, a radical shift from his previous hostility. He revealed the existence of a regional controller for their area in the Northeast. Though he couldn't pinpoint the controller's exact location, he did have secure communication methods: a phone and a laptop. With little hesitation, Nomad divulged the passcodes and phrases required to unlock both devices.

"Is the phone traceable?" Lucian asked, his voice tinged with caution.

"No," Nomad replied. "It's secure, untraceable. The Sodality wouldn't compromise its operations like that."

Nomad was now visibly cooperative, persuaded by Anja that he had been led astray by the organization he had pledged himself to. She gave him a bottle of water to drink. He even volunteered that he was due to check in soon. According to their original plan, they were to take Anja to a location to be selected by him and await further instructions from their controller.

Lucian weighed the information, his eyes narrowing in thought. Finally, he looked at Anja. "Can you handle this situation if we proceed with that check-in?"

Anja nodded. "Yes, I believe I can maintain control."

Lucian gave a curt nod, confirming his approval. "Very well. Let's make the call. Report that the mission was successful, with no complications—have him say they've captured a docile librarian and have no witnesses. That he's moving to a safehouse he had arranged for."

The air in the room grew thick with tension as Nomad made the call. Everyone listened with bated breath, sensing the importance of what they were about to undertake. A play this risky could either result in a significant advantage or, if things went awry, mark a perilous turn in their circumstances.

Nomad made the call and followed the instructions. A ripple of relief washed over the room as the call ended, but Lucian's eyes remained unyielding. This was a single, albeit significant, step in a much larger game. Now more than ever, the stakes were immensely high.

"Alright, let's get organized. Ian, I need you to handle the two bodies," Lucian directed, turning to his trusted aide. "Find a way to preserve them for now, maybe pack them in ice. We'll decide the next steps later."

Ian nodded, already scrolling through his contacts to find the necessary resources. "Understood. I'll handle it."

Lucian's attention shifted to Nomad. "Move him into the mansion. We'll need to find a suitable, secure location within the house to keep him. Assign a guard to watch him at all times."

Ian acknowledged the instruction with a slight nod. "I'll see to it personally."

Lucian's gaze then met everyone's in the room. "We also need to consider the possibility of luring the controller. We need a location that gives us the upper hand—somewhere they wouldn't suspect but would still consider safe for their operations. Start scoping out potential sites."

"I'll get on that," Emma confirmed. "Should I bring Ava into the loop?"

"If you need to, yes. We'll need all the manpower and expertise we can get. Delegate tasks to the rest of the team as you see fit, Ian," Lucian added.

Ian nodded again and quickly exited the room, leaving Lucian in the middle of a semicircle formed by Anja, Emma, and Zoe. The room fell into a pensive silence. Every single individual there knew that they had entered an irreversible path—a game of high risks and potentially even higher rewards.

Zoe retreated to her assigned room, her mind a swirling vortex of questions and uncertainties. Each passing second seemed to widen the gap between the life she had known and the one she was rapidly becoming embroiled in. The walls of her room felt both confining and infinitely distant as she sank into her thoughts.

After what felt like an eternity of contemplation, she knew she had to talk to someone who could perhaps illuminate the path ahead—or at least help her navigate its murky twists and turns. The first person who came to mind was Anja, of course.

She got up, changed out of her contemplative posture, and headed to find her. Her steps led her to a bedroom door, slightly ajar, where she heard low, intimate voices. Taking a deep breath to steady her nerves, she knocked softly.

"Come in," Anja's voice floated through the door.

Zoe pushed the door open and stepped inside, closing it gently behind her. Lucian and Anja were sitting together on a sumptuous bed, an array of papers spread out before them, their brows furrowed in concentration. But as Zoe entered, their expressions softened, becoming more inviting.

Anja was the first to break the silence. "Zoe, is everything alright?"

Zoe hesitated for a split second, wrestling with how to articulate the whirlpool of emotions inside her. "I'm not entirely sure how 'alright' is defined anymore," she finally said, a wry smile tugging at her lips. "I guess I'm just looking for some answers...or maybe just reassurance."

Lucian and Anja exchanged a brief, knowing glance before returning their full attention to Zoe. In that moment, she felt a strange mix of vulnerability and trust—a paradox that only heightened her sense of being at a crossroads.

Zoe took a deep breath, visibly composing herself before speaking. "I've been thinking a lot about everything that's happened...about the things you've told me and the decisions I need to make."

She hesitated, almost overwhelmed by the gravity of her own words. "I wanted to talk more about what you said—about this new world I'm seeing."

Lucian stood, gathered the scattered papers, and set them aside while Anja scooted over to the edge of the bed to sit and look over at

Zoe. Anja locked eyes with her, sensing the emotional gravity Zoe was trying to convey. "Please, have a seat," she gestured to a plush chair by the vanity. "We can talk about it as much as you need to."

Lucian took this as his cue to give them privacy. "I'll leave you two to talk," he said, striding past Zoe and toward the door. "Anja, Zoe, take all the time you need."

Zoe watched as Anja turned toward Lucian, who was already at the door. "Lucian, stay. I think you should be here for this as well. Call it a feeling, intuition, or what you will."

Lucian paused, his hand on the door handle, then nodded. He moved to lean against the wall, but his posture was more attentive now, fully engaged in the unfolding discussion.

Anja adjusted her posture on the bed and took a deep breath, meeting Zoe's eyes. "I've already told you most of the story, but you need to know a few more details before you choose."

Her words hung in the air, thick with implication, and Zoe found her heart beating a little faster. "Go on," she said, almost breathless.

Anja continued, her voice tinged with earnestness. "Zoe, I sense you're otherkin, too—a strong one. And I have an inkling of what that might be. You're not tied to an animal spirit, no. You're more like Lucian and me."

Zoe couldn't look away from Anja; a rush of mixed emotions flowed through her. Confusion, anticipation, a strange sort of relief. "Like you and Lucian? You mean, you think I'm…?"

"Yes," Anja interjected softly, almost as if she was hesitant to voice it. "More closely aligned with us, rather than an animal archetype. Our kind come in many forms."

Lucian stepped away from the wall, unable to be a spectator anymore. "Anja's intuition is rarely wrong, Zoe. If she senses this in you, it's there."

Zoe took a moment to process, her eyes shifting between Anja and Lucian as she absorbed the gravity of what had been said. "Otherkin," she finally spoke, savoring the word as if really tasting it for the first time. "I remember you talking about that. Looking at myself that way now…I didn't think…looking at it again; it explains some feelings I've had that I couldn't put into words or understand. Remember when I told you not to worry about losing control and that I could relate to that feeling? Like that."

"Yes, I remember, and I'm still working on it," Anja replied softly.

Lucian took a step forward, deciding it was the moment to interject. "Anja and I have had to navigate these feelings ourselves. It's disorienting and exhilarating in equal measure. But we've found strength, abilities, and a sense of purpose that we never had before. And we think—no, we know—you have that potential too."

Zoe looked at both of them, struck by the earnestness in their eyes. She knew she was choosing between the life she had known and a world unfathomable. Fear, curiosity, and a burgeoning sense of purpose wrestled within her. Zoe absorbed their words, feeling as though she was on the edge of something vast and unknown. "So what does this mean for me? What do I do now?"

Anja reached out, her hand landing softly on Zoe's. "It means you have choices, Zoe. Choices that will have profound implications. But know that we're here to guide and stand by you."

Zoe looked between them, her eyes meeting Lucian's and then resting on Anja's. A sense of gravity settled over her as if her next words would cement a path from which there would be no turning back.

"Alright," she finally said, her voice imbued with newfound determination.

"Wait, There's more." Anja held up a hand.

"Oh shit. More? Do I want to hear it?" Zoe asked hesitantly.

Anja observed Zoe, her eyes locking onto Zoe's as she continued to speak. "You should also know that we have everything here that we'll need to bring this out in you, to awaken you to your true nature. A legacy buried in your past, blood, and genes."

She leaned in closer, her voice softening but not losing intensity. "I know you, Zoe. After all you've seen, you won't be able just to walk away. It's not in your nature. What's holding you back now is mostly fear, particularly of the unknown. That's perfectly understandable, but I suspect your curiosity—your thirst for truth—will win out. Deep down, I think you already know this."

Zoe felt the words resonate within her, acknowledging her

hesitations and hopes. It was true. Her rational mind struggled to reconcile what she has learned and seen. Yet, a deeper part of her, perhaps not fully awakened yet, urged her to step into this larger world Anja and Lucian were a part of.

Lucian chimed in, his voice echoing Anja's sentiments. "Anja is right. You have a sense of pursuit, a drive for justice that has always defined you. Here, you can channel that energy into something far greater, far more impactful. The path ahead is certainly filled with uncertainties, but it also holds the promise of answers, of a fuller understanding of your being and the world around us."

Anja looked at Zoe, her eyes twinkling with mischief and sincerity. "Zoe, you know the source of my power, and let's just say the ritual involves tapping into that energy. Considering your preferences, Lucian will also play a role in this. The process is different for everybody, but for you, desire and pleasure are called for."

Lucian interjected, a playful yet respectful smile crossing his lips. "In this case, it appears that the path to enlightenment offers some, shall we say, indulgent intersections."

Zoe, momentarily stunned, burst into laughter, a release of tension that had been building up throughout the conversation. The awkwardness dissipated, replaced by an almost electric charge of anticipation.

"Ah, so the three-way could be more than just a fantasy; it could be transformative?" Zoe asked, her eyes shining with curiosity. "I've got to say, this is probably the most intriguing recruitment pitch I've ever heard."

Anja grinned, her eyes meeting Lucian's momentarily before returning to Zoe. "Let's just say it'll be a transformative experience that no other job can offer you."

Zoe felt the weight of the decision she had already made. It was unlike anything she had ever considered, yet she sensed this was right. With a smirk that matched Anja's, she replied, "Alright then. Let's do it. What now?"

At a nod from Anja, Lucian departed the room, his footsteps fading down the hallway. He returned shortly after, the door clicking softly shut behind him. In his hand, he held a small vial filled with clear liquid and a syringe beside it. Zoe's eyes darted to the needle, a shudder running through her.

"A shot? You left that part out… I hate needles," she exclaimed.

"It's a quick process, and I assure you, far less uncomfortable than what you've already endured tonight. Go sit with Anja on the bed," Lucian said, his tone calming.

While Zoe still looked apprehensive, Anja stepped up to her, easing her shirt off over her head. She gently rubbed Zoe's upper arms, working her way to her shoulders. The touch was soothing and reassuring, and Zoe's tension dissipated.

Lucian concentrated on the serum inside the syringe. For a moment, the liquid glowed a soft pink before returning to its original color. Catching Zoe's eye, he raised an eyebrow as if asking for permission. With a resigned but determined nod from her, he injected the serum with clinical precision as she turned her head away. Zoe eased herself down to sit on the edge of the bed and took stock of herself.

Still standing close, Anja leaned in and asked softly, "How do you feel?"

Zoe paused, assessing any immediate sensations or shifts within her. "I feel…okay. Different, but in a way that's hard to explain. Kind of tingly."

Anja smiled, her eyes reflecting satisfaction. "Then let's get ready for what comes next."

Zoe looked between the two of them, her expression filled with curiosity. "And what is that exactly?"

Lucian placed the now-empty syringe on a nearby table. "Transformation is a process, Zoe. The serum is just the beginning. Now you'll need to align your intentions and focus your energy."

He dimmed the lights in the room, leaving just a soft, warm glow casting gentle shadows on the walls.

Anja kneeled in front of Zoe, locked eyes with her, and guided her in removing the rest of her clothes. "Close your eyes. Deep breaths. Imagine your essence, your core, the most intrinsic part of you. See it as a ball of light somewhere within you. Got it?"

Zoe nodded, her eyes still closed. "Yes, I think so."

"Good," Anja said. "Now, you're going to let that light grow. Picture it expanding, filling you from head to toe. And as it does, allow yourself to let go of your fears, questions, and inhibitions. I will connect with you and guide your mind along buried pathways; for you, I don't think we will need the chants or other tokens."

A few minutes passed in this concentrated silence. The tension that had been lingering in the room seemed to dissipate, replaced by a thick sense of anticipation.

Finally, Lucian broke the silence. "Are you ready?"

Zoe opened her eyes, which now seemed to glint with a new awareness, and saw that Anja was naked, too. Lucian was also naked, his erection rigid and ready. "Very ready."

Anja smiled, her gaze shifting towards Lucian and then back between Zoe's legs. "I've been wanting to do this…"

Hardly believing her eyes, she watched as Anja kissed the inside of her thigh, Anja's hands reaching under her legs and over to rest on her hipbones, gently stroking her skin. Her kisses slowly moved up to her core before her tongue started to lick upward, opening her. Anja began to lick languidly, occasionally pausing to focus on her clit.

Zoe felt her mind being drawn inward, remembering things she never experienced. Pathways that were deeply hidden. The warmth of Anja between her legs dissipated. At the same time, a new warmth enveloped her back. Lucian, almost forgotten, has seated himself behind her and lifted her to lay on top of him. His erection now poised between her legs, his hands moving to her breasts to kneed and tease.

Twisting her legs back and moving up to kneel on top of Lucian, knees on either side of him, she looked down to see Anja smiling up at her, her hand over her pubic bone, her thumb stroking across her clit. She watched as Anja took him into her mouth and started to move.

Soon, Anja met her eyes, and she let Lucian pop out of her mouth, then took hold of it with her other hand, guiding it toward her entrance. Closing her eyes again, she sank slowly onto Lucian, savoring the feeling of being filled. A new urgency took over as she moved slowly at first and then faster as she felt Lucian trust up from below to match her. Anja's mouth found her again, teasing her clit as Lucian continued to pump into her.

She sucked in a breath and let it out with a moan and, "Oh fuck! That feels incredible."

Anja moved up onto the bed next to them and leaned in to kiss her deeply, their tongues entwining in a passionate dance, tasting her. Their hands moved to each other to caress and entice. Zoe felt her orgasm approaching and moved faster, feeling Lucian's rhythm beginning to get more ragged, and watched as Anja lay down beside them, spreading her legs wide to masturbate vigorously, watching as Lucian fucked her, eyes staring at their joining.

Zoe started to feel a change emanating from within, building alongside her imminent orgasm. It was not just a metaphorical shift—she felt her body was recalibrating, resonating with new frequencies.

Her senses intensified, expanding their reach into the environment around her—she could almost taste the air and feel the energy emanating from Lucian and Anja. Feel their pleasure rebounding off her own and reverberating back. That was it—she tipped over the edge and felt an orgasm like she never had before. She felt it consume her completely with echoes from Lucian as she felt him filling her with hot spurts. She sensed Anja feeding off of them both and reaching her peak. It seemed to last forever, drawn out beyond what she had thought possible.

Collapsing between Lucian and Anja, they moved up to lie, relaxed and gently touching while they all tried to breathe again. She felt deeply comfortable between them. She also realized that a new door within her had opened. With her eyes closed, she visualized her physical form, framed in a mirror of her mind's creation. It shivered and flickered as though waiting for a cue to metamorphose.

"Zoe," Anja called her back, "how do you feel?"

"I feel...different, yet still me...only more...," she replied, struggling to find the words. "It's like everything enriched. I feel more...connected?"

"Yes, it can feel like that," Anja replied softly.

Lucian added as he stood to close the curtains and turn off the lights, leaving the room in shadows. "Let's rest now; it has been a long and eventful day for everyone. We can explore more about you in the days to come."

Unable to resist, Zoe said languidly, "You two can explore me more any time."

As Lucian settled into bed with Anja in the middle, Anja replied with a satisfied smile, "Okay, Zoe, we get the idea. Now shut up and go to sleep."

That only worked for a little while.

Thirty

Anja's eyelids fluttered open, the comforting weight of Lucian's arm a gentle reminder of their shared slumber. The soft motion of his fingertips gliding over her skin coaxed her further into wakefulness. She turned toward him, nestling into his embrace for a fleeting moment, a quiet intimacy that Zoe—lying beside them—couldn't ignore.

As if cued by their motion, Zoe woke, her eyes squinting against the dim light of early evening. Her gaze had a new, vivid clarity, but a haze of disorientation veiled it. Her freshly awakened senses were still something she was learning to navigate.

Lucian released his hold on Anja, and the trio gradually disentangled themselves from the nest of sheets and each other. Anja rose and stretched, noting Zoe's slightly wide-eyed look as she took in the room as if seeing it for the first time through an enhanced lens.

As they went about the simple acts of gathering themselves—slipping into clothing, brushing through tangled hair—Zoe found her voice. "So, is this what it feels like to be 'woke' in a completely non-political sense?" she jested, her humor cutting through the weightiness of the transformation she had just undergone.

They all laughed, Anja and Lucian sharing an amused glance. Zoe's humor was like a balm, a way for her to process stressful or overwhelming changes while keeping the atmosphere light.

Grinning at Anja, "So, you seem more relaxed with casual nudity these days? When you decided to let go, you really went for it."

"And if I didn't know better, I would think that your humor got a boost," Anja remarked, a grin forming.

"Oh, you haven't seen anything yet. Give me a few more hours to acclimate to my newfound awesomeness, and you'll be wishing you had a mute button," Zoe quipped as she dabbed on some of Anja's perfume, her motions slightly exaggerated, as if she was exploring how her new form moved in the mirror.

Both women smiled as Lucian watched them from his position by the dresser. Anja sensed a new kind of relationship with Zoe, a shared experience that would indelibly link their paths.

Zoe gathered her discarded clothes with her usual lack of modesty and headed out the door to return to her room. "I'll be down shortly; I want to take a quick shower."

Lucian and Anja reached the door, preparing to head downstairs. There were plans to finalize and actions to be taken in the looming twilight. But for this moment, Zoe felt invigorated and recharged after spending time together with them.

Anja listened attentively as Lucian assumed his leadership role, cutting straight to the point. "Updates," he prompted, a single word that carries the weight of their current mission.

Emma was the first to speak up, her voice crisp and her report detailed. "We've found a suitable location. It's about halfway to Anja's estate and a bit to the south. Heavily wooded area, and we've secured it through a cutout to maintain anonymity."

Lucian's eyes narrowed thoughtfully at the information. "And accessibility?"

"Small jet accessible," Emma added, "It's close to a private airport, which will allow us a quick entry and exit if needed."

Anja mentally commended Emma's thoroughness. The nearness to an airport offered them a strategic advantage, adding an extra layer of options to their unfolding plan.

At that moment, Zoe entered the room, bringing a fresh wave of energy that seemed to disperse the room's focused intensity. She slipped into a chair, her eyes meeting Anja's for a brief moment. That eye contact spoke volumes.

Lucian took in Zoe's arrival but wasted no time. "Excellent work, Emma. Anything else? Ideas or thoughts?"

Anja listened as Ian suggested having Nomad propose a ruse to lure Lucian out to them. "Make it look like a high-stakes kidnapping profit, and with Lucian apparently desperate to get Anja back, it would likely work—sell it that way. The call should demand that Lucian come alone if he wants to save Anja and bring five million in unmarked bills. This way, they could present it like a kidnapping for profit."

It was a savvy suggestion, adding another layer of deception to their elaborate ruse. The plan wasn't just about capturing the controller; it was also about creating enough chaos and confusion to throw off anyone else watching or planning against them.

Lucian looked at Anja and Zoe, "Would this approach work?"

Zoe took the initiative. "We could bolster that with a recorded plea from Anja to make it more convincing for this controller. Have Nomad send an audio file to this controller to also lend credibility to having succeeded in taking Anja."

Anja nodded in agreement with Zoe's suggestion. "It'll make the situation seem more authentic and tempting, especially if I sound desperate. That should make the controller lower his guard."

The room settled on this course of action. The call was made, and details were finalized. The controller was set to meet Nomad and his team at five p.m. the next day, eager to be present when they finally succeeded in neutralizing the threat posed by Lucian and Anja. The controller would have Raven call Lucian to relay the ransom demands and deliver the money by ten p.m. the following night. As Zoe observed, an audio recording of Anja's plea was rehearsed, recorded, and then forwarded by Nomad. Anja's sway over Nomad only seemed to be increasing.

"Alright," Lucian commanded, "final preparations to leave. Emma, you'll drive the black van to transport the bodies and Nomad. Claire, you go with her for added security. I would like to have Ian out there tonight as well, surveying and making tactical plans to welcome our guest. Is there enough room in the van, or would that be too crowded?"

Ian commented with some dark humor, "There should be plenty of room with Smoke and Viper cooling it in the back."

Zoe winced at this suggestion but nodded.

Amid the final preparations, Lucian stepped aside to make a call. He kept it brief, nodding as he listened to the response on the other end. "Have the jet ready at the airfield by six p.m. We're flying to Iceland."

He hung up, sensing the startled stares that had settled on him from around the room. Zoe was the first to break the silence.

"I knew we wanted to keep them on ice, but Iceland? Isn't that a bit extreme?" Her words were tinged with playful sarcasm.

Lucian chuckled at Zoe's question. "Let's just say they'll need some cooling-off time, and my facilities there are well-suited for that purpose."

Though the room was charged with the tension of their upcoming mission, Zoe's humorous comment and Lucian's explanation allowed a brief, shared moment of levity. It was a small but needed respite, acknowledging the gravitas of their plans while holding onto the personal bonds that kept them united.

Anja, who had been silent for a while, suddenly spoke up, her voice tinged with urgency. "Lucian, it's critical that you're there with me when we meet the controller. I had a flicker of 'sight,' and if you're not there, someone will die. I can't say who or why, but…but even if you are, it might not be enough."

Lucian met her eyes, and the depth of understanding between them made it clear he took her words seriously. "Then we'll make sure I'm there. No questions asked."

Anja nodded, grateful for his unquestioning trust in her abilities. Zoe and Carlos shared a glance, each sensing the gravity of Anja's statement, while the rest felt an unwelcome weight settle amongst them.

"We'll depart in the morning, then," Lucian announced, turning to address the room. "Carlos, Aria, Zoe, Anja, and I will leave with the SUV to be there by noon. We'll finalize everything then and there."

As Ian, Emma, and Claire exited to coordinate their plans and prepare to leave, Anja felt a frisson of tense energy filling the room. It was a far cry from the morning's personal revelations, yet somehow connected.

The Sodality controller sat in the dim light of his secure office, walls lined with shadow boxes containing arcane artifacts. His hands were steepled, eyes narrowing as he listened to Nomad's voice through an encrypted line. The plan, a suggestion to lure Lucian away from his fortified sanctuary, brought a thin smile to his lips. It aligned perfectly with his machinations. It was as if the universe conspired to hand Lucian Miller to him on a silver platter.

He contemplated contacting the grandmaster for a moment, a fleeting notion that he swiftly discarded. The less the grandmaster knew at this juncture, the better. The controller would instead present a fait accompli—Lucian Miller eliminated, his inner circle shattered—rather than report another frustrating delay or setback.

He replayed the recording of Anja's plea, listening intently to the timbre of her voice, the emotion underlying each word. The scream at the end, a perfect note of desperation, should be the bow that tied this deadly gift together.

His fingers glided over his computer, bringing up a secure chat window. He typed a brief message to Raven, outlining the next steps. "Prepare for an untraceable call to Lucian Miller. Use voice modulation and relay the following threats," he typed, laying out the exact words he wanted to be used to scare Lucian into compliance. "Include the Anja recording at the end. That scream should ensure he comes running."

He leaned back in his chair, eyes reflecting the glow of the computer screen. Everything was falling into place, and it was time to bring the curtain down on this act. The controller felt a rare twinge of anticipation. Soon, all his problems would evaporate like morning mist under a rising sun.

Raven sat at her desk, swiveling her chair slightly as she read the controller's message on her encrypted device. A slow, pleased smile spread across her face; she always relished the moments that made her feel like the puppet master behind the scenes.

She thought back to how she helped create the first rift that led to Anja's capture. Now, she was pulling the strings for the finale, an intoxicating sensation of power and control. She relished the irony of it all; it was as if she was the conductor of a dark symphony, each movement leading to a crescendo of chaos and defeat for Lucian Miller.

She retrieved a burner phone from a drawer and attached a voice changer. She had gone through a lot of effort to secure Lucian's personal number, but her skills in cyber espionage had made that task trivial. She studied her notes one final time, ensuring all her lines were perfectly rehearsed. Her finger hovered over the call button for just a second before she pressed it.

The dial tone was short-lived. Lucian picked up, and his voice crackled through the phone's speaker. Her voice changer twisted her words unrecognizable as she delivered the threat verbatim, embellishing for maximum impact. She heard the audible shock in Lucian's voice, a sound that warmed her insides like a sip of fine bourbon. She hit the play button to transmit Anja's desperate plea, capped off by that piercing scream.

Raven's heart pounded in sync with the final moments of the audio. The brief silence that followed felt like an eternity. Then, Lucian's voice came through, tinged with an urgency that sang to her like a well-played violin. He agreed to the terms: to show up alone at ten p.m. the next day with the requested cash and bearer bonds.

She ended the call and tossed the burner phone into a drawer, her task complete. She would destroy it later. A momentary flush of triumph coursed through her, satisfaction lingering like a sweet aftertaste. Her part in this dark play might be done, but the final act promised to be something she'll savor for years.

In the soft glow of the study's lamps, Lucian sat at his mahogany desk, his attention divided between the file in front of him and the quiet activity around the room. He had already contacted Elín at Akar Labs in Iceland before their planned arrival. Zoe and Anja were engrossed in a subdued conversation on the leather couch, their words a soft murmur. Carlos, in contrast, occupied a corner of the room, focused on his laptop as he researched falcons in Iceland, a concern he had raised given their impending trip.

Lucian's phone buzzed, jolting him from his contemplative state. Glancing at the screen, he saw an unlisted number. He had a sense of foreboding, a knot of tension tightening in his stomach, answering the call. As the modulated voice outlined the ransom and instructions, Lucian played his part, his responses calculated to convey the right mix of desperation and agreement.

After hanging up the phone, Lucian placed it back on the desk, his eyes narrowing thoughtfully at the device: a slow smile formed, a moment of triumph breaking through the tension that had filled the room.

"They've taken the bait," he announced, turning to face Zoe, Anja, and Carlos. The energy in the room shifted instantly, their collective apprehension giving way to relief.

"Now let's get ready to finish this," Lucian said, the finality in his words making it clear that the endgame was near. The atmosphere was electrified, and each person was fully aware of the gravity of the next day's events.

As they left the study to retire for the night, their steps were lighter, but his resolve was steelier than ever. Lucian remained standing by his desk for a moment longer, his gaze trailing after them. He knew the stage was set, and all the players were in position. All that remained was to bring the curtain down on this perilous drama. "I think it's best if we all get some rest," Lucian suggested, rising from his desk. "We have a long day ahead of us tomorrow."

Carlos closed his laptop, Zoe and Anja ended their conversation, and the atmosphere in the room changed, charged with the weight of what lay ahead. They dispersed, each carrying their thoughts and uncertainties as they headed to their quarters for the night. But for

Lucian, sleep promised to be elusive, the next day's high-stakes gamble consuming his thoughts as he climbed the stairs, the specter of the unknown looming ahead.

The SUV rolled to a stop outside the safehouse, its occupants thankful for the quiet drive but well aware that the calm would be short-lived. A whiff of breakfast burritos and coffee still lingered in the air, a momentary comfort soon to be eclipsed by the day's events.

Ian greeted them, confirming that the area had remained secured and undisturbed. Carlos listened intently as Ian briefed him on the optimal vantage points for their operation, nodding as he processed the information. Once the briefing was complete, Carlos drove the SUV to a designated spot some distance away, hidden from view. After securing the vehicle, he hiked back to the safehouse, ready to join the others in their carefully orchestrated plan.

Everyone was issued a radio, set to a secure channel that ensured seamless communication. Final arrangements were put in place, with Claire and Ian positioned outside to keep a vigilant eye on the perimeter. Emma and Zoe would stay inside the safehouse, their eyes trained on Nomad, who would bait the controller into their trap.

The goal was clear: capture the controller alive. The weight of this mission rested on everyone's shoulders, and each participant knew their role must be executed with precision. There was a palpable sense of focus as they settled into their designated positions.

Anja took a moment to lock eyes with Lucian, a silent exchange that conveyed a world of understanding. It was as if they were saying to each other, "This is it, the moment we've been waiting for."

With radios in hand and hearts brimming with determination, they were ready. The trap was set, and now they waited.

As the clock ticked closer to the appointed time, the tension in the safehouse reached a new peak. Each participant fine-tuned their role, eyes sharpened, and senses heightened. Anja took her position on the couch, appearing as a vulnerable captive. Zoe's adept handiwork made her look battered and bruised, and her disheveled state added another layer to the illusion. The aim was to distract the controller, to make him underestimate the situation.

The radio buzzed to life, breaking the room's silence. Claire's voice crackled through, announcing the arrival of their quarry. "He's here, alone, in a nondescript sedan." It was go-time.

Nomad stepped outside, gesturing to the Controller to come in.

As he entered, his eyes locked onto Anja, and a self-satisfied smile spread across his face. "Good work," he murmured to Nomad, clearly pleased at the sight before him.

That momentary lapse of attention was all they needed. The sharp clicks of hammers being cocked reverberated in the air, swinging the controller's attention back to the room. His eyes widened as he realized the tables had been turned, but he wasted no time. Quick as a flash, he reached into his pocket and bit down on a capsule he had pulled out. Instantly, Lucian's instincts kicked into overdrive. He rushed across the room, expertly assessing the convulsing man's condition in the blink of an eye. Without hesitating, he tore open the controller's shirt and placed his palms on his exposed chest.

Lucian's face contorted with focus and a hint of desperation. A soft, ethereal glow emanated from his hands, casting a greenish light that flowed like water over the controller's form. Yet, even as he poured his energy into the dying man, he sensed it might not be enough.

"Damn it, it's not enough!" Lucian exclaimed, his eyes searching the room for a solution, landing on Anja.

Anja didn't hesitate. She moved swiftly to Lucian's side, and he felt her press close, joining her power to his, merging seamlessly. A different hue joined the green light, flickers of another color blending in as they focused intently on their shared goal. The convulsions slowly subsided, as if the two combined forces managed to pull the controller back from the brink. His features slackened, his body going limp as he lapsed into a comatose state. But he was alive.

Zoe let out a wry chuckle. "Well, too bad we didn't get to see Anja unleash her inner succubus again. A tragedy, truly."

Her words prompted grins from Lucian and Emma, who appreciated the attempt to lighten the mood. There was still much to be done, and they all knew it.

"Alright, let's get to work," Zoe declared, taking the lead as they started the next phase of their plan.

Lucian watched as the group quickly shifted gears to staging the safehouse to look like the aftermath of a deadly fallout between assassins. Given Emma's extensive background in undercover operations and Zoe's supercharged abilities in profiling, the two quickly crafted a believable scene. Stray bullet casings here, signs of struggle there.

"Ring, anyone?" Emma held out the sapphire ring, and Zoe carefully placed it back on Smoke, reinstating its prior position.

With the stage meticulously set, they moved outside to inspect the black van. Emma double-checked every nook and cranny, ensuring their earlier cleaning job left no traces. Satisfied, they loaded up the SUV with their two incapacitated captives—the controller and Nomad.

Finally, they were ready to move. Claire ferried them to the airstrip, where the jet awaited. Its engines hummed softly in the fading light, promising swift transport to the next destination. They boarded, ensuring that the controller and Nomad were securely restrained but kept in a state that would preserve their lives until answers could be gleaned.

As the jet ascended, everyone settled in. There was an air of tentative relief; critical steps had been taken, but the journey ahead remained fraught with questions and dangers. Nonetheless, for the moment, they could afford a modicum of respite. They've earned it.

As the jet cut through the sky, Anja glanced out the window at the blanket of clouds below, her thoughts meandering between the mission ahead and the intriguing dynamics of the team. The captain's voice came through the intercom, announcing, "Ladies and gentlemen, we have about five hours and twenty minutes remaining in our flight. We'll be landing at approximately five-fifteen a.m. local time. The weather in Keflavík is expected to be a balmy twenty-eight degrees Fahrenheit, warming up to near fifty degrees later in the day under sunny skies."

Anja processed this information, mentally recalibrating for the cooler climate. She felt a sense of time pressing down. Yet the promise of sunny skies seemed like an auspicious sign, and the temperature, while not warm by any means, was at least manageable.

She looked around at her companions, each absorbed in their thoughts or tasks. Lucian was reviewing some documents, Claire and Ian exchanged a few whispered words, and Zoe sat quietly, eyes closed, perhaps meditating or resting before what promised to be an eventful day. The air in the cabin felt thick with anticipation, each of them aware that their mettle would be tested in the hours ahead.

The thought stayed with her as she returned her gaze to the window, watching the clouds give way to a darker expanse. Despite the impending challenges, the announcement of their landing time reminded them that they were a well-oiled machine, ready to face whatever lay ahead with precision and unity.

As the jet ascended to cruising altitude, the cabin filled with the subtle rumble of the aircraft, creating a backdrop for the team's next round of planning discussions. Ian leaned forward in his seat, concern etched on his face.

"Firearms. We could smuggle them into Iceland, but that might complicate things. Given our, well, new skill sets, maybe we're better off without them. What do you think?"

Lucian nodded, considering the practicalities. "Agreed. The risk outweighs the benefit. We'll keep them onboard and have the jet depart as soon as we're cleared."

The issue of their two incapacitated passengers was raised next, drawing collective glances toward the securely restrained controller and Nomad in the rear section of the cabin. Lucian leaned back, thoughtful.

"I'll call Elín," he said, referring to a trusted contact in Iceland. "We can arrange a medical pickup at the Keflavík FBO. She has the resources to make it happen discreetly."

Anja listened intently to the discussions, her gaze alternating between Lucian and Ian. Though the crisis atmosphere had eased, the weight of responsibility remained. She observed the determination on

Lucian's face and felt a measure of reassurance. Their plans were solidifying, moving pieces falling into place.

Lucian reached for the satellite phone in his armrest and had an animated conversation. As he finished the call, his eyes showed a subtle but certain relief.

"Elín wasn't very happy with the short notice, and she was about to go to bed. She understood the importance and will get it done."

Anja met his gaze and nodded, feeling a fresh surge of confidence. While many questions loomed in the distance, the immediate path ahead was clear. It was a sentiment shared by everyone, each absorbed in their thoughts.

Seated in the plush upholstery of the jet, Claire looked up from her thoughts and turned her attention to Lucian. "What about the SUV and the airfield? We left it there. Should we arrange to have it picked up?"

Lucian nodded, appreciating Claire's diligence in tying up loose ends. He picked up the phone again and made a call. The murmur of his voice filled the space as he talked to Ava, his capable assistant.

"Yes, Ava, can you please arrange to have the SUV picked up from the airfield? Excellent. And thank you for the warm clothing you had delivered, the hotel booking, the limo, and everything else. You're invaluable."

He ended the call and placed the phone back in its holder, meeting Claire's eyes and nodding in affirmation. "Taken care of."

Anja observed this, taking a moment to appreciate how effortlessly Lucian managed the complex logistics and how each small detail added up to a plan that covered all angles. His actions were like deft brushstrokes on a canvas, each contributing to a larger picture only he fully understood. And yet, she sensed that the trust within the group, her included, was the foundation upon which their complicated mission rested.

Claire gave a satisfied nod as if ticking off another box in an invisible checklist and leaned back in her seat. Anja felt the atmosphere lighten a fraction. Every detail accounted for, every thread woven tightly into the fabric of their plan, allowed them a greater focus on what lay ahead.

Carlos looked up from his seat, a slight but welcoming smile spreading across his face as Anja approached. She took a seat opposite him and Zoe, settling in comfortably. Her eyes met Carlos' as she asked, "How do you think Aria will fare in Iceland?"

Carlos took a moment to consider the question, his eyes trailing off momentarily as she imagined he was envisioning Aria flying through Icelandic skies. "She should be just fine. Peregrine falcons are rare there, but they're not unheard of. Some even stop in Iceland as they migrate between the Arctic and warmer regions. It's off their typical route, but not drastically so."

His eyes met Anja's again, and he sensed the unspoken intention behind her question. Anja noticed that he understood she had other matters on her mind—matters that concern Zoe. With a nod and a polite smile, Carlos said, "Excuse me, I think I'll go check on Aria. Give you two a chance to talk."

Carlos left, his steps muted on the jet's plush carpeting, and Anja turned her attention to Zoe. The air seemed to shift subtly, the space now open for a more personal exchange. Both women understood the weight of the conversations to be had, and in this suspended moment, thousands of feet above the Earth, it felt like the right time to delve into them.

Anja took a deep breath, her gaze steady as she turned to Zoe. "How are you feeling, Zoe? You've been through a lot recently."

Zoe grinned, her eyes twinkling as she leaned back in her seat. "Honestly? If I'd known the supernatural realm came with private jets and exotic trips, I would've signed up ages ago."

Despite her levity, Anja could sense the genuine emotional struggle beneath Zoe's playful exterior. Zoe continued, "But in all seriousness, it's a lot to take in. I mean, do I leave the FBI? Work for Lucian? I've crossed lines that I can't just uncross, and as much as I like you guys, the stakes here are...colossal."

Anja listened attentively, nodding as Zoe spoke. She had watched Zoe wrestle with these dilemmas in the past, sometimes explicitly but often quietly, her eyes revealing internal debates even when her mouth spoke only of other things. "You're right, Zoe. The stakes are high, and the lines, once crossed, can't be redrawn. But, you know, sometimes we find ourselves on a path long before we recognize it for what it is."

Zoe looked at Anja, her eyes narrowing slightly, curious.

Anja continued, "I think you've already made your choice, even if you haven't acknowledged it to yourself yet. The person you've become, the lines you've chosen to cross—they've brought you here, to this specific point in time, in this specific place."

Zoe remained silent, her levity replaced by contemplation. The playful sparkle dimmed, giving way to a deeper, more earnest light. Anja could see her grappling with the words, weighing their truth against her complex web of thoughts and feelings.

Finally, Zoe spoke. "You may be right. Maybe I've been running so fast that I haven't had the chance to see where I'm going."

"And maybe it's time to consider that," Anja replied gently, "because wherever we're going, we're going together."

Zoe and Anja shared a moment of quiet understanding as the jet rumbled softly around them, carrying them further into the unknown. It was as if, among all the turbulence they'd faced, they had found a pocket of calm—a mutual recognition of the challenges and choices ahead.

Epilog

Within the dim chamber that had seen centuries of intricate plots unfold, Grandmaster Eamon Vale sat poised, emanating an air of unwavering confidence. Screens displaying real-time intelligence adorned the walls, their glow barely reaching the darker corners of the room. His fingers lightly touched the encrypted tablet before him, alive with arcane sigils and coded messages.

It had been some time since he'd dispatched Richard Kael on Operation Icarus, a mission of utmost significance aimed at Lucian Miller. A task whose success he awaited with keen anticipation. Recalling their only meeting when oaths were sealed, and loyalty ensured through arcane rites, Eamon had no reason to doubt Richard's effectiveness. The controller was bound to him by far more than just sworn words; their fates were interwoven with dire magical consequences.

Pausing, Eamon diverted his gaze to the large touchscreen map that occupied a segment of his chamber's wall. Digital threads linked assets, targets, and ongoing operations—each a critical component in his multifaceted web of global influence. Lucian Miller had recently become a new point on this complex network, a knot of variables and potentials. Richard's task had been to untangle that knot or, if necessary, cut through it.

Yet, his intuition told him there was more to this story, even though news of Richard's progress—or lack thereof—had not yet arrived. He was aware that Lucian Miller was a force to be reckoned with. For every asset like Richard, who navigated the corporeal world, Eamon had others who moved through shadows, gathering intelligence from the spectral and the arcane.

His tablet buzzed, alerting him to unrelated matters that required his attention. He responded with a few swift motions, constantly multitasking, forever orchestrating. But his thoughts returned swiftly to Richard and Lucian Miller, the two men who had now become so entwined in his calculations. His finger hovered over the tablet, contemplating whether to send a nudge, a reminder. But he refrained. Richard knew the weight of the mission, and Eamon would not allow doubt to cloud his judgment.

The grandmaster leaned back, the leather of his chair creaking softly under his weight. A shadow of a smile crossed his lips. The pieces were in motion, and the board was set. He had been a player in this intricate game for centuries, and he knew well that the key to victory lay not just in the strength of the pieces but in the mind commanding them.

The weight of ages rested lightly on Eamon Vale's shoulders as he pondered the complex dance of destiny, choices, and the delicate balance between dark and light. In his vast experience, he knew one truth remained constant: every player revealed their hand in time, and he would be ready when they did. His eyes settled on the digital rendering of the globe, its web of influence pulsing like the very blood through his veins. And so, he waited, for patience was his oldest and most trusted ally.

Eamon's thoughts transitioned seamlessly, pivoting toward the broader strategic landscape that Lucian Miller's potential downfall would create. His finger swiped across the tablet, pulling up various financial reports, charts, and analyses of Coruscant Technologies, Inc. If Richard succeeded in his mission, the gaping void left in Lucian's empire would become fertile ground for new influence and power grabs.

A shadow crossed Eamon's brow as he considered the disappearance of Howard Miller—Lucian's uncle and an individual who had always raised a red flag in his analyses. Supposedly gone on a "sabbatical," the timing seemed more than coincidental. He made a mental note to escalate this to a priority investigation. His eyes narrowed as he pondered the implications. Was Howard Miller a loose end, or was he another piece on the board, one that had yet to reveal its significance?

A few taps on the tablet initiated a search, dispatching spectral agents and trusted human resources to delve into the matter. It wouldn't do to have such a variable remain unaccounted for, not when so much was already in motion. People didn't just vanish, not without leaving traces that could be unearthed, and if Howard had indeed left something behind—a clue, a sign—it was only a matter of time before Eamon's expansive network would uncover it.

His gaze again shifted to the large touchscreen map, each node and connection pulsing with relevance, each an integral piece in his machinations. With Lucian Miller's future uncertain, Howard Miller's whereabouts unknown, and a slew of other interconnected events rippling through his network, Eamon felt invigorated. A lesser man might have been daunted, but Eamon thrived in complexity, and the current web of circumstances promised an intricate game indeed.

A soft chime signaled that one of his spectral agents had returned with preliminary information. Eamon opened the message with a flick of his wrist, eyes scanning the text. It was too soon for definitive answers, but the hints and partial truths now flowing into his chamber could be the beginnings of something illuminating. And as always, he would be prepared for whatever revelation came his way.

His eyes sharpened, his posture embodying the resolve that had kept him at the pinnacle of power for so long. Each player would show their hand in due course, each piece would move into place, and when they did, Grandmaster Eamon Vale would be poised to capitalize on whatever lay revealed. That was the art of the game, an art he had mastered long ago and one that he would continue to employ to ensure that the balance—his balance—remained unbroken.

The End

(To be continued in *Bound By Shadows,*
Book 2 of the Reclaimed Legacy Chronicles)

About the authors

The duo behind Morgan Emerson Fox is a husband-and-wife team that has ventured into the realms of urban fantasy. They weave tales that are not only entertaining but resonate on a deeper level with the readers.

Their journey into writing began as a shared passion, a way to create worlds and explore the complexities of characters and narratives together. During the dark days of the pandemic, they were running out of novels to read, audiobooks, and podcasts to listen to, and tried writing as a creative and emotional outlet.

Writing under a pseudonym has allowed them to blend their voices, thoughts, and ideas into a singular stream of storytelling that reflects both our imaginations. It's a partnership that challenges and inspires them, pushing them to delve deeper into the intricacies of plot and character development.

For more information, please visit morganemersonfox.com